BACK TO LAZARUS

A SYDNEY BRENNAN NOVEL

JUDY K. WALKER

ISBN: 1500916455
ISBN-13: 9781500916459

Cover design by Robin Ludwig Design Inc.

For Paul and Mom, who always believed;
And to my guys — for letting me in and then letting me go

BACK TO LAZARUS

CHAPTER ONE

On some level, I always associate suicides with Superman.

Truth, Justice, and the American Way. Wasn't that the opening of the old Superman series, the one in black and white? My brother and I used to watch the reruns on TV when we were children. We'd lie flat out on our bellies, propped up on our elbows, dead to the world until the end of the episode. By then the loops of my grandmother's cheap red-orange carpet would have carved deep grooves in our arm and elbow skin that tingled as they plumped and came back to life. It was our grandmother who told us once (or more likely, several times) that the actor who played Superman had killed himself. She was a reliable source for any sort of Hollywood scandal from the last 50 years. According to Gran, the actor lost touch with reality, began to believe that he truly was Superman. He jumped off a building—a skyscraper, no less—thinking he could fly away, and died when he found that he couldn't. I don't know if he was wearing his super suit at the time.

Noel Thomas's story began with the same ending, though the means weren't so dramatic. She sat in my office, slim black purse on the floor next to her, hands folded on her lap, and calmly related that her father had killed himself. She wanted to know why.

We sat in silence long after the sound of her steady voice had faded from the room. Finally I asked, "Was anything unusual going on his life? Had he been behaving differently in the past few months?"

"I'm afraid I won't be able to answer any of your questions, Ms. Brennan. My father actually committed suicide years ago, and we weren't what you would call close."

I waited, willing her to speak, but that's a skill that hasn't improved since I first tried it on a dog at age six. The dehumidifier in the corner started its low rumble, then began beeping the shrill alarm of saturation it repeated daily. It took effort for me to not flinch at the sound, but Ms. Thomas seemed unaffected. "How long had it been since you'd seen your father?"

"I don't know. A very long time. I was a child. I—" She paused, her gaze dropping as far as the surface of my cluttered desk.

"Ms. Brennan, when I was six years old my father killed my mother. He beat and choked her to death. I'm told that he was found hanging from a homemade noose in his cell. I want to know why he waited so long to do it."

I sat with my carefully cultivated non-expression, absorbing her words. Ms. Thomas stared at me aggressively, daring me to speak. But what was there to say? For most tragedies, even the most sincere words are meaningless. When we'd sat in silence long enough, her eyes and the hard line of her lips began to soften.

The tension became less palpable, and I slipped off my shoes with an audible sigh to clear the rest of it from the air. My "sensible" black flats were nearly as uncomfortable, but not half as sexy, as comparable heels. They'd tortured me all day because an attorney (currently heading up my shit list) asked me to be available for some last-minute negotiation. His civil case started tomorrow, and the information I'd found was his ace in the hole. He must have been successful because he'd called at 3:00 to say he wouldn't need me after all. At least I hadn't worn pantyhose.

My toes spread luxuriously, I slowly got to my feet and walked to the kitchenette area. Such a lofty title for a dorm fridge and a sink, but there's just enough counter space for a hot pot. I puttered around, making hot sweet black tea with milk. I could use a cup, and suspected Ms. Thomas could as well. When I returned with the mismatched but fortunately not chipped cups of hot tea, Ms. Thomas had slipped off her own shoes. Had she worn them all day since church, or put them on specially for me? She smiled, a little self-consciously, and thanked me. Settling into my chair, I held the cup in both hands, closed my eyes and let the steam condense on my eyelids. Only the warm glow of my desk lamp against my closed eyes kept me from drifting away. I opened them when I knew I was ready to listen, and hoped she was ready to talk.

"I prefer coffee to tea, but I've found that having a coffeepot close to hand is dangerous for any flat surfaces in my office, not to mention my nerves."

Ms. Thomas sipped her tea, nodded appreciatively, but didn't respond to the patter. Instead she launched directly into her story, reciting the facts of her life with no more emotion than if she had read them in a novel. Based upon the formality of her speech, it was a 19th century British novel.

"I'm the only child of Vanda and Isaac Thomas. As I said, I was only six when my mother was killed, so I remember very little of my childhood with them. We lived in a town called Hainey, about 60 miles west of Tallahassee. My mother and father had moved there when I was born, running from I don't know what. I'm not sure what my mother did, if she had job, but she wasn't a stay at home and cook type. In fact, she wasn't at home much at all. My father did something involving physical labor, not an office job. I remember him coming home close to dark, wanting to take a shower. I always thought he smelled sweet, like the outdoors, but he wanted to be clean. Sometimes our neighbor, Miss Johnson, would babysit for me until he came home."

She paused for another sip of tea, glancing briefly at the nearly blank legal pad on my desk in front of me before resuming her story. "When I was six years old, in October of that year, my father killed my mother. Apparently he had a habit of beating her, and for some reason that night things just got out of hand. He was arrested immediately, and I never saw him again. My father was an only child, so I went to live with my mother's relatives, grandparents and an aunt and uncle at different times. I don't recall ever meeting them before that."

"Did your family ever talk about what had happened?"

"No. They would talk about my mother occasionally, about what a vibrant young woman she had been, funny stories about her getting into trouble as a child, but my father was rarely mentioned."

"What about during his trial?" I asked.

"Not even then. I didn't know anything about his trial until years after his conviction. I'm not sure how I found out about it, but it wasn't from a family member. Again, it was not a subject we ever discussed. Then it was years after his conviction that he killed himself, and I didn't know he was dead until very recently."

Ms. Thomas picked up her tea again, waiting for me to say something, but I could have told her she'd be waiting for a while. (Except that would have required me to speak.) Now that she'd started, I wanted to see what she would say to fill the silence. She set her tea down, untouched, and turned it so the handle was perfectly parallel to the edge of my desk.

Waiting.

She reached for her tea again, then pulled her hand back to rest on her lap in a movement almost fidgety coming from her still form, and finally spoke.

"You must be wondering why I'm here, why now. I can't really explain it. I wish I could. My alarm went off for work Friday, just

4

like every other day, and I got out of bed, and I just suddenly wondered. Why? Why did he wait so long? So I called your number this morning, not that I expected you to answer on a Sunday."

And what did it say about me that I was here on a Sunday? But I was here to analyze a potential client, not myself. "Ms. Thomas, what do you remember about that night, the night your mother was murdered?"

"Nothing." She paused, and I knew she was resisting the urge to fiddle with her tea cup again. Instead she reiterated, "Absolutely nothing."

"What about the physical abuse, or even verbal abuse? What are your recollections of that?"

"Again, nothing. But its ongoing nature was confirmed by several people."

Yes, but which people? The family, of which she had no prior memory? She either saw the direction my thoughts were taking or had an equally suspicious mind.

"I'm certain the individuals in question were not related to my mother."

"When was your father's trial? What was he convicted of?"

"I don't know. I have the impression that he was convicted the year after the murder, but I don't know why. Maybe that's what I assumed."

"Are you sure that he even had a trial?"

"You mean could he have pled guilty instead?"

I nodded, and her head tilted in response. I couldn't read her expression, but it seemed this was a possibility she'd never contemplated.

"It's conceivable, but I don't know."

"When did your father die?"

"I'm not sure. Again, I have an impression it was four or five years ago, but I don't know why."

"How did you learn of his death?"

"It was an odd coincidence, really. A woman mentioned it in line at the grocery store several months ago. An elderly woman—I didn't know her name, but she looked vaguely familiar. She obviously knew who I was, knew intimate details of my life, and I was embarrassed to admit I didn't know who she was, or even the context of our acquaintance. And I didn't want to prolong the encounter."

"How did she know he'd died?"

"You know how small towns are. Gossip becomes deeply imbedded oral history in no time."

I leaned back in my chair, considering what she'd said, what she hadn't said, then returned my bare feet to the floor with a jarring slap. "Ms. Thomas, I'm not a psychologist, and I'm not a psychic. I don't know if I can get you the answers you're looking for."

The corner of her mouth curled. "I realize that, Ms. Brennan. I don't know that the answers can be found, but I believe you've got as good a chance as anyone else."

Noel had come prepared, handing me a typewritten memo in a manila envelope. By the time we reviewed it, we'd settled into first names, as I now knew more about her than anyone else not related by blood. ("Noel—it's spelled like a man's name, but my mother wasn't proficient in French.") It contained the basic facts she'd just related, as well as contact information for her relatives and for herself. She didn't know any friends of either of her parents in Hainey, but said her relatives may be of some assistance. They lived farther west, just on the Florida side of the Florida/Alabama border in Alastair. It looked like I was going to be spending some quality time in the Panhandle.

She may not have been exactly lying, but I was sure Noel wasn't telling me everything. Her grocery line encounter was conveniently vague, and her explanation for her sudden motivation to know the truth seemed forced. Having never actually encountered one before, I didn't put much stock in alarm clock epiphanies. Although to give Noel the benefit of the doubt and a well-worn cliché, stranger things have happened, as her family history was ample evidence.

Family history. That's something I wasn't looking forward to. A murder victim's family is seldom a cooperative source of unbiased information on the murderer. This was going to involve a lot of tip-toeing around sensitive family members, trying not to offend while gathering useful information, something my cloddish feet (and mouth) find challenging.

With that thought, my eyes strayed involuntarily to a pale blue envelope on my desk. I recognized the handwriting, if not the surname or return address. It had come three days before and lay on my desk like an undetonated bomb, all other correspondence removed from its blast radius. I had yet to find the courage to open it, but it had never been far from my thoughts. I still couldn't read it, but that night I gripped the expensively textured paper tightly in my hand and shoved it in my bag to take home with me.

Meeting Noel steeled me to do it. Ironic, isn't it? No, perhaps synergistic would be a more accurate term. Or synchronistic? Because of Noel, I was able to begin to face my own past, to pick up that letter and eventually read it. And it was because of my past that I agreed to take Noel's case. Not that I knew it at the time. In fact, a lot of rationalizations went through my head that evening, reasons to work for someone who wasn't being honest with me or with herself, agreeing to do what probably couldn't be done.

I told myself that I have a fondness for four walls and a pathological dependence on my exterminator to keep the worst of the six-legged creatures at bay in this insect Eden, neither of which comes free. And that was true. I told myself that part of me ached for the little girl who lost everything so many years ago, and yet kept living. I wanted to help her, this girl who'd grown up alone, a stranger to those who raised her, to the truth of her past, and to herself. Her story was so tragically unique, and yet felt so familiar to me. And that was also true, but uncomfortable.

I settled on a much more cynical justification, one that didn't require introspection and confirmed the identity I'd chosen for myself. Sure, my eyes glaze over in the supermarket checkout line, and I aspire to maintain my speed when passing flashing lights and wreckage. But a recent run of background checks and record searches had bored me senseless, and I'm only human. The Thomas family drama was too much, too many blanks to be filled in. It was like being handed the meaty part of a really good novel, only to have it snatched away before you could finish. I simply had to know the whole story of Isaac and Vanda, and I wouldn't stop digging until I did.

At least that's what I told my spunky investigator self as I headed carelessly out the door toward home, a bit of someone else's mystery to occupy my mind. It was a lot easier than admitting I wanted to fix Noel's broken family because my own was beyond repair. Some things just can't be fixed.

CHAPTER TWO

Home. Such an odd-sounding word, like a Sanskrit syllable chanted to bring one peace. I've certainly never had that kind of mythical or spiritual attachment to my surroundings. After years of living here, Tallahassee still doesn't feel like home, but neither does anywhere else I've been. I have gotten used to the city though, and perhaps that's as settled as I'll ever be. It grows on you, like the kudzu in neglected lots or the mold in your closets. Sometimes I think growing is what Tallahassee does best, although I fear the concrete and asphalt expansion may soon outstrip the organic. For now, if you go to the top of the new capitol building and look out over the city, lush green treetops still hide most of the human habitation. It's not nearly as pretty when you get to ground level, but then what is?

With the exception of portions of downtown, the architecture of the city isn't much to look at. My own modest house sits in one of the many wooded residential areas of Tallahassee. Typical of the neighborhood, it was built in the 1950s, plain brick with not enough windows and only one bathroom, but it's comfortable. There's a beautiful magnolia tree in the back whose broad shiny leaves and stately southern presence contrast nicely with the azaleas and camellias milling about in the shade. For a few months a year, their bright flowers bring a touch of Las Vegas to the back.

My front yard is a patch of lawn with a hodge podge of plants, appropriate in a city that can't decide if it's really north

Florida or south Georgia. A 20 foot palm tree and some young palmettos face off in the corners closest to the street, and flowering trees and shrubs are flung randomly about the lawn. One of my neighbors has blueberries in the spring and figs in the early summer, while another has a gorgeous live oak, the kind you see draped with Spanish moss in every southern postcard. Incidentally, despite postcard tropes to the contrary, Spanish moss isn't restricted to live oaks, at least not in Tallahassee. Silvery tendrils drape the trees indiscriminately, palms withstanding, making odd tinsel in a city that sees no snow.

In the dim street light, I could see that my teenaged neighbor Ben had been hard at work in my yard. I hoped the camellia nubs would grow back from their military cut. At least my personal favorite, the pampas grass, had been spared. The mass remained shaggy as ever, a slightly asymmetrical accent to my mailbox. In his destructive frenzy, Ben hadn't quite made it to the curb with the snarls of vines and trimmings. Instead he'd left it in my driveway, so I pulled alongside the curb and parked on the street.

I knew something wasn't right before I'd even stepped up on the curb. My door was apparently unlocked—ajar, to be exact—because a dim bar of light ran vertically in the doorframe. Now what? I could run across the street and ask to use Mr. Ginley's phone to call... someone. I couldn't even think of anyone. Certainly not the cops. I probably just forgot to lock the door this morning and one of the neighborhood cats snuck in. And if I went to Mr. Ginley, he'd start asking me again about my personal relationship with God. Mr. G means well, but 10 PM is a little late to be worrying about salvation.

Slipping my purse strap over my head and across my chest to keep my hands free, I advanced on the door. Since I hadn't parked in the driveway, the intruder may not even know I'd returned. If

10

there was an intruder. I paused on my front step. If someone lurked inside, was surprising him really a good thing? My eyes scanned the darkness for a weapon. Ben had left my shears on the front step, but 12 inches of pointed metal was a little more than I wanted to commit to, even if they were frightfully dull. Instead I picked up a freshly watered, six-inch terra cotta pot of impatiens and crept inside.

The light from a small table lamp kept me from tripping over my furniture when I entered, but was too weak to travel much beyond a three-foot radius. I stopped for a moment to let my sight adjust, but ended up seeing more with my ears than my eyes. The sound of movement in the kitchen ahead of me seemed ridiculously loud to my straining ears, but the nature of the noise was unclear. The refrigerator door was open, its bulb the only illumination in the room. Unfortunately the bar style counter blocked my view of whatever was scrounging in my refrigerator. I slipped around the counter and raised my pot. At the last moment, a squatting figure turned and looked up at me.

"Syd!"

It was too late to stop—my arms were already arcing down. I managed to hold onto the pot, but the flowers and muddy soil dumped out onto the kitchen floor. "Jesus, Ben, you scared the shit out of me!"

He grinned up at me. "Sorry, Syd. It was getting late, and I was worried about the fish. I came over to feed 'em."

It really was getting late, even for Ben, and it was rare that he let himself in when I wasn't at home. He probably had a fight with his mom, not that he'd ever say.

"So the fish drink Barq's and eat Doritos? No wonder Bruce looked so bloated this morning."

"Ha, ha."

11

Ben stood, stretching his legs to his full height. 5' 9"? 5" 10"? He must have grown an inch since yesterday. By the time he got his license next year, he wouldn't be able to find a car he could fit in. Ben turned to close the refrigerator as an afterthought. Then he noticed the mess on the floor. "Ohh, man. I just planted those."

"Yeah, well, no offense, kid, but I'm not a big fan of impatiens. Or anything else bubble gum pink. Give them to your mom."

"Yeah, right," he said. He was already squatting again, trying to scoop soil, leaves and petals back into the pot. I couldn't see his face.

"Just leave it, Ben. I'll get it later."

And I would. I'd put the pot in the windowsill where he could see it every time he raided my refrigerator. Warning or warm and fuzzy message? It would depend on my mood. I reached for the soda, chips, and a folding laminated chart next to the phone.

"C'mon. Let's go out back and feed the mosquitoes. What's our constellation of the day?"

Amateur astronomy was our latest kick. Before that had been field guides of birds, trees and shrubs, and reptiles. We'd learn one or two items a day, more as an excuse to sit in the back and hang out than out of any motivation to better our minds. We'd spend as many days or weeks as it took to master the backyard, our little chunk of the world. Reptiles hadn't taken long—with the exception of sunning anoles they're uncooperative little buggers—but there was an astonishing array of plant life, most of which I've since forgotten. (I can't remember people's names either, so I don't think the funky vines were offended.) We'd soon finish astronomy. Tree branches above us kept us in perpetual shadow and blocked our already limited view, although in our neighborhood, the humidity and cloud cover did more to obscure the night sky than the lights of the city.

12

When we'd gotten one under our belts, fudging a little to make the constellation fit what we actually saw in the sky, I tentatively approached the subject I knew he didn't want to discuss. "So, Ben, what brings you over this time of night?"

Even in the dark I could feel the suspicion of his gaze. "I told you. It was getting late, and I thought Jackie and Bruce might be getting hungry."

"Hunh."

I grunted noncommittally, nodding my head as I rocked up and back on a plastic lawn chair, its formerly straight legs buckling and bending. Ben should feel some responsibility toward Bruce Lee and Jackie Chan. He's the one who convinced me I needed some other living beings in my life, helped me pick out the fish (our compromise between ferrets and sea monkeys), and gave them the spectacularly nimble names they can never hope to live up to. Bruce and Jackie were a good choice, pretty and calming, something to talk at that has a heartbeat (I think) without being demanding. But they don't exactly bark or beg or even do somersaults when they're hungry. I sat rocking, counting my breath. When I got to ten, I spoke.

"So, Ben, what brings you over this time of night?" His head turned in my direction, but he didn't respond. "Fight with your mom?"

Ben lived alone with his mother. I had some vague notion of teenage angst and familial discontent, but I didn't know how they manifested their brand of dysfunction. All I knew was that when he wasn't with his friends, Ben spent a lot of time with me, and I suspected his mom spent a lot of time with someone else. Or various someone elses.

"Back off, Syd." There was an edge to his voice I didn't often hear, and I don't think he did either. It was gone when he spoke

13

again. "I got my dose of Oprah this afternoon."

"On my TV, no doubt."

"The boys were looking depressed. I thought they might feel better if they saw how bad the air-breathers have it."

I laughed before I could stop myself, and we passed the danger zone. He told me about the latest prank on his "fascist" math teacher, then drifted off into cafeteria adventures and who was caught making out next to the deep fryer by the grease stains on the ass of her jeans. I finally kicked Ben out around 11:00 PM. He had school the next day, and even if he didn't need to sleep, I did. Or so I thought. My active brain had other plans. I told myself I'd had caffeine too late in the day, but I really didn't want to go to sleep. I was afraid of my dreams.

I made use of my insomnia by going online to check out newspaper archives. Most didn't go back to the time of Vanda's death, but I still thought there might be something. I was sorely disappointed. Apparently the small town domestic killing hadn't held the media's attention. Nothing piqued my own interest until nearly 4 AM. There was no coverage of Isaac Thomas's case, but there was a short article on his death. He committed suicide by hanging, just as Noel had said. The article didn't say what kind of "homemade noose" he had fashioned, only that he had been found during a routine early morning head count. I wasn't familiar with the prison, but I did have a stroke of luck with its location. In a state littered with prisons, Isaac Thomas had been serving his life sentence for the 1980 murder of his wife in the Panhandle, near all of my potential witnesses.

My subsequent searching brought up nothing else, not even an obituary, so I downloaded the single article and printed it before shutting the computer down. Noel was coming by my office again tomorrow, and I wanted to have a copy to show her. My eyes and mind were losing their focus, but I forced myself to label a folder before heading to bed for a few hours. A disorganized person by nature, I love the illusion of organization that a labeled folder gives me. As I slid the article inside, my dry, fuzzy eyes caught something on the printed page that had escaped me on the computer screen— the date. Isaac Thomas had committed suicide on October 12th, 2002, not four or five years ago as Noel had said, but less than two. Why was my client lying to me?

CHAPTER THREE

The time discrepancy bugged me, although I couldn't imagine it made a difference when Isaac Thomas had committed suicide. The next morning in the shower I went through all my hot water trying to figure it out, and trying to flush the fuzzy remnants of night-mares from my mind. I emerged no wiser with wrinkled fingers, simultaneously flushed pink and shivering cold. No big deal. You can't stay cold for long if it's June in Tallahassee. The humidity would have my hair a frizzy red mass by afternoon, so I didn't bother with it. By 10 AM I was in my office, comfortably attired in jeans and a men's button-down shirt, but I could tell I'd be drag-ging by the time Noel arrived at 4:00.

The day slipped by quickly with me catching up on paperwork, wrapping up old cases and accounts and getting started on the new. I called to set up an appointment at the prison for the next day, then prepared a contract and releases for Isaac's records. Ready ahead of time and feeling virtuous with my accomplishments, I wandered outside to face the gorgeous if slightly muggy day. My office is downtown, but on the outskirts of total respectability, which suits me.

Downtown has some lovely older buildings, and some concrete government monstrosities, but nothing to rival the "new" capitol building. Erected in the late 1970s (pun intended), apparently the architect wanted to leave no doubt of its function as the source of power in a large and influential state. A tall, ugly tower of a building, the new capitol rises behind the more traditional columned and cupolaed old capitol, and is flanked by two rounded domes. I've seen Mad magazine folding covers that look less like a penis. It sits atop a hill, the hub in a hub and spoke traffic pattern, and entering the city by way of Apalachee Parkway it looms ever larger, like political porn.

Fortunately I didn't have that kind of office view, nor did anyone else in my neighborhood. My feet led me around the corner to my favorite coffee shop for some afternoon sustenance—carbs and caffeine. Most of the people sitting out front in the shade were familiar to me.

"Afternoon, Syd. Working hard or hardly working?" a grizzled older man asked me over the top of his cup of coffee. He wore his usual Veterans of Foreign Wars baseball cap, but I couldn't remember his name. Though he used the same tired line every time he saw me, he still seemed to think it witty.

"I aspire to do both," I replied with a slight bow. I reached for the door, but he wasn't finished yet.

"I'm surprised you have time to mix with the likes of us now. The riff raff!" A laugh exploded from his hoarse throat, and he turned to share it with the two pierced and jangling young men sitting at the table to the right of him. They made no move to join in, but stopped their own conversation and eyed him tolerantly.

"Why is that, Jerry?" I asked, having recalled his name.

He directed his answer to the young men. "Betcha didn't know our Syd here is a regular celebrity. TV, newspapers…"

He'd caught their interest now, and was enjoying the attention.

"Yeah, Jerry, I'm expecting the call from Hollywood any day."

The stringy blonde jangler broke his silence. "What for?"

Jerry's eyes flashed, and his bottom left the chair when he spoke, nearly jumping up in excitement. "You didn't hear? She's the one that told the world our governor is nothing but a dumb-ass cracker looking out for his own."

"I did not! What, are you trying to get me killed?" Jerry tried to look chastened, as I tried to look outraged. "It was the Attorney General, and I didn't say he was a cracker. I said he shouldn't rely solely on the word of elected officials whose daddies wore white hoods to say who was being racist."

Stringy Blonde's jangling friend, Brown Buzz-cut, forgot his nonchalant slump, grabbed the arms of his chair and raised himself to his full sitting height. "Oh yeah, I heard about that a few months back. The case over there near Destin with the Spring Breakers."

He turned to Stringy Blonde. "Remember, that kegger got a little crazy, and they arrested everybody. The white guys got released the next morning, but the black guys got charged."

Now he turned to me. Hopefully not on me. "That was you, bitching about it?"

It had been more complicated than that, and I wasn't the only one "bitching," but he was asking for a yes or no. "Yep, that was me."

Brown Buzz-cut sucked his cheeks in, tested his face, and sucked in his cheeks some more until he looked sufficiently bad-ass. He stared me down for a few seconds, then ruined his handiwork with a child-like grin. Well, it was child-like if you ignored the glint of metal in his tongue.

"Good. Fucking brats." He nodded his approval, and his grin faded. "Fucking cops."

Returning his nod, I took the opportunity to slip inside for my coffee and bagel before Jerry started up again. I thought I'd heard the last of that little fiasco, but leave it to Jerry to resurrect it three weeks after my phone finally stopped ringing. Buzz-cut had the basic facts right, but not the context. Once word of the unequal

19

treatment got out, charges against the black students were dropped. The State Attorney tried to bury the story, blaming it all on a computer glitch akin to Rose Mary Woods' 1973 postural twitch for Nixon, but it was too late. An FSU professor had been compiling statistics on racial disparities in the justice system from neighborhood surveillance to charging, trials to sentencing, and the preliminary results were troubling. Civil rights groups had been waiting for the appropriate moment to release the data, a time when the public was ready to listen, and they rightly recognized it was now or never.

Unfortunately the latest celebrity criminal trial occupied the national stage and refused to budge. However, at the state level, liberals called for a statewide investigation, a task force on race in the criminal justice system, and the generally apathetic citizenry began to agree. The governor refused, but knew he couldn't totally ignore the public outcry. Instead, he invited 50 community activists, criminal justice advocates, and "assorted screwballs" to a token "Day of Dialogue" with the Attorney General. "Day of Dialogue" was the governor's turn of phrase. "Assorted screwballs" was my friend Ralph's, being one of the chosen screwballs. He'd been unable to attend (he said he couldn't trust his temper; his wife said he was too sick) and sent me in his stead.

Ralph's turn of phrase turned out to hold more truth than the governor's. If the participants thought their presence would mean anything, they were screwballs. Idealistically naïve screwballs, the kind we need more of, but screwballs nonetheless. As for the day of dialogue, it wasn't a day, and there was no dialogue. It lasted less than two hours, beginning with a self-congratulatory statement on the import of the occasion and a lengthy ass-kissing introduction of the Attorney General by one of the governor's aides. The AG gave a prepared speech, then took three softball questions from the audience (obvious plants) before exiting the stage to make a statement to the press. I remember looking around at 49 other open-mouthed, speechless screwballs, all of us momentarily unable or unwilling to move from our seats. Everyone who worked for the AG or the governor had slipped out unnoticed when the AG had, so we had to find our own way out. By the time I'd navigated outside to the mocking sunshine, I'd found my voice again. And a reporter found me.

After that first reporter, I tried to be more diplomatic in my statements to the press, but I soon discovered that diplomacy wasn't in me, at least not in this case, and tried to keep my mouth shut. The Tallahassee paper is a horrid mish-mash of AP articles and state office propaganda, but a few central and southern Florida newspapers went beyond the flashy Klan accusations to the sub-stance—the current racial iniquities in our criminal justice system. If the government wouldn't have a dialogue with the public, at least the public was having one with each other. I can't say I was a media darling, but for once most of my phone calls didn't come from telemarketers.

Of course, Ralph found it all hilarious, at least in the beginning. ("Better you than me, Syd, better you than me.") Then the fall-out got serious. I often do contract work for court-appointed attorneys and even under-staffed public defender offices. Suddenly my bills were routinely audited and even challenged by prosecuting attor-neys in court. Attorneys, civil and criminal, became leery of hiring me for anything that might require my testimony.

The final straw, for me and for Ralph, was a letter from the Florida Department of Law Enforcement (FDLE) informing me that I was being investigated for my conduct in connection with an eight-year-old case. I'd been a lowly apprentice at the PD's office at the time, and the witness I'd allegedly coerced was now dead. When I showed Ralph the letter, he ranted and raved until his wife Diane

21

admonished him for the sake of his blood pressure. Then he marshaled his resources and a devilish grin, ordering me to go home and get some rest.

I don't know what was said, but Diane told me that before my headlights were out of sight, he'd called one of partners of the biggest law firm in Tallahassee. At home. Within a week, I had a letter from FDLE saying the investigation had been closed for insufficient evidence, and I was back to getting my bills paid on time (by government standards, that is). Now I could support my coffee habit.

Shaking Jerry took longer than I realized, and I had to chat with the barista and some of the other regulars while I ate my bagel. By the time I brushed the sesame and poppy seeds from my shirt, any chance of punctuality for my 4 pm appointment with Noel had slipped away. At 4:03, I did what any professional investigator would have done in the same circumstances—I slipped off my sandals and ran.

When I got to my office, Noel was already sitting on the front steps. Her expression was unreadable. "Sorry, Noel. I—anh!"

Pain shot through my foot. Better than any sweet mantra, the thought of my still technically "potential client" watching helped to suppress the expletives dancing on my tongue. Instead I settled for a squealing grunt through clenched tooth and hopped the remaining few feet to the front steps with as much dignity as I could muster. I'd stepped on the detritus of an overhanging tree, one of those barbed seed pods from a sweetgum shaped like a medieval torture device. Sitting down next to Noel, I used the cuff of my sleeve to gingerly tug the barbs from my arch while not embedding them in my fingers.

"Ouch!" Noel said, watching the operation.

"You've been given a rare gift today. I generally try not to make a fool of myself in front of a client until after we've signed the contract, but for you…"

The left corner of her mouth turned up in what I was growing to recognize as her smile. "If that's the best you've got, why wait? I can't imagine you'll scare anyone away that easily."

We went inside, and while I tended to my foot she walked around my office, glancing at the books and limited chachka on my shelves. She had just roamed to my desk when I emerged from the bathroom with a fresh band-aid.

"You don't have any family pictures," she said. It sounded more like an accusation than an observation. At least it did to me.

I sat down behind my desk and handed the folder with the article to her. "Your father died eighteen months ago." Actually, it was twenty, but who's counting?

Noel looked at the paper. "I didn't know that's when this was," she mumbled. She didn't take the time to read the article before closing the folder and meeting my gaze, her own face expression-less.

For me, math is one of those things like cleaning. I try to avoid it like—well, cleaning—but once I get into the groove it's hard to stop.

"When were you born?"

"October 6, 1972." Her response was automatic.

"So you were eight years old when your mother was killed, not six."

I gave her a moment to catch up with my lightning calculations. When her eyes narrowed at me I moved on.

"Noel, I'm going on the road tomorrow, to the Panhandle. Visiting your relatives, the prison where your father died. Is there anything else you want to tell me before then?"

Noel leaned over to reach in her bag, this time simple black leather the size of a briefcase, but soft and with no lock. She pulled out a manila folder and placed it on my desk.

"Here's a copy of my birth certificate. I thought you might need it to go with the releases. Shall we sign those now?"

I considered staring her down, refusing to answer, but I was beginning to think she was nearly as stubborn as me and it would get me nowhere. Instead I pulled out my own folder and my notary stamp, slid the papers across the desk, and indicated where to sign. I may have pressed my stamp with a bit more force than was necessary when she handed the signed papers back. Antsy with agitation, as well as the adrenaline of being late and foot-pierced, I went to the mini-fridge and rummaged among the sodas to give myself more time to breathe. I held up one, and Noel nodded her approval. My hands were steady when I handed her the can, then pried up my own tab, the gases releasing a satisfying ffssshhh.

Noel didn't open hers immediately. She set it in front of her and traced patterns in the quickly appearing condensation. She picked up the can, transferring it from one hand to the other, then set it back on my desk.

"My family isn't exactly on board with this. In fact, they may not be very happy to see you." This confessed, she opened her soda and took a quick gulp.

"How not happy to see me? Not offering lemon for my tea not happy, or turn out the dogs as soon as I open the car door not happy?"

She pursed her lips together and tilted her head back. "I'm honestly not sure." Then she smiled. "But don't worry—grandmother wouldn't think of owning such a filthy creature as a dog."

"I'm sure that's meant to be reassuring."

"No, not really," she admitted. "More prophylactic, I suppose. Grandmother can be a hard woman, but she may be less painful to deal with if you know what you're up against going in."

"And just what am I up against?"

"A woman of iron will, with little tolerance for the shortcomings of others. She loves her family fiercely, and protects them at all costs."

"Will she see me as a threat to her family?"

"She may. Grandmother doesn't understand this, why I want to do it, why I can't leave the past alone. She tried to talk me out of it. Well, that's a kind way of putting it. She doesn't talk anyone out of anything. She just forbids you from doing it."

"Do most people listen?"

"Oh, yes. She's the matriarch. She determines what's best—she always has—and everyone else falls in line. Even now, with her health failing, no one questions her right or her ability to govern our lives." Noel said this without the slightest trace of bitterness or irony.

Gee, so much to look forward to. Noel was going to speak to her family again this evening, to prepare them for my arrival. I doubt she was anxious to perform such a task, but she certainly didn't spend any time in my office procrastinating. Maybe she just wanted to be away from me. Within a few minutes, we had finished with our paperwork, and she gathered her things and headed toward the door.

Noel paused with her hand on the screen door latch and turned back to face me. "You know, Sydney, I don't know why, but my family acts as if they're afraid of the past."

Were they now? Somehow I didn't think her family was alone.

25

CHAPTER FOUR

My appointment at West Florida Correctional Institution (WFC) the next morning was for 9:30, but unlike Tallahassee, the prison was in the central time zone. That left me plenty of time to get there, with a getting lost cushion in acknowledgement of my spotty navigation skills. The warden's assistant, a Ms. Tanya (pronounced Tan-ya like the bland color, not Tawn-ya) Carroll, had been accommodating. Her north Florida twang sounded young, but she also sounded efficient. She promised that by the time I arrived she would at least know if Isaac Thomas's records remained, and where any records were being stored. Having some experience with prisons and law enforcement agencies throughout the state, that was a tall order.

My mind wandered on the drive, from Isaac and Noel to my unopened letter, from Noel's past to mine and back again and random destinations in between. I didn't attempt to control my thoughts, just watched my mind generate noise. The static was a necessary first step, priming my brain to recognize connections later. Lack of scenery on I-10 helped, providing a blank canvas for my brain spatter. The remaining 25 miles or so on state roads wasn't quite as monotonous, and I started to become aware of my surroundings again. Intermittent roadside markets carried everything from Vidalia onions to pecans, Native American trinkets to bonsai trees. Restaurants with country names promised home cooking, whatever that meant. Meat in your vegetables? Approaching the incorporated areas, the businesses were replaced by convenience stores with enough gas pumps for a Nascar race.

The driving gods were smiling on me. I made good time and found the prison with no wrong turns. Since I was early, I went to a nearby Handi-Way (not quite as many gas pumps within the town limits) for a drink and a bathroom break. It must have been close to shift change at the prison. Everyone inside the market was wearing a uniform. I roamed back and forth in front of the drink coolers, eavesdropping, trying to get a sense of the people I'd be dealing with.

The woman behind the counter was plain, in her early 50s, with flat hair the color of smoked cigarette filters and an eye-catching mole on one plump cheek. Penciled-on eyebrows were her only make-up. She seemed to know the whole town and traded good-natured jibes and modest innuendo with everyone who walked through the door. I picked up a bottle of water and some peanut butter cookies (my compromise between total crap and something nutritious) and went to check out.

I smiled at her as I set my purchases on the counter. "Shift change?"

She chuckled. "It sure is, honey. Three times a day this is the safest place in town to get gas and smokes. All these big burly men hanging around to protect ya. Isn't that right, Charley?"

The buzz-cut young man waiting next to me blushed to his earlobes and began to fidget with the pack of gum and soda in his hand. He looked like a skinny high school kid, if you ignored the crisp khaki corrections uniform and all of its aggressive accoutrements.

"Well, I would hope to do so, yes, ma'am."

Another uniformed man, older and bulkier, bumped me on his way to the door. The bell on the door rang as he opened it, and he

28

turned back to speak before leaving.

"Shit, Annie, he couldn't stop a one-legged thief. He'd have to quit his goddamned jawing first. You better not be late again, Charley. If I write you up one more time, the warden's gonna have your ass."

Charley's head dipped unconsciously, and the blush that had begun to fade pinkened his ears again. "Yes, sir," he said, to the already closing door.

Annie rolled her eyes. "Just ignore him, Charley. Anybody as mean as him shouldn't be let out off his chain."

Annie handed me my change. I thanked her and said to Charley, "I'm with her. Like my Gran always said—don't let the bastards get you down."

I looked again at his uniform as I passed him and laughed. "And my Gran never had to work in a prison with turds in brown uniforms."

Annie's chuckles followed me out the door, and I could still feel the warmth of them as I left the parking lot.

WFC was on the outskirts of town. There was public access to the parking lot and one administrative building, but the rest of the facility was enclosed by chain link fence topped by razor wire. I drove past the ubiquitous black men in blues washing down cars. There may be some minor stylistic variation, maybe a crew neck versus v-neck shirt, but most prison inmates in Florida wear blues: blue pants and a blue shirt, usually with a white T-shirt underneath. You'll see guys in blues scattered over most prisons, washing cars, pushing carts of laundry or cleaning supplies. Of course, the one dress code exception is death row. Death row prisoners in Florida wear orange, but you won't be seeing them out washing cars.

I greeted the men rinsing car suds as I walked past them to the administration building. I'd never been to WFC, but experience told me the warden's office would be in that building rather than inside the razor wire, and a uniformed receptionist just inside the door confirmed my suspicions. The receptionist must have phoned ahead. I was greeted by Tanya Carroll before I could even make it to her office. She had over-permed short blond hair and just enough too much make-up to slightly cheapen her pretty face. Ms. Carroll was as young (mid 20s?) and efficient as I had supposed. She was slowed down only by the extra syllables she invariably added to her vowels, and the perky well-bred politeness that wouldn't allow her to speak in the brusque monosyllables and sentence fragments that are good enough for the rest of us.

"Yes, ma'am, I am happy to say that we still have copies of Mr. Isaac Thomas's records. I've pulled those and someone is making copies of them for you right now. It's a lot of records, but she's been working on it since we spoke yesterday, so if you'd like to come back after lunch they should be ready."

For the first time there was a slight shimmer in her veneer of composure as her gaze involuntarily turned to the unseen office of an unseen supervisor. "Of course, we do have to charge you for the copies, and I'm afraid we require payment when you pick up the records—checks only, no credit cards. I should have said something when we spoke on the phone, but I'm sorry to say it slipped my mind. If that's a problem, you can send us a check and we'll mail you the records."

"No, that's no problem at all. I'll write you a check this afternoon."

Her head did its unconscious supervisor swivel again, but Tanya seemed relieved. "Good." She clasped her hands and swiveled one last time. "Oh, good."

That settled, I left her office, but not before visions of baby shampoo bottles with twisting heads began flashing through my head. I stood for a moment in the hazy bright light outside the admin building, shaking the image away and getting my bearings. When I passed the men washing cars in the parking lot, nodding, I noticed that they hadn't even had time to finish their rinse.

The timing suited my plans. Alastair was only about 40 miles west, so I could go meet Noel's family and stop by the prison on my way back to Tallahassee. I decided to top off my gas tank and chat up everybody's friend Annie at the Handi-Way on the way out of town. I wasn't hungry, but I'm never above putting something by for the cause, in this case a green sports drink and a bag of freshly roasted peanuts (freshly warmed under a heat lamp, that is). When the last customer left, I headed to the counter. Annie recognized me.

"Well, hello again."

"Hi." I smiled as I handed her a credit card with a tricky strip that doesn't always work. I'm almost, but not quite, ashamed to admit that I keep it primarily as a tool for bonding with cashiers, slowing down the transaction and increasing the interaction. The card went through this time, but I didn't need it with Annie anyway.

"I thought I'd live on the wild side and get my gas after all the cops left."

She smiled and looked at the plain black clock on the wall. "Yep, they're all gone. Won't have that many customers again for another seven hours."

"So does everybody here work for the prison?"

"Just about. It's a job, and a pretty good job at that. 'Course, anything more than minimum wage is a good job around here, and you get benefits too."

"Yeah, but what a work environment. I don't think I could do it."

Annie leaned across the counter toward me. "You and me both.

That's one of the reasons you'll find me right here behind this counter. I hear about what goes on in there every day, twice a day. Don't get me wrong—it ain't that bad, not like in the movies. It's maximum security, but they're not all a bunch of murderers. The way I figure, most of those guys in there aren't that different from you and me. But the ones that are... Mmm, there are some scary people in there."

She let out a harsh laugh. "And between you and me, not all of 'em are inmates."

The drive to Alastair didn't take as long as I had hoped it would. Mind distracted, I probably drove too fast. Annie's parting words bounced around my skull, teasing me as she'd probably meant them to. My gut had told me not to follow up yet, not to push her. She knew I'd be back. And I knew I was right to wait, but I was still on edge. As I sped toward Alastair, I realized Noel's little talk with me the day before had done more harm than good. The thought of facing her grandmother made my stomach queasy. Fortunately I take the band-aid approach to such situations—rip it off quickly and it won't be as painful. Or at least not as prolonged.

I was meeting with Noel's grandmother, Mary Harrison, and her daughter Ginny. According to Noel, Mr. and Mrs. Harrison had given birth to three daughters. Noel's mother Vanda had been killed in 1980. Vanda's sister Viola had died a few years later from some sort of cancer, and Mr. Harrison had passed away himself about three years ago. There were living grandchildren, those born with Noel's generation, but only Mrs. Harrison and Ginny remained at the Harrison homestead.

It was a lovely old place. I took the drive slowly to keep from kicking up dust, and to take in the view. The property was circumscribed by an unpainted ranch-style fence. A couple of ancient live oaks, their branches grown heavy enough to seek the earth again, flanked the entrance. Rainfall had been on the low side for several months, so the grass wasn't as lush as it might have been, but it was still hanging on. The fields in front had been subdivided, some enclosed by barbed wire, but there was no evidence of livestock or cultivation. An outbuilding, perhaps an old barn, looked structurally sound but had long ago lost any decorating paint. It had weathered to the color of pine bark.

There was a large vegetable garden to the left of the house, now likely hosting peppers and tomatoes, squash and beans. Another enormous live oak grew to the right of the house, shading that side of the yard and most of the structure. What looked like a pecan grove began about 50 yards to the back of the house, and stands of pine created a visual barrier on its periphery.

I parked alongside the only other car in evidence—a dark blue sedan, several years old but with little evident wear, and sat long enough for the dust to settle. Car door open, I was stretching across the seat for my bag when I heard the front door and saw a figure step out onto the deep porch. She waited there until I had exited the car, bag in hand, before she walked down the steps to meet me.

"You must be Miss Brennan." She extended her hand with a small smile. "I'm Virginia Ludlow, Ginny everyone calls me."

Shaking hands is one of those social customs that's always felt bizarre to me. I've never been able to do it naturally, and generally just mimic whatever form and pressure is given me. Ginny's shake was blessedly quick, her fingers overlapping and claw-like. Our fingers barely made contact. "I'm Sydney."

We turned toward the house and mounted the steps. "Can I get you anything, some iced tea or water?"

"Iced tea would be great. Thanks."

She led me through the door into a sitting room that seemed

dark after the bright June day. There were no lights on, and the sunlight that came through the windows was mottled with shade. A ceiling fan whirred high above us. It was cooler than I had expected without air conditioning. The house had been built before such modern conveniences, when people used the elements to their advantage instead of creating a hermetically sealed space of constant temperature. A great deal of thought had been devoted to things like ventilation, orientation, and shade.

We crossed the sitting room and I found myself facing an elderly black woman in a high-backed armchair. Her arthritic hands were folded in her lap. She inclined her head a bare fraction of an inch to look up at me when Ginny introduced us, then gave a slight nod. Ginny left to get my tea. I sat down in an overstuffed chair catty-corner to Mrs. Harrison's.

"This is a beautiful place you have here, Mrs. Harrison."

"Yes. Yes it is."

Her voice was hard, without a bit of the quaver common to the elderly. Her unblinking eyes were equally hard. I began to wonder if Ginny's offer of hospitality was all that altruistic, or if she had just wanted to escape her mother's formidable glare.

"It's a shame to bring ugliness into such a beautiful place, don't you think?" she demanded.

Definitely not altruistic. "Yes, ma'am, it is."

She turned her head slightly, as if measuring me for my coffin. "Why are you doing this?"

"Your granddaughter hired me for reasons of her own, Mrs. Harrison. If she can't explain them to you, then I certainly can't."

"Oh, I know why she's doing it. Or why she thinks she's doing it. I asked why you are. What makes a person want to meddle around in another person's business for money?"

Some inexplicable puckish urge almost brought a smile to my

face, but I repressed it. "It's what I do."

"And is that something you're proud of?"

When I didn't respond, she tried another tact. "Just how much is she paying you?"

I took the time to breathe before answering.

"Mrs. Harrison, I didn't come here to pick a fight. I just came here to meet you, to let you know what I'm doing and see if you have any questions I can answer. Noel is going forward with this. I don't know your granddaughter very well, but I have a feeling that when she puts her mind to something it gets done." I paused. "I also have a feeling she takes after you."

For a moment her eyes softened, and I thought she would smile, but it was just a moment. Still, I knew it was the closest thing I'd ever have to an opening. "What can you tell me about the relationship between your daughter and her husband?"

"I assume you mean my dead daughter. My dead, murdered daughter." She watched to see if I'd flinch; I didn't. "Her name was Vanda."

"Yes, ma'am."

"He killed her. That was the extent of their relationship. What more is there to know?"

"They had a daughter."

"I thank the Lord for that every day."

"They were married for several years."

"Until he beat and choked her to death. Blissful years they were not. Young lady, let me tell you that you have never seen a woman more beautiful than my Vanda. She could have had any man, any man she wanted, and what she ever saw in him, I shall wonder until the day I die. That's all I have to say."

I wasn't sure I had the strength to respond. I could feel myself shriveling like a worm on the hot sidewalk under her gaze. She went on.

"You think you got some kind of magic in that little finger of yours, you can wave and make me say my Vanda was a bad person, you go right ahead and try. You… who do you think you are? What gives you the right to come in here and say I don't know my own daughter?"

Not understanding her defensiveness, I opened my mouth to respond, but she barreled on.

"You don't have to say it. I can see it in your eyes. And let's just say I got a little magic of my own. I know one day you're gonna come in here and try to break my heart with your lies. Go ahead and try; you can't touch me. But if you hurt my Noel…"

"Mrs. Harrison, think what you want about me, but the simple fact is that if I don't do this, she'll just get someone else. You can't scare everyone away."

I wasn't really so sure of that last part; her glare made my chest hurt. "Or she might just do it herself."

For the first time, I saw a crack in her composure, and she became what she always was but refused to let anyone see—an old woman. When she spoke this time, her voice trembled with anger.

"Get out. Get out now, and don't come back."

I rose and left the way I'd come in. When the door shut behind me, I paused on the porch long enough for a few deep breaths of hot humid air. I never did get my iced tea.

CHAPTER FIVE

Tanya was true to her word. When I stopped by WFC on my way back to Tallahassee, she was at lunch, but the records were waiting for me at the front desk in a banker's box with an invoice. I tried not to outwardly cringe at the figure and wrote the check out slowly to give myself time to consider whether it would bounce. Probably not. The man behind the desk watched me lazily from his straining reclined chair. I couldn't decide if the poor chair or his uniform buttons were in more agony, stretched against his massive bulk. He hadn't even bothered to speak when I arrived, just nodded toward the box. Perhaps he was contemplating my account balance as well, dreaming idle correctional officer dreams of thinner days when he could have apprehended me in the parking lot before I made my felonious check-writing escape. No, I realized, as I tore the check from my book. He'd been staring down my blouse as I leaned over the desk. Asshole.

The box wasn't quite full and I'd managed to snag a spot near the admin building, so it gave me great pleasure to refuse his half-hearted offer of assistance to a "little lady." Even better, I was able to lug the box balanced against my hip in one hand so I looked like a bad ass. (You can bet he hadn't moved it, so he didn't know how heavy it was, or wasn't.) My desire to throw the box at him to see how fast he could move was a strong itch in need of scratching.

A life lived in the South taught me long ago to take offensive chauvinistic offers and diminutive titles as well-intentioned but misguided remnants of a chivalrous code that wasn't all bad. I often used those fossils to my advantage, and sometimes they even gave me a touch of the warm and fuzzies. I can't say my irritation with the man was out of character for me, but it was disproportionate to the quick peek he'd had. I suspected my bad temper was a result of Grandma Harrison's animosity.

What was with the paranoia? Her accusations that I was lying about her daughter before I'd even started my investigation made me wonder what I'd find. What could be so bad about a child that her mother could refuse to accept it as truth, nearly 25 years after her death? No point speculating; it just made me dwell on the woman's ill will. A little music therapy (singing along with my favorite road trip CDs at the top of my lungs) flushed the prickles out of my system. I managed to not think about Mrs. Harrison or anyone related to her by blood or marriage for the remaining hour drive back to Tallahassee. No doubt about it—the woman was a distraction I wasn't being paid enough to deal with. For that matter, I wasn't being paid to deal with her at all, as I'd remind Noel at the next opportunity.

When I got home, I set the box of records on my desk in the living room. In my gallivanting around the Panhandle I'd forgotten to eat lunch, or even my dried-up peanuts, and my tummy was gurgling. Tallahassee is a town that eats depressingly early—try finding a restaurant that's open after 9 pm and you'll end up at a 24-hour diner—but at 4:00 it was early for dinner even by Tallahassee standards. Since Ben wouldn't be coming over this evening (he had some kind of sports things at school) I embraced the flexibility and eccentricity of the self-employed. Grabbing a couple of slices of leftover pizza, I added a Mexican beer with a slightly shriveled lime to round out the meal and took it all to my desk.

Three hours later, I had stale pizza crust, a stiff neck, and a few pages of notes to show for my efforts. The box representing the last years of Isaac Thomas's life had gained some color too. A tagging system for reviewing records is essential—I use yellow for useful information I may need in the future, green for items of interest that require more investigation, and red for knock your socks off revelations. The color scheme was skewed toward yellow and green, as is usual, but there were a couple of items in red as well. Generally what red lacks in quantity, it makes up for in quality.

Although only a few pages in length, the Pre-Sentence Investigation Report (PSI) was the most colorful section of the box. A PSI can be requested by the sentencing judge or one of the parties, and it's always prepared by the Department of Corrections. It often includes a statement from the investigating officer that headed the investigation, and may also include a statement from the defendant. There was nothing from Isaac Thomas in this one, but there was a brief statement from the investigating officer, Rudy Nagroski. His words weren't nearly as personal or as vengeful as some I've read. It sounded like standard language, and only requested generally that punishment be commensurate with the crime. Mr. Nagroski definitely went in the green column.

The statement of the facts of the case must have been from one of the case reports or from an informal discussion with one of the investigating officers. The source wasn't identified, and the summary was brief with little detail. Vanda Thomas was discovered in the evening hours of October 6, 1980, by a neighbor. She was lying fully clothed on the bed. There were some signs of struggle in the bedroom. Isaac had struck her several times in the face, then manually choked her to death. Although it technically couldn't be used in his "score" (to lengthen his sentence) because there had been no conviction, another section of the PSI noted that there was a previous complaint of domestic violence against him. The

39

complaint number was provided—big green tab. The complaint had been less than a year before Vanda's murder.

Also in the green column was Isaac's public defender, Sam Norton. I wasn't familiar with the name, but I knew Ralph would be. Sam Norton had pled Isaac out before they could go to trial. Isaac got 25 years to life for first degree murder. Didn't sound like much of a deal to me, but what do I know? In the 80s, parole might have sounded like a real possibility. In fact, with prison overcrowding in the mid 90s, some guys were getting five and 10 times or more of their time served as gain time, only serving a fraction of their original sentence. It wasn't until building prisons overtook building schools as a priority that the legislature was able to really "get tough" on crime. Now with a myriad of sentence enhancements and minimum mandatories, sentences were longer to begin with, and inmates had to serve 85% of their sentence before they're eligible for parole. And good luck getting it then.

The rest of the information in the box was mostly yellow, for example, all those magic dates and numbers that would hopefully enable me to access every bit of information about Isaac Thomas. Still, a picture of the man began to appear in his incarceration records. He had only two DR's (disciplinary reports) in his 20 years of incarceration. One of these had nothing to do with Isaac's conduct. There'd been a minor incident of vandalism in his wing, and when the officer was unable (or unwilling) to determine the identity of the perpetrator, he wrote up everyone. The other was for a fight on the yard. There were statements from 7 inmates swearing that Isaac had intervened to stop the fight, and he wasn't seriously disciplined.

Isaac's inmate request forms were always respectful (as were the responses from the officers in charge), and they were rarely for purely personal benefit. Many of the prisons in Florida aren't air conditioned in summer and are poorly heated in winter, so sometimes he asked for extra fans or blankets, depending on the season. Other times it was something as trivial as permission for the wing to stay up an extra half hour to watch the NBA play-offs. He'd been issued an extra T-shirt—could he give it to so-and-so next door who was short one? Would it be possible to get their legal mail delivered earlier so they had more time to respond before the next pick-up? All the minutiae that make up day-to-day life in a prison.

It wasn't until I got near the back of the box, or closer in time to the present, that red flags appeared. There were only two, and one of these was an optimistic categorization—it didn't exactly knock my socks off, but my gut said it could with a little more digging.

All prisons have their own medical facilities, but treatment of illness obviously isn't the focus of our prison system (I'm not even sure it's the focus of our health care system) so these facilities are limited. Often an inmate requiring specialized tests or suffering from a serious illness is sent to a separate prison medical facility. A couple of weeks before Isaac committed suicide, he received a medical transfer. He was returned to WFC the next day, so it was probably just for testing. Still, there could be a connection to his death. Southern prisons aren't exactly known for their oncology wings. Isaac wouldn't be the first person to choose the time of his demise rather than suffer the pain and humiliation of a protracted illness.

The other one was a true red flag. Isaac's PSI reflected that he had no living family. This information didn't come from Isaac, so it probably came from his trial attorney, and it was consistent with what Noel had told me. However, a few months before he committed suicide, Isaac added someone to his visitor's list for approval, a

41

JUDY K. WALKER

woman named Ida Pickett. Well, to say he added her name is misleading. Hers was the only name he had ever submitted as a potential visitor during his 20 lonely years of incarceration. There was no other mention of Ms. Pickett, and no indication that she had ever actually visited him, but she was listed there, along with her address. Interesting enough, but her singular status wasn't what knocked my socks off. Isaac's identification of her was. Under the heading of "relationship to inmate," Isaac had written in impeccable block letters "SISTER."

Noel had just gained another aunt.

CHAPTER SIX

My head spun from hours of looking at photocopies of small type and barely decipherable handwriting, not to mention the latest revelation about Noel's family. Noel was either mistaken or lied about when her father died and how old she was when her mother was killed, but I was willing to give her the benefit of the doubt on this one. It's possible she didn't know about her aunt. It looked as if her father and his sister hadn't been in touch for years, and Vanda's family was unlikely to bring up the subject. That didn't change my conviction that Noel wasn't being straight with me about everything else, but I needed more information before I started attributing devious motives to her omissions. All I knew right now was that Noel and her entire family made my Sydney Sense tingle like crazy.

So I did what I always do when my head is spinning. I made Ralph's favorite cookies.

I'd already been an investigator for a few years by the time I met Ralph Abraham, but I still feel like he showed me the ropes. He knew how things worked at the local level, who's important and how to get the community on your side. His connections (and convictions) go back to his days as an idealistic young black man in the civil rights movement. He's in semi-retirement now, doing consulting work once in a while on projects and issues that still ignite those young fires, but his health isn't what is used to be.

Ralph was diagnosed with diabetes a few years ago. Although

she tries to hide it, I swear his wife Diane cringes every time I walk through their door. I try to tell myself it's because I still bring him forbidden chocolate peanut butter oatmeal cookies. The truth is, I only ever bring them when I need Ralph's help, so I can't really blame Diane's anxiety on sugar alone.

It was 9 PM when I arrived on their doorstep, but Diane managed to swallow her emotions quickly as she welcomed me inside. I held up my little baggie in an effort at full disclosure. "See, I only brought four—two for each of you."

She smiled. We both knew she'd be lucky to get her hands on just one. I paused for a moment before heading toward the den. "How is he?"

Diane started to speak, then made a face that caused her head to tilt and one eyebrow to rise. I recognized it as a variation on the "men are such dumbasses" expression and mirrored it with the ease of much practice. Diane let out a surprisingly girlish giggle for a woman of her mature years.

I tossed the bag of cookies on Ralph's lap as I crossed the room to my favorite armchair. "Hey, old man. I brought your stash."

It took Ralph a moment to tear his eyes from the TV. A big-haired woman was leaning against a police cruiser, wailing about her man in a twangy voice while mascara streaked down her face. It wasn't a country music video, so it must be Cops. "Ever see anybody you know on there?"

"If I'm such an old man, how do you expect me to remember? What do you want, Syd?"

"Just to bask in your sunny disposition. Have a cookie, codger. If you've got your teeth in."

He tried to scowl at me, but his natural good humor won out. Ralph could never maintain a bad mood for long. "So who's got your world in a whirl this time, kid?"

I told him all about Noel and her shrinking and expanding family. "You check the body?" he asked. Little chunks of chocolate covered some of the gray in his mustache and settled on the pooch of his slightly bulging belly.

I simply blinked. "Her dad's body. Check with DOC and see what they did with it. If the lady's really his sister, maybe they released the body to her. Not to mention your client might want to know where her dad's buried."

I nodded. "The sister—if she is his sister—lives in Lazarus."

"Lazarus!" Ralph lurched forward and I was afraid his tatty black recliner would flip before settling into its full upright position. By his tone of voice, you'd think I'd said Baghdad. In the off season.

"Yeah, Lazarus. What about it?"

"You never heard of Lazarus?" He shook his head in disgust. "Let me tell you a little story about a shitheap called Lazarus. A bunch of industries moved to Lazarus in the 1940s to help with the war effort. Close to the coast and to the interstate so you got cheap transport, close to the air force base, and lots of unemployed poor people, so you got cheap labor. Well, Lazarus was so friendly, those companies told a few friends, and on and on. Before you knew it, business was booming and Lazarus had just about the lowest unemployment rate in the south."

"And then the other shoe dropped?"

Ralph mock-glared at me. "Who's telling this story?"

I grinned and he went on.

"Hell, yeah, both shoes drop-kicked their asses at the same time. In the late 1970s and early 1980s, companies started going belly up or moving out of state. But people didn't notice all at once. See, they were suddenly preoccupied with their parents and spouses

45

and children getting sick and dying. Turns out for Lazarus, the unusually low unemployment rate went hand-in-hand with an unusually high mortality rate, just on a slightly delayed timetable."

Ralph relaxed back into his chair and took a sip from the glass at his elbow. "It was a hell of a thing. I went up there for a while, trying to help collect the stories so somebody could file suit—the kinda thing you and I did in Beaufort—and I've never seen anything like it. Just about the whole damn town is a Superfund site now, full of PCBs and mercury and lead and—oh, wait. I forgot. There is no Superfund 'fund' anymore, so that designation isn't worth the triplicate paper it's filed on."

Uh-oh. I knew if he got going on one of his rants I'd be lucky to get out by midnight, and I'd have to be even luckier for Diane to let me in the house next time. "But you digress...."

"Digression is an old man's prerogative."

"You're not really an old man."

He took the hint, and I asked him what he knew about Isaac's attorney, Sam Norton.

"Screaming Sammy? He was a piece of work. They don't make 'em like him anymore, thank God."

"Was—past tense?"

"Yeah, Sammy died years ago. When would this have been?"

"The murder was October of '80, so we're looking at 1981."

"He was already in his declining years by then. I think he died in 1983. Screaming Sammy was known for his cross-exams and his closing arguments. He was absolutely merciless with cops and snitches, not to mention State Attorneys. I swear to God, I saw him call out the prosecutor one time. It was a plea day—no jury. 'Mr. Curtis,' he said, 'you have insulted me and you have insulted my client. How about you and I stop bothering the Court with this nonsense and take it outside?'" Ralph chuckled. "He was almost as bad in front of the jury, but he usually pulled it off with an air of righteous indignation."

"So he was a decent attorney?"

"I'd have asked for him myself *in his day*, but I'd say by 1981 his day was long past. Find out if he had a second chair. If so, that's who did all the work."

Ralph shook his head and laughed condescendingly. Or maybe it just sounded condescending to me. "Sydney, as usual, you sure know how to pick 'em. Screaming Sammy, a Superfund site, a client who lies to you with a family who hates you—"

"She hasn't really lied to me."

"If that's what you think, then you're just lying to yourself."

"What is that, a koan? Thank you, Obi-Wan, for your astounding insight." He'd touched a nerve, and I smiled to take the edge off my sarcasm.

"You just watch yourself over there. The cops cleaned house a few years ago, as they do periodically, but there's bound to be a few assholes left. Around the time of your murder, they ruled Stetler County like a cracker cartel. Anybody who didn't go along ended up behind bars or wishing they could be so lucky. Don't do anything stupid to piss them off."

"Come on, Ralph. You know me better than that." As I left, he gave me a face that looked suspiciously like Diane's "men are such dumbasses" expression. I chose to ignore it.

47

CHAPTER SEVEN

I hate it when Ralph is right. Of course I'd said the same thing, had the same doubts about Noel's candor, but to hear Ralph say it out loud... Yep, Noel and I were definitely having a talk.

I spent the next day on the phone, starting with my buddy Tanya at WFC. She got back to me within half an hour about Isaac's body.

"Yes, ma'am, Mr. Thomas's remains were released to a Mrs. Ida Pickett, who was identified as Mr. Thomas's sister."

She insisted I call her Tanya but kept calling me "ma'am." I was starting to understand Ralph's ageist paranoia. There had been no autopsy prior to the body's release. Tanya confirmed that Ida Pickett's address was the same one on the visitation request, and was about to hang up when I remembered the other reason I called.

"Oh, Tanya, one other thing. I noticed when I was going through Mr. Thomas's records that he had a medical transfer not long before he died. The paperwork on the transport was there, but that was it. I didn't see a referral or test results—I can't even tell what tests were done."

"Mmm, that's odd. We copied everything we had in our files and gave it to you. Was he sent to Latham?"

"Yes."

"Well, I don't know how it happened or why, but they must have kept his medical records. Maybe Mr. Thomas was supposed to return for more tests or treatment, and they didn't want to risk the

49

records getting held up if they went back with him. It wouldn't have been proper procedure, but unfortunately not everyone is as careful as we are about our records."

She'd been very good to me, so I bit my tongue on a sarcastic reply that was pure reflex. "I'm sure you're right. Thanks again, Tanya."

That done, I stared at the phone for a while. I checked my email, then checked outside for the snail-mailman. I straightened my desk and washed my teacups. When I reached for the broom to sweep the front steps I decided enough was enough. I'd been putting off my last (and most important) task before seeing Noel this evening. Band-aid, I thought, picking up the phone and dialing the numbers so fast I had to redial. Besides, it couldn't be as bad as Grandma Harrison.

She answered on the third ring.

"I'm calling for Ida Pickett."

"This is she."

"Ms. Pickett, my name is Sydney Brennan. I'm calling from Tallahassee. I'll be traveling around Lazarus soon and I was wondering if I could come by and speak with you."

"You don't sound like you're selling anything."

"I'm not."

"And you just want to talk?"

"Yes, ma'am," I reassured her.

"You're not a reporter, are you?"

"No, ma'am. I'm an investigator."

I could hear her sigh on the other end. "This is about Isaac, isn't it?"

"Yes, ma'am, it is."

The seconds dragged by. Finally she spoke again. "Sydney, did you say?"

"Yes, ma'am. Sydney Brennan."

"Well, Sydney, when should I expect you?"

She gave me her address and directions to her home from the interstate, and I told her I'd call when my plans were settled, but I hoped to see her by the end of the week. She hadn't asked any questions, and that surprised me. Perhaps she was writing out a list and saving them all for when I showed up on her doorstop. Latham Correctional Institute, where Isaac had been transferred, was also on my road trip schedule. I called to let them know I'd be coming by soon with a release to pick up his records.

Noel tapped on the screen door just as I was hanging up. The door was unlocked, as always, and she let herself in, peering around the door first, as if the screen were opaque. "Am I interrupting?"

"No. Just planning a road trip."

"Really? For little old me?" Noel tried to deliver a coquettish drawl, but perfect diction clung to her speech tenaciously.

"Yes, in fact, for little old you. Come on in. I have news."

I told her about the records from WFC, that they appeared incomplete but I was checking on the rest. "Your father went to Latham C.I. for something medical a couple of weeks before he died."

"What do you mean, something medical?"

"I don't know. That's the information I'm hoping to pick up. It was a medical transfer for only one day. It could have been for tests or treatment. The records weren't at WFC."

"Do you think it had something to do with his death?"

"I don't know. It could have. Considering the proximity in time, we can't rule it out."

"So he could have been diagnosed with some sort of terminal illness, or a debilitating disease."

"It's possible."

Noel raised an eyebrow and creases appeared on her mouth. My unwillingness to commit was beginning to annoy her. She took a deep breath. "What else?"

I didn't respond.

"What is it that you're having such difficulty telling me?"

"It's pretty big."

"By your demeanor I'm certain it is, but I'm a grown woman, and so are you. Just cut the games and tell me."

It was my turn to take a deep breath. "Noel, your father was not an only child." I paused to let this sink in. "He had a sister. Your aunt. She's still alive. Her name is Ida Pickett, and she lives in Lazarus."

Noel stood up and walked out the door.

At first I thought she'd left, but when I rose from my own chair I could see her silhouette through the screen door, settling down on the concrete front steps. I crossed to the fridge, retrieved a baggie of fresh cookies from home, and went out to join her.

"Cookie?" I offered.

She took one and broke off a piece, leaving chocolate marks on her index finger and thumb. "Mmm. Good. Peanut butter?"

"Yep." I broke off a piece of my own. "They're no-bake."

"What do you mean no-bake? You have to bake cookies. If you don't they're just dough."

"Not these. You heat the gooey stuff on the stove, and then when you mix it with the oatmeal it cooks."

"Freaky."

"Magic."

We sat in silence through another cookie each, staring at the trees and buildings silhouetted against the orange dusky sky.

"Sydney, I don't know about this."

"They're actually not that bad for you."

"That's not what I'm talking about." Noel was serious again. "It's not going to get any better, or any easier, is it?"

I wanted to tell her the truth, but my eyes were transfixed by a smear of chocolate on her full lower lip. It made her look so young, so vulnerable. It made me want to lie. I compromised.

"I don't know."

She shook her head at me, much the way Ralph had the night before. "You don't know much, do you?"

"Nope." I licked my lips and ran my tongue across my sticky teeth, checking for obvious bits of oatmeal. "Noel, what was Hainey like?"

She considered for a while, or maybe she was just trying to decide whether to answer. When she did, her voice was strong and neutral, the voice I was used to hearing her hide behind.

"We lived on the outskirts of Hainey in an older house. It was gray or light blue, and it had a small, square front porch with white railing. Sometimes I'd do my homework there. The houses in that area weren't very close together, but I don't remember them having big yards either. You could walk to a couple of businesses—bars mostly, but maybe a church too."

"Was it a big town?"

"I don't really have a sense of how many people lived there. I've never been good at estimating things, and I don't think I saw much of Hainey as a kid. I can tell you that it was big enough to have strip malls and pawn shops, and small enough that at that time it still had vacant fields and mom-and-pop country stores as you left the center. When we lived there, the asphalt was just starting to win out over farmland. I think it was a sad time, a time of transition. Even as a child I could feel it, a kind of hopelessness that made people ugly."

"I didn't like it." With that last bit, her eyes and voice lost the distance they always held when she described her childhood. Noel rose and stretched out the concrete kinks and numbness. "I'll see you in a few days, Sydney."

"I want to go talk to her. Your aunt."

She stopped with her hand on her car door, then turned to face me. From where I sat, I couldn't see the chocolate any more. "Then do it."

CHAPTER EIGHT

Ten miles after exiting I-10, I had yet to see a sign announcing my imminent arrival in Lazarus. In fact, I had yet to see much of anything. My jeans were sticking to my legs, and I needed to stretch. I'd had a long day of driving already, the boring kind that made me wish I was a dental hygienist or a cable guy (cable gal?).

The pine corridors of the interstate, where a few trees effectively screen the clear-cut fields on either side, had given way to weeds on State Road 31. There were weeds in abandoned industrial parks, weeds in fields with lone rotting oak trunks and doorless barns of dishwater gray. Barbed-wire fence fragments curled at the edges of empty pastures, their years of rust the most vivid color in the slowly passing landscape.

I never did see a sign for Lazarus, but eventually one-story buildings of corrugated metal and concrete block appeared, along with motor homes and simple brick apartment complexes. I turned left when I came to a convenience store with two gas pumps, as Ida Pickett had directed. The word "diesel" was painted in white stenciled garage sale letters on one pump. The other pump appeared unlabeled and, looking at my half-empty fuel gauge, I was glad I was driving a rental car today. I try to be careful what I feed my own dear Cecil.

Maple Street had a few trees but none that looked like maples to my untrained eye. The houses were modest, almost uniformly painted white, with neat front porches and browning but appropri-

55

ately cropped lawns. I thought I'd made a wrong turn when the street dead-ended at a twelve-foot high chain-link fence. Then I realized the street hadn't dead-ended, but split so its lanes wrapped around the obstruction. A large sign on the chained gate had a "Warning" in red capital letters, followed by an alphabet soup of government agencies and numbers. It wasn't until I had nearly passed the restricted area that I noticed the empty monkey bars and riderless swings swaying in the breeze.

Having just missed 915 Maple, I pulled the rental to the curb to walk back. I'd occasionally had glimpses of figures behind curtains and screen doors, but at 917 Maple I had my first confirmed human sighting since leaving the interstate. The man's hair was fully gray, but the freckle-like moles spattered across his dark cheeks gave him a boyish appearance. He poured water from a gallon jug into a watering can, then walked to some soil-filled buckets and began watering the plants inside. It looked like mustard greens from where I was standing, but I couldn't be sure. He noticed me as he began watering, gave a small nod of acknowledgment, but continued to watch as I walked up the front steps of 915.

The screen door rattled under my knuckles when I knocked. I could see the shadow of a form approaching, backlit from what appeared to be the kitchen. Isaac's sister unlatched the door and pulled it open, standing back to let me enter. She wiped her hands on a dish towel as she spoke.

"Come on in. I figured you'd be thirsty after the drive so I made some iced tea." My face must have reacted because she laughed as she put a hand on my shoulder and turned me toward the kitchen. "Don't worry—I used bottled water. For the ice and the tea."

Before stepping into Ida's kitchen, I got a fleeting impression from the rest of the house of tidy surfaces, walls of photographs, and the faint scent of some kind of flower. She led me to a formica-topped table, the kind with an inch of stainless metal fringing the edge. As a child, the narrow parallel grooves had made me think of lanes in an ant racetrack. Ida indicated a chair for me while she went to the refrigerator. She returned with a pitcher of tea and a Tupperware container of ice cubes.

"See, I wasn't kidding about the ice cubes." Ida gestured at an array of full water containers in the corner. "It's a shame to have to live this way, but..." Her voice trailed off and she shook her head.

"I hope you don't mind sweet tea."

I sipped appreciatively and sighed. "Mother's milk."

That drew a chuckle from her. "I knew I heard a hint of the south in your voice."

Her own voice was like slow velvet. She leaned back in her chair, draping one arm over its wooden back. "My tea used to be the talk of the neighborhood. I always put a little bit of fresh mint in it—blasphemy around here, but it tasted so good everyone pretended not to notice."

Ida set her tea glass down and rested her elbows on the table. "I don't grow fresh mint anymore. I guess you saw Mr. Phillips next door, with his greens and tomatoes in buckets. The EPA man told him it wasn't safe to eat anything that grew in the ground around here, but Mr. Phillips can't give up his fresh vegetables. So he buys bags of soil along with his bottled water. He says it's still better than the fake stuff they sell in the grocery store."

"Ms. Pickett, I—"

She interrupted. "Please, call me Ida. I never was a 'Ms.,' and my husband Ernest died a couple of years ago. I haven't felt much like a 'Mrs.' since then."

"All right then. Call me Sydney." She nodded and I went on. "Ida, I noticed the playground when I came in."

Her eyes grew shiny with tears. "Kids can't even play outside. If we had any kids left around here, that is. Most of the families moved away when the truth started coming to light."

"How long has it been like this?"

Ida let out another throaty chuckle. "Well now, that's the $64,000 question, isn't it? It depends on whose lawyers you're talking to. The plant's been here for about 60 years, but it's only in the last 20 or so that we started to notice the people dying of cancer, women with miscarriages and children with birth defects. And there were other things too. More subtle things that nobody'll ever prove."

"Like what?"

Ida considered for a moment. "Well, I don't know how else to put it. People acting crazy. Getting violent for no reason, or not much of one. I'm sure someone could come up with some big, societal explanation for it, and that's probably part of it, but I can't help but think... I don't know. I don't know how anyone could turn out right. I always wondered about Isaac and Vanda, growing up in the middle of this."

Ida leaned forward to pour me a refill from the sweating pitcher. "So Sydney, why exactly are you here?"

I considered her question, as I had during the hours of driving that morning. It's one I'd known she would ask, but I could never quite come up with an answer. "Well, I'm not really sure. To tell you the truth, I think you might know better than I do."

I waited. Ida began twisting the edges of the napkin she'd used as a coaster, shifted in her seat. She looked down at her handiwork and spoke in such a soft voice I had to ask her to repeat herself.

"What about the little girl?" Her head had sunk in her shoulders until her neck was barely visible, and she braced herself as if for a blow.

"Noel?" I asked.

"So it is Noel. I thought so, but then I felt sure they'd change her name when they got her."

"She's fine. Of course, she's not so little any more. She's about my age."

Ida had the napkin in her hand now, gripping it, and nodded her head over and over. A sob exploded from her, an anguished sound from deep in her belly that would leave her throat sore when she was done. She left the room. I didn't follow.

When she returned five minutes later, she had washed her face and had a damp washcloth in her hand that she occasionally applied to the back of her neck. Her eyes were swollen, and from the shadows beneath them I suspected she'd had about as much sleep as I had the night before. Two women who'd never met, lying awake staring at the walls, contemplating the ghosts of the past. I got lost in the image, and Ida's voice startled me.

"You said she's about your age, huh? So you're what, 19?"

I blushed and started to protest, but Ida held up her hand and went on. "No, I've done the math. You've got one of those faces that doesn't show its age for a while. Mine was like that. Everybody thinks you're still in school until you hit 45. Then all of a sudden, time catches up with you."

"So how many years until you start looking your age? Four or five?"

"Oh, honey, I like you. I do have a mirror, but I still like you. It's true though. I didn't have a wrinkle or a gray hair for the longest time, but the last few years just about did me in. Ernest being sick, and Isaac... So Noel wants to know about her daddy?"

"Something like that. When was the last time you heard from Isaac?"

"Oh, Lord. It must have been about six months before he died.

59

I don't remember how or why, but somehow he got in touch with me. Ernest was in the last stages of cancer then—he died just a few months before Isaac did—so I didn't have much to spare for Isaac. But he was a comfort to me, in his letters."

Ida's eyes began tearing up. Her grief was so raw, I tried to take her farther from its source.

"How did you know about Noel?"

She smiled. "I met her once. She couldn't have been much more than five years old. Isaac brought her with him when he came home for our mother's funeral, and they spent a couple of days."

"They?"

"Just Isaac and Noel. He didn't bring Vanda. She didn't exactly get along with the rest of the family. Truth is, I was surprised to see Isaac show up at all, much less with Noel."

"Was that the first time you'd seen her?"

"First and last time in person. Isaac had sent me a picture after she was born. No letter, no return address, just a picture. He couldn't."

Ida must have felt my skepticism because she rushed to defend her dead little brother.

"He'd made a deal with Vanda. Vanda felt that we disapproved of her. In hindsight, we probably did treat her that way, but I couldn't see that at the time. And Mrs. Harrison had made her feelings about Isaac very clear."

I tried not to laugh and ended up snorting. Ida grinned and said, "So you've met her?"

I nodded.

"Isaac and Vanda had gotten married young, and I guess they thought all their marital problems came from their families. Doesn't seem that crazy if you've met Mary Harrison. In order to save their marriage, they left Lazarus and broke off contact with all of us.

They didn't even tell anyone where they'd gone. It was all very sudden. I suspect they'd just found out that Vanda was pregnant with Noel and wanted a fresh start."

"How'd you track down Isaac to let him know about your mother?"

"Oh, it wasn't that hard. When he sent the picture of Noel, Isaac didn't use a return address, but there was a postmark. It was a small town. I called the post office there, and someone got a message to him."

"Was that in Hainey?"

"No. No, I can't remember the name, but that wasn't it. I think they moved again right after Mom's funeral. Noel mentioned that while they were here, something about going to a different school soon."

"What was she like?"

"Noel? She was a quiet child. Not shy, but just not chattery like most children are. Very intelligent. When she spoke it was like talking with an adult. I don't remember her playing with the other children either. She just seemed more comfortable with adults. I think she read a lot. When she and Isaac drove up, I remember she was reading a book in the car."

She paused, leaning back in her chair and closing her eyes to call up the memories. After a few moments, she opened them again. "She made me sad. She wasn't a very physically affectionate child. I wanted more than anything to give her a hug, but I was afraid to."

"You said Isaac and Vanda thought their marital problems were because of the family. But you thought it was something else."

Ida pursed her lips and tilted her head, trying to see me from a different angle. "Do you work for Noel or not?"

"Yes, I do."

"Can you come back tomorrow? I need to think about some things."

"Okay," I said. After all, how could I say no to another day in lovely Lazarus?

CHAPTER NINE

Richard Frey, Screaming Sammy's second chair during Isaac's trial, still worked at the Public Defender's Office. He was now the Chief Assistant, basically top dog under the elected Public Defender. Frey was out of the office, but I got him on his cellphone.

"Yes, of course I remember who you are. Where are you?"

"I was just over in Lazarus and I'm on the interstate headed in your direction right now. Well, the direction of your office. Where are you?"

He'd been in Carlton Springs that morning, less than 20 miles from Lazarus, and had just caught I-10 on his way back to Hainey. I wasn't more than a few miles behind him.

"Listen, there's a great little diner just off the next exit. It's a place called Mirabelle's—cinder block painted red, big windows. How about we grab a bite there?"

Mirabelle's was only about a quarter of a mile from the exit, and I pulled into the gravel parking lot a few minutes later. I recognized Frey before the door had even finished dinging my arrival. He was sitting in a booth in the corner. He'd taken his jacket off, but he was still the only man wearing a tie.

Frey was one of those men probably more attractive now at age 50-ish than he had been 25 years ago. The lines gave definition and interest to what was likely an unremarkable face in his youth, and the gray in his hair gave distinction to what had been just plain brown. He seemed a little short of average when he stood to greet me, maybe 5' 8", but when he smiled I lost all thoughts of average-ness. His smile must work magic with juries. For his clients' sakes, I hoped the rest of his expressions were as charismatic.

"You must be Sydney. I'm Richard." His handshake was firm and comfortable, as if he offered his hand a million times a day. We settled in and ordered. I got the club sandwich at his insistence, and I wasn't sorry when it arrived. The lettuce and bacon were crisp, the tomato ripe, and there wasn't a hint of sogginess to the toasted sourdough bread. I ate slowly, savoring my sandwich, and found it difficult to focus on his words.

"I was pretty green when the Thomas case came in. Of course, I didn't think so. I guess I'd been working at the PD's office a couple of years. I'd already gone through misdemeanors and worked my way up to felonies. This was my first capital case."

"So they did seek the death penalty?"

"Oh yeah. They'd already gone through discovery and it was close to trial by the time I got called in. You ever work capital?"

"I've done a little contract work on appeals—specific witness interviews, that kind of thing—but nothing at the trial level. I don't really know much about it. In fact, assume I don't know anything and you'll be pretty close."

"Well, a capital trial has two parts. The guilt phase is basically like a normal trial, but if the jury finds your client guilty there's a second part, the penalty phase. The jury hears evidence from the State about why your client should die—aggravation—and evidence from you about why your client should live—mitigation. Then the jurors vote, but unlike the guilt phase it doesn't have to be unanimous. At least not in Florida. If a majority of the jurors vote for death, just 7 to 5, your client gets a death sentence."

"Why only a majority?"

I nearly choked on my sandwich when Richard grinned at me.

Wow, that'll melt your panties.

"Don't get me started," he said. "If you ever want a diatribe on the Vagaries of the Criminal Justice System, just give me a call and set side a few hours."

Richard gave a nod to the waitress and she began making her way to our booth. "I was brought in on the Thomas case because it looked like it was going to trial, and Sam Norton needed help. We try to put two attorneys on capital cases, and seconds cut their teeth on the penalty phase stuff. Look at the defendant's family, at his childhood, at whether he has mental health issues. That was supposed to be my job."

"Supposed to be?"

"Yeah, well, we never got that far, did we?" Richard shook the clotting ice cubes in his nearly empty glass of iced tea.

"And?"

"And what?"

I didn't answer. Just used my trademark Sydney Stare and waited.

Richard lowered his voice. "You ever think of becoming a cop? No, forget I said that. I've got enough screwed clients as it is. Damn, I'd confess if you were interrogating me."

I'd like an opportunity to interrogate him all right. Whoa, where had that come from? Focus. For example, on his wedding ring. Richard cleared his throat.

"It's funny. Now that I'm Chief Assistant, I end up fielding a lot of administrative and personnel type problems." He leaned across the booth.

"I hate it. Makes me feel like a babysitter. Lately there's a lead attorney who hasn't been pulling his weight, and his seconds have been picking up the slack. Yesterday I had one of the seconds in my office. I wanted to know why she hadn't said anything, and she blamed it on something she half-jokingly called 'second chair syndrome.' Some sort of co-dependency, covering up for and enabling the lead's behavior. I told her that was the most ridiculous thing I'd ever heard."

The waitress filled Richard's glass, and I covered the mouth of my own just in time. If I had any more sweet tea today, I was going into orbit. Richard took a sip and went on.

"I'm going to have to track her down this afternoon and apologize. I've been doing this for 25 years now, and Norton's been dead for 20. Working with him just about drove me insane, but it still feels funny to talk about it."

"He was your first," I said, before I realized how it sounded.

Richard laughed. "Yeah, in a way I guess he was. I learned a lot from him, most of it being what not to do, and to trust my own instincts. When I got called in on the Thomas case, it was a mess. Norton was a mess. He'd already gotten two continuances. He hadn't finished the depositions yet, and I don't think he'd even read the discovery. I was supposed to be doing the penalty phase, but I wasn't getting far with Thomas on his family history, and it seemed to me the most important thing was to get it together for the trial. If he wasn't found guilty, we wouldn't need to have a penalty phase. So I started organizing the files, reviewing materials."

"Was there a chance he'd be found not guilty?"

Richard graced me with another panty-melting grin. "Remember, I was young. I didn't understand yet that our justice system is made up of people. The law is just a bunch of words on paper, the rules you hope everybody will play by when no one's there to watch them."

"Ouch, a cynic."

"That's wisdom speaking, not cynicism. I'm still an idealist. I have seen everything, every kind of deceit and corruption of the system, many times over, and I'll tell you nothing can surprise me. But I'm still surprised, every time. Surprised that someone's not doing the right thing."

Richard chuckled and looked embarrassed. "I warned you about getting me started. If I were on a jury, Thomas would've walked. There simply wasn't what I would consider to be evidence beyond a reasonable doubt. But people like me don't end up on juries. Thomas would have been convicted, especially with Norton representing him."

"And that's why you made a deal?"

"Yeah. Well, to be honest, I was out of the loop on that one—found out after the fact and boy, was I pissed—but in hindsight it makes sense. And you have to remember that this never should have been a death case to begin with. In theory, the death penalty is reserved for the worst of the worst. Child killers, hit men, serial killers, that kind of thing. All murder is offensive to a civilized society, but we're talking about the truly repugnant killing here, the kind of crime you just can't get your head around. Not to diminish the very real problem of domestic violence in our country, but a man choking his wife to death just didn't fall into that category."

"Really?" I asked, my tone dry.

"I'm going to tell you a dirty little secret," he said. "For a long time, Florida was even less enlightened than the rest of the country about domestic violence. People used to joke about the 'one free wife' rule here, that you could get away with killing one of your wives, but the next one would get you prison time. At some point in the 1980s that changed. There was a big swing in the other direction, and I suspect we've got a few guys sitting on death row—or executed by now—for that very reason. They were the public example. It could be that Thomas fell into that timeframe, and that's why the State sought death."

"Who was your investigator?"

"I'm embarrassed to admit this, but I don't think we had one. Of course, we should have had for a capital case. We were probably short-staffed on investigators then—it feels like we always are. I know we were sharing. It wasn't like you had designated teams, or particular investigators always worked with particular leads. You also have to keep in mind that by this point in his career, Sammy was pretty isolated. He'd managed to piss off most of the decent investigators, and he tried to avoid having one if at all possible, doing the legwork himself or having a second do it. Oh, he might have an investigator do a specific task, but he didn't want them taking over his case."

He glanced at me quickly, to see if I'd been offended. "His words, not mine. I don't know if he got paranoid at the end or he was always like that. Anyway, I suspect Isaac's case was seen as a penalty phase case rather than a guilt phase one by everyone but me, so maybe 'the powers that be' didn't push it. Shows you what a mess the office was back then—that's when you really need some-body, is for penalty phase. Then again, we never made it to trial, and Sammy was a notorious procrastinator. It wasn't unheard of for him to wait until a couple of weeks before trial, beyond the very last minute, to draft an investigator. That's probably why they were all pissed off at him."

"I know it's a long shot, but would the office still have your file on Thomas's case?"

His undivided attention made me feel short of breath and tingly, like a mild food allergy. "Sit back, and enjoy the moment, because I'm about to make your day. Drum roll, please. We do have his file, and I've already had it pulled."

"Really?"

"Yep. Since he didn't get the death penalty, our office normally wouldn't have kept it this long, but as it turns out I'm a slightly anal retentive type about those things. My secretary is having it copied right now, so if you want to follow me back to Hainey, I can give you a copy of your very own this afternoon."

CHAPTER TEN

We got back on I-10 for a few miles, then took the 231 exit toward Panama City. It took us about an hour, driving conservatively, to get to the PD's office in Hainey. I wondered if Richard drove that way because he assumed I was a slow driver and didn't want to lose me, or because he'd just pissed off too many of the area cops on cross-examination to risk getting pulled over.

The PD's office was in a building so new, the landscaped palms and shrubs looked stubby and fresh from the nursery. "Nice," I said, as Richard pressed a buzzer by the door to gain admittance.

"We shut the doors for lunch, and I forgot my key," he explained. "Yeah, I'd rather have spent the money on something useful like more attorneys or investigators, but you can't fight bureaucracy. Believe me, I tried."

Richard opened the door when the lock clicked in release, but before we entered he leaned back with the door to point around the side of the building. "Did you notice that other parking lot, and the other entrance?"

"No," I admitted.

"Probably couldn't see it the way we came in. We only have half the building. The State Attorney's office has the other half. If you want to pay them a visit sometime, we share a stairwell."

"You're kidding!"

"No. Wish I were. You can bet I raised holy hell about that, too, for all the good it did." He grinned. "As if we're all not paranoid enough."

We took an elevator to the second floor. When the doors slid open, I was surprised to find myself facing a large room with about a dozen cubicles in the center and a few offices along one wall. The other wall was bare. Most cubicles were empty for lunch, but a few brave souls, attorneys and investigators by the sound of things, sat hunched over documents or phones.

Richard's own office not only had walls, but was actually two offices in one. The outer room housed a desk, metal filing cabinets, and a woman filing papers who was presumably his secretary. I'd guess she was about Richard's age, though she seemed older. She was dressed in a simple white blouse and teal blue skirt, and while her eyeshadow was a bit too dark and too blue, her make-up was otherwise unremarkable. It was the slightly frizzy perm in her short, dark blonde hair that set her age. Her hair made me think of grandmothers wearing polyester scarves over their rollers.

"Millicent, dear heart," Richard said. "How goes the fort-holding? Any major catastrophes this morning?"

She wiped her hands on her skirt and shut the drawer she was working in. "Nothing I couldn't handle."

She held her hand out to me. "It's Melinda, not Millicent," she said.

"That may be what your birth certificate says, but trust me on this. You're a Millicent, through and through. This is Sydney Brennan. So she says. I haven't decided what her real name is yet."

I tried not to cringe. I changed my name legally over a decade ago, but it still felt like a deep, dark secret I could be arrested for. Oh, the irony if he managed to guess my real name. I stammered a "nice to meet you."

"Ah, Sydney of the Thomas case. Well, I've got good news for you. Since he was out of the office all morning, I was finally able to get some work done. The Thomas trial attorney file, the original and one copy, is on Richard's desk. No, I take that back. There's no room for anything on his desk. But it is somewhere in his office."

Richard was surprised to find that it was only one box—full to the gills, but one box nonetheless. "I'd like to think there would have been more materials if we had gone to trial, but I doubt it. My files on capital cases generally run from 2-5 boxes, so that should tell you something."

He offered to find me a place to review the file, but having seen the office's layout I declined. Any space Richard could find me was sure to infringe on the cramped people who worked there on a daily basis, and I didn't want to spend all my office capital at once. I did allow him to introduce me around. When Richard was paged for an important call (the high-tech page consisted of relayed yells across cubicles), I took the opportunity to chat up a few of the older attorneys and support staff, people who'd been there long enough to know Screaming Sammy. No one I spoke with had been very close to him, and they all confirmed what I had heard already. I was surprised that no one offered to tell me war stories. Melinda's response was typical.

"I'd heard that Mr. Norton was called that, but I can't say that he was screaming much when he worked here. Mr. Norton was in private practice in the Panhandle for years, and by the time he came to work at the PD's office he wasn't in good health. I think that's why he came here, so he could have a steady check and health insurance. I didn't see him often, but the poor man always had bad color. He took a lot of sick days, and from what I heard he didn't make it to court very often except on plea days."

"Were you his secretary?"

"No, not usually. His secretary, Rita, was an older woman. She died a few years ago herself. At that time, I was assigned to a couple of other attorneys who've since retired." Melinda seemed to lose herself for a moment, then blinked at me.

"It's enough to make you feel old. Sometimes if there was a big trial, something high-profile or a death penalty case, I'd pitch in to help out the regular secretary, but that was never an issue with Rita. She was incredibly efficient, and I don't think Mr. Norton ever gave her that much to do."

"Did you ever see him hang out with anyone in the office, commiserate about cases?"

"No, I didn't. I got the impression he didn't spend much time with people here, in or out of the office. I'd say he spoke to Richard as much as anyone else, but even then I wouldn't say they were close. Richard could tell you better than I could."

Eventually I gave up on Sammy and went to hang out with a young investigator named Mike Montgomery. When introduced, I'd been told if I had any need of technological assistance, computer searches, etc., Mike was the man. By the looks of him, pallid under chin-length hair and small-framed glasses, he was able to find out most things without ever leaving his cubicle. (Like I had room to talk about the pigment-challenged, with my fluorescent white skin.)

"So, how long you been working here?" I asked.

His eyes rolled back a bit as he thought about it. "Must be going on six years. God, time flies."

"You come here straight out of school?"

"No." Some personal thought that went unexpressed seemed to amuse him. "No, I started out going to grad school for computers. I didn't finish. Decided I needed a little fresh air and sunshine."

Now it was my turn to be amused, but apparently my thoughts weren't so obscure.

Mike laughed. "Yeah, I know you can't tell it to look at me, but I do set foot outside from time to time. I've just had a dry spell lately. But I might go out on the water with a buddy this week. I don't know. Anyway, I quit grad school, messed around for a while, did some traveling. Eventually I ended up here."

"Do you like it?"

"Yeah, for the most part I'd have to say I do like it. If I won the lottery tomorrow, I'd give my notice, but if I have to work I can't think of anything I'd rather be doing. I don't get bored here, or if I do I just move on to something else for a while. When I can't stand to look at the computer screen any more, I go track down some records, or interview witnesses. You know yourself that being an investigator isn't nearly as glamorous as it sounds to everyone else. Sometimes it's downright tedious. But then you move on to some-thing else. I just don't think I'm cut out for a 'normal' job, doing the same thing day in and day out. You know?"

"Yeah, I know exactly what you mean." I was sitting on the edge of Mike's desk while he sat in his chair, and I lowered my voice and leaned toward him conspiratorially when I spoke again. "What's the office vibe like?"

"Not bad. We've had a few rough spots, but nothing you wouldn't find anywhere else. I think the key is to be sociable, maybe have a beer once in a while, but not try to be everybody's best friend, to maintain our own independent lives so we can get away from this shit. Richard and I do stuff together once in a while, but that's about it."

"What's he like?"

"Okay, for an attorney." He couldn't hold the deadpan and broke into a smile. "He's a good guy. I guess you could say he took me under his wing when I got here, and we work together a lot. When I—"

Mike broke off suddenly, and I wasn't sure he'd go on. He kept his eyes on his hands, tracing a bump on the side of his index

75

finger. "He's always been there when I needed him. His wife's a good cook too."

We sat in silence for a few moments until he recovered enough to turn the tables on me. "So what about you? What brought you to the business? The *search for truth*?" His voice lent an ironic air to the last phrase.

"Something like that." He raised an eyebrow, and I reluctantly went on. "If you hear enough lies, they start to leave a bad taste in your mouth. I wanted something simpler, something cleaner."

"And you decided to become an investigator? First day of work must have been a real shocker."

I laughed. "Yeah. Yeah, it was. But it still fits the bill somehow. I wouldn't do anything else."

As I perched on Mike's desk, I felt content, warm and fuzzy. Camaraderie, that's what it was. Now that I'd gone private, I missed sharing my work, the excitement and the frustration, with colleagues. Wasn't I a little young for nostalgia? Maybe, but—the sudden realization of an actual physical warmth next to me would have made me jump if my feet could touch the floor. Richard had finished his phone call.

"Find everything you need?" he asked.

I looked at my watch. Much of the afternoon had slipped away, even by central time, and it was time to load up the file and drive around for a while, get a sense of the area. My slide from Mike's desk was relatively graceful, which for me meant I hadn't fallen.

"Like you said, time flies. I really ought to be going." I reached for the box I'd left on the other corner of Mike's desk.

"Let me take that," he said, and scooted his chair back to rise.

"That's okay, Mike." Richard grabbed the box before Mike could stand. "I'll walk Sydney out."

I nodded my thanks, but said nothing. It wasn't like me to do feminine demurral. I told myself I let Richard take the box because it was too heavy for me, but who was I kidding? My office was full of such boxes, with no burly men around to move them for me.

A sudden impulse made me turn back before Mike's cubicle was out of sight. He was still watching us.

"You should go. On the water. Wherever. Get a little Vitamin D for both of us."

Mike's face looked conflicted.

"Just do it. Call your buddy right now."

His face cleared. "You're right. I will." He reached for the phone. "Thanks, Sydney."

Richard led the way out of the PD's office to my car. He walked ahead of me, and I tried, mostly unsuccessfully, not to look at his ass in his slacks. When he set the box on my back seat and turned suddenly to face me, I felt myself blush, sure that could see where my eyes had been pointing. If he did he gave no indication of it, and I hoped he'd think the flush was from the sudden heat of the asphalt.

"Listen, I'll review my file tonight and give you a call about meeting tomorrow. That should give you time to come up with some tough questions I can't dodge. Sound like a plan?"

"Yeah, that sounds good."

Richard held out his hand. I offered my own awkwardly, and he took it in both of his. My hands were chilled from air conditioning, and his warm hands felt good around mine. My eyes nearly closed with the pleasure of it.

"Tomorrow then," he said, giving my hands a final squeeze before releasing them and heading back inside. I didn't watch him go. I swear.

CHAPTER ELEVEN

The public defender's office was located on the edge of downtown Hainey. The heart of the town was a square about four blocks by four blocks. Like a lot of old downtowns, it was undergoing restoration. The main street was lined with new planters and park benches and freshly planted trees, while one of the side streets was being repaved. Not all of the buildings were occupied, but none of them were derelict. Most were two stories, with none above three. I know nothing about architecture, but the mix of styles and building materials was pleasing to the eye.

The mix of occupants, or rather the lack thereof, was less pleasing. I saw a couple of upscale restaurants and a few sandwich-type eateries that were only open for lunch. They were obviously catering to the courthouse crowd. As someone who spends a fair amount of time around courthouses, there are few crowds I like less than the courthouse crowd. Their spoor was everywhere here. There were several law offices and an expensive-looking one-hour dry cleaner. The bail bonds place right across from the courthouse must have been grandfathered in to the newly fashionable area. (In their defense, they had painted the building an eggshell with kelly green trim and toned down the neon signs.)

As I left downtown, it became apparent that the rejuvenation effort hadn't spread far. Most of the places on the main street into town looked respectable, meaning they mowed their grass and didn't have burglar bars, but they looked faded. Beyond main street, things got downright depressing. Like so many towns, the only vitality (i.e. money) was at the seat of power, with none left for the people who were subject to it.

Mike had given me a map, so I headed in the direction of the Thomases' old neighborhood. The scene of the crime. In the last 25 years, the mom-and-pop stores Noel mentioned had been swallowed up, and the only evidence of vacant fields was an occasional empty weedy lot. As near as I could tell, the spot their house had stood on was now a Dollar store. There were a few loiterers, and even a few residences left in the area, so I did a quick canvas, expecting to find nothing. I wasn't disappointed. No one remembered them; no one remembered the crime.

It was time to find a place to roost. Prison visits were on the schedule again tomorrow, so I drove about half an hour up 231 to be closer to the interstate in the morning. Just finding a clean place that didn't reek of cigarettes or have dead roaches on the AC unit gave me a little thrill. (Being an investigator lowers your standards pretty quickly.) Having gotten my bag and the trial attorney file settled on the extra bed, I was eyeing the unsullied mattress with longing when an alarm went off.

The noise filled my ears with the insistence reserved for electronic devices and small children. Like most people, my instinct and great desire was to blame the disturbance on a neighbor, but it seemed to originate in my own room. When I followed the shrill repeating noise to one of my bags, it occurred to me that the sound must be a cell phone. Next thought—wait for it—my cell phone. Oh yeah, I do have a cell phone. I hate it and only use the beast on road trips. Even then I have a convenient habit of leaving it in the car. I must have forgotten to forget it.

"Hello?"

"Sydney?"

80

"Yes?"

"You're new to the world of telephones, aren't you? This is Richard."

"Oh, hi Richard. Just cell phones. What's up?" I'd forgotten I'd given him my cell phone number.

"What are you doing for dinner?"

I walked to the window and looked out at the strip of fast food hell. "Well, I hear there's this great French restaurant right across the street, but I don't have reservations and this is the high season."

He laughed. "Forget it. You'll never get in. I got René off on a stalking charge a few months ago and even I need a reservation. I've got a better idea. Where are you staying?"

I told him. "My wife has plans tonight, and the kids are off being teenagers, so what do you say to some heavy-duty carb loading? There's a decent Italian restaurant a few miles from your motel. I'll pick you up."

I agreed. After he hung up, I automatically pulled the waist of my pants forward, tugging at the top of my underwear to see what I was wearing. Good—nothing grandma or ratty. I blushed, whether because the ritual was automatic or because it was triggered by dinner with a married man I wasn't sure. Men aren't the only ones sometimes governed by organs other than the brain. At least I hadn't sniffed my pits, I thought, right before heading to the bathroom to apply more deodorant.

Richard drove a silver late model Toyota sedan, like so many others on the road until you peeked in a window. Then its owner-ship became unmistakable. Richard's car was definitely his domain, not his wife's or his children's. Empty dry cleaner bags puddled on the floorboard of the back seat, and a slightly wrinkled dark suit hung on the passenger side. Bulging accordion files, yellow legal

81

pads, and other attorney-type detritus fought for space with an illegibly labeled banker's box. I had to toss a garish Tabasco tie in the back before I could sit down.

"Sorry. Got that in a conference in New Orleans," he explained. "You ever been there?"

"New Orleans?"

"No, Avery Island. The home of Tabasco. Here it is in the heart of Acadiana, and they've got this enormous Buddha statue that looks out over a pond full of alligators. Amazing. No, maybe its back is to the pond. I'm not sure."

"And maybe the pond isn't full of alligators?"

Richard laughed. "Yeah, maybe. But I did see a few little ones when I was there. Got this on that trip too."

He reached into the console between us, which was filled with two neat rows of CDs. His hand inadvertently brushed against my bare forearm where I'd rolled my sleeves up, prickling the hairs. It took every ounce of self-control to keep from moving my arm, to pretend I didn't notice his touch. Or was I just hoping for another jolt? Without looking, he ran his fingers along the spines, withdrew a CD, and placed its jewel case back in the space it had vacated. The lazy voice and nimble fingers of Dr. John filled the car.

"You've got an eclectic mix here," I said, thumbing through them. "Warren Zevon, Greg Brown, Jill Sobule, Talking Heads…."

"I like storytellers," he said. "Please don't move them around. It's one of the few things I'm obsessive about. I know where each one is, so when a mood strikes me I don't have to pull over or wipe out to indulge."

Rosalia's Italian Restaurant was next door to the Good Times bar, and they shared a large parking lot. When we got out of the car, I could only hope that Rosalia's had good sound-proofing. For a Thursday night, Good Times was really hopping.

"Unique name," I said, nodding toward the whooping and honky-tonk. I could feel Richard's amusement in the dark. "I've been hanging around the Panhandle too long. Some of these guys are starting to look familiar."

"Have you been to WFC?"

"Yeah, a few days ago, and I'm heading back tomorrow."

"That explains it. I've heard a lot of the guards head over here when they get off work."

Rosalia's was a pleasant surprise. The lighting was warm, aided by red-glassed table votives, and it was cozy without being crowded. Our waitress, a cute pony-tailed brunette barely old enough to drive, led us to a table almost immediately. The menus had hand-written addendums, cards with daily specials and notes about availability of regular items.

"What are you having?" Richard asked.

"I'm leaning toward the angel hair marinara," I said virtuously.

"Her alfredo sauce is to die for."

"I think you're the first man I've ever heard use that phrase —'to die for.'"

"But it is."

I suspect fettuccine alfredo heads most women's lists of date food don'ts. Fettuccine can be hard to handle if you're nervous, or just a klutz, slapping against your chin or flinging sauce on the clothes you've calculated are most likely to impress. And the alfredo... why not just get reverse liposuction while you're at it? You'll spend the whole dinner wondering if you've eaten so little of your entrée he'll think you're anorexic or eaten so much he'll know you're destined for a life of loose-fitting garments. What neurotic creatures we women are, or at least this woman. Good thing I wasn't on a date. I ordered the fettuccine alfredo.

The evening passed pleasantly, with the kind of conversation you enjoy at the time but can't recall later. The wine was good, the food even better, and I didn't get a drop of either on my chic clothes. I wore my usual road uniform of a men's button-down shirt (white) and jeans, but I had put on sandals and pulled my hair back with a scarf to signal my brain that it was off the clock. I guess it didn't get the message.

We made it to coffee before I reverted to shop talk. I'd reviewed the police reports while waiting for Richard, and now I took the opportunity to ask him about some of the players.

"You know," he said, "Rudy Nagroski, the lead detective, is retired, but he's still around. I'm surprised he's not here at Rosalia's tonight. He's a pretty good guy, as cops go. He was a transplant from up north, so he wasn't brought up with the local politics, and he didn't take every crime in his jurisdiction as a personal affront. How long are you sticking around?"

"At least tomorrow, probably through Saturday."

"I'm busy tomorrow, but I'd be happy to go see Rudy with you on Saturday. If I wouldn't be stepping on your toes."

"Not at all. Local or not, he might be more relaxed talking to somebody he knows. But are you sure you want to? It's your day off. Your wife might actually want to see you sometime."

Richard laughed. "Angela's used to me working on Saturdays. I'm sure she has her own plans. She's learned to be very independent, if that doesn't sound too chauvinistic."

"How chauvinistic is too chauvinistic?" He looked momentarily stricken so I added, "Just kidding—I know what you mean. The marriages where two people become one unit scare me. Although I have to admit, if my husband were out at all hours with adoring young seconds I may get the teensiest bit jealous."

"Angela used to in the beginning, but it's become sort of a running joke with us, which young thing I'm having an affair with now. My wife knows I've always been faithful."

I avoided Richard's eyes. For the first time all night I felt un-comfortable, but I wasn't sure why, whether it was because of his thoughts or my own. We left a few minutes later, and I wondered if the timing was a coincidence.

The party was still going at the Good Times, but a few people left as we did, heading home so they could start all over again tomorrow. Just as we would. Tired and slightly wine-sluggish, the thought made it hard for me to move from the car when we arrived 15 minutes later. The motel I was staying in was an older one, with no interior access. My first floor room opened directly onto the parking lot, and when Richard dropped me off at the motel he insisted on walking me to my door. The lock was a tricky one, the kind that requires you to pull the door toward you and give an appropriate grunt before it opens. A truck's headlights blinded me as it pulled in the parking lot, and I nearly dropped my keys. Great, was there anything else I could do to add verisimilitude to my impersonation of a drunk person? For some reason it bothered me that Richard might think two glasses of wine with dinner would knock me on my ass.

I finally managed, with the proper profane incantations, to coax my door open. The table lamp was on, as I'd left it, and everything was as it should be. Pulling the door back toward me as I removed the key, my body turned slowly to face Richard. I opened my eyes wide, straining to make out his face as it drifted toward my own in the dark.

His lips hovered near my own—I knew they must—so lus-ciously close that his head blocked the little bit of light in the parking lot. His features began to take shape, but his expression was still indecipherable. I held my breath until my lungs burned and tiny open circles appeared in my vision. Finally, I feel his breath

85

expelled from his nostrils, a quick sigh, as he tilted his head to kiss my cheek. His warm lips lingered for the space of several heart-beats, but the way my heart was racing, that wouldn't have been long. He rocked back on his heels and said a soft good night. I responded in kind, and hoped the darkness hid the flush that spread from my cheeks to the base of my neck.

My mind was racing in time with heart, blood, and other organs, and yet a tiny piece of it remained aloof, unaffected, as always. I visualize that fold in my gray matter as a tiny old school-marm type, perched on a rocking chair in the back of my skull, muttering an occasional "hmm" and taking notes of things to share with the rest of the class when the time is right. Mrs. Bibbystock, I call her, when I'm feeling whimsical. It was Mrs. Bibbystock who noticed the blinding truck leave the parking lot right after Richard.

Neither of us noticed the note that had been slipped under my door, pushed out of the way with the door's opening arc, nor did I notice it the next morning.

CHAPTER TWELVE

The kinds of places I stay when I'm working don't have much to offer in the way of luxury, but they do have the panacea of hot water. The next morning, I showered until the steam billowed from the bathroom when I opened the door. Then I wiped the mirror with a hand towel, reveling in the streaks.

Once I'd dressed (light blue shirt with khakis this time—it was too hot for jeans) I walked next door to Denny's, my notes tucked under my arm. I had some OJ and an English muffin while I tried to gather my thoughts. This is also typical road routine, which explains the jelly smears on many of my note pads.

Noel had talked about her old babysitter and neighbor, Miss Johnson, but she hadn't even known her first name. Last night before turning in, I'd channeled my insomnia and unruly thoughts of married men into completing my initial review of the trial attorney file. I'd jotted down everything I could find on Miss Johnson and was hoping the police reports had given enough identifying information to track her down. Or rather, for me to have Mike at the PD's office track her down. He struck me as the efficient type, so I should have just enough time to get an address on her before heading out to Ida's place in Lazarus in the evening.

My first stop of the morning was Latham C.I. to check on Isaac's medical records. I got nothing there but dirty looks. Well, almost nothing. The records administrator was a stern woman in a plain navy ankle-length dress and cardigan. From her demeanor, I suspected she valued economy in thought as highly as economy in dress. She remained standing behind her desk, but I pretended not to get the hint. I sank down in a metal folding chair as if it were plushly upholstered and began removing items from my bag, including a notebook and pen.

"You won't need that," she told me.

I ignored her words and waited expectantly like an eager pupil. She pushed on.

"Isaac Thomas was processed and spent exactly one day here at Latham Correctional Institute. He was returned the same day he arrived, and he was not treated or tested, nor did he in any way receive attention from our staff. If he had, we would have a record of it. Further, regardless of what you may have been told by ill-informed individuals at other institutions, any records that come in with an inmate leave with him, and Mr. Thomas would have been no exception. At Latham, we keep records of those actions actually initiated at our institution, but if we maintained full medical records on everyone who passes through here we'd have no room for the inmates. Now if you'll excuse me."

I didn't have a chance to speak, even if I could have thought of something to say. She left her office before I'd even gathered my belongings. Honesty compels me to admit that when I have all my paraphernalia (official-looking bag, pads, pens) I'm often the last person to leave a room. It started as a natural behavior, taking time to put everything in its place, but then I began cultivating it. I've heard and seen a lot of things I otherwise wouldn't have without my apparently abstracted tardiness. This was to be no exception.

As I closed the flap on my bag, I noticed an inmate in blues loitering in the hallway by the door. He was a youngish black man —that is, about my age. Still young by outside standards, but old enough in the prison population to start knowing better, start settling down and maybe even start feeling old. I remembered nodding to him when I walked in. He'd been mopping the hall, and it looked like he was still cleaning the same spot.

"That Miss Hinckley knows everything there is to know about records," he said.

"Yeah, that's what she told me. In fact, I think those may have been her exact words."

He smiled and leaned on his mop. "'Course, that don't mean she knows everything there is to know about prisons."

"No, I wouldn't think she would."

I noticed he also pulled a big garbage bin behind him, so I picked up Miss Hinckley's wastepaper basket and took it to him. He dumped the basket, giving an extra shake for those particularly sticky documents.

"You don't work for the state, do you?"

"No, I don't."

"Didn't think so, and I can usually tell." He walked slowly into the office to return the empty basket. "Sometimes we get some mighty healthy-looking people in here. Seems to me like not everybody that comes here on a medical is really here because they're sick."

He replaced the can and stood in the doorway. I finally picked up my bag and moved to join him.

"What else would bring someone to this fine institution?"

He looked slowly up and down the hallway before speaking. "Personally, I don't know. But I hear things. Like maybe if somebody wants to have a private chat with you, the kind you don't want nobody to know about, they suddenly decide you don't look so well and get you a medical transfer. Just long enough to talk to you. Then you have a miracle recovery and get sent back home. You follow me?"

Fortunately I did, because I figured that was all he was saying. "Yeah. Thanks, man."

He nodded and loaded up his cleaning supplies. "It ain't gospel, but that's what I hear."

He moved down the hall away from me, then turned with a grin and did a half-skip backwards. He cupped a hand around each ear, both of which stood out straight without any help.

"And like the ladies always say, I got me some damn fine ears."

His words occupied my thoughts as I drove to WFC. Without an autopsy, there was no way of knowing if Isaac's organs were eaten up by cancer or some other terminal illness. Of course, even with an autopsy the M.E. may not notice ill health in a suicide, much less the suicide of an inmate. But if Isaac hadn't been sick at all... Nothing in Isaac's visitation records indicated a visit from a cop, but that didn't mean anything. Someone could have looked the other way on the sign-in, or the medical transfer could have been their first meeting. But why? After 20 years of incarceration, what information could Isaac possibly have that was important enough to justify the charade?

The most obvious answer was information about another inmate, something he'd overheard or something someone had confessed to him. It was obvious, but it didn't feel right. First of all, common sense says snitching is more common in jail than in a prison. Elaborate systems develop in some jails, pipelines of information to satisfy the law enforcement wish list, with that information occasionally coming directly from the officers. Inmates find out who's ripe for snitching, what needs to be said, and jump on board for reduced sentences. It's pretty simple, and everybody knows about it. Everybody, that is, except the jurors who convict people based on snitch testimony.

It gets more complicated in prison. The guys there have already been convicted and sentenced, so no one in a position of power cares about their cases anymore. Plus chances are good that you're looking at multiple jurisdictions with the snitcher, the snitchee, and the place they're incarcerated. Like I said, complicated. I suspected that in prison, you'd have to hold some pretty compelling information to get noticed and make it worth the effort of following up.

Aside from the practical considerations, Isaac just didn't strike me as the snitching type. He hadn't made a statement of any kind in his own case. Richard told me he'd refused to either confirm or deny his guilt, to the court or to his own attorneys, even when it could have helped him get a more lenient sentence. Often when a defendant pleads guilty as part of a plea agreement, he's required to make a statement to the court, setting out the circumstances of his case and his part in the crime. Isaac had avoided that by pleading nolo contendere (no contest) to the charges against him, not admitting responsibility but agreeing to not contest the charges.

The State had been unable to produce any jailhouse snitches against Isaac, or at least none worth using. Isaac apparently was not a chatty guy, so it seemed unlikely that he'd encourage others to unburden themselves to him. And he had no known history of snitching over decades of incarceration. It didn't make sense. In order to get my head around it, I needed to have a better understanding of what kind of inmate, and what kind of person, Isaac had been.

CHAPTER THIRTEEN

Tanya was unavailable when I got to WFC. I had a funny feeling that from now on, no matter when I dropped by or why, Tanya would always be unavailable. Ms. Ricker, the woman standing in for her, was older than Tanya, probably in her late 40s, and not nearly as pleasant. I had a sneaking suspicion she was related to the records woman at Latham.

"I'm familiar with your *requests*," she said. The way she said it, you'd think I'd asked her to hitch up and be my lead dog for a little dogsled race in Alaska. Nude. "We've given you all of Mr. Thomas's records."

"Yes, ma'am. You've all been very helpful, and I do appreciate it, but I'm sure there are additional records. I still haven't seen any medical records for—"

"Ms. Brennan, I assure you, we have given you all of Mr. Thomas's records. I can't tell you where your hypothetical records might be, should they exist, but they are not here. Now, I have other obligations."

Although she looked ready to spit on me, or more likely run me down on her way out the door, I managed to maintain my own pleasant façade. When I told her that Tanya had promised me access to the guards who'd interacted most with Isaac, I could swear I heard Ms. Ricker's teeth grinding. So maybe I was stretching the truth a little, but I'm sure Tanya would have done if I'd thought to ask. The woman pretended to consider my request.

"I'm sorry, but that won't be possible. Excuse me."

"I'll only take a few moments of their time. I'm just trying to find something—anything—to tell his daughter. She was the victim of such tragedy. Can you imagine? For her father to kill her mother, and then take his own life… anything that could give her insight into his last days may help her find some peace."

Perhaps I was laying it on a bit thick, but there were other administrators milling about. Ricker would look like some kind of bitch if she challenged me now.

"I understand, but it's just not possible. We're short-handed, and they're about to do a count."

I've never been to Los Angeles, but I've often thought of counts as the prison equivalent of the infamous L.A. traffic. Inmates in prisons are individually counted at regular intervals, and during those counts you cannot have an inmate visit. In addition, if you've passed through at least some portion of prison security, you're often trapped at that location until the count is finished. However long that is. I generally figure on half an hour, more or less. That's not so bad. It's like rush hour in its predictability. You can plan around a scheduled count.

However, there are random counts as well. Perhaps they're not truly random, but they seem so if you don't know the reason for them, and as an outsider you rarely do. Weather is sometimes a culprit. I've learned not to schedule visits before 10 AM at certain times of year because of the fog. Even in good weather, the count can be "off," and they have to start over. I once waited two hours for a scheduled visit when a count turned into a recount for a reason that was never divulged. It reminds me of rubber-necking slowdowns, where you get past the snail's pace traffic only to find that either there was never an accident or anything else to gawk at, or it's now long gone but people are still looking, just in case.

I wasn't about to be thwarted by a count. "I'll wait," I told her.

She looked at her watch. "Officers start breaking for lunch in half an hour. You're welcome to wait in the cafeteria and question them there."

She left before I could thank her. Good. My smile was wearing thin around the edges.

The cafeteria had long tables with bench seats rather than individual tables, perhaps to avoid the feeling of high school cliqueishness that seems as inherent to large eating spaces as bad food and plastic trays. I got a soda from a machine in the corner and settled down to wait. There was no guarantee employees would eat here instead of going out for lunch, so I was hoping Ricker hadn't lied about the officers being short-handed. If they were short, they'd be less likely to have the time or freedom to leave the facility to eat.

I saw the occasional inmates in blues and a group of geeky, stocky men in short sleeve dress shirts and ties that must be contractors from outside, but the brown-uniformed corrections officers didn't begin trickling in until about noon. The first few I approached either hadn't worked there long enough or didn't work in the right areas of the prison to have had contact with Isaac. Then a sandy-haired young man I recognized sat down at the end of a row.

"It's Charley, right?"

"Yes, ma'am." When he blushed at the attention, I decided I could forgive him for calling me ma'am.

"We haven't met, but I saw you at the Handi-Way around the corner a few days ago, talking to Annie."

He smiled. "Oh, yes, ma'am. I remember now." Then he must have remembered the way his superior had tried to humiliate him because he blushed again. The poor kid blushed so much he reminded me of an exotic lizard or octopus, some sort of creature gifted (or in his case cursed) with an excess of appearance-altering pigment.

"I'm Sydney." I sat across from him and explained that I was looking for people who knew Isaac Thomas. I was trying to get information for his daughter.

"Did you know why he was sent to prison?" I asked him.

"Yes, ma'am, I did, not that he ever talked about it. To tell the truth, I found it all kinda hard to believe, but then you never know what somebody can do."

"His daughter was very young when he was sent to prison, and she never saw him again. She didn't even know he was dead until recently." As I suspected, his sense of southern chivalry helped bring Charley out of his shell.

"That is a shame. I was pretty new to the job when I worked on Isaac's wing. He seemed like a real nice man. I never knew him to cause anybody a bit of trouble. He was good with the new guys, helping them to settle down, to understand how things work and what'll get them in trouble." He smiled. "Not just the inmates either. He told me a few things too, about how to deal with the inmates, how to deal with the other guards. And he always did it private-like, so's nobody would hear."

"Would you say Isaac was a leader?"

He considered this for a moment. "Well, not really. At least, not the way most people mean leader. Isaac looked out for people, and he got things done, but he never took credit for it. He was sorta quiet. I mean, he'd have conversations, but he wasn't one of those guys who talks just to hear the sound of his own voice. Mostly he just listened. He had a way of getting you to do the right thing, without ever telling you what it was."

"Do you remember him having any visitors? Family or

anyone?"

"No, no I don't. I guess I just figured he didn't have any family left. I didn't know about his daughter."

Charley looked down at the remaining spaghetti on his plate and played his fork around it. "Now you know, somebody who might be able to tell you something more is Sue Ellen. Seems to me like she spent a lot of time around Isaac. I know she was real upset when he died."

"Were you around then?"

"When he died? No, I wasn't. They were moving us around a lot about that time, and I think I was at some sort of training when it happened. I hadn't seen much of Isaac for at least a few weeks, maybe a couple of months."

"Were you surprised when he killed himself?"

"Well, I was and I wasn't. Any time somebody dies it's a surprise, and Isaac never struck me as the type. But like I said, one thing I've learned here is you just never know what somebody will do. And I can't say I ever saw him depressed, but there always was something sad about him. You ever meet somebody like that? It's like they've seen something or done something that no matter how hard they laugh or how big their smile is, the sad in their eyes won't go away. I just thought that's the way he was."

We sat without speaking for a while, me sipping my soda and Charley finishing his spaghetti. He suddenly rose, putting his napkin over his mouth and chewing vigorously so he could speak without choking or spitting food.

"Sue Ellen!" he called, and beckoned a petite young woman to join us with her food.

She exchanged blushes with Charley as she sat next to him. Once she had her tray down she turned her shy gaze on me, tucking her short dark hair behind her ears.

"Sue Ellen, this is Sydney." Charley went on to explain why I was there. As he did, Sue Ellen's face grew expressionless. She locked her eyes on her salad, cutting an unripe cherry tomato with surgical precision.

"So I thought maybe you could tell her about Isaac," Charley concluded. Sue Ellen still didn't meet my eyes, but she glanced at Charley. Her mouth hung open, as if she were about to speak but couldn't remember how.

"Charley! Goddammit, boy, do I have to stand over you all the time? You know we're short. Quit jawing and get back to your post." It was the officer who'd made fun of Charley in the convenience store.

Charley rose without a word and left, tray in hand. I watched him leave, then turned back to face Sue Ellen. Her lips were colorless, and her voice came through them at a whisper.

"I have to go too."

She stumbled getting up and left her tray on the table. Then she exited the cafeteria, opposite the direction Charley had gone. I followed her on a hunch. As I suspected, she'd gone to the ladies' restroom. I went through a lounge area with vinyl furniture and a mirror, through another door and into the "business part" of the arrangement. Sue Ellen was leaning over one of the two sinks, looking sick. She didn't even seem to realize I'd entered.

"Sue Ellen?" When she turned to look at me I saw that the blood had left the rest of her face too. "Are you all right?"

She didn't answer so I went to the neighboring sink and wet a couple of paper towels in cold water. Then I took Sue Ellen by the arm, led her back out to the lounge and set her on a vinyl chair. The cushion squeaked in response to her meager weight. I folded the cold paper towels and pressed one to her forehead. Her brown eyes were dilated and seemed too large for her thin face. She had the look of someone who'd been gradually wasting away.

"Here," I said, handing her another towel. "Put this on the back of your neck."

She closed her eyes and took a few deep breaths. "Better?" I asked. She nodded.

"I'm sorry. Something I ate this morning must have disagreed with me. Thank you."

"No problem. I have to admit, the sight of the food in there was almost enough to make me sick too." She tried to smile. We sat for another minute before Sue Ellen looked at me.

"Thanks again, but I really do have to go."

"Are you sure you'll be all right?"

She didn't answer, but got up, smoothing her hair and the front of her cargo-type uniform pants.

"Look, Charley was wrong. I don't know anything. I knew who Isaac was, but I don't talk much to the inmates, or anybody else."

She stopped, facing the door with her hand ready to pull it open.

"I feel bad for Noel, I really do, but I can't help you."

I waited long enough to ensure I wouldn't run into Sue Ellen in the hallway. I didn't want to push her. Not yet. She would talk to me in time, just as I knew she had talked to Isaac.

I hadn't told anyone at the prison that Isaac's daughter was named Noel.

CHAPTER FOURTEEN

Before heading down to the PD's office in Hainey, I stopped by the Handi-way for a snack and another quick chat with Annie.

"Well, hello," she said as I came through the door. "You've spent so much time around here lately, the rumor is you're moving in."

"Must be all that southern hospitality at WFC keeping me here."

Annie snorted. "That'll be the day. You can bet you got most of them boys jumping out of their shorts over there, they're so wound up."

"Really? Anyone in particular?"

"If there is they wouldn't tell me. From what I've seen, if you work at that prison long enough, you start to figure everyone you meet is either a criminal or about to accuse you of being one. Which one you think they take you for?"

I raised an eyebrow. "Probably a little of both." I told her that I'd spoke with Charley and Sue Ellen.

"That Charley's just a doll. He used to have a thing for Sue Ellen. They'd come in here twice a day, along with everybody else, seeing which one could outblush the other. But I haven't seen Sue Ellen around here at all in the last few months. Maybe Deacon's teasing got the best of her."

"Deacon... is that the guy that was in here the other day giving Charley a hard time? In his mid 40s, maybe 5-foot-10 and running about 230. Brown hair and moustache just starting to go gray?"

Annie folded her arms over her chest and looked at me. "What are you, a cop?"

Any anonymity I might have was already long gone, so I told her.

"Shit, girl, no wonder they're paranoid. Probably think it's about some kind of lawsuit."

I assured her it wasn't.

"Well, it makes no difference to me. I got a nephew that landed in jail for a little bit of nothing, and if something happened to him or they didn't treat him right, you better believe I'd go after them."

"About that guy…"

"Oh, yeah, that's Deacon all right. He's meaner than hell, but like most bullies it's all talk. There's a few like him over there—always is in those kinds of places—but I've never heard of them getting up to anything serious."

Mike wasn't in his cubicle when I got to the PD's office. I thought maybe he'd gone to lunch, but the guy in the adjacent section said he was in Richard's office. Richard's secretary was nowhere to be seen, but his door was ajar and I could hear voices from inside. Raised voices.

"That's crazy, Richard. Why would I do that?" Mike's voice was raised, but he sounded more perplexed than angry.

With my usual tact, I knocked once on the door and pushed on through. Mike didn't look angry either, but Richard was agitated. His face and neck were flushed, and his mouth shone with saliva. He looked at me, licked his bottom lip distractedly, then held it with his front teeth. His eyes flashed with pain, and he released his lip and his pent-up breath simultaneously.

"What's going on?" I asked.

Neither spoke. Richard's eyes darted back and forth between

Mike and me, but Mike just shrugged and gestured for Richard to go on. Richard put his hands on his desk, palms down, and took another deep breath before speaking.

"Someone, a man, called my house late last night. My wife answered the phone."

Richard breathed deeply again and sat down. "She was told to be careful of you, Sydney, if she valued our marriage."

I tried to be nonchalant. "Sounds awfully catty for a man."

"He said he saw us kissing outside your motel room, and from what he saw, the next time it wouldn't stop there."

"You did kiss me."

It was Mike's turn to flush. "On the cheek," I clarified. "So much for chivalry."

"Mine or his?" Richard asked, and started to smile. "My wife actually took it much better than I did. I may be an attorney, but she's the one in our family who always thinks logically. She said it was highly unlikely that any man who called our house at midnight and refused to identify himself had anyone's welfare in mind but his own."

I casually took a seat, but I wasn't ready to let Richard off the hook yet. "And you thought the anonymous caller was Mike?" My voice was a carefully calculated mix of incredulity and disgust. Richard flushed in embarrassment.

"Well, not really. I know it doesn't make sense, but my wife just told me about the call, and I wasn't thinking clearly, and Mike was the only person I could think of who knew I was taking you to dinner."

"It wasn't Mike."

"Well, I know that now, but—"

Richard was still defensive, so it took a few seconds for the implications of my certainty to sink in, but they did.

"Who was it?"

I finally listened to Mrs. Bibbystock's voice whispering in my ear. "I don't know, but he was driving a pick-up. Someone must have followed us from the restaurant. A pick-up entered the parking lot behind us. I can't tell you the make or color. It blinded me when I was trying to unlock my door. Then the same headlights left right after you."

I let my words sink in before going on. "You've got a tail. Who have you pissed off lately?"

"Besides you and Mike? Who else have I spoken to? I'm sure the list is endless. But it's an odd sort of call, isn't it? It wasn't a threat. If it was harassment it was very subtle. It sounds more like a colleague with a twisted sense of humor than a former client with a grudge."

"Still," Mike said, "it's worth having a patrol car swing by your house periodically. I'll make a call."

I left with Mike. After he made arrangements for Richard, I told him what had really brought me there—not the latest installment of office melodrama, but an address for Claire Johnson.

"You try the phone book?" he asked.

Of course I hadn't, but I was saved from humiliation when he failed to find a listing for Miss Johnson there. We moved on to the computer, where he pulled up the latest version of Autofind. I told him we had used an older version years ago at the public defender's office.

"Oh, well this is amazing! They've done so much to improve it since then." Mike's eyes sparkled behind his glasses. "It's much more accurate, and it draws on more sources of information. What's your birthday?"

I tried to speak normally, but my throat had gone dry. I wondered if my report would look suspicious, like one of those "a-ha" moments on TV shows around minute 38 where suddenly the hero and audience realize nothing is as it seems.

"No self-respecting woman would tell you that."

Mike had no interest in repartee. He shrugged. "Whatever. You're not going to believe how much information they have on you in here. It's pretty scary, really."

"Let's just skip the demo. You can show me how to use it while you look up Miss Johnson."

I had her birthdate from the old police report, so Mike had pulled her up before he was done complaining that I was no fun. There was no question that we had the right person when one of her previous addresses matched up to her address in the report. She had no work address listed, so I'd see if I could catch her at home that afternoon. Mike printed out directions for me.

Fifteen minutes later, I pulled up in front of a brick duplex on a residential block. I'd say it had seen better days, but "better days" had avoided this neighborhood entirely. Spaces that were once front gardens were almost universally under concrete now, like broad sidewalks, often oil-stained from their conversion to parking. Some of the parking looked long-term. A rusty old Impala sagged on flat tires two doors down. I've been around enough really bad neighborhoods that I couldn't say I felt unsafe, but I did feel unwelcome. I also couldn't say how much of that feeling came from the residents and how much was a projection of my own white middle-class guilt.

One half of the duplex I'd parked in front of was an exception to the predominate drab deadness. Ferns hung from macramé planters, and petunias brightened window boxes. The ground in front was sealed with concrete, but it did host a birdbath filled with colorful rocks and surrounded by salvaged containers of every sort. Some had living plants, others were filled with plastic pinwheel flowers that sat motionless in the heavy air. A flock of pink flamingoes congregated at a crack in the concrete. Tacky, but colorful.

That was not where Miss Johnson lived.

My destination was the other half of the duplex, dull as the rest of the block with burglar bars and heavy curtains on the windows. A woman answered the door almost immediately. I'd parked on the street rather than her concrete yard, and she'd had plenty of time to observe my approach.

"Claire Johnson?" I asked.

"Yes. What do you want?"

"My name is Sydney Brennan." I handed her a card. "I'm an investigator and I was wondering if I could speak to you about some people who used to be your neighbors."

"Ohh. This'll be about that no-good little Damian down the street. It's about time somebody did something about him. Playing that loud music all the time and his drawers down below his privates, there's no question what he's up to."

She let me through the door, then shut and locked it behind me as she rattled on about Damian. She indicated a seat on a sofa and sat in the neighboring armchair. The large flowers that patterned the furniture had faded beyond recognition, but each piece was bedecked by a bright solid-colored afghan folded into a triangle.

"Little punk drug dealer, that's what he is."

Now that I'd gotten in the door it seem like a good time to let Damian off the hook. "Miss Johnson, I'm not here about Damian."

"Must be one of his cousins then. Lord, I don't even begin to know how many children they got over there."

"No, ma'am. This is actually about some of your old neighbors, from a long time ago. Over on Patience Street. The Thomases. Do you remember them?"

I had her birth date, so I knew before meeting her that Claire Johnson was 51. Otherwise I might not have been able to guess her age beyond a 10 or 15-year range. The darkness of her skin and within her home masked most signs of aging in her face, but she wore the garment of an older woman, a shapeless thing that hung from her ample chest and fell in folds to her knees. When I said the name Thomas, she somehow looked both older and younger simultaneously. She was momentarily animated, perhaps possessed by the memory of inhabiting her 25-year-old body. Then she sighed deeply, and while the memory of youth remained in her eyes, her posture began to sag and her cheeks seemed to slide off their bones.

She nodded, and I thought I saw the ghost of a smile. "Oh, yes," she said. "I remember them."

She leaned back in her chair, smoothing the folds of her house-dress and picking at a speck of fuzz. "Isaac and Vanda. I used to babysit their little girl Noel. Of course, I guess you knew that already, didn't you?" I nodded. "What do you want to know?"

"What do you remember about them? Were you there when they moved in?"

"Yes, I was. Let me see. They'd only been there a couple years when—well, you know. I was living back home with my momma when they moved next door. I had me a little bit of trouble about a boy, but that's neither here nor there." She grinned a bit as she alluded to her notorious past.

"Looking back, it's sad. They seemed so happy then, like they had a whole new life ahead of them. Noel was such a sweet little thing. A little odd, always with her nose stuck in a book, but a good kid. Never a bit of trouble. Sure didn't take after her momma on that count."

"What do you mean?"

"You don't know? Oh, that Vanda was a hell raiser all right. She couldn't have been much older than me, but into the kinda trouble that women weren't getting into around here then, if you know what I mean."

"Men?" I asked.

Miss Johnson laughed. "Well, I done told you, even I knew about that kind of trouble. But yeah, she was into men, but not just *for being into men.*"

She spoke those last words slowly, and when I still looked at her blankly, lowered her voice and looked around her living room for spies. "She was into men *for the money.*"

"She was a prostitute?"

Miss Johnson gave me a disgusted look, but whether it was for saying the word aloud in her home or saying it so loudly as it burst out of me, I couldn't be sure. "I wouldn't use that word. It wasn't that she did it professional-like. She just needed the money."

"I thought Isaac had a job."

"I didn't say *they* needed the money, now did I? I said *she* needed the money. See, she had herself a drug problem. Might not sound like a big deal now, with those kids out there dealing on the corner." I hadn't seen any kids dealing on the corner.

"What kind of drugs?"

"Well, I can't say for sure. I can tell you she was messed up on something most all the time I saw her, not that I saw her that much. Seems like she slept most days, and she went down to Jimmy's bar of a evening. To get high or get some money to get high."

"Did her husband know?"

"Isaac would have to have been a blind man not to. Yeah, he knew. Such a good, kind man. Handsome, too. Always working, always taking care of the little girl, and trying to clean up after Vanda besides. I'm sure he tried to get her to stop early on, but then I guess he gave up, just tried to keep her from doing too much damage."

"Did they argue about it?"

"From time to time, but not as much as you would think, with her out every night of the week. Like I said, I think he gave up on her. Or at least gave up on trying to change her. But some nights you'd hear 'em—mostly Vanda really—screaming such filthy things. She coulda taught them kids on the corner a thing or two, with that mouth."

"Did you ever see them fight?"

"You know, I can't say that I did. I seem to remember after it happened that people talked about him beating on her. Somebody said he even went to get her from Jimmy's once and made a scene, but I can't say that I ever saw it."

She settled back, shaking her head, then suddenly sat up so straight she almost stood from her chair. "No, wait, I tell a lie. There was one night, musta been a few months before she died. Lord, I never seen that man so angry. I was sitting in the front room reading a novel, like I always do."

She pointed to boxes full of what looked like lurid-covered romance novels in the corner.

"I don't know where everybody else was. In bed maybe. I heard this racket, and the porch light was on next door. There was Isaac, dragging Vanda out the front door. She was crying, but he wasn't saying a word. At least not until he got her out of the house. I ran over to see what was going on. I was afraid she mighta done something, that something might have happened to little Noel. I used to worry about that a lot. Anyway, Vanda was crawling, hanging onto his legs, and Isaac pushed her away and down the front steps of the porch. He went after her and stood over her. I thought maybe he was checking to make sure she was OK. Vanda was just sobbing and carrying on."

Miss Johnson stopped for a moment and hugged her arms around her body without seeming to realize it. "You know, the Lord says to love thy neighbor, but I'm just a flawed human being and I never did like that woman. I didn't like what she did to Isaac, and I didn't like what she did to the child. But it hurt my heart to see her in that state. And then, he looked down at her, like he could spit, and said, 'Whore.' That was it. Just that one word. And she kept wailing."

"I didn't know what to do," she admitted. "I just stood there. Isaac went in the house and came out again with a paper bag of something, metal and glass by the sound of it, that he threw in the trash. I followed him when he went back in the house, to see if Noel was okay. He got on the phone, and I heard him say, 'Come get your daughter. She's not welcome here any more.' Her folks came to pick her up that night. She was still sobbing in the yard when they showed up."

"What about Noel?"

"I don't know. I never did see her that night. She wasn't standing around, and I didn't feel like I should go nosing about, so I left. Vanda was gone a couple weeks, but she did come back. I didn't see it. She was just there one day. And she did better for a while. Things quieted down, and she quit going out all the time. But it didn't last out the month, and she was at it again."

"Miss Johnson, what was in the trash can? What did Isaac throw away?"

She looked offended. "What makes you think I woulda looked in somebody else's garbage?"

"I would have."

She grinned. "Yeah, well, I guess maybe we have something in common then."

"What was it?"

"Just what you think. Drug stuff, for smoking it. I might not know how to use it, but I could figure out what it was used for easy enough."

I checked my watch and saw that it was time to leave for Ida Pickett's. "Well," I said as I rose, "thank you, Miss Johnson. You've been a big help."

She walked me to the door and looked out carefully before opening it.

"Damn kid pushers," she said. "You know, I just don't get it. I don't know what they put in that stuff to mess people up so bad, make 'em so stupid. Just like Vanda. I thought she had everything when they moved here. She was a beautiful woman then, before she stopped eating and drinking anything that wouldn't get her high. And here she had a good-looking, hard-working man who adored her, a sweet child and another on the way…"

I'm sure my mouth dropped in a rather unattractive fashion. "A what?"

"Oh yeah. You didn't know that? When they moved here Vanda was pregnant, just barely showing. Maybe four or five months along."

"What happened to the child?"

"Vanda had a miscarriage."

CHAPTER FIFTEEN

I stopped on the way out of town at a place Mike had recommended and got a bunch of fried chicken and sides to take to Ida's. The smell nearly drove me insane on the trip up there, but at least it took my mind off everything else. I was having making sense of this new picture of the Thomas family home.

Lazarus didn't look any better the second time around. It's not that I expected the EPA or somebody to run and do a quick clean-up while my back was turned, but I'd hoped some of what I felt last time was the shock of seeing the degradation for the first time. Ida's neighborhood did seem a little less X-Files deserted, maybe because people were coming home and getting ready for dinner. There were lights in windows and cars in driveways, but still no one abroad except Ida's neighbor Mr. Phillips, watering his greens. He must have recognized me. This time he smiled as he nodded. I gathered up my bag and the box of wafting goodies and walked to the fence at the front edge of his property.

"Hello," I called to Mr. Phillips.

"Good evening," he said. "Mighty fine weather."

"Yes, sir, it is. What are you growing in there?"

"Well, I just started some squash and peppers, but I don't know how well the squash'll take. They like a lot of space. Then I got tomatoes here—beefsteak and cherry—and mustard in the back. I'll be starting the chard soon."

"Frilly edged or broadleaf?" I asked, referring to the mustard.

"Broadleaf," he replied, with a scandalized look. I didn't know there was a hierarchy among mustards. As I walked toward Ida's front steps, Mr. Phillips glared at her house, perhaps wondering what kind of frilly edged element she was bringing to the neighborhood.

It hadn't occurred to me until knocking on her door that my impulsivity might be considered rude. What if she didn't like chicken, or thought I was insulting her cooking? What if she kicked me out and I ended up eating it all myself? Okay, so the way I was drooling right now, the eating it all part didn't sound so bad. What if I had something really important to worry about? I still looked at Ida apologetically when she opened the door.

"My stomach's on eastern time, and I thought you might be ready for an early dinner too."

"Is that from Lorna's?"

"I think that was the name of it. Used to be an old Tastee Freez. The signs are still in the parking lot."

"Did you get biscuits or hush puppies?"

"Both. And cole slaw and collards."

"Honey, what are you waiting for? Come on in."

We went in to the kitchen, where Ida set out paper plates, tall glasses of iced tea, and a roll of paper towels. She grinned. "I'm really living high now. I won't even have to do dishes."

I put a little of everything on my tripled up paper plates and dug in. "Mmm," I moaned, through a bite of juicy well-seasoned chicken breast. "Just like a picnic. Except inside."

"I can't remember the last time I ate outside." Ida's gaze went involuntarily in the direction of the quarantined playground.

I put down my food. "Ida, if I'm being too personal you can kick me out and keep my chicken, but I have to ask. Why do you stay here?"

A smile brushed her lips. "Well, I guess that is hard for you to understand, young as you are. But this is the first and only house my husband and I ever owned. This used to be a nice neighborhood, full of life. My husband and I couldn't have children of our own, but we used to walk to that very park in the evenings, watching over the neighbor kids and waiting for the sunset. We did that every day for so many years, until close to the end when Ernest got too weak to leave the bed." Ida looked down at her plate and gripped her tea glass tightly with both hands. "We lived our lives in this house, and my Ernest died in this house. It's been over 2 years since he's died, but I'm nowhere near ready to let go yet."

She released her grip and took a small sip from her glass. "You know what's so strange to me? This earth, this air and water is no different today than it was 15 or 20 or even 30 years ago. The damage was already done by then. We just didn't know it. To think of all that life going on, when really everything around us was as dead then as it is now. We just didn't know it yet." I looked away as she dabbed her eyes with a piece of paper towel.

"I'm sorry, Ida."

She stretched her arm out and patted my hand. "Aren't we all, honey aren't we all?"

After another fortifying sip of tea, she went on. "You know, even if I wanted to leave, if I was ready to leave, I couldn't. I can't afford to. I couldn't give this house away, much less sell it. And I don't have any children or anyone left to move in with. Unless we can get the government to buy us out, a lot of people around here'll be stuck."

We sat for a while, pushing our food around on our plates. It seemed we'd both lost our appetite. "Boy, I am just a ray of sunshine. What do you say we leave this stuff here and go look at family pictures? I pulled all of my old photo albums down. I thought you might want to look at them."

"That sounds nice," I told her. And it did.

As we flipped through old albums and boxes of loose pictures, I learned more about the Thomas family. Ida and Isaac's parents, John and Iris, were long dead. Their father John had died in an accident when Ida was 15 years old. Their mother Iris had died several years later. It was her funeral that had brought Isaac and Noel to Lazarus on the one occasion that Ida had seen them together, the only time she'd met Noel and the last time she'd seen her brother alive.

There had been another Thomas child, the eldest son named Jacob. Three years separated each of the children, with Ida in the middle and Isaac the youngest. Jacob died of leukemia at age 11. It had been diagnosed late, and Jacob had died within a matter of months, but they still incurred a significant debt of medical bills. With the grieving family pinching pennies and John working a second job, they had nearly paid off the bills when John himself died. Of course, his death had left them in an even more precarious financial position. Iris got work at one of the factories, and the children did odd jobs for money until they were old enough to be consistently employed.

Ida held out a picture and indicated a handsome, broad-shouldered young black man posing as a sort of he-man in the grassy front yard of a house. Small children hung from his flexed arms and clung to his thick legs. A head tilted next to his own where another child hung down his back from his neck. Everyone was laughing.

"Lord, he was strong. He always wanted to play football. He tried once, I think it was his sophomore year, but he couldn't skip work for the practices."

She laughed. "I think the coach was even more disappointed

than Isaac was. He came over and talked to momma about it, and she would've tried to work something out but Isaac wouldn't let her. He said putting food on the table was much more important than a bunch of guys getting their pants dirty trying to knock each other down."

At the next picture Ida sucked in her breath. This showed a slightly older Isaac, still a teenager but starting to show the man he would become. His straight black eyebrows, full without being bushy, were softened by the kind eyes they framed and a mouth reminiscent of a child's doll, cupid-shaped and just short of femi-nine. He stood facing the camera, his mouth closed but smiling, with his arm around a woman, his eyes focused on her rather than the camera lens. The woman had an hourglass figure, her tiny waist blossoming into full hips and breasts, and her short skirt showed off long tapered legs. Her dark hair was cut short, fluffed out about an inch all around her head. Her face was radiant, her brown skin flawless with the exception of a dark mole that brought even more attention to eyes that were almost too large for her face. She was gorgeous, a black Marilyn Monroe.

"That's Vanda," Ida whispered, transfixed by the image of the woman her brother had murdered. "I'd forgotten how beautiful she was."

"How did they meet?"

"I'm not sure. She was a year older than him, and I think he'd just started his senior year. She could have had any man she wanted."

Ida gave a short laugh. "In our less charitable moments, some of us jealous females said she'd *already had* every man she wanted. Now, with the benefit of age and experience, and an absence of raging hormones, I'd have to say that was unfair. I doubt she slept around any more than any other girl back then, which incidentally

117

wasn't much despite what was going on in the rest of the country. Whatever brought her and Isaac together, I'm sure she was faithful to him. At least, in those early years when I saw them."

"Were they good together?"

"At first, but everyone is at first. They seemed very happy, but gradually Isaac starting behaving differently toward everyone else. He and Vanda seemed to focus all their energy on each other. His grades had never been much more than average, and they started slipping."

"That's not that uncommon in a graduating senior."

"True, but he also started missing work. We didn't see him at home as much. Not that I was at home much either. I went through a couple of bad boyfriends around that time. I think maybe we were both, Isaac and I, going through the teenage rebellion that we'd put off for years of being responsible children."

"He did manage to graduate, barely. Then he got a factory job —not where mom worked, he made sure of that—and started making some money. He and Vanda were always together. They still seemed okay for a while, but after about six months or so, I started hearing about problems."

"What kind of problems?"

"Well, the thing about Vanda is, she was her momma's favorite. She was headstrong and probably a little spoiled, and she always got her way. She wanted more for Isaac and for herself than just working at a factory in Lazarus. I don't know what exactly, but she always had dreams in her eyes. When it didn't happen right away, I think she got frustrated. She and Isaac started hanging out in bars, first on weekends and then during the week. Isaac didn't spend many nights at home anymore."

"One night he and Vanda came in, half-drunk, to pick up some of his clothes. They had a big fight with momma, and she blamed all of his 'wicked ways' on Vanda." Ida smiled. "As you can imagine, that didn't go over very well. Isaac moved out, and apparently they had the same fight over at the Harrisons, because Vanda moved out of there too."

Ida sighed and rubbed her eyes. "Things got worse before they got better. I don't know if this is true, but bad news usually is. I was told they were living in some dump because all of Isaac's money was going to drugs for the two of them. Hard stuff. Then he lost his job. I don't know if that knocked some sense into him, or he just couldn't support their lifestyle as easily without a job. About a month later, Isaac showed up at the place where I was waitressing. He said he and Vanda were getting married at the courthouse and he wanted me to be there. Of course I went. There was another young woman there, I think one of Vanda's cousins, but no one else from either family."

She started flipping through the box on her lap, without success. "There should be a picture of them in here. Vanda was too thin, but they seemed happy. After the ceremony, the four of us had cake and champagne, and they announced that they were leaving Lazarus. They didn't say it in so many words, but they'd decided to cut off contact with the families and wouldn't tell either of us where they were going. I'd get an occasional letter, and a few years later I think Isaac started sending momma money, but there was never a return address, and not even the postmarks stayed the same."

"I never thought they'd make it. To be honest, I don't think poor Vanda would have been happy with anybody for long. There was just something missing in her, something she could never fill, no matter how beautiful she was. But..."

Ida had to stop and take a deep breath before she could force the words out.

119

JUDY K. WALKER

"I never in a million years would have guessed it would end that way. For any of them."

CHAPTER SIXTEEN

The vending machine at my motel didn't have water or root beer, so when I reached the turn at the convenience store, I pulled over to get both. That's probably where I picked up my tail. They were waiting for me, either there or somewhere else just past Ida's.

The business was small, only the two gas pumps outside and three aisles of goodies inside. One aisle was taken up by items ranging from motor oil to feminine products. Not the kind of goodies I was looking for. I roamed for a while, discontent. I'd forgotten to bring a novel with me this trip, and I really wanted something suitable for vegging. The literature section consisted of a wire rack that lurched dangerously and screeched when it turned. Selection was limited to romances and some sort of religious fiction, a combination apparently only I found ironic. I settled for an entertainment magazine and a novel that looked, quite literally from the cover art, to be a bodice-ripper.

I didn't notice any other customers when I checked out, so they must have been parked around back. It was around 9 PM, recently dark with the moon either not yet risen or hiding among the clouds. The road was nearly deserted. Although there were headlights behind me, I didn't meet a single car, driving in content if not blissful ignorance for about 20 minutes. The road was narrow, largely policed by a double yellow line, and when I came to a short passing zone the vehicle behind me zipped by without hesitation. I was glad to have his headlights out of my rearview mirror, but my relief was short-lived when I realized there was another vehicle behind me, a pick-up or something with similarly torturous high headlights.

Shortly after passing, the driver in front of me braked hard for a deer.

At least that's what I thought, having seen a doe and fawn earlier by the edge of the highway, partially screened by the over-grown grasses. I braked hard as well, and a slight rush of adrenaline buzzed through me. The bright headlights looming behind me in my rearview mirror added to my adrenaline. I wondered what my insurance coverage was like on a rental. I didn't wonder why the lead pick-up's headlights went off, or why no dome light came on inside the pick-up when its doors swung open.

The knock on my window startled me. I hadn't seen anyone approach from behind in the blinding headlights. A figure was standing directly next to my door, so close that all I could see was dark clothing on a torso. Was he waiting for me to get out? I rolled down my window. A gruff voice asked if I was all right. Years of cultural conditioning won out over baser instincts of self-preserva-tion, and I unbuckled my seatbelt and opened my door. I was even apologizing, for what I can't imagine, as I slid out.

"Hey, I'm sorry, I didn't—"

Didn't have a chance to finish. As soon as my head emerged from the rental, the world went even darker. A musty, scratchy hood was thrown over my head. An arm hooked around my throat in a V, dragging me the rest of the way from the car. I tried to get my feet under me to kick out, get some sort of control, but all I could do was hang on to the crooked arm to keep from choking. One of my sandals caught on the edge of the car and came off. Miraculously, the other stayed on as my feet left the ground and my calves smacked hard against what I suspected was a pick-up's tailgate. I could hear heavy boots stomping on the metal bed around me, and even through the hood I could smell the sour body odor of the man who'd grabbed me.

The smelly man pulled me firmly against him. He was sitting, probably with his back against the cab of the truck, and he had his legs raised on either side of me. His position was offensively intimate, and I flailed my arms around and pulled my feet toward me to try to get some leverage. Hands gripped my forearms and ankles tightly, pulling my legs straight, and there was a sudden bony weight upon my shins.

The smelly man's arm moved slightly into a chokehold, squeezing on either side of my throat. Spots danced across the darkness of my wide-open eyes as the hood brushed my eyelashes. Going limp just before I actually fainted, I pulled my hips forward slightly as I slumped, creating a little space between my rear and his groin. If I had to keep feeling the bulge in his pants, knowing that me being a helpless captive caused it, I'd lose the tenuous hold on my control.

Handlers on nature shows place hoods over animals' heads so they aren't unduly stressed by their capture. My hood seemed to have the same effect, although I'm sure that wasn't intended. Unable to see, to visually assess the risks to me and determine what persona to present to my captors, there was nothing to do but wait. My lower back started to cramp, but I stayed motionless as we continued down the highway.

I had no sense of time, except that of increasing discomfort. Eventually we pulled off onto a bumpy road, one that was either poorly paved or not paved at all. The pick-up slowly maneuvered over and between bone-jarring ruts and potholes, its springs creaking in protest. The soft flesh of the torso behind me kept my upper back and head from smacking any edges, but there was no friendly

123

fat between my tailbone and the ridged metal of the pick-up bed. I gasped in pain once before I could stop myself. Hopefully the sound was lost among those of the engine and tires and metal bits. I tried to reach out with my senses, to become grounded enough in the world around me that I'd have my wits when the hood was removed. They'd remove it. They'd want to see my terrified face. The hum of insects was audible over our mechanical sounds, but I was unable to smell anything except heavy, humid air and the stinking man who held me in a chokehold.

Sure enough, when the pick-up came to a stop, Stinky Guy moved from behind me and I could feel bodies shifting around, presumably to block my escape. I did a quick crab-walk until my back was against the cab, and a moment later the hood was ripped from my head, along with some of the curly delicate hairs that grew along the base of my neck.

There are certain kinds of immediate pain that trigger a rage in me totally disproportionate to the amount of damage actually done. These triggers include hard head bumps getting in or out of cars, jammed bare toes and fingernails, barked shins, and just about anything where it seems an inanimate object has expressed malice toward me, or I've been really dumb. I discovered that night that hair pulled out at the root is another trigger.

"Ouch! You stupid shit!"

My hands flew to the back of my neck, to protect it from further outrage and massage the sting away. So much for keeping my wits about me, and encouraging the image of a helpless, frightened little woman.

My outburst shocked the men into silence and gave me a chance to look around. The pick-up had turned its headlights off, but there was just enough ambient light from the sky to tell that we had pulled off a dirt road into a small clearing in the trees. The arboreal silhouettes looked different in size and shape, more like forest than the tree rows of timber land. There were three men crouched in the back of the pick-up with me, and slamming, rattling doors announced the imminent arrival of at least one and possibly two more men from the cab. All of them wore black clothing, gloves and ski masks. The raw tingling in my neck had momentarily burned the fear away, and I wondered where they'd found ski masks in Florida. I took my time looking them over. They all looked really big.

"Hot enough for you?" I asked. My God, I really was insane.

The man nearest me abruptly smacked me across the face. I was surrounded, but not in any way restrained. Once one of them crossed the line and struck me, I had no reason not to be physical as well. So says rationalizing hindsight. At the time all I knew was that my face ached and I'd just found another trigger.

My remaining sandal was a sensible shoe, with a hard chunky heel about an inch thick, so it had a bit of heft. Because of the way they crouched, the men's most coveted and vulnerable targets were tucked out of reach of my short legs, but that posture did bring a couple of heads within striking distance. I braced myself on extended arms, raised my ass and kicked my leg out hard. I didn't get much power behind it, and I lost my shoe, but I did manage to connect with someone's chin. It wasn't the man who'd slapped me.

Then I flipped over onto my knees and scrambled back toward the cab, hoping to climb over the top. As I did, I could feel a presence behind me and swung my leg up and back. This time the gonads gods were smiling on me and I heard a warbling yell. I hoped it was my slapper, but I couldn't be sure. Whoever it was, he should be thankful I hadn't been wearing my shoe.

Finally on my feet, I started climbing the cab, but Number Three grabbed my left arm, squeezing so hard I could feel bones and tendons grinding. Like many women, I haven't cultivated arm strength, so with him too close for kicking I fell back on my favorite fifth grade defense—fingernails. I raked from the elbow toward the wrist, but, while he had some choice words for me, he didn't let go. Then I dug in, squeezing my fingers into his squishy flesh with all my might, feeling one of my nails bend. Number Three maintained his hold on my arm with one hand but let go with the other, reaching for my scratching hand and clamping it with his own. I tried to hang on, but heard myself yelp with pain as he twisted my hand free.

I'd forgotten about Chin Guy. By this time, he'd recovered from my wussy kick and approached me from behind. He clamped his large hands on either side of my head, squeezing hard for a moment. His hands were so large they overlapped, and I felt the straight metal post of my right earring jamming into my head. Then he threw my head forward, smacking my forehead into the cab window. I bounced. My body fell at an angle, as if on a tether, until Number Three let go of my arm. My body came to rest on the truck bed on my side.

Meditation has never been my forte, but that moment of stillness, of freedom from pummeling, was bliss. In my scrambled brain, the seconds stretched on for eons, and I felt some great transcendental something. I was on the verge of Enlightenment, Nirvana, whatever, and I must have smiled.

"Lady, you are some kind of fucked up," I heard from far away.

I kept smiling until someone shoved his hand into the curly mass of my hair and began dragging me to the end of the pick-up. Some part of my brain knew to scuttle along to minimize my need for a hairpiece, but I still wasn't doing any higher order thinking.

Soon I became aware of someone slapping my face, lightly this time, to bring me around. My body was lying across the lowered tailgate. I'd lost track of my attackers, but when the man slapping my face stopped and leaned close, I could smell his familiar body odor.

"What do you want to go passing out for?" he asked, pinching my cheek hard with rough fingers in a faux caress. "We're not done with you yet. Nowhere near."

He pushed my hair back from my forehead. "Be a shame if you lost all that pretty red hair. Don't suppose any of you boys happened to bring a razor?"

I was still lying flat on my back with Stinky Guy at my head and another of the men at my feet. At the word razor, I could feel my stomach go hot and my skin go cold. My chest grew tight and I thought I'd suffocate. It wasn't my hair I was worried about.

"Nobody? Ah, well. We'll just have to think of something else."

He stroked my hair again. The masks covered their mouths as well, but I knew he was smiling. He'd seen my fear, and he enjoyed it. I breathed deeply through my nose, trying to stay calm without outwardly panting.

"Red hair, huh? Are you a real redhead or is that one of those dye jobs? Looks real, but that's why you pay the big bucks, so it'll look real. I hear there's only one way to tell for sure."

He buried his right hand in my hair, gripping it tightly, and inserted the index finger of his left hand behind the top button of my pants. They were button fly. He gave one great yank and my pants ripped open, exposing my underwear. I could feel the bile rising in my throat, and I thought I'd either throw up or choke on it soon. The base of my throat burned with the acid. Stinky Guy was transfixed by my underwear, and I knew he'd forgotten about the other men surrounding us.

"Leopard print, huh?" There was movement behind his mask and I could hear him swallow. "I bet you just fuck everything

127

coming and going in those beauties, don't cha?"

It's amazing the things you can do to trick your brain, like a magician with a little misdirection, a shift of focus. For example, I don't like to cry in theatres, so when I feel tears coming I'll keep looking about 10 degrees to the right of the screen. Gets your emotions under control and nobody can tell you're doing it. Your brain can do that for you, too. It latches on to things that are trivial or meaningless, 10 degrees right of center, to keep you functioning when you just want to shut down from sheer terror. And you don't even see it coming.

My underwear was not leopard print. It was my favorite pair, cotton and well-worn with the pattern fading. I hadn't been able to find a replacement, so I hand-washed them and hung them to dry every time in a vain attempt to stave off their disintegration. With this misapprehension on his part, my brain had something else to focus on. Or my psychotic nature reasserted itself. Take your pick.

"No, it's not leopard."

I rolled toward him, swinging my legs down and reaching for his eyes. I missed and settled for his nose instead, and as I twisted it and dug my fingernails through his mask into his face I screamed at him.

"Leopards don't have stripes, you stupid pervert son of a bitch!"

Stinky Guy gave a girly squeal of his own and backed up, throwing his hands up to shield his eyes from my berserker rage. When he backed away, I ran for the trees. One of the other men— Chin Guy?—grabbed me, but someone else shook him loose. I think it was one of the guys from the cab. I kept running.

Instinct kicked in. I jumped, barefoot, over obstacles I never really saw, fallen trees and rocks and who knows what. My right hand was no longer functional, so with my left I gripped the waist of my pants, not wanting to stop to button them but afraid they'd fall down and take me with them. I counted in my head as I ran.

When I got to 500 and saw there was no one on my heels, I stopped, panting. I couldn't hear anything over the sounds of my own labored breathing, and my vision was clouded with spots and darkness. Bending over, hands on thighs, I breathed in through my nose and out through my mouth until I could see again. Then I fumbled with one useless hand to get my pants buttoned again. Fortunately they were worn enough that the buttons slid right in. Otherwise I'd never have managed it.

I closed my eyes and listened. Nothing. Wait—damn, there was something, and close. The canopy above was thick, but there wasn't much undergrowth here to provide cover. Still, I'd have to make do. I couldn't outrun anyone anymore. I was exhausted, and I thought I was going to throw up. I hunkered down behind a large tree trunk in a patch of ferns.

He was quiet. If I hadn't heard him before, I wouldn't have seen him, all dressed in black in woods so dark the only shadows were the silhouettes of objects rather than cast by them. I breathed through my nose until that started sounding loud and I got paranoid that my nose would whistle. Then I literally held my breath. He stopped a few feet away, looking in every direction but miraculously not seeing me. Or so I thought.

Then he spoke.

"Wait until I'm gone," he whispered, "then keep heading in that direction."

He tilted his head up a fraction, like a dog scenting the wind. "Eventually you'll hit another road. Pray he doesn't come back."

He said all this without ever looking at me, then turned around and walked away. I counted to 500 again. Around 175 I thought I heard yelling far away, like someone reporting in from a search, but

I might have imagined it. I didn't hear anything else, real or imagined, and at 500 I set off again, stumbling through the trees.

CHAPTER SEVENTEEN

The following hours are a half-remembered dream, with disjointed bits and pieces in no apparent order. Occasionally the pain of stepping on something not meant for my soft urban feet would bring my mind into focus, but like the pain, the focus rarely lasted longer than a few moments. I threw up at least once. I recall looking up to see several raccoons sitting on their haunches, watching me as I wiped my mouth on my sleeve. One tilted his head and rubbed his chin in thought, before turning to share his thoughts with his friends. He was a wise raccoon, or a wealthy one, because all of the other raccoons nodded their heads in agreement with his staccato chatter. Then they waved little paws, dropped to all fours, and wobbled away.

In time, I came to another road, as the hooded man had promised. Minutes or hours later, all I knew was that it was still dark. The growth was tangled close to the road with thorny vines and branches. Although an occasional set of headlights pierced the leaves, I felt pretty well screened from view. Sometimes I'd become aware that time had passed, but couldn't tell if I'd been awake or asleep during that time. The only thought I was able to hold in my mind was that nothing in this world could get me to set foot on that road before daylight.

The slow arrhythmic popping of a diesel engine brought me to my senses soon after dawn. My body was vibrating like a high-strung dog, but I got to my feet with the aid of a nearby tree.

Fortunately the engine sound was from a slow-moving tractor, and by the time I made it to the road it had only just passed me. I tried to speak, to yell to the driver, but the flesh in my throat was stuck painfully together and no sound would come out. The hard paved road was torture on my bruised feet, and anything more than a fast, careful walk was beyond me.

I got lucky. Somehow the man driving saw me. I guess tractors have rearview mirrors. He stopped, put on the hazard lights and climbed down. I knew I must look like a wandering lunatic, so I tried to smile as I slowly approached him, but I couldn't tell if my facial muscles were actually responding. The man stood next to his tractor, one hand on his hip and one toying with a crisp Atlanta Braves cap, and looked me over. He took off his cap and raked his hand over wisps of gray hair and a mostly bare skull. Then he slammed his cap back on his head, decision made, and walked back to his tractor.

Once again, I tried to call out, but my voice failed me. My eyes started to tear at the thought of him leaving. I could almost touch the tractor. The tires were close, but probably too large to grab. Before I could decide whether to try, the man climbed back down, this time with a tall metal travel mug in his hands.

"My wife fixed this for me this morning, but it looks like you need it a damn sight worse than I do," he said, handing me the mug. His voice shook slightly when he spoke.

I held the mug in my left hand and balanced it with my swollen useless right. After a couple of sips of strong coffee, I thanked him, but that was the extent of my verbal talents. The man took the cup from me and placed it in an improvised cupholder while he helped me up. The seat was slightly bucket-shaped, but wide enough for two. He told me his name was Joe Fisher, that his little farm was less than a mile back down the road. His wife Maggie would know what to do with me.

I had taken up the coffee again and managed a few more sips before we started our rumbling, popping progress.

"I know Maggie," I said.

My voice sounded far away to my own ears, and a very small voice inside my head (good old Mrs. Bibbystock) reminded me it was very unlikely Mr. Fisher was married to my cousin from Birmingham. We didn't speak often, but I suspected my cousin Maggie would mention it if she had moved to the Panhandle and married a farmer 30 years her senior.

Mr. Fisher looked at me askance. I could tell he didn't want to touch me, probably out of concern for me more than his own fastidiousness, but he had doubts about my ability to keep my seat. Either my comment or its delivery decided him. As soon as he had gotten the tractor turned around, he placed one arm firmly around my waist as if I were an unruly sack of potatoes.

The pressure of his arm against sore ribs that gave me a moment of intellectual clarity, or perhaps it was the diesel burbling I could feel in my bones. I poked Mr. Fisher's arm and asked him to stop. When he had I pointed to the red bandanna hanging from his front shirt pocket. He looked at me dubiously but pulled it from his pocket. Just then a wave of nausea hit me, and I realized that even if I got down from the tractor without inflicting more damage on myself, I wouldn't make it back up under my own power. I breathed deeply, eyes closed, until I knew I could speak.

"We need to mark it."

It only took him a moment to comprehend. He climbed down, walked to edge of the road and picked a tree. I nodded painfully and he tied his handkerchief to a sapling very near where I had emerged onto the road. I managed to stay upright until he got back in the seat and resumed his firm grip. Then I slumped against him and allowed myself to check out for the rest of the ride.

I hate hospitals. I hadn't set foot in a hospital for 18 years, so it's not all that surprising that I had to lose consciousness to find myself in one again. Lying on an examination table staring up at icy fluorescent lights, I realized where I was and tried to explain that I didn't belong there, that I was actually just fine and would be on my way now. Big surprise that didn't fly. I have a vague recollection of making a nuisance of myself, flailing and shouting, and yet they still wouldn't let me leave. Another big surprise.

The subsequent hours are a collage of metallic smells, the strobe effect of passing overhead lights as I was wheeled around for tests, and interminable questions about what had happened. I was exhausted. I wasn't aware of specific pain, just an overall feeling of rawness and pressure in my skull that blacked out every-thing else. I just wanted to be left alone to sleep. While tending to my feet, they asked where my shoes were. I didn't know. Then they asked what kind of shoes I'd been wearing. I didn't know. In fact, I couldn't think of a single pair of shoes I owned, now or ever. Apparently that's when I began sobbing uncontrollably.

Eventually I was taken to a room of my own, and the pestering decreased from non-stop harassment to periodic pokes and prods. These pokes and prods were scheduled to occur any time I fell asleep. After several of these intervals, I began to come out of my haze. My thoughts were less jumbled, and I recognized the purpose and logic of actions around me. The world had edges again, and so did my body. The pain helped clear my mind.

The head of my bed was slightly raised, and I fumbled for a button to raise it further. I grunted when my right hand bumped against the bedrail, which only made my head hurt worse. When my vision cleared, I lifted my hand slowly to look at it. There was a bandage covering the fleshy portion all around, leaving only my thumb and fingers protruding. My fingers were thick and discolored, like sausage gone bad, and I had to suppress an involuntary gag. It was enough to make you a vegetarian. My thumbnail was intact, but most of my other nails had been torn or broken and showed evidence of bleeding.

A nurse came in before I could catalogue the rest of my injuries, or inflict any more attempting to get comfortable. I tried to speak, but my mouth wouldn't cooperate. She anticipated me, offering a sippy cup of water and the admonishment to "sip slowly." The suction made my head hurt more, and I felt a twinge at my cheek, but no champagne could have tasted sweeter than that tap water. She held the cup for me, and after a few sips she set it on a stand beside my bed.

"Thanks," I managed. It felt like I hadn't spoken in years.

She smiled. "I'm Marie. I know you're probably used to this by now, but I'm going to check you out real quick."

She demonstrated by checking my eyes and my pulse, and doing several other things that might not have made sense to me even if I hadn't been knocked on the head.

"Are you in pain?"

"Some," I answered. She waited for elaboration, but I gave none.

"Describe your pain for me."

I closed my eyes and started at the top, picking my words carefully. My goal was to demonstrate with my articulateness that I really was hunky dory and they could let me out right now.

"I know you've heard this before, but I'm afraid I can't manage any fresh metaphors right now. My head feels like it's in a vise, and if I do anything out of the ordinary, like breathing or blinking, things tend to cloud over at the edges. My hand is throbbing—" It was then that I opened my eyes to look at my left hand. There was an IV line taped to the top. Marie followed my gaze.

"You were a little dehydrated. There are some antibiotics in there as well."

"Ah, I guess that brings me to my feet. They feel like they're on fire, or they've been beaten by a two-by-four. Make that both."

"Were they?"

I paused to consider, but I didn't want to force it. "No, I don't think so. The rest of my body just feels like a big bruise."

"That's a pretty accurate assessment."

"When can I get out of here?"

Marie grinned. She looked to be in her early 40s, with short brown hair done daily with curlers or an iron, but her grin was much younger than her hair style. Almost mischievous.

"I'll see if I can get Dr. McCauley to stop in."

Dr. McCauley was attractive in a generic doctor right out of central casting kind of way. Close-cut respectable hair, long angular face, white coat and stethoscope. Without the white coat or in a non-hospital context outside, I probably wouldn't recognize him again. The Hollywood actor association led me to expect someone a bit more… malleable? Someone with a soft touch in his bedside manner. Within moments he shattered that illusion, and I began to suspect that Marie's grin had been at the prospect of the good doctor putting another challenging patient in her place.

He stood over me and repeated many of the tests Marie had performed. The metal legs of an institutional chair screeched on the floor as he pulled it toward my head and settled in. He sighed, leaned back and rubbed his eyes, then crossed his legs widely, ankle to knee.

"You have a closed head injury, a concussion. Basically you, or someone on your behalf, slammed your brain against the inside of your skull. If he'd done it again with that kind of force, you'd most likely be dead or a vegetable. Either way we wouldn't be having this conversation. There doesn't appear to be any major bleeding, but rather than have you drop dead in the parking lot, we're going to monitor you for a while. At least for tonight, probably longer. You may experience post concussion syndrome—we can talk about that later—but I don't think you're going to have any permanent brain damage. Not that I can make any guarantees."

"You have a stress fracture in your left ulna. Your right hand is such a gnarly mess that we won't be able to tell the extent of the damage until the swelling goes down. Lacerations and contusions, a sprain or possibly more serious ligament damage. You have lacerations and contusions all over your body, but your feet are the worst. Not quite shredded, but pretty close. The cuts are superficial, but it took us a while to get all the foreign matter out of your feet, and we have to watch for infection."

He leaned over and carefully removed a large bandage from my forehead. The tape didn't pull, but it still hurt. Then he produced a round mirror from one of his voluminous pockets and placed it in my left hand. I gripped it gingerly, afraid of disturbing the IV on the other side. I'm not crazy about needles. I didn't want to look in the mirror, but part of me couldn't resist, and the doctor was watching.

When I was a sophomore in high school, I caught an elbow playing pick-up basketball after school and ended up with a hell of a shiner. It was centered on my cheekbone, but the swelling and discoloration extended to my eyesocket. It was beyond make-up, even if had owned any and known how to use it. Instead I wore a brand-new skirt to school, a cute black and white checked thing with a wide black waistband that really popped. I never wore skirts or dresses in high school, and I don't know what had possessed me

137

to buy that one, but I was glad I had. The next day I kept hearing compliments from behind me or from my "good side," and when I'd turn to thank my unsuspecting classmate she (or he) would gasp. I was uncomfortable at first, but somehow the two things that drew attention to me seemed to cancel each other out.

An Oscar gown would not mitigate the damage to my face this time.

My forehead was split and swollen, all the better to show off a color wheel of red and blue make purple. It had a nasty wet look. One cheek (right or left? I couldn't make sense of the mirror image) was similarly accented. My nose was pink and had a slightly crusty look around the nostrils, as if some of the fluids dried there had been stubborn to remove. My lips were dry and cracked, bits of skin sticking off at right angles. Topping it off was a tapestry of angry red scratches scattered all over my face.

The face in the mirror that could not be my own was mesmerizing. I knew I'd stared too long when I saw tears leaking from the inside corner of one eye, the eye above the most bruised cheek. I could feel the moist drops creeping, itching my face, but I still couldn't figure out which cheek it was. I set the mirror face-down on my sheet-covered lap.

"Could I get some lip balm?" I was proud and amazed that my voice only cracked a little bit, no more than could be explained by my parched throat. I shouldn't have spoken.

"I don't know if you remember this, but after you were brought in you had... an episode. Despite your head injury, I took the risk of giving you something because I was afraid you would do yourself more damage. That's something not uncommon with head injuries, and some people experience it for weeks or even months afterward. Unprovoked irritability or anger, mood swings and loss of emotional control."

He scrutinized my face, and I broke eye contact first. I remembered, and I also remembered what he didn't say, that among other things I begged him not to tell anyone I cried.

"You are incapable of taking care of yourself right now."

I felt like I was about to lose that precious control again. I don't cry, and crying twice in one day was unacceptable, even for a shitty day like this. But I couldn't help it. Emotion and the smell of strong cleaning agents made my chest constrict; after 18 years it smelled the same. This time when I spoke I couldn't look at him, and my voice was barely above a whisper.

"I hate hospitals."

"I know." Something in his voice made me look up. I wondered what else I'd said. His eyes were almost sympathetic. He started to say something, then abruptly changed his mind, sliding his implacable manner back into place.

"Just do what I tell you and we'll have you out of here in no time."

He scooted the chair noisily to its original position and turned to leave. In the open doorway he fired a final shot.

"And don't do anything stupid to get yourself in here again. I might not be so nice the next time."

CHAPTER EIGHTEEN

Don't do anything stupid, huh? But what had I done, stupid or otherwise, to land myself in the hospital? I had to have done something. This hadn't just been random violence. Despite what Yankee fans of "Deliverance" might think, the South is not patrolled by roaming hordes of rednecks looking to enjoy some good ole boy fun. This was a planned, coordinated attack. Two vehicles with several men in protective clothing followed me to an isolated area they knew well to execute their plan. Why? What was the motive?

I had nothing of value, and as far as I knew they hadn't taken anything except me, and maybe one of my shoes. They hadn't said much, hadn't asked me any questions, so they couldn't be after information. Not that I'm exactly James Bond anyway. The biggest secret they could get out of me is my Aunt Faye's recipe for potato candy, and even that only if I could find the little index card. But they didn't ask me anything, and they didn't really tell me anything. They just scared the shit of me. That's what we professionals call the motive of intimidation. A not very professional motive, I might add, indicating I was probably dealing with someone either stupid or psychotic. Which brought me full circle back to why.

By this point I'd blown my remaining brain fuses and was just about at intellectual blackout. The pressure in my skull was getting pretty intense, but at least it was making my throbbing hand and burning feet less noticeable. When Nurse Marie came in, I intended to ask her for some assistance in the distraction department (if I couldn't think straight I might as well be pharmaceutically happy) but changed my mind when I saw she was wearing her serious face.

"The police are here to speak with you, if you're up to it."

My pulse abruptly picked up its pace and my blood pressure rose. My vision started going fuzzy again. I felt like I'd done something wrong. It was an involuntary reaction, like taking your foot off the gas at the sight of a state trooper when you're already driving the speed limit. I've always had an unreasoning distrust of law enforcement, and I'm sure working at the PD's office and hanging out with defense attorneys hasn't helped. It's a good way to hear about the worst law enforcement has to offer. Rationally, I know the evil acts that most people wouldn't believe if you told them are perpetrated by 1% of law enforcement (okay, maybe 5% on a bad day), but the bad guys aren't considerate enough to wear big C's for "crook" on their chests. And, like the proverbial bad apple, if unchecked the rot spreads pretty easily in the dark.

"Yeah. Sure. Okay." As she left to let the cops in, I remembered my need for assistance.

"Marie!" Bad move calling loudly. (I couldn't have managed a yell.) My vision went dark and I waited for it to clear.

"Could I get something else to drink, maybe a Coke to settle my stomach? Thanks." Not exactly a happy narcotic, but it was something.

Two men in button-down shirts and khakis entered. They were both in their early 40s, clean-shaven with dark hair and enough physical resemblance to be brothers. One made the introductions while the other screeched chairs over to my bed. I found their synchronicity slightly disturbing, as a suspect might.

"Sydney Brennan? I'm Detective Drake and this is Detective Sutton. We're with the Stetler County Sheriff's Department. How are you feeling?"

"Well, I'm just thrilled to be here."

I wasn't sure if I was being sincere or sarcastic, and by their expressions I could tell the detectives weren't either. It seemed to throw off Drake a bit. One point for me.

"We'd like to speak with you about what happened last night."

I was glad to see Marie return with a styrofoam cup of soda over crushed ice. I felt so worn out. I thanked Marie and took a sip. She smiled at me, then turned to the detectives with the stern look she'd used on me earlier.

"Don't be too long," she told them.

"Yes, ma'am," responded Drake, ever accommodating. Sutton hadn't spoken at all yet. When Marie had gone, I nodded my head and Drake continued.

"We found your rental car, Ms. Brennan. It doesn't appear that anything was taken—your bag and other personal effects are there —but we'll need you to confirm that nothing is missing. Can you tell us why you were out there?"

"I was visiting someone in Lazarus." He waited, but I didn't volunteer anything else.

"Ms. Brennan, you are a private investigator. Correct?"

"Yes."

"Were you working on a case?"

"Yes."

Again, he waited, but as mule-headed as it might sound I wasn't about to do his job for him. This time Sutton spoke.

"Ms. Brennan, could you tell us what happened?"

I took another sip of soda to give myself strength.

"I'll try. Things are still a little fuzzy. I was meeting with some-one in Lazarus at her home. When I left there, I stopped at a convenience store—"

"The Shop-n-Save on 98?" Sutton interrupted.

"Yes. I think that's the one. I was in there for a few minutes. When I left, it must have been around 9 PM. It was dark. I'd probably driven about 20 minutes when the pick-up in front of me stopped short. There was another vehicle behind me, I believe also a pick-up. I wasn't thinking. I wasn't suspicious at all. I just thought there was something in the road. Someone from the vehicle behind me knocked on my window. I couldn't see him because he was standing too close and he'd left his high beams on. When I opened the door, he yanked me out, threw a hood over me and dragged me to the bed of the first pick-up."

"Did you see anyone?"

"I didn't see any faces if that's what you mean. When they took my hood off, they were all dressed in black, wearing gloves and ski masks that covered their mouths."

"Go on."

"They drove for a while. Just in the one truck. I don't know how long, but probably not more than 15 minutes and definitely not more than half an hour. Then we pulled off onto a little dirt road. There was a clearing in the woods there, and that's where they took my hood off."

"Would you recognize the place if you saw it again?"

"I don't know. I might."

"How many people were there?"

I closed my eyes. "One held me in a sort of chokehold while we were driving. He had strong body odor. When we stopped everyone moved around—they were wearing heavy boots and the metal truck bed was bare—and there were three men in the back with me. I'd guess there were two more in the cab, but I'm not sure. It could have been as little as one or as many as three. So total, between four and six men."

I opened my eyes. "I don't really remember much after that. Flashes, but nothing that makes much sense. Obviously they knocked me around quite a bit. I don't know how I got away, but I probably got in a few shots of my own."

I looked down at my hands. "My nails are a mess. I don't know if anyone took samples—"

"We have swabs and clippings. It's the hospital's standard procedure for potential, uh, well." Sutton trailed off.

"I wasn't raped. I'm not sure what did happen, but I know I wasn't raped."

"Yes, ma'am. We're aware that you weren't sexually assaulted."

I tried not to think too hard about that one. "Somehow I got away and ran into the woods. I must have been there all night. I think there was a farmer the next morning."

My eyes slid shut again. I was so exhausted that tears leaked from the outer corners of my eyes. I just wanted to sleep. My arm was too heavy to move to reach my soda.

Sutton spoke. "Yes, ma'am. Mr. Fisher. He and his wife brought you in this morning. We've spoken with him and he's going to take us out there this afternoon, out where he found you."

I had a quick flash of memory and opened my eyes. "We marked it."

"Yes, ma'am. We'll see if we can back-track from there to the clearing."

My eyes were closed again, and I thought they must have taken the hint until Drake's voice cut into my doze.

"Ms. Brennan," he said sharply. I opened my eyes. "What were you working on?"

"I can't imagine it had anything to do with this."

"With all due respect, Miss Brennan," and Drake's expression told me how little was due, "that's our job, deciding what is or isn't

145

relevant."

I tried to glare at him, and it made my head hurt worse. I almost told him to fuck off. Probably not a smart move, but under the circumstances, who could hold it against me? After another good look at Drake, I felt sure he would. I fully intended to stare him down for as long as I remained conscious, but was saved from such a dramatic gesture by Sutton.

"Ms. Brennan, you said you were here working on a case. We know you live in Tallahassee, and my guess is you don't take many pleasure trips to Stetler County. In fact, correct me if I'm wrong, but I'm guessing you don't know a single person here that's not connected with what you're working on. Doesn't it make sense that we should start with your investigation?"

I sighed. Put that way, I knew he was right, and I was too tired to argue. It was getting more and more difficult to speak, and I wasn't sure what I could ethically divulge.

"I can't give you details until I've spoken to my client. I'm looking into her—family background."

Drake leaned forward. "Anything illegal in it? Any criminal history?"

I knew this was an area that would make the case, and my client, pretty easily identifiable, but I didn't care anymore. I just wanted to be left alone. "Someone in her family was convicted of killing his wife 20 years ago. He's dead now. There are no active issues. There was nothing… unresolved. That's why it doesn't make sense. It must be something else."

I closed my eyes, and this time I wasn't opening them again for anyone or anything. Fortunately I didn't have to test my resolve. Marie came in and asked them to leave. I was asleep before they left the building, if not before they left my room.

CHAPTER NINETEEN

When I opened my eyes, there was someone sitting in a chair next to my bed that I didn't immediately recognize. His floppy chestnut hair was still parted in the middle, but it only fell to the top of his ears. Even more surprising, his skin was tanned, with a slightly reddish tinge that promised to turn brown within days. And he wasn't sitting in front of a computer.

"Mike?" I asked.

"Sydney!" His magazine slid off his lap onto the floor and he bent to pick it up. He was still wearing his glasses, or I never would have recognized him.

"You're awake."

One of my eyes seemed to have swollen even more. I blinked several times but it remained a slit. I narrowed the other eye at Mike.

"You got a haircut."

He blushed, deepening his sunburn.

"And a tan," I went on. "How many days have I been out?"

He laughed. "Just a few hours. I went fishing in the Gulf yesterday. Per your suggestion."

He looked down at his forearm, pressing with a finger until his tan turned white, then looked up again. "Richard's here too. He just went to get us something to drink. In case anyone asks, we work with you. That's the only way they'd let us in."

"Who, Marie? Is it past visiting hours?"

"I don't know who Marie is, but the sheriff has somebody posted in the hall. They're not letting just anyone in to see you."

"And you said we work together? If that gets back to Drake, he'll be all over my ass the next time he interrogates me."

I told Mike about my visit from law enforcement, that Drake had been the bad cop in the routine, acting suspicious of everything I said. The thought of going another few rounds with him exhausted me. I tried to look for my cup of soda, but my field of vision had decreased as the swelling around my eye increased, and when I turned my head I was swamped by nausea.

Mike stood from his chair. "Are you okay? Do you want me to get the nurse?"

Normally I'd tell him, or anyone else, I was fine until I dropped where I stood. Of course, I wasn't standing right now. I'd been beaten into submission, and that thought more than the pain itself brought tears to my eyes. I tried to smile and said, "Please."

I wasn't sure any sound came out, but Mike understood and waved a nurse down from the doorway. Closing my eyes and breathed deeply through my nose, I tried not to cry. It wasn't pride; I knew how painful a bout of sobbing would be. A nurse, not Marie, came in and gave me something in my IV. I sighed and slipped away again.

The next time I opened my eyes, Richard was next to my bed. He was wearing reading glasses and had a paperback book in his hands. Mike sat a little beyond him, flipping through another magazine. I must have moved or made some sort of sound because they both looked up.

"Hey, Sleeping Beauty." Richard smiled, but it was a half-hearted attempt. In the harsh fluorescent lighting he looked his age, his brow marked by deep lines. He leaned forward, and I heard Mike's chair scoot closer.

"How are you feeling?" Richard asked.

I swallowed thickly. "Thirsty." He held a straw to my lips and I took a few sips of water.

"I was hoping for something stronger."

Richard turned to Mike and clapped him on the shoulder. They both laughed. When Richard turned back to face me it was with a real smile, the kind that made my pulse race. For a moment my inner ears grew numb with the rush of blood, but that passed and my spirits lifted. The not-Marie nurse must have heard them laughing. She came in before the smiles had faded from their faces and introduced herself as Lily. After she checked me out, I asked her for a soda.

With the first sip, I noticed a different kind of discomfort. I had to pee. Bad. I didn't have a catheter (thank god) and no one had mentioned anything about bodily functions. Maybe they expected me to use a bedpan. Well, that wasn't happening. I looked at the two men sitting next to me. Maybe it was the drugs talking, but modesty be damned.

"Lily, I have to pee like a big dog."

Both men blinked hard, and I saw Lily's eyes move to an elongated plastic kidney bean on a stand nearby.

"In the bathroom," I continued firmly.

We didn't argue because I didn't say anything. I knew it was going to take a lot out of me to walk to the bathroom so I saved my strength. I simply refused to change my mind.

The room was a double, but there was no one in the other bed. Fortunately my bed was the one closest to the bathroom. Lily pulled down my sheet and helped me swing my legs to the floor. I waited for the blood to stop roaring in my ears. When it did, I noticed the breeze on my backside.

"You guys better not look at my naked butt."

149

I could tell they were both trying not to laugh. Laugh, cry, hospitals, funerals, it's all the same. Anything to release the tension.

My legs were too short to reach the floor while sitting on my bed. I'd have to slide off the edge of the bed. No problem. Lily stood in front of me to my left side. She apparently favored Broken Arm over Sausage Hand. (Stress Fracture Arm just doesn't sound as sexy.) Sitting at the edge of the mattress like a kid on the high dive, with Lily waiting to catch me, I finally took a deep breath and plunged.

Unfortunately I'd forgotten about my nearly shredded feet. I cried out when I landed on them, and I would have crumpled to the floor if she hadn't steadied me. Mike and Richard moved forward, but she waved them away. I stood there catching my breath, getting used to the bruised, fiery pain in my feet. With the sheet pulled up, I don't think Mike and Richard had seen my bandaged feet. They certainly hadn't seen my bruised shins and calves, and my gown's thin cotton sleeves had slid up to reveal more cuts and bruises. I found out later that even my back was black and blue, so it's just as well that they heeded my admonishment not to look at my naked butt. One of them sucked in air involuntarily, but I didn't look. I didn't want to see their expressions.

Lily helped me shuffle to the bathroom. She went in with me and closed the door, but I didn't feel self-conscious. I was too glad for the assistance. I couldn't use the handicapped bars effectively with my injuries, so my descent was an exercise in controlled falling. Before long I had an empty bladder, and I'd accomplished my goal with nothing more than the expected delays caused by head rushes and cloudy vision. I didn't even pee on my feet.

When Lily and I emerged, Mike and Richard were singing Creedence Clearwater Revival's "Have You Ever Seen the Rain." They couldn't agree on the words to the verses, so they'd just sung the chorus over and over, in at least two different keys.

"We didn't want you to think we were listening to you tinkle," Mike explained in a stage whisper.

I may have only known them for a few days, but Mike and Richard made good hospital buddies. They managed to chatter at me until Lily kicked them out, without ever touching on anything too heavy. They left an assortment of magazines and comic books behind, apparently chosen at random from the hospital newsstand. It was sweet of them, but I didn't have the energy or the inclination for reading yet. All I wanted to do was sleep. My slumber was so heavy that night, I didn't see the third shift nurse at all. It was like someone had flipped the power switch in my head to the off position. I didn't dream, and I doubt that I even rolled over. In fact, considering my injuries, I'm sure I didn't. I opened my eyes the next morning just long enough for Marie to give me some juice. Then I went right back to sleep.

Mike and Richard came by around lunch. Apparently they'd called ahead and found out I'd be allowed to eat outside food. They brought me a cup of rich potato soup with a piece of crusty bread. I didn't ask where they'd gotten it, but it was still hot, and it was delicious, with just a hint of smoky cheese. Eating it was a bit of challenge. My right hand was still too swollen to manipulate, and because of the stress fracture I didn't have my usual range of motion with my left either. Fortunately, they'd foreseen the difficulty and brought one of those flattened ladle-like spoons that you use in Asian restaurants. It took a while, but eventually I got more in my mouth than on my gown.

When they went back to work, I went back to dozing. During one of my waking periods, I realized they hadn't been on their lunch break; it was Saturday. No, wait, it was Sunday. I was supposed to do something today, or yesterday, but I couldn't remember

151

what, and I didn't care enough to try very hard. It was sweet of them to visit, but they hadn't said if or when they'd be back. I felt an uncharacteristic twinge at the thought of leaving without saying goodbye.

Mike and Richard did return in a few hours, but to my disappointment they hadn't brought food. Having kept the soup down, I was starting to get hungry for real food again. Dr. McCauley came in while I was chastising them for the oversight. They remained in my room, but retreated a discreet distance away while he poked and prodded, checked vitals and bandages. Once the doctor pulled my sheet back up and patted it absently, they resumed hovering.

It never even occurred to me to ask them to leave. Dr. McCauley said a lot about my injuries, and they hung on every word. Of course, the only words I heard were "recovering nicely" and "home tomorrow."

"No driving, for at least a week. We'll set up a follow-up appointment for you in Tallahassee and take it from there. Have you made arrangements yet for transportation?"

I hadn't anticipated the driving ban, although I probably should have. Blame it on the head injury. Before I could protest, Richard spoke.

"We've taken care of it. Thank you, doctor."

I waited until McCauley left. "What do you mean you've taken care of it?"

"We're driving you back tomorrow, you and your car."

"It's a rental."

"Good. Then we'll just drop it at the airport." Richard turned to Mike. "We can do that this evening, if the cops are done with it."

My strength must have been returning because my stubborn streak definitely was. "Look, not that I don't appreciate your help, but were you thinking of consulting me?"

"It makes sense. Just don't worry about it. Let us take care of it."

Richard's words sounded like condescension to my addled brain. "I'm quite capable of taking care of myself."

"Look, I know you're exhausted and you're in pain, but don't be unreasonable."

"Unreasonable? Well, isn't that a typical male response? I'm not just some helpless female victim—"

"Sydney." Mike had moved next to my bed and put his hand on my shoulder briefly, just long enough to establish eye contact. His voice was soft but firm. "You were a victim. I can't imagine you ever being helpless, but you were a victim. Right now you can't hold a steering wheel, and you can't press the brakes. We're your friends. Just let us do this for you."

My irrational (I could admit that to myself but never to Richard) anger and frustration evaporated, and I felt watery inside. Before I could make a spectacle of myself, we had another set of visitors. Intruders. Drake and Sutton. The four men may have all been associated with our justice system, but they didn't move in the same circles. It was more like a Venn diagram, with friction where the circles overlapped. Right now I was the overlap.

Mike and Richard stood together at one side of my bed, while Drake and Sutton moved to the other. They eyed each other warily, like wolves over a carcass. I guess that made me the carcass. Drake said they'd heard that I was leaving town tomorrow, making it sound as if I were making a prison break instead of going home.

I didn't rise to the bait, nor did my appointed protectors. We were on our best behavior. Richard explained our anticipated check-out plan. Sutton said they weren't done with the rental car, but they'd take care of returning it, and if Mike and Richard came by this evening they could get my belongings.

"What about your client?" Drake asked.

I'd started to drift off again and was caught by surprise. "What about her?"

"Have you spoken with her yet?"

"No. I didn't think to tell my kidnappers to wait while I grabbed my day timer."

Drake looked at me blankly. Normally I would assume he was just being an ass, but in the past 48 hours I couldn't always be sure that my thoughts emerged from my mouth intact.

"I don't have her number," I clarified.

"We can't let you leave until you give us that information," Drake said.

"What makes you think you have the authority to stop me? You think you can run this place like your own little backwater fiefdom —" Fortunately Mike saw where I was headed and once again stepped in as the peacemaker.

"She won't be leaving until tomorrow afternoon. Sydney, was your client's contact information in your car?"

"Yes, but—"

"John, we'll come get Sydney's things tonight. That should give her plenty of time to contact her client. If you return tomorrow at, say 11 AM, I'm sure she'll have the information for you."

That seemed to work for everyone, and Sutton escorted his associate from the room before Drake could remember to be uncivil. Mike had a hand on my bed next to me, presumably to keep me from launching myself at the cops. I was still agitated and chafed at my physical weakness, my apparent fragility. In short, I was spoiling for a fight. The adrenaline momentarily penetrated my brain fog to jolt a few synapses, and I found myself calling after Sutton and Drake.

"I will tell you one thing about my client."

154

Sutton and Mike looked at me apprehensively, but Drake licked his lips in anticipation. The truce had been withdrawn.

"My client is a black woman. Is the KKK still active in Stetler County?"

It was a shot in the dark, but it seemed as likely to me as an attack over investigating a 24-year-old domestic killing. Drake's lips grew tight. It was Sutton who answered, with a careful non-answer, as the two men retreated from the room.

"That's certainly something to keep in mind, ma'am."

Mike and Richard followed so they could get my belongings, Mike hanging back just long enough to get a whispered dig in at me. He raised an eyebrow.

"Fiefdom?"

I tried not to grin because it hurt so much. "Maybe I got a little carried away."

"You think?" His own grin was unrestrained.

CHAPTER TWENTY

Finally alone, I became aware of a gnawing feeling in my gut and in my brain. I didn't know what to tell Noel, and I didn't know how she'd take it. I also needed to give Ben a call. The fish wouldn't starve tonight, but Ben would give me grief if I didn't call. There was nothing I could do until Mike and Richard returned with my stuff. At the moment I wasn't sure I could remember my own phone number, much less anyone else's.

By the time Mike and Richard showed up, I'd feasted on jello and broth and had another nap. They'd brought my belongings from my rental car and my motel room. The motel owner, Mrs. Waters, had packed up my things when she'd heard (as I'm sure everyone in the town had) of my near demise. My bag was waiting at the front desk, along with a plate of homemade brownies and a get well card. She hadn't charged me for the nights I didn't made it back to my room, and she hoped I wouldn't let a few hooligans keep me from coming back to stay with her again. Hooligans, huh? At the moment I didn't feel like arguing with her assessment.

Once Mike and Richard left, with Mike taking the brownies with him "for safekeeping," I made my phone calls. All I told Ben was that I'd gotten held up for an extra day and I'd explain when I saw him. I could hear the TV in the background, apparently something interesting enough that he didn't take the time to ask me any questions. I didn't tell Noel much more, just said that I'd been involved in an altercation that required police involvement. They

157

wanted to know what I was investigating in case there was some connection. She readily agreed to me telling them anything they wanted to know, and, unlike Ben, when I told her I'd fill her in later she made it clear she'd hold me to my promise.

Mrs. Waters' hooligans were a subaudible hum, a recurrent mantra that evening during my waking moments, tickling at my brain. Fortunately I was getting pretty good at ignoring extra noises in my head, and if they disturbed my sleep, I didn't remember it next morning. I woke feeling rested and hungry for something more substantive and more flavorful than hospital oatmeal. When I tired of morning talk shows and tormenting Marie about how much she would miss me, I asked her to bring me my motel bag.

My case of toiletries sat on top. Opening it was like finding a long lost box of treasures under the bed. The fresh scents were reassuring. Chief among the treasures was my toothbrush and little bottle of mouthwash, sitting on top. Below this were matching little bottles of make-up and skin care products. I wear very little make-up as a rule, and nothing I'd brought with me would alleviate my current colorful condition. I doubted anything outside of a movie set special effects department could help. Deodorant, some tinted lip balm for my chapped lips, and a tube of rich almond lotion would do for now. I couldn't apply the lotion with one hand, but at least I could flip off the cap and smell it.

The clothes below my toiletries case were neatly folded, much more so than if I had done the job. Even more surprising, they'd also been freshly laundered. Bless Mrs. Waters. I didn't know what had happened to the clothes I'd been wearing that night. They were no longer fit to wear anyway, but it was an odd feeling, knowing that my clothes could be sitting somewhere in a police locker. Torn, with traces of my blood, evidence of my terror. I metaphorically shook off the macabre sense of melodrama. (No more actual shaking for my poor tender head.)

The sight of clean underwear lifted my spirits. A button down shirt was next. I didn't want to try to pull anything over my head, and the shirt was loose enough not to draw attention going bra-less. Who was I kidding? I'm not flat-chested, but I'd have to be a topless Pamela Anderson for anyone to notice my breasts before my face in my current state. The bottoms department wasn't as easy. My khakis were now gone, with my only remaining pair of pants being jeans. Reasonably respectable jeans too, not coming apart, falling off your ass comfortable jeans. The thought of someone (I couldn't do it) pulling jeans over my ripped feet, buttoning them up to constrict my bruised, aching limbs was too much.

Once again, my guys came to the rescue. Richard's wife sent some sort of microwave-friendly quiche or casserole and a pair of comfy gray drawstring sweats. Mike brought most of the brownies and a pair of garbage-green Oscar the Grouch slippers for my feet. They had Velcro so I could fit them over my bandages. I couldn't imagine where he'd gotten them, and I chose not to take the choice as an insult. The guys left to track down the piles of paperwork required to secure my release while Marie helped me dress.

It seemed I'd never get out of that damn hospital room. The doc came by for a last visit. He said a lot more stuff that I ignored, gave me some tubes and prescriptions, and changed my bulky bandages for smaller versions. Then Drake and Sutton dropped in to pay their respects. Sutton did all the talking this time, so it was relatively quick and painless. I told them why I was in their lovely county and whom I had spoken with, but no specifics on what I had learned. As far as I was concerned, they didn't need to know. Apparently they agreed, because they didn't ask any follow-up questions about my case. Or perhaps they had another theory.

159

"Can you tell me if this is familiar to you?" Sutton asked.

I heard the rustling of plastic as he pulled something from an inside pocket. Rather than handing it to me, he set it on the bed next to my hip. It was a newspaper article in a clear evidence bag. The headline read, "Racial Discrimination Still a Reality." I didn't bother to pick it up.

"Not this particular one, but I was quoted in a lot of newspapers about this. I'm sure you remember all the media attention."

Sutton's smile was strained. "Oh, yes. But take a look at this one. Please."

The IV was gone from my left arm, but I still picked up the article gingerly. My name was circled in red pen, and someone had scrawled in the margin, *"Go home, bitch! Next time there won't be enough left of you to bury."*

If I'd had more in my stomach, I would have thrown up. Sutton must have seen my queasiness.

"I'm sorry," he said. "I thought you should see this. The KKK thing might not be that far off base. I don't think you'll be in any danger when you return to Tallahassee, but if you'd like we can call Leon County and have a car—"

"No, thanks. I'm sure I'll be fine."

He nodded, as if he'd expected my response. Sutton rose from his chair, retrieved the article from the bed and replaced it with one of his business cards.

"I'll keep you informed of any progress. And please, feel free to call me if you need anything."

Sutton gave me another strained smile, but I thought it was a genuine one. Drake left on his heel, without ever saying a word. The two cops had to squeeze past Richard and Mike at the door. I hadn't noticed them before, but their grim expressions assured me that they'd been standing there all along and heard everything. If they didn't resist the temptation to vocalize their concerns, it was going to be a long drive back to Tallahassee.

I begged one last bathroom break before we left. This time I leaned on Marie in transit, but once I made it to the bathroom it was all me. My right hand was still useless. It and my forearm were encased in a kind of strap-on splint to ensure immobility and give everything a chance to heal. My left arm would also need to be babied for a while, but with my necessary reliance on it, I hoped to be well on the road to ambidexterity soon. I'd always wanted to be ambidextrous, so the optimist in me (probably still under the influence of drugs) noted that getting my ass kicked hadn't been a total loss.

I continued my streak (no pun intended) by not peeing on anything that couldn't be easily wiped off. Unable to tie my pants, I was still bursting with optimism and self-esteem as I held them up left-handed. That is, until I caught a glimpse of my reflection in the bathroom mirror. Luckily I was standing at the door leaning on the straight metal handle at the time, far enough from the mirror to be spared the details of my face and wise enough not to move closer for a better look. What stopped me in my tracks was the dirty red halo of nastiness I called hair. Maybe they could shave my head before I left.

Marie came to help tie my pants when I emerged from the bathroom. I looked past her at the guys, about to speak, but the sight of them stopped me. Mike and Richard stood side by side, doing some kind of white man jive, singing without making a sound.

"Let me guess—Milli Vanilli, 'Blame it on the Rain.'"

They grinned like a couple of fourth graders with a new poop joke.

"Well, aren't you just too cute and clever. I've got a serious

161

question for you jokers."

Their grins faded as they looked at each other, wondering if they'd somehow crossed a line. I sat on the edge of the hospital bed while Marie slid my Oscar slippers over my bandages.

"Have you ever in your life seen anything like my hair?"

Mike took a bag from a nearby table and approached me. "There is no safe answer to that question, except maybe this. I got you a little something else." He reached into the bag and handed me a Red Sox hat.

It hurt my face to smile, but I couldn't help it. "How did you know?"

"You must have mentioned it."

I expanded the size a few notches and pulled the hat gingerly down over my hair. The brim just touched the edge of my forehead bandage. Marie pulled a wheelchair over from the corner, and I settled in and looked at Mike.

"All right. Marie, thanks for everything. It's been real, but we're outta here. Like a Roger Clemens fastball."

"You do know he hasn't played for the Red Sox for years?" Mike said.

I shushed him so loudly, I saw lightning flashes across my open eyes.

"Don't speak such blasphemy around a person who's unwell. You could have a detrimental effect on my recovery."

Chapter Twenty-One

Richard drove his car to Tallahassee (he'd cleaned it out for the occasion) and Mike rode shotgun. The idea was that I'd have the entire backseat to stretch out. I fought to stay vertical on principle, but riding as a passenger puts me to sleep under the best of conditions. I dozed against the window for a while, but soon gave up any pretense of consciousness and lay down to doze horizontally. It's never that much more comfortable to lie down squashed than it is to sit up, but at least your head doesn't bob and you're not fighting gravity.

Mike navigated to my house without ever once asking directions, and when I came around it was only because we were pulling in my drive. I'd left my car in the carport, but Cecil, a light blue Volkswagon Cabrio, didn't take up much room. Richard pulled up as close as possible behind Cecil so I wouldn't have to walk as far. There's a door to the kitchen from the carport, and I was hoping to slip in unseen that way rather than through my front door. Some of my elderly neighbors are nosy and have poor eyesight, a bad combination for my reputation. The last thing I needed was for Mrs. Kimball to watch two men carrying me home drunk in the middle of the day for an orgy. That's what her prurient mind would see, and she'd pass it along to the rest of the spinsters and widowers at the curb. They all met there every morning with their cups of coffee to get their newspapers.

The house was a little stuffy when we walked in, but Jackie and

Bruce weren't floating at the top of their aquarium, so things seemed in good order. I hope I thanked Mike and Richard, but all I know for sure is that I went straight to bed and was asleep again within minutes.

Ben was in my room when I woke. He'd brought a chair from the kitchen and was sitting next to my bed. I rolled over painfully to find him staring at me.

"Wow, you really do look like shit!"

From the mouths of children. "Kiss your mother with that mouth?"

"No, but the girls at school never complain."

"Yeah, well, the girls at school are a bunch of sluts."

"Don't I know it."

We smiled at each other.

"Good to have you back," he said.

I was lying against several pillows in a semi-raised position. I didn't know who'd had such foresight and engineering know-how, but I was glad for it. It made sitting up easier. "Thanks for feeding the boys. Hand me my hat?"

He did, and I shoved my hair under it a bit too hard. "Lip stuff?" He handed me that as well, and I smacked my lips with just a bit of color. "Better?" I asked.

"Well, yeah, if the Red Sox weren't such a loser team."

"Come help me up, you twit."

It was as difficult as I'd expected, with much rushing of blood and screaming of nerves, and I was glad for the assistance. We walked together to the living room, Ben angled slightly ahead of me in the narrow hallway. He settled me in a chair, then went to the kitchen to get us something to drink. That was when I noticed Mike.

"You're still here," I said.

"That's Syd, master of the obvious," Ben said. I tried to give him a scathing look, but only managed a worse headache.

Mike was pulling dishes down from my cabinets, but he stopped long enough to give Ben's shoulder a guy squeeze. "Remember, she's not quite firing on all cylinders yet."

Mike ran his finger in circles next to his head. "We gotta cut her some slack."

"What are you doing?" I asked. "And where's Richard?"

"I'm getting some of your dishes down so you don't crack your head open again trying to reach them. Richard went grocery shopping with Noel. They should be back any minute."

"Noel?"

Ben answered. "Yeah, Noel. Are you supposed to be taking some kind of pills or something?"

I didn't have any idea, but of course Mike did. He and Ben consulted about my medical condition—Mike was putting a list on the refrigerator—while I tried to make sense of my life. Too many people I barely knew, who didn't know each other at all, suddenly seemed to know each other very well. Perhaps I missed seeing Rod Serling when I woke up, or more likely there was a simple explanation. Of course Ben would have come over as soon as he saw the activity. I must have told Noel I was coming home this afternoon, and she'd have come over to interrogate me after my mysterious phone call. Then Mike and Richard stuck around to get me settled in, and everyone got chummy while I was sleeping. I felt a vague uneasiness about the situation, but I wasn't sure why.

Soon after I'd made these brilliant deductions, I heard a car pull in the driveway. Richard and Noel staggered through the door, arms loaded with grocery bags. Noel spoke first, glancing in my direction as she scooted her bags onto the kitchen counter.

"Well, if it isn't Sleeping—oh my God!"

The top of one bag tilted, and bags of pasta spilled on the floor. By the time she'd picked them up, Noel had returned to her usual composure. She left her bags and walked toward me.

"And I thought I was looking better."

"I'm sorry. Richard tried to warn me, but after speaking to you last night I thought he was being melodramatic."

She lifted my cap gently to get a better look at my forehead. "Obviously I was wrong."

She put her hands on her hips while she looked me over, then turned back toward the men in the kitchen. "If you guys can handle that, I think it's time Sydney got a bath."

Noel helped me up and we headed toward the master bath. "And order some pizzas while you're at it."

I sat on the toilet while Noel started the bath. For once I was glad for the tacky fuzzy toilet lid cover. I couldn't remember where I'd gotten it. Surely I wouldn't have paid money for it, but the alternative (that I was putting my bum on a tacky fuzzy thing that came with my house, a tacky fuzzy thing that had previously hosted the bums of strangers) was even worse. My mind grew so fixated on the thought, I didn't notice Noel's brief departure until she returned with a carton of Epsom salts.

"I figured you probably wouldn't have these," she said, dumping salt generously into the churning hot water. "It's a generational thing. My grandmother swears by them."

When the tub was full enough, she turned off the water and began seeing to me, starting at the bottom. She removed the bandages gently, leaving a small pile on the floor.

"It's all right to get your feet wet, but I wouldn't let them soak the whole time."

Next was the splint on my right arm, which Marie had strapped on over my shirt sleeve that morning. It had Velcro straps on the forearm and then slid off over my hand. Fortunately my fingers weren't as swollen, but they and the rest of my arm had grown much more colorful and were still no fun to look at.

Noel placed the splint on the floor next to the pile of bandages and went to work on my forehead. "Any more?" she asked.

"I'm not sure. Maybe some small ones."

Noel pulled a couple of towels from the rack and set them next to her. Then she began trying to pull my sweats off without pulling me off my toilet perch. My underwear came off with them, but got hung up at my knees. It hurt trying to stay upright, but the absurdity of it all made me giggle, and Noel grinned. There were some small bandages on my calves, and my legs were covered with nasty bruises. I thought she'd say something, but after her initial outburst, Noel had given no sign of surprise.

She draped the bath towel on my lap while she undid my buttons, then pulled the towel up over my chest as she removed my shirt. Whether for the sake of her modesty or my own I didn't know, but I appreciated it. I was never one of those women at the gym who felt comfortable flashing my breasts and furriness at everyone in the locker room until I'd sufficiently aired out and felt like dressing. Maybe if I'd gone to the gym more than half a dozen times in my life, I'd feel differently, but I doubted it.

One of the men called out from the kitchen, and Noel went to check on the crisis, telling me not to move until she got back. I was starting to chill and took the opportunity to wrap the other towel around me. When she returned, she got me sitting on the edge of the bath and asked me if I needed any more help. I assured her I could handle it. She nodded and flipped the switch on the bathroom fan.

"I'll be back in about 15 minutes to help you out. Don't worry about your hair. We'll wash it under the tap after you bathe. If you need anything, just let me know."

A wicked grin touched her mouth. "We Southern Baptists aren't much on nudity, but if you fall in I think I can help you out without endangering my immortal soul."

After Noel left, I slid awkwardly into the warm bath water. I could hear laughing in the kitchen. Had that been a sarcastic remark, Noel's first joke? People really were loosening up around here. Nothing like a helpless, nasty-looking friend to unleash one's goodwill and sense of humor.

I tried to resent them all, resent their intrusive presence and condescending helpfulness, their apparent wholeness. I'd turned my back on my own family years ago, or rather I'd returned their favor. I had my reasons—good reasons—and I hadn't regretted it for a moment. Well, I hadn't seriously regretted it. I also hadn't regretted being wholly independent. In case you're wondering, yes, wholly independent does look an awful lot like alone. At least from the outside. You get used to it, and you get territorial. The presence of other people in your life is annoying. It scrapes on raw nerves and taxes social muscles that are content to be atrophied.

Now my kitchen was full of people laughing, fixing food, making themselves at home. They'd never asked if they could come in, and I tried to be angry about that too. I tried, but I couldn't. If they'd asked, I'd have turned them away, like I do everyone. And I was glad they were here. I was glad. There, I said it, to myself if no one else. It didn't even hurt that much. In fact, it was nice to be taken care of. Just for an evening.

I got out of the tub carefully, dried off and wrapped myself in a towel. Sitting on the fuzzy toilet lid, I looked down at the stopper in the tub and wondered if I'd pitch in headfirst if I tried to take it out. Noel came in and saved me the trouble. She'd found a shirt with a zipper for me, and after washing my hair I carefully dressed myself in clean clothes. Progress.

The five of us spent the evening hanging out and eating pizza from paper plates I didn't know I had. Maybe they'd arrived with the groceries. I kept dozing off in my armchair, and occasionally I'd catch scraps of conversation out of context. The synaptic dislocation was almost enough to wake me up, but not quite. Instead the sound of familiar voices was reassuring. Mike and Richard left first. They still had to drive home to the Panhandle, but said they'd be checking in periodically. Ben left soon after, and Noel got me settled in for the night, preparatory to leaving.

She actually tucked me in, or the adult version of such a procedure. She left a glass of water and a bottle of pills on the nightstand by my bed, just in case.

"There's a chart on the fridge that tells you when to take your medication. Richard and I filled the prescriptions, and they're on the counter by the fridge. There should be plenty of food, but if we missed something, I'll be over tomorrow after work. I left my work number in case of emergency, and Ben's next door if you need something. I think he finishes school this week, and he gets home early pretty early. Of course, you know that."

Noel smiled. "Richard and I had an interesting talk when we went shopping. He's a good man. You know, he really cares about you."

"He's married."

"True." She shook her head and started to rise. "True."

The discussion of Richard's marital status cleared my head enough to make me realize what had been nagging me all evening.

"Noel, does Richard know who you are?"

"You mean, does he know I'm your client, or does know he defended my father for murdering my mother?"

She smiled. "It hasn't come up yet. And I only told him my first

169

name."

For a while after Noel left, I thought I'd finally had my fill of sleep. A short while. I couldn't get my head around what was going on, and I couldn't make myself care. My head got wooly again. I didn't think about tomorrow. I didn't think about anything. I just lay there until sleep came, and with it, dreams.

Pain woke me once, probably the result of an ill-advised sudden move in my sleep. I was still breathing hard with a vague recollection of being chased in the darkness. Once I'd stopped flailing around the pain left, and with the pain and the memory of the dream gone, I was able to get back to sleep pretty easily. Then I dreamed of Allan.

It had been 18 years since my brother died, and for the first few years, I dreamed of him often. Sometimes I relived real moments from our past, actual conversations with him. In those dreams, I knew he was dead, and there were so many things I wanted to tell him, but our past scripts constrained me. I was trapped in the same words and couldn't change anything, except by the end tears would be streaming from my eyes as I said my lines. Eventually I started to think he knew what was coming too, that he was trapped in the script, and his chocolate eyes looked like they were melting.

In other dreams, I'd create new memories. I'd remember while dreaming that Allan was supposed to be dead, but think my greatest wish had been fulfilled. The waking world where he was dead became the dream, the nightmare. We never lived very dramatic moments, just the everyday things we used to take for granted. When I woke from those dreams, I'd have a few cruel moments of happiness, thinking Allan really was alive and my years of grief the dream. Then the truth would creep in again, and the emptiness would return.

I hadn't dreamed of Allan for a while, and I don't know what triggered this one. In my previous dreams, he'd looked as I remembered him, a beautiful 19-year-old with his whole life ahead of him. This time he looked closer to the age he would be had he lived— 37. I wanted to ask him what he was doing, if he had a family, but I don't remember either of us speaking. I don't think we could. We just looked at each other, smiling, and in the way of dreams we did that for a fraction of a second that was forever. At the end of forever, both our faces were wet with tears. We embraced. His arms were strong, lifting me up onto my toes. It lasted forever, and forever ended again. I fought to stay asleep, to stay with him, but I couldn't. My eyes opened to see the red numbers of my alarm clock. 2:14 AM. My pillow was damp and my face itched with tears.

It hurt to move, but I got up to splash water on my face anyway, only to discover that task was too complex for my feeble left hand. I settled for a damp washcloth instead. The coolness was reassuring, and I took the cloth with me to the living room to sit in front of the TV. Even manipulating the remote was painful enough to take the fun from channel-surfing infomercials. I flipped the television off and set the remote on the end table next to me. A bit of pale blue on the other side of my hula girl lamp caught my eye.

That damn letter. How many days had it been since I'd brought it home? I couldn't remember any more. It was still unopened. Why not? I was feeling masochistic. I reached for it and spent a good half minute fumbling to get it open with one sore hand.

Dear Sydney,

You know I'm not much of a writer, but you've never seen fit to grace me with your phone number. God, why do we bring out the worst in each other? I was angry before I even finished that first sentence, angry just at the thought of you, at the sight of your chosen

171

name. And I know your blood pressure will rise at the sight of my handwriting, if you still recognize it. Believe it or not, it wasn't my intention to batter you with dysfunction right out of the gate. For some reason, I'm a fully functioning adult in every other aspect of my life, but when it comes to you I'm still a bitchy teenager. I'm married now. Did you know that? His name is Britt. He's a wonderful man, and I'm sure I don't deserve him, but there you are. I'm happier with him than I have any right to be. We're coming up on our fourth anniversary.

Dad is still dad, but less so, if that makes sense. He's even less present than he used to be, more in his own world, or just totally out of it. I can't tell the difference. I'm worried about him. He's retired now, and he's out in the Lab at all hours, doing whatever it is he does, with no phone and no one to check on him. He doesn't eat right, when he bothers to eat at all. I think he sleeps out there. Sometimes I drop by and I'm not sure that he even knows who I am. Ten years without speaking, and I can still read your mind. "Not that he ever did." Know us, any of us. And you're right. He didn't. Poor misbegotten us. Whoops, slipping into dysfunction again.

I don't know what I'm doing. I don't know why I'm writing to you. Maybe I'm maturing, or at least aspiring to. I still feel like you betrayed us, but I'm starting to understand now that you thought we'd betrayed you. I'm not saying that I can ever forgive you, or that I expect you to forgive me, but I can't imagine mom or Allan would want it this way. It's been far too long already.

Call me. There are things we need to talk about. Current things, like dad, not the past, since we know we can't speak reasonably about what's gone before. Just call me, sis.

Lisa

My left hand strayed involuntarily to my forehead. I only became aware of its movement when my fingers felt the unexpected texture of a bandage. I couldn't remember why the bandage was there. Then I found myself looking at my trembling hand, wondering how something so pained and pathetic could have moved of its own accord.

I went to the kitchen and inspected the row of pill bottles on the counter. The ones I wanted were in my bedroom, where Noel had left them. She'd left the cap loosened for me. Unable to use both hands, I dumped a couple of pills on my nightstand, then picked them up and downed them with a sip of slightly stale-tasting water. I had no more dreams that night.

CHAPTER TWENTY-TWO

I spent the rest of the week convalescing, or as Ben said, being lazy. I slept a lot and watched videos. My brain didn't feel up to reading yet, but toward the end of the week Ben brought a computer video game over, and that occupied a little of my time. It was one of those slow-paced strategy games, something I could actually play left-handed without getting carpal tunnel syndrome. Ben came over after school, and by mid-week we'd finished off Mrs. Waters' brownies while picking apart the last of the day-time soaps. After that, I'd have my daily excursion to the mailbox. My feet still caused me a lot of pain when I walked, but it no longer felt like the pain was a harbinger of something horribly wrong. It was just pain.

Noel often arrived before we made it back to the house. She'd drop by after work, and we'd play rummy until Noel had completely slaughtered us. By the end of the week, I could use the fingers of my right hand to pluck individual cards from my left. Ben's fingers never got any more dexterous in his clumsy attempts to cheat.

We also ate dinner together every night. Noel cooked, with some assistance from Ben. How she coaxed a teenager addicted to pizza and junk food into the kitchen I'll never know, but they made a pretty good team. Their chatter and the steaming smells always lulled me into a doze.

Sounds idyllic, doesn't it? In a way it was, while they were there. If I picked at my food, I still ate enough to allay any concerns. If I slept a lot, seemed a little fuzzy or grumpy sometimes, needed sunglasses to get the mail, who could blame me? I was healing. And I was chafing at the inactivity. But most of all, I was taking a lot of pills. A lot for me, anyway. I don't shun western medicine when I need it, but my need threshold is probably a little higher than most. I was never a recreational drug user, even in college. It wasn't a matter of morality or legality. Again, I guess I just never felt the need. But I felt the need now.

Once Noel and Ben left in the evenings, my mind would wander where I wasn't ready to go—back to the clearing in the woods, back to the moments before or the years after my brother's death. So I'd go to bed. I'd have my nightly dose of narcotics and go to sleep. That worked for a day or two. Then I found that the silence of the day was too much for me to bear, and I started my morning dose.

For the first couple of hours, I'd watch the drugs take effect, like an intellectual exercise. There, there it is—the bit of vertigo in my brain, like I'm falling but only stepping a few feet off the edge of a deck before hitting the ground. It's controlled falling, trying to find the next step on the stairs in the dark, a step you know is there but your brain thinks disappeared forever when you turned the light off. Amazing. Feel my blood accelerate briefly through my body, then slow down. And the pain isn't as close. It's still there, but doesn't make me claustrophobic, doesn't feel as if it's sitting on that same next step down, waiting for my tentative foot to smother me again.

Then I'd sleep, or pretend to myself I was sleeping. It was such a fine line, after a while I didn't know if I was asleep or not, but it didn't matter. Not as long as I didn't have dreams. I found as the days wore on I couldn't play Ben's computer game. It was too frustrating, perversely getting more difficult rather than easier. And the sun in the living room was too bright for my eyes, so I started going back to bed. Or not leaving the bed. Most days I remembered to clean up, or at least move to the living room, before Ben showed up after school. The presence of him and later Noel began to be less of a comfort and more something intrusive that kept me from my sleepy haze. Part of me knew that was a problem, but I didn't care. The most I could do was try not to let my irritation show while Ben and Noel were there.

One evening I was jolted from what may have been a fake doze by a variation on the cocktail party syndrome. I'd call it the "I'm a Lying Bastard" syndrome. I wasn't awakened by the sound of my name, but instead by the knowledge that a lie I'd told was being passed along to someone else.

Ben was saying, "Sydney doesn't have any family."

"None at all?" from Noel.

"I don't think so," Ben responded. "She said she's an only child."

I'd been trying not to think about my family since dreaming of Allan and reading Lisa's letter, which of course mean on some level I'd been thinking of them the whole time. That's probably why the conversation caught my ear, not because of my impressive polygraphic abilities. And because Lisa's pale blue envelope, now lying on the floor beneath the end table, suddenly seemed fluorescent, pulsing like a paper telltale heart.

I didn't even remember telling Ben the lie, but I must have done. For years I'd told anyone bold enough to ask that I was an only child. I always rationalized the lie by telling myself that in a way it's true. The three of us may be related by blood, but we haven't been a family for a long time. When my brother Allan died 18 years ago, he pretty much took the idea of family with him. Now for the first time, my "partial truth" felt wrong. I was unable to call it anything but a lie.

177

My sister Lisa and I haven't spoken since our mother's funeral. In her letter, Lisa said it had been 10 years, but it's more like eleven. We hadn't spoken for years before that either. Lisa and I never got along very well. I always thought she was a bitch, and she always knew I was right. I'm not in contact with our father either, so when I got Lisa's letter I thought he might have died. You'd think she would have called for something like that, let me know about the funeral, but with Lisa you never knew. Of course, as she said, apparently I hadn't given her my phone number. And I hadn't opened the letter for days, knowing it could contain the news of father's death. Guess the bitchiness gene is common to the entire female line.

I wanted to say something, to stop Noel and Ben and explain all this and more, but there was so much to tell, and I was so tired. It took too much effort to care. I couldn't face it, couldn't face them, and feigned sleep. Again, rationalization, excuses, for taking the coward's way out and not telling them when I had the chance. If I had, I could have saved us all a lot of grief. Maybe. Maybe not.

That night I took the last of the vicodin—only one, and my sleep was fitful. I got out of bed the next morning, feeling raw, and thought a little food might take the edge off. When I tried to heat a mug of water in the microwave for some instant oatmeal, I found myself staring at the microwave uncomprehendingly. I pushed every variation of the buttons I could think of, with no response. Then I realized the damn thing was unplugged. It must have gone unused all week. Had I eaten at all when Ben and Noel weren't here?

The microwave stand was too heavy and awkward for me to move to get to the outlet, so I struggled with a kettle of water on the stove instead. The whistle of hot water pierced me between the eyes and probably contributed to my lack of control as I sloshed water into my bowl and made apple cinnamon soup. I forced myself to eat it anyway and felt I was on the road to recovery until I dropped the bowl while trying to rinse it and splashed myself with oatmeal water.

"Fuck!" I screamed, recovering my grip on the bowl and bringing it down hard on the counter. Nothing but pain shooting up through my arm. I threw the bowl on the floor. The painful action of my arm was met with a satisfying breaking of ceramic, and I screamed again, a wordless shriek until my breath ran out and my throat felt bloody. I left the shards on the floor and went back to bed.

My sleep was deep and undisturbed, and when I woke up I was feeling more like my self. I seemed to have finally slept myself out of my lethargy and into restlessness. Monday was my follow-up appointment where I hoped for a reprieve from my local doctor, but I couldn't drive before then. Mike and Richard had made doubly sure of that by taking my car keys. They had called a couple of times to check in, and when they said they were coming to Tallahassee Friday evening—this evening—it was one of the few things that had managed to penetrate my haze. Now I was looking forward to their visit, for the car keys and the company. I'd been hiding long enough, and to butcher my metaphors it was time to get back on the horse before I became equine-phobic. It was time to focus on Isaac again, and it was time to tell Noel what I'd learned about her family.

Mike and Richard were meeting me for coffee when they got in town Friday evening. The coffee house I'd chosen is sort of hippie/suburban bucolic, hippie because a lot of the alternative types hang out there, and suburban bucolic because it adjoins a park frequented by yuppie families feeding the ducks. I was looking forward to getting out of the house, to caffeine in familiar friendly surroundings. Noel was taking me there after she got off work. That gave me some time alone with her, time to get her up to speed before the guys arrived for a strategy session. In hindsight, my cabin fever and temporary drug-free euphoria made me look forward to the outing with unjustified naïve optimism.

This was my first sojourn into public since the accident (attack, Syd, it was an attack) and I was going bandageless and hatless. A scarf over my hair and big sunglasses hid some of the fading minor bruises, but most were still easily visible to the most casual observer. I didn't care. The more furtive you are about anything, injuries or your relationships or your finances, the more interested people become. If you're hiding something, it must be because you've something to hide. I put on lipstick but no other make-up, and my short-sleeved blouse and knee-length skirt exposed more healing bruises and scratches. Nosy parkers be damned.

Ready half an hour before Noel was supposed to arrive, I decided to unpack my motel bag before I tripped over it. It was on my bedroom floor, and only my tentative, aching baby steps had saved me tripping so far. I put the clothes away first, then moved on to toiletries and the manila envelope from Mrs. Waters. In it was a printed itemized bill, but I was surprised to also find a short handwritten note paper-clipped to a sealed envelope.

According to Mrs. Waters' note, she'd found the envelope under a chair by the door when tidying my room. "*S. Brennan*" was scrawled on the outside of the envelope in an uncertain hand. It appeared those fingers had trembled as much in addressing the envelope as my own were in trying to open it. I took it to the kitchen, sidestepping the remains of my ceramic bowl, and slit the top open carefully with a knife. Then I got a pair of latex gloves from under the sink, nearly toppling over, before realizing I didn't need a whole pair. My right hand still wasn't that consistently functional (as my attempts at sliding a glove over my left hand demonstrated) and good luck getting a size "small" glove over the awkward splint.

I settled in a bum-numbing kitchen chair and took a deep breath, letting the residual spots and blotches fade from my eyes before sliding the single sheet of paper from the envelope. It was plain paper, the kind you'd find in any printer or copier, folded three times. The words were printed clumsily, as if the writer knew he or she should disguise her handwriting but wasn't quite sure how to go about it. The message itself was unexpected.

Please go home—its not safe here and your not helping anyone.

Chapter Twenty-Three

The misspellings could be deliberate, like the clumsy handwriting. I didn't think so, though I couldn't say why. The letters were big —masculine? Feminine? I could guess, but it would be only that. The sound of Noel's car in the driveway interrupted my thoughts. Rising from my chair more quickly than I thought I was able, I tucked the letter away in a book in the living room, then threw the glove in the trash. I was still trying to wash the powdery rubbery smell from my hand when Noel walked in.

"What happened here?" she asked, as the kitchen door shut behind her.

I felt trapped. My heart pounded and my vision went dark from the top down. I leaned forward slightly until I could feel the reassuring solidity of the sink in front of me. When I spoke I could make out Noel's figure again.

"What do you mean?"

"This." She pointed at the mess on the floor.

"Oh, that!" I realized too late how relieved my voice sounded. "I dropped a bowl."

Noel looked at me askance, perhaps wondering why I'd left it long enough for the remnants of oatmeal to dry on the fragments. "Are you ready?" she asked.

"Yeah, I just need to get my bag."

"I'll clean this up while you do." I thanked her and went to get my things.

Noel was just finishing up when I returned to the kitchen. I watched her. I could feel my anxiety festering, but I couldn't bring myself to speak. I don't know why I didn't tell her about the letter. We drove to the coffee house in silence.

There was a nice breeze that evening, and the raised wooden deck was shaded by a live oak, so we sat outside with our heavily iced drinks. The university students and legislators were gone for the season. We had our pick of tables and chose the far corner. The few people braving the heat were quiet, reading, typing on laptops, or talking in hushed tones. Although public, it seemed very private.

Noel was dressed Friday bank casual in a fitted navy blue top and unwrinkled khaki capris. She sat straight in her seat, but she closed her eyes and tilted her head back to catch the breeze. "When do you expect Mike and Richard?" she asked.

"Probably about an hour, maybe more, maybe less."

She lifted her head and sat even straighter, waiting.

"I wanted some time to talk to you first, to let you know what I found out before I got... distracted by the hooligans." I tried to smile when I said the word, but I wasn't entirely successful.

"I wondered, but I didn't want to ask." She looked down at her napkin coaster, straightening the edges. "Not until you were ready."

I started with the easier stuff. "I spoke to your father's sister, Ida Pickett. Twice. I was actually leaving her house when, uh, when it happened. I like her. She's a kind woman, someone I think you'll want to meet." Noel didn't speak.

"She said your father contacted her about six months before he died."

"Did she say why?"

"She didn't know, and he didn't tell her. Ida's husband was dying of cancer at the time. Maybe he didn't want to burden her any more. I think it's important though. She hadn't heard from him since before your mother's death. In fact, the last time she saw him was at their own mother's funeral. She said she met you there. You must have been about five years old, and your father took you there for a few days. Do you remember that?"

Noel shook her head without speaking. I went on to tell her an abbreviated version of her parents' self-imposed exile from their families, glossing over the darker bits. She was going to need some time to assimilate everything.

"Is Miss Johnson still alive?" she asked.

"Yes. She still lives in Hainey." I smiled at the recollection. "I do believe Claire Johnson had a thing for your dad, and no wonder. Ida showed me pictures. He was quite a handsome man."

"A handsome man and a wife beater."

I stifled my initial impulse to defend a man I'd never known. How could I? He'd killed his wife, beaten and strangled her. Still, Noel had asked for the truth.

"Maybe. I don't know. There were no previous complaints against him, and you said yourself you didn't remember it happening."

Someone knocked over a plastic chair a couple of tables away. We both turned to look, and if I flinched away from the sound Noel didn't seem to notice.

"I wouldn't, would I? I don't want to. But it happened. Grandmother told me about it. One time he beat my mother so badly the family had to go get her, to take her away from him."

Noel leaned forward and lowered her voice. "She lived with them for weeks until she'd healed, and they begged her not to go back to him. She wouldn't listen, and he killed her."

Suddenly the conversations around us seemed louder, closer. My head kept turning involuntarily, listening, looking over my shoulder. I struggled to maintain my focus on this person who'd

185

been so kind to me, this person whose heart I was about to rip out. "Noel, don't take this the wrong way, but your grandmother is probably not the most unbiased observer of your parents' lives."

"Are you saying she's a liar?"

"No. I'm just saying people often remember things the way they wish they were, the way they think it should have been. Or the way that's least painful."

"Do you?"

I didn't answer her question. Below us a Black Lab mix harassed the ducks, and his barks reverberated in my ears. "I heard another version of that incident. In it, your father did get very angry. He did lose his temper, and he did throw your mother out. But he never struck her."

"According to whom?"

I hesitated. "Miss Johnson. She heard the shouting, and she was worried about you. She witnessed the whole thing. She said she'd never seen your father so angry, and he dragged your mother out of the house, but he didn't strike her."

Noel settled her arms across her chest, and her mouth tightened. "Why?"

I waited for her to elaborate.

"Why did he kick her out?"

"Miss Johnson didn't get there until the fight was already under way, and your father didn't say. She heard him call your grandparents, but he didn't tell them either."

"You're lying."

Strictly speaking I was telling the truth. I never lie to a friend or a client unless I absolutely have to, so I decided it was a good time to keep my mouth shut. Noel wasn't ready yet, or maybe I just wasn't ready to tell her.

"You know, Sydney, I have a picture of my father, and he was

186

handsome, but I've seen many pictures of my mother. He wasn't half as handsome as she was beautiful. He thought she having an affair, didn't he? And that's why he killed her."

"It's possible."

"There's more though, isn't there?" Once again, I held my tongue. Her voice grew husky and blood sprang to her face.

"Who the hell do you think you are? You work for me. You are my employee. Do you understand that? I'm paying you to get information for me. How dare you dole it out in bits as you please, like treats to a dog?"

I closed my eyes against flashes of… something. Bits of something that kept pushing into my brain and made my ears roar. It felt like my airway was the size of a straw. My own voice was a husky whisper as I leaned forward.

"Me? What about you? You tell me you can't remember anything because you were six years old when your mother died, but you were eight. You tell me your father died four or five years ago, and it's only been 18 months. Then you tell me this ridiculous story about a stranger in a grocery store breaking the news to you. Come on, Ben could do better than that, and he's in high school. If you want results, you have to be straight with me."

"Results? Sydney, I admit you've had a good excuse for sitting on your ass for the past week, but what about before that? From what I'm hearing, you haven't done a whole hell of a lot."

I tried to calm myself before I spoke, but it was getting more and more difficult. "Noel, your mother had a substance problem."

She seemed to be holding her breath. When she spoke, it was nothing I expected. "Well, you should know."

"What's that supposed to mean?"

"Oh, come on!"

Our voices had gotten loud with emotion, but now Noel fought to control her voice, and it came out a whisper again.

"Do you think I'm blind? You think I can't see how out of it you've been all week, haven't noticed the empty pill bottles? That shit's not candy, Sydney."

I had to fight for control myself, fight not to be defensive because I knew she was right. "I know that, Noel, and I'm done."

"What—until you get a refill? How dare you judge my mother?"

She paused to get her breath again, gripping her glass hard enough that I thought it would shatter. When she looked up at me, her eyes were so angry that my own heart began to pump faster, and I could feel my anger rising to meet Noel's.

"I didn't judge your mother. I'm not judging your mother. You wanted to know what I found out, and I'm telling you."

"Because you're taking prescription drugs, because you're—"

White, that was what she wanted to say. I could see it in her eyes. She could see it in mine as well and pulled back. Somehow I knew that Noel would slit her own wrists before saying anything that could be interpreted as "playing the race card."

"Because you're middle class, you think it's somehow different. But it's not different. A drug addict is a drug addict."

"I am *not* a drug addict. I had one week—*one week*—of hiding from my bad dreams after someone beat the hell out of me and tried to rape me. That doesn't make me an addict."

She flinched slightly when I said the word "rape," but her anger had taken her too far to turn back now.

"And how do you know my mother wasn't hiding from the same? So she turned to drugs after my father beat the hell out of her. That's what happened, isn't it?"

I didn't respond quickly enough. "Answer me, Sydney!"

I don't respond well to shouting, and I don't respond well to ultimatums. In the end I told Noel what I did about her mother the way I did not because, as she said, she had the right to be answered, although she did. I told her for a lot of complex psychological reasons that I don't quite understand, and because my blood was pounding and my nerves were jagged edges and I felt like someone was standing behind me with an axe. But I think in its simplest form it came down this: she'd pissed me off, and she'd hurt me. I wanted to hurt her back.

"You want to know what happened? Fine. Your mother didn't turn to drugs because your father beat her. She was already using. According to Mrs. Johnson, your parents fought because she was having sex with other men for money. To feed her drug habit. Your mother was a—"

I stopped, my brain belatedly catching up with my mouth.

Noel's dark skin grew ashen and her lips paled. She stood up and left, without uttering a single word.

CHAPTER TWENTY-FOUR

Mike and Richard arrived a few minutes later. I was still sitting in the same spot, staring at the melted ice water that had pooled on top of my coffee.

"What's wrong? Where's Noel?" Richard asked.

"She left. Do you mind if we get the coffee to go and head back to my house? I'm a little tired."

Of course they agreed. When neither of them offered to help me to the car, I surmised that no one could see my shaking but me.

On the way home, Richard told what should have been a funny story about Mike trying to serve a subpoena for him earlier in the week at some down at heel strip club. I tried to laugh in all the right places, or any place at all, but I couldn't. My mind was preoccupied with thoughts of Isaac and Vanda and Noel, and also (but less so) with men hiding behind masks. By the time we turned on my street, I knew what I had to do, and I knew I was going to need help.

"I'm not sure why the two of you are here," I said, once we'd settled in with our drinks. Mike and Richard both opened their mouths, but I went on.

"Just let me finish. You've both been good friends to me, and I appreciate your support. What's less clear is your position, your involvement, in my case."

This time they didn't try to interrupt, so I went on. "At the risk of sounding like a Charles Bronson movie, this investigation has become personal for me. There are two reasons for this, one you

191

know and one you don't. First of all, somebody—or rather five or six somebodies—tried to scare the shit out of me a week ago, and did a damn fine job of it. Obviously it had something to do with my investigation, but I don't have a clue what. They went to a lot of trouble to make sure my nightmares would keep me out of Stetler County for a long time. I don't appreciate that."

"Second is the one you don't know. Or at least I don't think you do. Isaac Thomas's daughter, my client, is Noel."

Mike seemed to take this revelation in stride, but when Isaac's case was tried he was probably still playing kickball, blissfully unaware that such things happened in the world and that he would soon be a part of them. Richard, on the other hand, having lived through it, was clearly shaken. He ran his hands over his face a few times, up and down from forehead to chin and back.

I considered stopping and making my pitch, but I couldn't yet. If I was going to get anywhere, I needed to secure their help. Mike and Richard were friends, and I wouldn't lie to them, but I wasn't above resorting to some guilty manipulation in service of the greater good.

"Noel and I had a bit of an argument this afternoon. That's why she left. She doesn't know what to think any more. With her mother dead and her father in prison for killing her, Noel was raised by her mother's side of the family. Noel didn't even know she had anyone left on her father's side. In fact, that's one of the lies her grandmother told her, that her father was an only child. She's in a position where her grandmother is telling her one thing and I'm telling her something else. Yes, she knows they've lied to her, but they're family, and I'm telling her things she doesn't want to hear."

"Like what?"

"Like her mother had sex for money to feed her drug habit."

192

Mike blew out his breath. "So what do you want us to do?"

"I'm going to fix this, for Noel and for me. She can't go through her life not knowing the truth, and I can't go through my life detouring around Stetler County every time I head west. I've decided to start over, from the beginning. I'm going to treat Isaac's crime and his suicide as if they just happened and I'm investigating them from scratch. That's the only way I'm going to find whatever it was I missed the first time around. It's not going to be easy, and not just because the cases are so cold. As recent events have demonstrated, I'll need to watch over my shoulder the whole time."

I paused for a sip of my drink. Caffeine courage. "And I could use some help."

Richard looked at Mike, and he nodded. "We're in."

I smiled and nodded my own head. I had expected their cooperation, but my eyes filled with tears anyway. "Good. Let's get started."

We had my living room looking like it had been hit by a paper cyclone in no time. I told them everything I'd learned so far, and together we went through the trial attorney file (Richard's file) and prison records. I didn't have a copier at home, so we used my scanner to copy individual pages important enough to require that much time and effort. My living room floor was sown with discrete piles of pages, waiting to be stepped on. My big dry erase board hung from a couple of nails on the wall, listing slightly. A vertical line divided it more or less in half, with the left side showing a timeline and the right a to-do list.

Looking around the room at the chaos, my eyes came to rest on the bookshelf. It was then that I remembered the note. I retrieved the box of gloves from the kitchen before removing the note from the book. "Mrs. Waters found this when she cleaned my room."

Richard spoke after he'd read it. "I'll pass this on to law enforcement so they can run forensics on it. But don't get your hopes up."

"I'm not. I'm more interested in your impressions. Who do you think wrote it?"

This time Mike spoke. "I think we can assume it was left before you were attacked—little late to worry about your safety after the attack. Could be one of your attackers didn't really have the stomach for it."

"Could be," I agreed. "That's the most logical explanation, with what little information we have so far. And yet, I don't think that's who it was."

"Who then?"

"I don't know."

No one volunteered anything else. I was grateful that neither man played the "what if" card. What if I'd found the letter, as the writer probably intended, before I was attacked? Questions echoed in my head enough without hearing them from their mouths as well.

We hadn't eaten yet, and when we realized how late it was, Mike volunteered to whip up an omelet and threw some steak fries in the oven.

"My salsa's moldy," I warned Mike as he began pulling ingredients from the refrigerator.

"Yeah, I noticed, but Richard and Noel bought some."

"So's my cheese."

"You can cut the mold off cheese."

I cringed. Creating a hospitable environment for mold was one of my fortes. Eating it was not. I needn't have worried. Even Mike blanched when he pulled the block of blue (formerly cheddar) cheese out of the fridge and threw it in the trash.

Cheese or not, within a few minutes we were eating a savory

concoction that I could not believe had been produced in my kitchen. I didn't ask Mike how he had managed it. I preferred to believe it was magic, perhaps because that gave me an excuse for not being able to produce such things myself. After all, I wasn't a magician.

As we ate, we devised our game plan. Mike and Richard would stay the night with me. In terms of my reputation with my elderly neighbors, I couldn't decide whether having two men sleep over was an improvement over just one. It either showed that it was clearly a platonic arrangement of convenience, or that we'd moved beyond simple adultery into the realms of serious naughtiness. I was also concerned about Richard's wife, but apparently she felt comfortable that it was the former.

"But I do have to be home by lunch tomorrow," Richard said, dumping more ketchup on his plate and generously dipping his fries. He was working hard to reach his 4-6 servings of vegetables.

"Some kind of family get-together," he continued. "My wife is a wonderful, understanding woman, but if she has to face the groping brother-in-law alone, I'll be wishing I was only in the dog house."

"That's cool. I'm supposed to go out on the Gulf with a buddy." Mike rubbed his face and I could hear the late-day scratchiness. "Got to work on keeping my base tan."

"Lucky you. Well, my doctor'll give me the all-clear on driving Monday morning, so I should be heading in your direction by that afternoon," I said, ever the optimist.

"Need a ride?" they asked simultaneously.

I grinned at the harmony, but they didn't see the humor. "No, thanks. I already have a ride."

Which was true, in an aspirational sort of way. I was hoping to get a ride from Ralph, which would give me a chance to pick his brain again. If he couldn't take me, I'd just drive myself, now that I had my keys again. Of course, that little contingency plan went unmentioned. I'd rather drive to the Panhandle on Monday by myself anyway. My brain needed the space, the room to wander that I only find while driving or showering. That's when I have some of my best insights, and I could use some insight.

I hadn't told Mike and Richard, but I had a third reason for continuing my investigation. It was something so crazy I wasn't about to tell anyone else until I had some hard proof. I didn't know where the idea had come from, what had triggered it, but I needed to think it through, figure out if it was just unsubstantiated fancy. That's what someone else would call it. I'd call it gut instinct, and my gut had a pretty good track record. It was only a whisper, but right now my gut was telling me it thought Isaac Thomas hadn't killed his wife. It was telling me he was innocent.

CHAPTER TWENTY-FIVE

I gave Ralph a call after the guys left on Saturday. His wife Diane said he'd gone away for the weekend, fishing with some old buddies (what was it with these guys and fishing?). She didn't expect him back before Monday afternoon. My appointment was Monday morning. So much for Plan A.

The phone rang around 9:00 Sunday night. I expected it to be Mike or Richard. It was Noel.

"How are you feeling?" she asked.

"A little tired, but I'm doing okay. You?"

"About the same. I—" Seconds ticked by as I waited for her to finish. She changed direction. "You have a ride to the doctor tomorrow?"

"No."

"Let me guess. You're driving yourself."

"Probably."

"I'll take you. See you around 8:30?"

"Yeah, that sounds good. Thanks."

"Sure. See you then."

"Noel?" I was afraid she'd hung up already.

"Yes."

"Are you really okay?"

"No, but I'm getting there."

Comforted by the thought of progress with Noel, I wandered around my house getting things together for my return to the

197

Panhandle. I came across a plastic bag in a corner of my living room that must have been overlooked all week, a consequence of my relaxed approach to housekeeping. The back of my neck went hot and my stomach lurched dangerously when I looked in the bag.

Inside was a bottle of water, a root beer, and a paperback. Pretty innocuous items. Innocuous items I'd bought at the convenience store that night, before things got crazy. Before I was attacked. I still couldn't bring myself to say that out loud. Working as an investigator for going on 10 years, I'd been threatened regularly, pushed around occasionally, and I'd even had a gun pointed at me once or twice. But it wasn't really malicious, and it was rarely personal.

I was a stranger who got in someone's face one too many times asking uncomfortable questions. I was an annoying force that provoked a reaction, a flesh embodiment of the system that had ground them and theirs up indiscriminately for generations, no matter which side I technically worked for. But I was never a target because of who I was, and I was never a victim. Until now. It was an uncomfortable thought, one I preferred to ignore.

The water and root beer went in the trash, unopened, but the cover of the paperback caught my eye. A bodacious brunette, with long flowing hair that provided more coverage than her torn blouse, was mounted in front of an impossibly muscled man with similar hair. Their manes contrasted with that of the perfectly white horse. I almost laughed, but I could understand the appeal. I didn't care for the pretty boy on the horse, but maybe Oded Fehr or Viggo Mortenson.

This time I did laugh. Even in my current state, I couldn't imagine wanting anyone real, anyone I knew, to protect me that way. The appeal was still pure fantasy. It didn't even rise to the level of reality of winning the lottery. I wanted to win the lottery, but I didn't want to be safe if it meant I had to be protected. Maybe I hadn't quite been broken yet. I started to throw the paperback in the trash, then packed it away with a smile. I knew someone who might enjoy it.

I'd spent Saturday and Sunday going through Isaac's boxes, and when I crawled into bed around 10 PM, I was ready to be there. It was that wonderful rare feeling, just short of exhaustion, of being satisfied with what you've done, not feeling like you needed to do any more to "deserve" rest. It was unusual for me to get such contentment from intellectual rather than physical work, but while I was reading my body was healing, so I guess I'd covered both fronts.

I set my pillow vertically against my headboard, feeling the usual lurching inch of poor workmanship or a loose screw when I leaned against it. The air conditioning was working hard enough to justify a thin blanket in addition to my usual sheet, and as I slowly raised my knees I pulled the blanket up with them. It was an awkward job with my splint, but I didn't mind. I gently tucked my arms around my knees and leaned into them. I couldn't hold the position for long, but it felt good, like a bookend to my day. Settling down in the covers and turning out my little lamp, I fell almost immediately to sleep.

I dreamed of broken unicorns, fragile figures that had fallen from Vanda's dresser and cracked on the floor, to be captured in crime scene photographs.

Noel was on time the next morning, as I knew she would be. We didn't say much on the drive to the doctor. We needed to talk, but we needed to have the kind of conversation that you couldn't have in a few minutes while driving. I considered risking it in the doctor's office, having never made it to the inner sanctum in under 40 minutes before, but I barely had time to get settled in my chair before I was called back.

Dr. Brandon Malcolm, my doctor with two first names, is the the best kind of doctor. By that I mean he doesn't go into technical medical details you don't need, he doesn't make you feel guilty for bad habits or not following ridiculous instructions to the letter, and, most importantly, he doesn't give you ridiculous instructions in the first place. He asked what had happened, but his slightly lisping voice was laced with curiosity rather than disapproval. I made a flippant reply about seeing the other guy, and he laughed and was satisfied. As I'd expected, he released me from all restrictions, including the driving edict.

Noel looked genuinely pleased to hear that my doctor agreed with my prognosis that everything was cool. (My words.) I was about to suggest that we stop on the way back to my house for coffee, but she beat me to it. I took this as a positive sign. As we sipped and I played with scone crumbs, we fumbled through half-apologies before tacitly agreeing that we were okay and not to speak of it anymore. I could tell there was still something on her mind, and we had nearly finished our coffee when she blurted it out.

"You were right about the story. About how I learned of my father's death."

She eyed my fidgeting fingers. Her own plate, and shirt front, were immaculate.

"Was I really that transparent?"

"Well, maybe you just get to be particularly suspicious in my line of work."

Her mouth twitched. "And diplomatic. I think Ben would say it was a pretty lame story."

Noel handed me an envelope. "I received this about a month before I contacted you. It took me a while to decide what to do about it."

I opened the envelope and removed a clipping. It was the same article I'd found about Isaac's death on the internet, but it had been cut from the original newspaper. The paper was slightly worn and there was a pinhole near the top, as if from a thumbtack.

"If you'll notice, the article was from the middle of the page so the date isn't on there. I asked my grandmother about it, and she said it had been four or five years since he'd died. That's why I was so surprised when you told me how recently it had happened. I really didn't know, Sydney."

"I believe you."

I pulled another piece of paper from the envelope. It was unlined, a small scrap of paper about the size the article had been, perhaps cut with the same scissors from a piece of copier or printer paper. Written in pen in a wide slanting script were the words, "*Don't you want to know why your father died?*" I wasn't sure if the handwriting matched my own note. I hadn't thought to keep a copy when I gave the original to Richard.

"I don't know who sent it," Noel said.

"It looks like a woman's handwriting."

"Yes, I thought so too."

I examined both papers for a while longer, but there was nothing else to be learned from them, not by me at any rate. I'm sure some modern-day Sherlock Holmes could have taken it to his lab and cracked the case, but I didn't have that kind of money or scientific aptitude. Noel told me to keep the papers anyway. I'd give them to Richard.

"Noel, why didn't you just tell me?"

"I don't know. I really don't. It just seemed so surreal. An anonymous note, a newspaper clipping about a dead father I didn't know."

She began to press on her eyebrow with an index finger, tracing a few millimeters along the inner edge before applying pressure again, then releasing her finger and repeating the process.

"Sydney, I never asked for this. I never asked to be born into an episode of Dateline. I don't want people to pity me and my family or try to analyze us, as if we're indicative of the breakdown of society. We're not a symbol; we're people. And it's no one else's business. I'm not even sure it's mine."

I had no response, and, having unburdened herself, Noel was done lingering. She still had to go to work. When we reached my house, she walked me in and was immediately transfixed by the state of my former living room, now the Thomas War Room. I left her examining the whiteboard while I went to the bathroom. I'd gained mobility in the past week, but it still took me longer than usual to perform the appropriate function. I thought I heard the phone ring, but wasn't concerned about answering it. If embarrassment at my near-elderly bathroom tardiness wasn't enough to make me hurry, then the opportunity to speak to a telemarketer certainly wasn't. Unfortunately it wasn't a telemarketer.

I could tell when I returned to the living room that Noel was pissed, but I couldn't imagine what I could have done while in the bathroom to piss her off. It didn't take long for her to tell me, albeit somewhat indirectly.

"Your sister called. She said not to worry, that nobody's dead."

"Lisa?"

How she had gotten my number? Come to think of it, I was probably listed in the Tallahassee phone book. Easy enough to access from the internet. For someone who wants to bother, which I wouldn't have thought included Lisa.

"Unless you have more than one sister you don't have."

I looked at her blankly, trying to make sense of the syntax of the sentence and Noel's intent.

"Ben idolizes you. He loves you, and he trusts you more than he does his own family. How could you lie to him?"

It was then that I remembered the bit of conversation I'd overheard the night before. "I didn't exactly—"

"Don't even think about finishing that sentence. There's no getting around the fact that you denied the existence of people related to you by blood. Little Orphan Sydney. You did lie to him."

"Noel, it's not a big deal."

"Like it wasn't a big deal for my grandmother to tell me my father was an only child, that I had no other family?"

"It's not remotely the same thing."

"Oh sure, there's a difference in degree, but it is exactly the same thing. A lie is a lie. You of all people should know that."

"What's that supposed to mean?"

"You're so goddamned self righteous about it. That's what kills me. You and your 'justice in fact, not just in theory.' And all the time you're just a hypocrite, like everybody else." She grabbed her purse and opened the door to leave.

"I put your sister's number on the counter."

The door was already shut, and I considered shouting after Noel, but I settled for muttering about my family under my breath while I willed the dizziness away.

"I didn't lie to them; they lied to me."

To help calm myself, I focused on Noel's actual words, peeling the emotion away from them. "Justice in fact, not in theory." The phrase was from one of my newspaper quotes a few months ago. So that's why Noel had chosen to hire me, not just, as I'd assumed, because Brennan is near the beginning of the alphabet. I was still standing in the same spot, staring at the door Noel hadn't slammed, wondering at the sudden injection of melodrama in my life, when

Ben walked through it.

"Why aren't you in school?" I asked.

"We finished last week, remember? What's wrong with Noel?"

"I don't know," I said. Was that a lie? Was I lying to him again?

"Ben, sit down."

He looked at me apprehensively and slid one of the chairs from beneath the kitchen table. "What's up?"

I sat directly across from him and fought not to look away from his eyes.

"You know how I told you I was an only child, and that I didn't have any family. Well, that wasn't exactly true. In fact, it wasn't true at all."

He didn't look particularly stunned, so I took a deep breath and went on. "I had a brother who died when I was about your age, and I have a sister. We had a falling out when my brother died, or I guess you could say I had a falling out with everyone else."

"What happened?"

"They lied to me."

My words came out more forcefully than I had meant them to, as if I had resumed my argument with Noel, and I took a deep breath before going on.

"I took off and didn't see much of my family for a while. Then my mom died about 10 years ago, and I haven't spoken to my dad or my sister since then. Not that we were ever very close."

"How'd he die? Your brother, I mean."

"Car accident, late one night. He was—" He was what? Young? Handsome? Betrayed? "Well, you know how it goes."

"Yeah." Ben started picking at a callus on his hand. "Sorry about your brother. How old was he?"

"Nineteen."

"Man, that really sucks. The rest of it doesn't surprise me

though."

"Really?"

"Nah. I could see you doing that, just walking away. You know, there are times when I've wanted to do that myself, just walk away and be done with it."

He was still looking down at his hand, admiring his handiwork, but for the first time I could see the pain in his face that I'd ignored so easily. For the first time, I wondered why he'd eaten dinner with me every night this week, why he stopped by every evening even when I wasn't laid up. He seemed to feel my stare and looked up, but the vulnerability was gone. He was a teenager again, with things to do, energy only just held in check.

"I gotta go. I'm riding with Kelly over to the car place."

"Kelly, huh? Guy Kelly or Girl Kelly?"

He grinned. "Girl Kelly. You don't think I'd ride across town and sit in the car shop for Guy Kelly's ugly face, do you?"

I was glad to see his good cheer return, but at the risk of squelching it I still had to ask him one more question. "Ben, you're not mad at me, are you?"

He looked surprised. "Why, 'cause you lied about your family? No, of course not. It's obviously something you don't like to talk about, and it's not important. I mean, I guess it's important to you, but it's not important to me. And I know you'd never lie to me about anything important."

Ben paused at the door. "Don't go getting all morbid and old fogey on me."

I laughed, with more relief than humor.

"I won't. I promise."

CHAPTER TWENTY-SIX

The drive west was uneventful, both physically and intellectually, meaning I had none of my hoped for great revelations or insights. I drove my own Cecil rather than taking a rental. Perhaps I needed the comfort of the familiar, including the same motel I'd stayed in before. Mrs. Waters was glad to see that I was well and that I'd returned to her humble business despite my bad experience with those hooligans. Being a big believer in the restorative powers of chocolate, I assured her that I owed my recovery entirely to her luscious brownies.

Mike and Richard picked me up for a working dinner after I got settled. We ate at a Mexican place where everything was drenched with cheese and the iced tea tasted slightly of sulfur. It was no Rosalia's by any means, but when I switched my beverage to a Corona, the taste of the food improved dramatically. Maybe it was the interaction with my antibiotics—good thing I didn't read those labels after all. We sat in a corner under a precariously hung rotting sombrero, making plans. After reassuring myself that the sombrero would disintegrate rather than cause injury if it landed on our heads, I was better able to concentrate.

Richard told us he had a good friend who was an Assistant State Attorney, someone he had gone to law school with that, according to Richard, had not yet been corrupted by the politics or the power of the position.

"Jim Gilbert is fair and impartial, the kind of guy who actually thinks he's going to the office to see justice done.'"

"Poor misguided soul," Mike said.

Richard pretended not to hear, but I gave Mike a conspiratorial grin. For some reason, Richard seemed to be stuck with the role of parent tonight. Poor misguided soul. I tried not to giggle.

"More importantly, Jim owes me. Big."

"How big?" I asked. "This is likely to burn up a lot of good guy capital. The kind where he doesn't take your calls anymore when we're done."

"As big as it gets. Let's just say I rendered a favor to Jim, the magnitude of which probably cannot be paid off in this lifetime."

Mike and I looked at Richard with interest, and respect, but no more details were forthcoming.

"I've spoken to Jim and explained the situation. Sydney, you're scheduled to meet with him in the morning, and he'll let you review the State Attorney's file from Isaac's case while you're there."

"Sounds good."

"Yeah. He's a nice guy. Don't abuse him." Richard's sudden stern gaze made me feel even more like a naughty child.

"I also talked to Rudy Nagroski. He was the original investigator in charge," Richard explained for Mike's benefit. "He's available all afternoon to speak with us. Mike, if you don't mind sitting this one out, I thought Syd and I would handle it. Rudy's pretty laid back, but three people might feel too much like an ambush."

"Makes sense, and I've already made plans of my own with the lovely Serena. She works records at the police department. Most people call her 'The Gatekeeper,' but she's always been pretty accommodating with me," Mike explained.

"I'll bet she has," I said.

Ben would have had a smartass reply. Mike pretended he either didn't hear me or didn't care, but his flushed face betrayed him.

"The trick is to bring candy as a peace offering, preferably those miniature Dove bars. I've gotta take care of some stuff at the office in the morning, but I thought I'd camp out in her office for the afternoon, see if I can find anything on Vanda or Isaac."

"Look for the incident in the bar. Miss Johnson said it was a place called Jimmy's."

"Will do."

A few minutes later they were dropping me off at my motel. The only other car in the lot was a silver mini-van piled with a contradictory mix of blankets and beach umbrellas. My eyes automatically examined the license as we slowly drifted by. New Mexico. I always like New Mexico license plates, the bright yellow Land of Enchantment. My room was four doors down from the van, and Richard parked directly in front of it. It wasn't dark outside yet, but the edges of the sky were just turning to citrus. I drank the air as I slid slowly from the car, and for a moment I was surprised by the weight of it. Nope, definitely not in New Mexico any more.

"Are you sure you want to stay here? Again?"

Richard had obviously mistaken my Corona languor for uncertainty. My initial reaction was to play dumb, or offended. But why? Why play anything?

"I have a different room."

"Yes, but—"

"I wasn't attacked at the motel."

"Still, the association—"

"By that logic I'd never be able to eat at Lorna's again." I couldn't resist a smile. "Then the terrorists really will have won."

Richard's left lip curled. It reminded me of Noel. "All right, I give up."

He called good night as he folded himself into his car, but he didn't leave until I was secure in my room, or at least inside with the door locked. In fact, I must have felt secure, ignoring the siren song of motel cable and going straight to bed. It was early (especially by Central time) but I slept immediately and soundly.

I was up bright and early for my appointment with Gilbert. Because the State Attorney's Office was in the same building with the Public Defender, I had no difficulty finding it and was actually a few minutes early. I didn't have to wait long before Gilbert met me in the lobby. He insisted that I call him Jim, but I found that difficult to do. With his dark, graying good looks he somehow didn't look like a Jim. Richard's name games must have been rubbing off on me. As he introduced himself, Jim held my hand just a few heartbeats too long, but I felt certain it was habit rather than an intentional message.

When we got to his office, I saw that his chair was no more ostentatious or comfortable looking than my own. That was one point in his favor. He had decorated his office with pictures of his family, including his dogs, rather than ones of him glad-handing politicos. That was another.

"Richard says you're a good guy. That's high praise coming from a PD."

"High praise indeed. Of course, he has to say nice things about me. I know all the secrets from his younger, wilder days," he said as he raised an eyebrow. I'll just bet he did.

"Were you with the State Attorney's Office when Isaac Thomas was prosecuted?"

"I was, but I didn't rise as quickly here as Richard did at the PD's office. I had just started doing felonies and wouldn't see a capital case, even as a second, for a couple more years. Chet Hawkins prosecuted the case, and I don't think he had co-counsel for it. Probably would have if they'd made it to trial, but since it was plea bargained there was no need. Unfortunately Chet died a few years ago. I'm afraid the file will be your best source of information."

"Will the people in your office wonder why I'm here?"

"No, probably not. Postconviction appellate counsel in capital cases is always provided with a copy of our file. It's not uncommon for them to have someone come by to look at the originals. I doubt anyone here now would remember the Thomas case, and they certainly wouldn't remember the disposition."

Jim smiled. "Besides, I sent out an email this morning letting everyone know an infidel would be in our midst today to look at files. I doubt anyone will speak to you at all unless absolutely necessary. Richard and I are the exception. Here at the State Attorney's Office, we can be pretty chummy with private attorneys, but when it comes to true blue public defenders, there's not a whole lot of fraternization. And vice versa."

He led me to a small, spartan room where a single banker's box sat on a lonely folding table, accompanied by an office chair. "If you need copies of anything, ask for Renee. She'll take care of you."

I didn't know what I was looking for, but whatever it was I didn't find it in that box. Going through everything quickly but thoroughly, I didn't see anything of consequence that I hadn't seen in the trial attorney file. I even double-checked against the trial attorney file inventory I'd done over the weekend. Nothing. That struck me as odd. Where was their case? Come to think of it, where were the handwritten notes by the Chet Hawkins, or memos to his investigator? Who was his investigator? I saw no reference to one in the file, but in a capital case he wouldn't have been without one.

Worst case scenario, if Hawkins hadn't had an investigator he would have been asking the police or sheriff's officers for help on things like following up on evidence testing, checking out the suspect's priors. But there were no notes to LEOs, and no references to Isaac's priors. Conviction or not, if there had been an incident at Jimmy's, it should have been in the ASA's file. There was no correspondence at all, to law enforcement, to the defense, to Vanda's family to inform them of progress or disposition. Nothing.

Renee, as Jim's "Girl Friday," must have had him microchipped. She apparently knew where he was at every moment and led me to a conference room where he was meeting with some other attorneys. She asked me to wait outside, then returned a moment later saying he would meet me in his office in a few minutes.

He was once again true to his word, and in about five minutes I was experiencing déjà vu, sitting in the same chair I'd been sitting in a couple of hours earlier. Perhaps it was my general paranoia exacerbated by the missing file items, but I felt as though I were meeting him again for the first time, that this was a man I really knew nothing about.

"Mr. Gilbert—" I began.

"Jim," he interrupted.

The interruption annoyed me, and I felt, as I often feel with men in power, that his cordial insistence that I use his first name was actually a not-so-subtle display of power. I was tempted to continue using his last name, but I didn't. Probably because I also wondered if I wasn't just looking for an excuse to be pissy to a prosecutor.

I explained about the items I felt were missing. He looked genuinely perplexed. "You're sure?" he asked. I told him I was.

"That doesn't make sense. In case you didn't notice, we're sort of flying under the radar here. I didn't review it, but I retrieved that file myself. No one knew I was getting it, and as best as I could tell it hadn't been touched in years. I even had to wipe the dust off the box when I retrieved it from storage. Everything should be in there."

"What about the investigator? Do you know who his investigator was?"

"He may not have had a dedicated one at that time, but you are onto something. Even if he didn't he would have been getting assistance from the investigating agency."

Jim leaned forward, tapping his cupped hand against his upper lip. "And there was nothing handwritten in the file? Nothing at all? Or typed?"

"No."

"Chet was meticulous about his files. He used to drive the secretaries crazy because he insisted on typing his own memos, one finger at a time. He used carbons so he'd have copies for the file, and he always made a mess. I don't like this."

Jim tapped away a while longer, long enough for me to decide my recent animosity probably was just me being pissy. Having finally come to a decision, he rose to shake my hand again and escort me out.

"Sydney, I'm going to make some calls, do a little digging and see what I can find out. If you don't mind, I'll just contact you through Richard. It's a little less... obvious."

I thanked him for his help and left the building, only to walk around to the PD's entrance. It was nearly lunch, and I was hoping to grab Mike and Richard for a quick bite and update. They were both out, but Millicent—I mean Melinda—said Richard should be back soon and let me into his office to wait. There was a small sofa along one wall, upholstered in coarse navy fabric.

When Richard returned 20 minutes later and found me sleeping, I had the presence of mind to hope the upholstery hadn't given me a waffle face, but that was the extent of my embarrassment. A couple of weeks earlier, I would have been mortified to be caught napping in someone else's office, but now it didn't seem to matter so much. I was still just concentrating on doing whatever it took to get me through the day. Right now that was a nap, hopefully followed by copious quantities of food.

Richard was happy to oblige on that count. We went to Lorna's, where I gorged myself on fried chicken and mashed potatoes. In between bites, I told him what I'd found, or rather hadn't found, at the State Attorney's Office. His confidence was reassuring.

"Jim will figure it out. I'm sure I'll hear from him within a couple of days. Look, I've got to go back to the office after lunch. A couple of minor depositions got pushed up, but it shouldn't take more than an hour or so. Why don't you head back to your motel and get some rest? I'll pick you up when I'm finished, and then we can go see Rudy."

My failure to argue was an indication of how tired I really was. Must have been all the chewing. Returning to my room, it took all of my meager stores of discipline to pull the envelope of crime scene photos from the trial attorney box and settle down at my cramped little motel desk. (I couldn't be trusted to sit on the bed.) The photos were tagged with sticky notes from my previous reviews, but I wanted to glance through them again before meeting with Rudy Nagroski. My intentions were good, but when I realized that I was on my second round of the stack without noticing that I'd finished the first, I decided I wasn't really seeing anything and allowed myself to settle on the bed and fall instantly to sleep.

Perhaps the photos hadn't done much for my conscious mind, but they certainly stirred up my subconscious. Forty minutes later. my eyes opened suddenly with that frustrating feeling of having dreamt important things, but upon waking the images slipped through my fingers like sugar through a sieve. The only one I remembered was both familiar and unexpected, the tactile sensation of a finger gently tracing the side of my face. I could feel the hand turn against my face to expose the palm.

I had often dreamed of my brother Allan doing that precise motion, but this time when I'd opened my eyes I hadn't seen his familiar fingers with their perfectly rounded nails and their half moons at the base. The deep creases on Allan's knuckles always seemed such a contrast to his unlined palms, but I didn't see those either. Instead, I opened my eyes to see a pale callused palm contrasting with a rich brown hand. The fingers had similar moons, but these nails were a little longer than Allan kept his, and slightly curved under on the end.

It was Isaac, of course, young and handsome as he had been in Ida's pictures. Isaac before the death of his wife, before his own slow death in prison. His head tilted sideways, as if trying to see around an obstruction, or compensating for an astigmatism. Or trying to get his eyes to assimilate what his mind could not. His mouth parted slightly for a moment, but he didn't speak. His lower lip started to tremble until he squeezed his lips together, forcing whatever had nearly escaped deeper inside. His breath caught on a deep intake of air, but his lips relaxed into fullness on the exhale. Then his mouth started to curve on one side. Just like Noel.

Despite my rapidly firing synapses, I woke from my nap feeling rested and with plenty of time to freshen up. The swelling had gone down, but one side of my face was still bruised enough that there were limits on what make-up could do. I stuck with a white tank and button-down shirt, but I did put on a long skirt in a delicate flowered pattern, hoping to soften my image for Mr. Nagroski. I'd rather look like a sweet little thing in need of assistance, in this case information, than a loser from Monday night Smackdown.

215

Once I'd done all I could with my face, I headed to the motel office to wait for Richard. I knew Mrs. Waters would be there this time of day and thought I might pick up some good gossip. She was sitting behind the front desk knitting. I always think that's an odd occupation for Floridians, even north Floridians. Perhaps it persists because of the northern transplants. I watched Mrs. Waters for a while, not wanting to startle her. When she looked up I told her I was just waiting for my ride.

"Really? A gentleman caller? You do look nice."

I laughed. "Well, thank you, Mrs. Waters, but Mr. Frey from the PD's office is picking me up for some work. I don't think he qualifies."

"Frey, Frey… oh, yes. Richard Frey." She lost her concentration and dropped her needles while searching her memory, and now one hand went unconsciously to her bottle brush gray hair.

"He is a handsome man—such a radiant smile—and very nice besides. Too bad he's married." She looked at her lap for a moment and went back to knitting.

"Yes, he's much nicer than that last gentleman," she said.

"What gentleman?" I asked.

"The one who came asking for you last night. Didn't you see him? He didn't leave his name. He was asking what room you were staying in this time, but of course I can't give out that information."

"What did he look like?"

"Oh, I'm afraid I can't say. I was cleaning my glasses when he came in, and I couldn't see a thing. Kind of like when you're at a restaurant and the waitress asks you if you need anything when your mouth's full. Customers are always doing that to me with my glasses. A few times a day I use this special spray and it takes a few minutes for me to finish with them. But I can tell you he wasn't very nice. Didn't stop to chat at all."

"Do you remember anything else about him?"

"Well, I feel kinda funny saying this…"

"Please, Mrs. Waters. It could be important."

Until that moment, she obviously didn't have any idea that the stranger could be anything more than a bad blind date. When I said "important," she looked at the fading bruises on my face and the splint that was to remain on my right arm for another two weeks, and the light switched on. Her eyes got big and her mouth dropped open with a gasp, as if her whole face was on a hinge. She remained that way for what should have been the space of a few breaths, except that she had forgotten to breathe. When she remembered, she also remembered her dignity, closing her mouth and trying hard to talk normally.

"Well, I should have known he wasn't here for a date. I know it's tough sometimes in Florida in the summer, which of course lasts at least six months of the year, and some places still not having air conditioning, or working outside—"

"Mrs. Waters—"

"I'm sorry, dear. I do tend to yammer on when I get flustered. It's just that, well, if it had been a date I'd think he would have taken a shower, and he definitely did not. I didn't need my glasses to smell his—"

She lowered her voice and looked around, then went on in a whisper as if she were uttering a profane word.

"You know. His B.O."

217

Chapter Twenty-Seven

I was able to set Mrs. Waters' mind at ease by telling her that everything was going to be okay, that it probably wasn't anything to worry about but that I would be checking out tonight just in case. Setting my own mind at ease was much more of a challenge. It felt like a pen full of screaming monkeys throwing feces. I was able maintain a façade of composure until Richard arrived a few minutes later. I watched the parking lot, and when I saw him pull in I waved my arms like a mad woman. In other words, like me.

His car had barely stopped when I threw the door open and hopped in, as best as I could hop with the heavy bag I probably shouldn't be carrying.

"Hey, Sydney. How was the nap? Listen, I was thinking that tonight—"

"Richard, he's found me. He's after me again, and he knows where I am."

"Who? What are you talking about?"

"I don't know who, do I? But he was here last night, and I didn't even know it. He was right here, Richard. Right here."

Richard hadn't moved the car yet. He took my left hand in both of his, and I tried not to flinch.

"Okay, Syd. Slow down. Take a few deep breaths for me."

I closed my eyes and did as he asked. Eventually the monkeys stopped throwing crap, but they were still making piles of turd balls to have at hand. Just in case. I smiled at the image.

"Thanks. I'm all right now. Let's just get out of here. I'll tell you on the way."

I relayed what Mrs. Waters had said. We weren't far from Rudy Nagroski's house, so Richard pulled over in the parking lot of a boarded-up fast food joint to give me a chance to finish. I hadn't told him much about my experience that night, and even now, to save time I only told him the significance of the body odor. We were due at Nagroski's, and I also figured I'd have to tell the whole tale again soon enough. I may have missed something, and Richard and Mike would want to pick apart the details.

Richard didn't speak for a while after I finished. He kept his head turned, watching the young men loitering outside another bankrupt business across the street. It had gone through numerous incarnations, each leaving a bit of itself behind, generally architecture or advertising, like a commercial fossil. Considering the apparent age of the signage, the latest scheme had been a check cashing place.

"Richard, we need to go. We're going to be late."

For a moment, I thought I heard his teeth grinding. That seemed a fanciful idea until he turned to face me. The anger in his features hid his vitality and made him ugly.

"We're getting you out of here."

"I told Mrs. Waters I was checking out tonight."

He looked as if he wanted to say more, but thought better of it. He started the car, catching a little tire rubber as we left the parking lot, and I heard the teenagers across the street whoop. Hooligans, Mrs. Waters would say. I should be so lucky.

We arrived at Rudy Nagroski's home less than 10 minutes later. We had the trial attorney's file in the trunk, but I preferred to travel light whenever possible. I had a binder in my bag with all of the police reports and the ME report, as well as the envelope of crime scene and autopsy photos. Besides, I was afraid lightning might strike me dead if I took a trial attorney's file into the home of a law enforcement officer. At the very least, the ACLU would revoke my membership.

According to Richard, Rudy's wife had died a few years back, which was one reason he spent so much time at Rosalia's. It's true that a bachelor couldn't get better food, but he was also rumored to have a thing for Rosalia. When he opened the door, my first impression was that Rosalia could do worse. He was a handsome man.

"Hey Rudy," Richard said when the door opened. "Good to see you. This is Sydney Brennan, the investigator I was telling you about."

"Well, come on in."

Rudy stepped aside and informally motioned us inside so he could close the door. It could be that he wasn't a hand-shaker as a rule, but I didn't think so. Rudy hadn't actually stared, but when he looked at me I could feel his quick assessment. I felt certain that he'd decided against shaking hands because of my condition, whatever he perceived that to be. Bruised. Tender to the touch. Fragile and afraid. Strong and angry.

And then he surprised me.

Rudy took my right hand gently in both of his and raised it to his lips. His eyes flicked to mine for my reaction. I don't know what he saw. For him it was an effortless gesture, over before my brain could engage. My whole hand tingled, and I wasn't sure if he'd kissed the fingers, the back of my hand, or both. I'd never had a man kiss my hand before—not seriously anyway—and I found the sensation both thrilling and repulsive. Not trusting myself to speak, I settled for a meager smile and nod of acknowledgement. Then I let him see the assessment in my own eyes.

Rudy was taller than Richard, and broader, a little heavy but with the extra pounds spread out uniformly across his body rather than bulging in any one place. His closely cropped hair seemed the color and consistency of chrome. Eyebrows of the same shade seemed incongruous over hazel-green eyes, and his face was softened by a cleft in his chin and a little extra padding on his strong jaw. He wore a white button-down shirt with navy blue slacks, and his white socks seemed to blaze on his otherwise bare feet. I wondered whether I should take off my own shoes.

I continued to wonder when we entered the heart of his home, an unremarkable one-story brick house, ubiquitous to suburbs across the country. For an old bachelor, Rudy was pretty civilized. He led us into a study that was not immaculate, but much cleaner than any room in my house, while he went to get us some fresh iced tea. (We had declined his offer of beer.)

There were no torso-less animals or ancient firearms mounted on the walls, nor was the furniture heavy brown leather. Sage green chairs were grouped around a coffee table laden with magazines, Scientific American and an unfamiliar birding magazine on top. Matching green curtains were open to view a backyard maybe two or three times the footprint of the house in width, but extending about a hundred yards. Binoculars and a field guide sat on a small table at the center of the window. There was no chair, so presumably Rudy stood while watching.

The far wall of the study was a bookshelf that contained nothing but books—no chachka, no photos. The book spines didn't match, but they were all muted tones, and the books seemed to be arranged by size, making smooth, even rows of uniform height on each shelf. Before I could examine any of the titles, Rudy returned with a tray of three glasses. He served us first, and I noticed the liquid in his own glass was of a slightly different color. I didn't doubt that it contained iced tea, but iced tea of the "improved" variety. I couldn't be sure of how improved, unable to smell it from where I was sitting. Perhaps the smell of improvement permeated the study on a molecular level. Something certainly gave the room an undeniable if subconscious feel of masculinity, and it wasn't the furnishings.

"Rudy, I saw your boat there along the side. She's a pretty little thing. You been spending much time on the water lately?"

"Oh, she's a pretty little thing all right. Pretty to look at and not good for much else. You better believe I'd be out on the water if I could ever get the goddamned motor to work."

He looked over at me. "Beg your pardon, miss. 'Course, I'm sure in your line of work you've probably heard much worse."

For a northern transplant, he sounded the part of a local admirably. Such affectation had probably been essential to his job. I realized that he was playing a game with me. That's okay. I knew my part too.

"Yes, sir, I'd have to admit that I have heard worse. In fact, I'm ashamed to admit that on occasion I may have even said worse. In a fit of pique, of course."

We chatted for a few more minutes, Rudy flirting gallantly and me parrying with a hint of over-the-top, demure southern wit. Richard seemed to be enjoying the show. When I decided I'd amused them both long enough, I got down to business.

"Rudy, what do you remember about Isaac Thomas?"

"Quiet man. Devoted to his daughter. I wouldn't have fingered him for murdering his wife if we'd had any other suspects."

"Why is that?"

"I don't know. I could say he didn't seem the type, but we both know that doesn't mean anything, especially in a domestic. It just didn't feel right."

Rudy sipped his "iced tea" slowly. "Thomas never said he did it, but more importantly he never said he didn't do it. He didn't say much of anything. How many clients have you had, guilty and innocent, who swore up and down they didn't do it? At least to the cops, if not to you."

Richard smiled. "Most of them."

"Exactly. Now I don't know what he said to you in confidence, and I don't want to know, but Sammy used to talk a bit. A bit more than was good for him and his clients, if you want the truth of it, especially toward the end. I was having a beer with him one night. I'm sure he thought he was picking my brain about the case, but at that point he wasn't picking anything but his next drink. Sammy was frustrated. Frustrated hell, he was pissed. He said Thomas wouldn't tell him a thing, not a goddamned thing. He wouldn't say where he was that night, he wouldn't say what happened, and he wouldn't talk about his relationship with his wife."

Rudy paused for another sip. "I'm a cop. It sure as hell wasn't my case, but I said maybe he ought to have a head shrinker look at the guy. But you know how Sammy was. Said there wasn't anything wrong with his client a good smack upside the head wouldn't fix."

"Did he invoke *Miranda* when you spoke with him?" I asked.

"No, he didn't refuse to speak to us. He just didn't speak. I mean, he wasn't rude about it. He kept asking if his daughter was okay, and what would happen to her, but that was it. He wouldn't talk about his wife or the crime."

I appreciated that Richard sat silently while I continued to question Rudy. "What happened when you picked him up?"

"Well, really, that was the strongest thing we had against him. We showed up at the house not long after he killed her. I think we had an anonymous tip."

"What kind of tip?"

"I don't know. Whoever was working the switchboard would

have taken the call, and I don't have a clue who that would have been. I guess it was the usual—some neighbor heard the altercation and got worried."

"Man or woman?"

"I don't know. Anyway, I can't remember why, but I was in the area, along with the Sarge. Richard, you remember Sergeant Wiggins?"

Richard nodded, but didn't speak.

"Asshole moved to south Florida a few years back, and I haven't heard from him since. So me and Sarge drop by the house and see someone leaving out the front door. It was Thomas, and when he saw us he panicked and took off running. We didn't know his wife was dead, but when a man runs from the cops, it tends to make you suspicious. I was no spring chick even then, but I chased him down. Not that it took much chasing. When I got close enough, I told him to stop and he did. He never put up a fight. By that time Sarge had gone in and found—what was her name? Wanda?"

"Vanda."

Rudy ran a hand over the back of his skull, as if stimulating brain cells, and nodded in agreement. "That's right. Vanda. He found her dead."

"Was the daughter there, in the house?"

"No. I couldn't tell you where she was. With family or friends, I guess."

"Were you there when they processed the crime scene?"

"Oh yeah." He shook his head and gave a cringing smile at the memory.

"That was a late night. We were short-handed, and we had to wait for the crime scene techs and the ME. Seems to me like there'd been a fire somewhere. Nothing serious, nobody died, but I think

225

that's where everybody was."

We took some time to go through his reports, but there really wasn't much there. I hadn't seen much about Vanda in particular, so I asked him about her.

"Well, we never got far on her. There was a neighbor that said the wife used to mess around a lot—prostitute herself, really—but she admitted she'd never seen her bring a man home with her. The prostitution thing could be true, but we never got more than rumors, and those rumors usually came from women."

"Jealous women," I said.

"That's what we suspected. The victim was a very beautiful woman. And you have to remember, once we picked up the husband running away from the scene, nobody was pushing us to find things that would make the victim less sympathetic to a jury. Like it or not, that's just the way it is."

I pulled out the envelope of crime scene photos and selected one that I had tagged. It was a shot of Vanda lying on the bed, from far enough away to get the whole bed in the picture, but close enough to clearly make out the way her head had fallen to one side.

"Can you tell me if this picture shows exactly the way she looked when you found her?"

"Well, if you want to be technical about it, Sarge found the body, but I'm pretty sure this is what she looked like when I walked in."

"Was there any indication she'd had sex recently?"

Rudy sipped at his drink and rubbed the bridge of his nose between his fingers, considering.

"We definitely didn't have DNA, but I don't know if we were doing that whaddaya-call-it, acid phosphatase test back then. Even if most places were, our ME wasn't the brightest bulb in the box, so I wouldn't count on it. Sheets were rumpled, but they could have just been bad housekeepers. I don't remember seeing a condom but I do remember—I don't know how—that she wasn't wearing any underwear. Maybe her dress was hiked up when we got there, or maybe it was later when the ME got there. Sorry, I just can't say."

"What was your impression of her physical condition?"

"It didn't take a medical degree to see she'd been strangled, face bulging and dark. Petechial hemorrhaging. She'd been struck, but not more than a couple of times. I wouldn't say she was beaten. I think all the marks were on the same side of her face. Let me see, that would have been the left side, because her face was turned away to the left and you couldn't see the marks right away. Not until she was moved."

I pulled out another photo, a close-up of the right side of her face. Her cheek had a dark spot under the eye. "What about this mark? It's not a bruise?"

"Certainly looks like it, but I'm sure she was only struck on the one side. What's the ME's report say?"

"He doesn't say it was a contusion, but he doesn't mention its presence at all."

Rudy snorted. "Big surprise." He examined the picture again. He was trying hard to keep his hand from shaking, but there was still a slight tremor as he held the 4 x 6 print. He set the photo down, closed his eyes and leaned forward to rest his elbows on his knees with bowed head. He remained in that position, breathing slowly, and I was about to ask if he was all right when he sat upright so quickly I heard something pop.

"I've got it. It was some kind of dirt. It smeared right off. There were some spots on her neck as well, and when we picked him up his hands were dirty. He was kinda dirty all over. He wouldn't say why."

"The spots on her neck—were they isolated spots or more like lines or bands?"

"Just a couple of small spots, and before you say anything else I know where you're going. If his hands were dirty and he strangled her, why were there only a few small spots, spots high on the neck near the jaw I might add. Not where I'd strangle someone. The theory was that he strangled his wife, killed her, but he thought he'd only choked her out. He leaves her, comes back after he's done something to get his hands dirty, and checks her pulse, maybe even tries to revive her. That's when he leaves the spots. Or he does think he killed her, goes out and digs a hole to put her in, then checks her pulse to make sure she's gone before burying her. 'Course we never found the hole. Neither one's a great explanation, I'll admit, but probably good enough for a jury."

At this point Richard began asking Rudy questions, but my mind was elsewhere and I had problems following the conversation. There was this nagging itching feeling at the back of my brain, and not just a "did I remember to send my mortgage payment" kind of itching. This was something big. The more I concentrated, the more it itched, so I finally gave up and tried to listen to what the men were saying instead.

"What about priors? A history of violence with his wife?" Richard asked. "I don't remember seeing anything, but it's possible we had a report and Sammy mislaid it before I could get my hands on it."

"Nope. Nothing. I know I was surprised by that. You expect a domestic murder to be an escalation of violence that's already there. The neighbor—what was her name?"

"Claire Johnson?" I volunteered.

"Yeah, I think that's it. The baby-sitter." Rudy's grin would have seemed lecherous on a less attractive man. "She was a saucy young thing. She didn't think there was any violence to speak of either, but she did mention something. I don't know, maybe about a bar, but I never heard anything else about it."

I'd been swinging my pen back and forth between my thumb and index finger, and I suddenly lost my grip. On my pen, that is. It flew across the room and cracked against a glass-fronted liquor cabinet. Rudy and Richard looked at me as if I'd lost my mind. On the contrary, I'd just found it. I could feel Isaac's touch and see his crooked smile in my mind's eye.

"Rudy, you said there was a fire that night, the night Isaac killed Vanda."

"Yeah, that's right. Pretty big fire, if I recall…" His voice trailed off and his eyes lost focus.

"Where was that fire?"

It took him a moment to see me, but he eventually managed to marshal his thoughts. "It was a bar, not very far down the road. A place called Jimmy's."

CHAPTER TWENTY-EIGHT

Pieces were starting to come together, but there were still gaps to be filled. As we'd expected, it was now late enough for dinner, so we called Mike and asked him to meet us at Rosalia's. There was much to discuss, but Rudy had invited us to eat there with him, or invited himself to eat with us. I wasn't sure which. Either way, we couldn't get rid of him after he'd been so helpful. Besides, I had a feeling he knew something else important. I just didn't know the right question to ask.

Rosalia's was close, and Richard was unusually quiet on the drive. Rudy's car was in front of us, and when I saw the sign for the restaurant and Rudy's blinking turn signal I spoke.

"As soon as we get rid of Rudy, we've got to put our heads together," I said.

"As soon as we get rid of Rudy, we've got to get you checked out of that motel and checked into someplace safe."

I'd been so involved in our discussion of Isaac's case, I'd forgotten about my stinky visitor. Obviously Richard hadn't forgotten. My stomach did a few flip-flops, and I wished he'd reminded me after dinner. Deep breath. Let it out. Okay. I refused to let some perv with body odor ruin my decadent carb-loading. In fact, I might even have dessert.

We'd beaten Mike to the restaurant, so the three of us got a table and ordered a bottle of wine while we waited. I sat next to Richard with an empty chair for Mike directly across from me.

Although wearing a long skirt, I was taking no chances putting my knees within Rudy's reach. Mike made good time and arrived just as the bottle of wine did. He and Rudy had met once or twice before, but they'd never worked the same case. By the time Mike had joined the PD's office, Rudy was spending most of his time behind a desk. I tried to get a few whispered words in with Mike while Rudy and Richard flirted with the waitress. Rudy was a bad influence.

"Productive day?" I asked.

"Definitely. We need to talk. And you?"

"The same."

Rudy's voice cutting in was like a bellow after our soft words. "Turn your back for two minutes to order food and the next thing you know the young people are whispering sweet nothings in each other's ears."

I gave Rudy an icy smile, and Mike blushed.

The food was excellent, as I had expected. We started with surprisingly good salads, more than just the dreaded iceberg lettuce and grated carrots, and a basket of crusty pungent garlic bread. We were on our second bottle of wine as we finished our salads, and halfway through our entrée Rudy ordered a third. Not surprising since he put away most of the second single-handedly. My entrée was a luscious mushroom ravioli in a creamy sauce, and Mike and I split an order of tiramisu for dessert. Rudy restrained himself, making no comment but raising his eyebrows significantly. He'd actually been on his best behavior all evening, regaling us with stories from his years in New York law enforcement. There was less danger of offense that way, since we were technically on different sides and may have our own dramatically different versions of any of his Florida stories.

Once Mike and I finished our dessert, we ordered coffee all

around. The waitress told us it would be a few minutes, that they were making it fresh. Richard took advantage of the opportunity, saying he had something in his car he wanted to give Mike before he forgot, if we didn't mind.

"I think we can bear your absence," I said. I thought I knew what he was going to talk to Mike about and I was a little annoyed.

"Subtle," Rudy remarked when they'd left.

"Always," I replied. "Speaking of subtlety, you seem to have lost your southern heritage over dinner." His accent and mannerisms had gradually neutralized during the evening, then reverted to a slight hint of his northern antecedents.

"You caught me," he said. "It must be the wine." With that, he finished the last swallow in his glass with a flourish.

"You've slipped a little as well. And you didn't have as much wine," he noted. "That's what being a good, I mean a really good, investigator is all about. Persona. You have to figure out what kind of person the person you're interviewing will talk to, whether it's a witness or an attorney or another investigator. I can tell you've got a knack for it. Not everyone does. Especially women. Women's lib or feminism or whatever you want to call it has ruined some fine female investigators. As an investigator, you have to use every tool in your box, and there are some roles now that women won't assume. Because they're not supposed to. Because it's demeaning or chauvinistic or—oh hell, I don't know. It seems damn silly to me to throw away half the tools in your box just because they happen to be the ones that work."

I secretly agreed with him, but I wouldn't admit it to Rudy. Fortunately Mike and Richard returned and saved me from having to say anything. By the set of Mike's jaw, a slightly quivering straight line, I could tell my suspicions had been right. Damn Richard for not being able to wait five minutes until we finished our coffee to tell Mike about my smelly friend. At least he had waited until the end of dinner. Well, I refused to participate in the gloom and doom.

"Rudy, there was one other thing I meant to ask you. During the Thomas case, do you remember if Chet Hawkins had his own investigator?"

"No, no I don't think he did. He probably would have used one of us for his leg work, but as I recall there wasn't much to be done. I know I didn't do it… give me a minute."

He closed his eyes and assumed what I was beginning to recognize as his thinking pose, fingers massaging the bridge of his nose. Mike looked at me questioningly, but I nodded my head to let him know that Rudy hadn't passed out from the wine, that if we were patient he'd get there. Sure enough, he lifted his head a minute later.

"I can't remember his name, but he used a young guy, somebody who hadn't been with us long, and I don't think he stayed long after. I thought he was an obnoxious little shit, but I always thought that about the young guys. I'll let it roll around in my head for a while, and if I think of his name I'll let you know."

Once we'd paid the bill (Rudy chivalrously insisted on paying for my meal but said the men were on their own), we said goodbye to Rudy and met in the parking lot by Richard's car.

"All right guys, what's the plan?" I tried to keep the tone light, but Richard's mood was like a black hole. Mike made an effort of his own.

"Well, we could always have you stay with Rudy." Mike had raised his eyebrows at me when Rudy kissed my hand good night, but being my second hand-kiss in a day, and having some wine in my veins, I'd kept my own composure. Fingers, actually, I realized this time. He kissed my fingers between the middle knuckle and the hand.

"Have you no respect for my virtue, whatever remains of it?"

Richard didn't bite and continued to suck up all happiness and light. "The first thing we need to do is get Sydney checked out of the motel. I'll go on ahead. You two ride together. Give me a five minute head start and then follow. And keep your eyes open."

We did as he asked. In Richard's current mood I wasn't about to contradict him, and Mike apparently felt no reason to.

"Don't you think he's being a little too Spy vs. Spy?" I asked when we left the parking lot.

"I don't know, Sydney. I hope so. Better—"

"I know, I know, better safe than sorry."

"I was going to say better annoyed than dead, but close enough."

With that, Mike checked the rearview mirror yet again.

"I've recruited a bunch of paranoid lunatics," I mumbled as I stared out the window. I'm sure Mike heard, but he didn't contradict me.

CHAPTER TWENTY-NINE

Richard was waiting for us at the motel, as expected. It only took me a few minutes to gather my belongings and check out. It helped that a teenager with no inclination for conversation more stimulating than "credit or debit" was behind the desk instead of Mrs. Waters. I set my bag on the ground between Mike's and Richard's vehicles until we decided where I was going to spend the night.

They both offered their homes, which I vetoed immediately. If there was some danger to me, I certainly didn't want to bring it home to Richard's family. Then I said that after 3 bottles of wine, I might try to take advantage of Mike. That wasn't exactly true, but I did think it would be too weird to stay with a single male friend I'd known for less than two weeks. Besides, I didn't know how long I'd be staying here, and we needed a solution for more than one night.

We settled on a place in Hainey in a block of active businesses that tended to get a lot of traffic. Room access was interior by key cards only. That decided, Richard said we needed to get rid of my car. A light blue Cabrio is cute, but conspicuous.

"For now, I don't think we need a rental. I think we should just trade out your car with one of us. Mike, if you don't mind, yours isn't any less conspicuous but it is less likely to be known."

"No problem." Mike turned to me. "My piece of crap is your piece of crap. Just so you know, the gas gauge doesn't work, but it gets decent gas mileage. Unless you're driving to California and back, you should be okay on a tank of gas a week."

"Cecil shouldn't give you any problems either."

"Cecil?"

"Yes, my car's name is Cecil, and he speaks with a cockney accent. Don't worry, he's not that chatty with strangers."

Mike's little yellow Jeep may not have had some of its more cosmetic parts intact and wasn't the smoothest ride, but it was an automatic and cute in a rugged sort of way. We weren't thinking and took the time to switch our belongings and our bodies even though everyone was going to the same place. I followed Mike, and while we were playing musical duffel bags Richard slipped into the motel. He was concluding a discussion with the desk clerk when Mike and I arrived, having already arranged for my room on the third floor.

I could tell immediately that we had moved up a class or two in accommodations. The night desk clerk wasn't the typical bottom rung motel teenager or skeazy fifty-something wearing an undershirt and a permanent 10:00 shadow, but instead a clean-cut fairly attractive twenty-something. I didn't know what Richard had told him, but the clerk watched me intently while trying to avoid looking at me. The lobby mirrors helped.

The guys followed me upstairs and I dumped my bag on one of the room's double beds. The bathroom layout was such that the toilet and shower were in an interior room, with the double sink vanity area in a buffer zone leading to the bedroom. A coffee maker sat on the counter. I picked up the carafe and walked back to where the guys were sitting, Richard at the desk and Mike on the bed with my bag. I held the carafe aloft.

"Caff or decaf?" I asked.

We all looked at each other, looked at the clock (11:43 PM) and simultaneously said, "Decaf." Richard smiled for the first time since he'd picked me up that afternoon.

I was anxious to hear what Mike had to say. Since I'd had an opportunity to share the discovery experience with Richard while Mike had kept his news bottled up for hours, I suggested Mike go first. He'd gone in early and spent the morning doing the work he was actually being paid for at the PD's office, then took a sandwich to the police station so he could review reports on his lunch break. Time got away from him, and he hadn't made it back to the PD's office until about 4 pm. Mike had checked under Isaac and Vanda's names, and under Vanda's maiden name, but hadn't found anything not related to the murder investigation.

"I remembered what you said about the bar incident, so I asked one of the old timers what the likely spots would've been around that time, and he said the same—Jimmy's. Eventually I found a report." Mike started digging through the papers in what looked like a computer bag.

"Isaac did hit her, but she never pressed charges, and neither of them spoke to the cops. It sounds like Isaac came in looking for Vanda, and she was messing around with some other guy and really rubbed his face in it. The witnesses didn't say much, except that they were surprised he didn't deck her earlier. I didn't have a chance to check it out yet, but I think I've got good addresses for two of the witnesses."

"Good. We'll add them to the list." Richard looked at me and smiled. "Too bad we left the whiteboard in Tallahassee."

I raised an eyebrow in acknowledgement. He'd ridiculed the monstrosity when I first pulled it out at my house, but now it looked like I had a convert.

"Now for the really interesting stuff." Mike's pushed his glasses farther up the bridge of his nose. His face was so eager he looked too young to buy beer.

239

"While I was looking through the reports on Jimmy's, I came across something else."

"The fire?" I asked.

His jaw dropped. "Dammit, Syd, how did you know that?"

His face had gone from a ten-year-old five minutes before opening Christmas presents to the same ten-year-old five minutes after getting several pairs of socks and underwear, and I couldn't hold back my laughter. Thankfully I regained control quickly. As exhausted as I was, I would have laughed until I cried.

"I'm sorry, Mike. I'll explain later. I don't know any of the details, just that there was a fire. Please go on."

He seemed mollified and even managed a grin. "There was a fire the night Vanda was killed. I don't know her time of death, but it had to be close to the time of the fire. It was suspicious, but it was eventually ruled accidental because arson couldn't be proven. They were really lucky. It was almost a major tragedy. Apparently the building wasn't up to code, didn't have any windows and only one or two exits, no sprinkler system. Jimmy's was packed, and if the fire had burned a little more quickly or someone had panicked, dozens of people could have died."

Mike handed each of us 10 or so photocopied pages, our copies of the reports. "I know there doesn't seem to be a ready connection, but there's something there. I can't believe it's just a coincidence."

Richard was silent, so I chimed in. "I agree, and I can give you a little piece of the connection."

I summarized what Rudy had told us, finishing up with the spots of smeared dirt on Vanda's body. "I think the dirt on her face and her neck was soot, soot from the fire at Jimmy's."

"Shit, that could be," Mike agreed.

"Can you do me a favor tomorrow morning and run an Autofind on some of the fire witnesses?"

"Already taken care of," he said, handing me and Richard small stacks of print-outs. "That also includes the two witnesses to the bar incident. Once you start asking questions, I wouldn't be surprised if there's some overlap on the witnesses."

I started leafing through the pages. "Let's just hope the barflies haven't drunk themselves to death yet."

It was nearly 1 AM, so we adjourned for the night. Mike and Richard had to be at the PD's office bright and early the next day, and while I might be able to sleep in a little longer, I did have a long list of witnesses to contact. We would touch base tomorrow after work (their regular work at the PD's office, that is), and if I had anyone left to see, we would divvy up the remaining witnesses then. I looked affectionately at the two sets of tired eyes that were not my own. I hoped we finished this up soon. In addition to the stress of being stalked by stinky perv, I was in a constant state of exhaustion, and I didn't know how much longer these guys could keep working two full-time jobs.

As tired as I was, I couldn't think about sleeping until I looked over the report from the fire at Jimmy's. Like Richard, I wished I had my whiteboard with me. The timeline would come in handy right about now. I pulled out my binder of reports and concentrated on two things, Vanda's time of death and the time of the fire.

Despite TV shows to the contrary, time of death is by no means an exact science even now, and certainly not in 1980 in the Florida Panhandle. It can best be determined by outside factors—when the body was discovered and when the victim was last seen alive. Rudy and the Sarge apprehended Isaac and discovered the body at 10:45 PM. It'd be nice to know when the anonymous tip came in, but if it wasn't in the files I'd already reviewed (and it wasn't), chances were slim that it would show up in the future.

The exact time the fire at Jimmy's started was similarly elusive. The fire department had gotten the call at 10:06 and responded to the scene at 10:15 PM. The first police officers had arrived 10 minutes later, with additional officers trickling in over the next half hour. Let's say for the sake of simplicity that the fire started at 10 PM, and let's assume Isaac actually did get soot on his hands at the fire. He wasn't listed in the police reports as a witness. That meant either he was gone from the scene at 10:25 when the police started to arrive, or he was there and no one ever spoke to him, not unlikely in the chaos of a fire scene. The report I was looking at was by an Officer James, but it looked like the whole force had been there, and I'm sure a lot of what they'd done hadn't been reduced to writing.

So how had Isaac gotten to Jimmy's, and why had he gone there? I had a vague recollection, from a report or my conversations with Noel, that Isaac and Vanda had only owned one car. From her reputation, I found it hard to believe that Vanda had stayed home all evening. Perhaps she'd gone out earlier, Isaac returned home and went to Jimmy's looking for her, but by that time she'd already left for home and they missed each other. Assuming she'd even been to Jimmy's. And where had Noel been that evening?

I could ask Noel, and I would if I had to, but that didn't seem like a very good idea right now. I didn't know for sure if I was at the top of her shit list, but I probably wasn't the best person to ask her questions about such a psychologically sensitive subject. She may not remember immediately and get defensive, and she may end up remembering things differently simply because of her anger at me. I also didn't want to muddy her family waters any more than I already had until I felt sure it would lead to some answers, preferably answers that I could anticipate.

I didn't know where Mike lived or how long it took to get there, but I doubted he'd had time to fall asleep yet. He answered his cell phone on the second ring. I told him I need another favor.

"If you get a chance tomorrow, I need you to check something out for me. I want to know how many cars Isaac and Vanda owned when she was murdered, and if you can get detailed information on the vehicles that would be great."

"Sure. No problem. I'm writing it down so I actually have a shot at remembering this conversation took place when I get up in a few hours. Can I ask why, or is it to complicated to explain this early in the morning?"

"Yes, and yes. It's just a little hunch that may or may not pan out. I'll explain later. Thanks, Mike."

CHAPTER THIRTY

After I hung up, I put on my jammies and went to sleep almost immediately. My sleep coma lasted until the alarm clock cut through my skull like an ice pick at 7 AM. Tired as I'd been the night before, I'd thought to open the drapes before tucking in. Good thing. Without some natural light in the morning, even the ice pick alarm could not have roused me. After a shower and some orange juice, I might feel almost human.

I found OJ and coffee in the lobby and wrote out my game plan while I waited for the sugar and caffeine to enter my bloodstream. As I fumbled with my map and witness list, I glared at the two Styrofoam cups. I wasn't sure which was more watered down, the juice or the coffee, but neither was doing its job. I'd have to count on the sound of Mike's rattling Jeep to keep me awake as I went on my rounds.

I struck out with the first two on the list. One was a bad address; the other didn't know what I was talking about and threatened to sic the dog on me. It was a yippy little thing, afflicted with mange and missing half its teeth, so it was an empty threat, but it didn't do much to help my mood. As I pulled up in front of the third address, I decided if I didn't get somewhere with this guy I was going to have to take some drastic measure to salvage the day. Maybe ice cream for breakfast.

My hips and digestion were saved when Robbie Johnson (no relation to Claire) opened the door. He was an attractive man, slim but not thin, with dark skin and not a hint of gray in his neat close-cropped hair. I identified myself and he invited me in, full of hospitality, as a good man of the cloth should be. I had been surprised by the collar.

He offered beverages, but I declined. He led me to the living room where we sat in comfortable over-stuffed chairs. There was a slight scent of lemon furniture cleaner in the air.

"I'm guessing you don't go by Robbie any more."

His white teeth flashed as he laughed. "Well, there are a few people who still call me that, but to most people I'm the Reverend Robert. Just plain Robert will do."

"Robert, I'm here about something that happened almost 25 years ago. Do you remember a bar called Jimmy's?"

He sighed. "Oh yes, I remember Jimmy's. There was a period of my life when I spent a lot of time and money there. I'm not proud of it, but I was young and eventually I had the sense to get out. I was very fortunate. A lot of lost people never find their way out of places like Jimmy's."

Religious people make me nervous, and for a moment I was afraid he was about to launch into a sermon. Robert read my mind, or more likely my expression. He smiled.

"Don't worry. I'm not going to give you a sermon on the wages of vice and sin. I'm going to let you in on a little secret." He lowered his voice accordingly. "I get the impression my God is a lot more forgiving and understanding than the one a lot of people around here pray to."

I had to smile back. He was absolutely charming. "So what is it you need to know about?"

"Do you remember a woman named Vanda who used to hang out at Jimmy's?"

For a moment he seemed to forget I was in the room and

246

muttered, "Vanda. That's like Wanda, but with a V."

"Excuse me?"

He blinked and looked at me. "Oh yes, I remember her too."

"What can you tell me about her?"

"Some of my less forgiving colleagues would call her a Jezebel. I'd say she was a very unhappy woman, perhaps trying to deserve what she'd gotten in life. She was physically beautiful, one of the most physically beautiful women I've ever seen in my life, but she could be a very ugly person."

"She spent a lot of time at Jimmy's, more than I did. I think she was probably there every night. I was working on a road crew, and I'd come over to Jimmy's with my friends after work. As I said, I was a young man, and naïve. At first I didn't know what she was up to. I noticed she would disappear into the bathroom with one of the men and come out a few minutes later. It never occurred to me that she was selling herself. The bathroom didn't even have a door, just a curtain, and I couldn't imagine someone would have sex there, with all those people on the other side of the curtain." He blushed and grinned. "Plus I thought it was supposed to take a lot longer."

"Did you ever see her husband come in?"

"Just once. That was the night I finally figured out what was going on. In fact, that might have been the last time I went to Jimmy's."

"Did they fight?"

"I suppose you could say that. He eventually struck her, but until that point it was very one-sided to be called a fight."

"Can you tell me what happened?"

"Vanda had just come back from the bathroom with a friend of mine, I think his name was Tony. He was an older man, and I shouldn't really say he was a friend. We worked together, but I didn't like him. He was mean-spirited, the kind of man who thinks physical injuries, especially to women, are funny. There must have been about six of us sitting around a table, and we were drinking beer while we waited for a pool table. Vanda went around the table, touching everyone in turn, just a shoulder or cheek. Then she plopped down on my lap. She was wearing a short skirt, and she was drunk. She sort of over-balanced and her legs went up in the air."

Robert shook his head at the memory. "Everybody started whooping, so I started whooping too. I didn't know they were yelling because she hadn't been wearing any underwear. All of a sudden a man came out of nowhere and grabbed her arms and dragged her off my lap. Vanda fell to the floor, but he kept dragging her toward the door until she bit him."

I was almost afraid to ask. "Bit him where?"

"The calf, fortunately for him. I don't even think he knew what he was doing until she did that. Then she spit on him and started screaming, f— this and f— that. I'd never heard a woman speak like that before in my life. He said it was time to go home, and she said f— you, I'll go home when I damn well please."

"Did you know who he was?"

"No, I didn't have a clue. She got up from the floor and walked back over to our table." He paused. "This is really important, isn't it?"

"Yes, it is." I didn't explain. I knew he didn't need an explanation, just assurance.

Robert took a deep breath and tried to smile. "At least my wife is out doing the shopping now. I don't know if I could tell you this if she were here. You have to understand, it's not because this was sinful or sexual or embarrassing. It was just ugly. It was a very hateful, ugly situation, and I'm glad to say I've never experienced anything else with that kind of negative intensity."

He took another deep breath. "Vanda came back to the table, and started flirting, talking about which one of us she should be with. Then she wanted to know which one of us could give her the most pleasure, which one of us had the, uh, largest penis. In that moment, things changed. It wasn't funny or sexy anymore. It was just uncomfortable."

"Was that when he hit her?"

"No. I think he grabbed her arm. He kept telling her it was time to go, but she wouldn't listen. Then something got into me. I must have thought I was being gallant or macho. Both probably. He was a very large man. I asked him what business it was of his what the lady did with her time. He could have broken me in half, but he did much better. He told me he was her husband, and she was the mother of his child. That put me in my place. I didn't even know she was married."

"Then Vanda began screaming at him again, insulting his, uh, prowess. I think she said something about their child, their 'brat' she called her, and he slapped her. It was so fast, I didn't even see it happen. One minute she was standing, and the next minute she was on the floor. I think he was as surprised as she was. He just left her there on the floor."

"Did he say anything before he left?"

Robert sat, fingers interlaced, trying to capture the words. His voice deepened slightly as he spoke, and his inflection changed, as if trying to reproduce Isaac instead of merely Isaac's speech.

"He said that she was a no-good whore, and that if she ever hurt their child he would kill her."

With that sound of cold assurance, goosebumps broke out all over my limbs. Robert, still lost in his memories, didn't notice. My voice brought him back.

249

"Do you know if Vanda was using drugs?"

He considered for a moment. "I never actually saw her or anyone else using drugs at Jimmy's, but in hindsight I know it went on. Ironically, in my current position with the church, I'm much more familiar with the signs of drug use and abuse than I would have been as a young man. It certainly would explain a lot about Vanda—her dramatic mood swings, her self loathing, why she'd do the kinds of things she was doing when she had a husband and child waiting at home."

"Do you remember the fire at Jimmy's?"

"I heard about it, but I'd left Hainey by then. My road job ended and I went to stay with an aunt in Georgia for a while, and then I went to seminary. I came back to Hainey about five years later. I have to say, if anything surprised me about that fire, it was that no one was killed. Jimmy's was a corrugated metal shack with a tar paper roof and no windows. My goodness, it got hot in there. And smoky. They did cut out a hole and install one of those window air conditioning units, but you can imagine how much good that did."

I asked Robert about his friends from that time, and the other people on my list.

"I'm afraid I lost touch with everyone, and when I returned I didn't try to reestablish contact. That was a different life, a different me."

Robert rubbed his hands over the wooden accents on his armchair, back and forth. We both rose, and he walked me to the door. Once he'd opened it, he stood in the doorway, dazed by the sunlight. I'd begun to wonder if I'd have to push my way around him to get out when he stepped aside suddenly and turned to me.

"Vanda was killed soon after that, wasn't she? By her husband?"

I nodded. He looked pained, and I could see his lips moving as

250

he muttered some sort of prayer. "What about the child? What happened to their child?"

"She was raised by relatives."

"It is fortunate that she had family. But that poor child. To grow up with the knowledge—of what? Of uncertainty, I suppose. What other lesson could a child take from such senseless suffering, but that life is uncertain. I shall pray for her tonight."

We were standing on his front step now, and he turned to grasp my left hand gently but firmly in both of his.

"And for you."

CHAPTER THIRTY-ONE

Great, now I had two motives for Isaac to have killed Vanda, or at least two variations on a theme—anger at her sexual escapades or anger at her treatment of their daughter. It seemed more important than ever to find out where Noel had been that night, but I was still hesitant to contact her directly, for all the reasons I said before and one more. I'm just a big wuss. I hate confrontation, at least in my personal life and on my own account. I can handle and even thrive on confrontation if I'm helping a client, although Noel's case was proving an exception even on that count. I compromised. I knew she'd be at work, so I called her home number and left a message. Regardless of our personal problems, I needed to talk to her about what happened the night her mother was killed. I needed to know where she had been that night.

I didn't have Noel's work number with me, and she wouldn't get the message until this evening. Even then, I wouldn't hold my breath waiting for her call. I couldn't wait for Noel to forgive me enough to speak to me. Instead Claire Johnson moved up a few spots in priority on my list. I gave her a call and made an appointment to see her at 1:30. Afternoon was perfect. I'd missed breakfast and didn't want to have to rush our interview because I was about to faint from hunger.

I still squeezed in three more short interviews before lunch, two men and a woman who had been at the fire. No one remembered seeing Isaac or Vanda at the fire. In fact, only the woman had ever set eyes on Isaac, and that hadn't been at Jimmy's. A few months before he killed Vanda, there was a period of a couple of weeks that she saw him dropping Noel off at school every morning when she dropped off her own child. They'd spoken a few times, just small talk about their children, and the woman said she could tell who the involved parent was in that household.

All three of them remembered Vanda, though with slightly different interpretations of her behavior. The men said she was beautiful, wild and crazy, and a lot of fun to be around. The woman said she dressed like a w-h-o-r-e, and that she was no better than she should be. She hadn't spent as much time at Jimmy's as the men had, generally only going in to remind her husband to come home, so she couldn't give me specifics about Vanda's behavior. Both men admitted that they had suspected Vanda was having sex for money and drugs, that she was rumored to have a bad habit, but emphasized that they had no personal experience with her, or with the drug trade there. Yeah, right.

I went to grab some lunch after that, both because I was hungry and to get the taste of their hypocrisy out of my mouth. I was of two (or three or seven) minds about Vanda and Isaac Thomas. Whether he killed her or not, I found it hard to muster up much anger at Isaac. I'd never use the words out loud for fear of hurting Noel, but it appeared that her mother had been a crack whore. Murder can never be excused, but she had given Isaac a lot of provocation. There was no evidence he had physically harmed her when, to be quite honest, many men would have. Until, that is, he killed her. If he killed her.

On the other hand, I thought of what Ida and the Reverend Robert had said. For whatever reason, it sounded as if Vanda had been a genuinely tortured soul. Isaac had stayed with her throughout her crap, perhaps for Noel's sake, or perhaps because he still loved her, still saw a bit of the person she used to be. With my defense background, I was conditioned to think about the person she used to be, about what brought her so low. Or maybe I was just a sucker.

I left off with musing and headed over to Miss Johnson's, sure I could count on her to muddy the water a bit more. She must have seen me coming because she had disengaged an impressive array of locks by the time I got to the door.

"Hello, Miss Johnson. Thanks for taking the time to see me again."

"Well, come on in. Don't stand in the door yammering. It's not safe for a body to be out of doors any more."

"The street looked pretty quiet when I drove up."

"Maybe the crack dealers are on their lunch break," she said, without a hint of a smile.

I took a seat on her familiar afghan-accented sofa. "Miss Johnson, I had a few more questions for you about the Thomases, and what happened back then. Do you remember a bar called Jimmy's? I think you mentioned it the last time we spoke."

"You better believe I do. I only set foot in there two or three times, but if my momma had known she woulda tanned my hide. Don't get me wrong, I was no angel. I had my share of boy problems and those kinds of things, but ladies did not go in Jimmy's. It just was not done."

"I've heard that Vanda spent a lot of time in there."

Miss Johnson snorted. "Like I said, *ladies* did not go in there. But you're right. Vanda was in there all the time. She spent her time there while I'd babysit her child."

"Do you remember when Jimmy's caught on fire?"

"Oh yeah. It pretty well gutted the place. I think they tried to re-open a few months after the fire, but it didn't take. Wasn't too long after that they tore it all down."

"What do you remember about that night?"

"Oh, it's been so long. Let me think. I saw it. I was over there, but why did I go over there?" She clapped her hands together and touched her index fingers to her bottom lip, almost as if she were praying. Apparently her prayers, and mine, were answered.

"Oh, lord, I remember now. I went over there because of little Noel. I was worried to death about her."

"You weren't keeping her that evening?"

"No. That is, I was supposed to, but her momma picked her up. See, Isaac had to work late, so Noel came over here to stay. It must have been around 8:30 or 9:00 that night when Vanda dropped by. She said she wanted to take Noel with her. She didn't say where, but I figured she was going to Jimmy's. That's where Vanda always went, and I think she took Noel there a couple of times before. Of course I didn't approve, but I didn't have any say-so. She was Vanda's child."

"Then about 10 o'clock I heard a car pull up, and a little later there was a knock at the door. I remember I looked at the clock before I answered the door, wondering who could be knocking so late. When I did, I realized there was a program I wanted to watch —Dynasty maybe? I don't know. So I went to the door and it was Isaac, still in his work clothes. One of his buddies had just dropped him off, and he was coming to pick up Noel. I said, what do you mean? Didn't Vanda talk to you? We looked over to the house and didn't see any lights, so we figured Vanda and Noel were still at Jimmy's."

"Ooh, that man was mad. His friend had already left, and I didn't have a car, so he just took off walking down the road toward Jimmy's. It's not that far, and I know for a fact he'd walked over there before, looking for Vanda, or picking up the car when she left

256

it behind."

"Are you sure he hadn't been in his house yet?"

"About as sure as I can be. It was only a few seconds after I heard the car pull up that he knocked on the door, and like I said, he still had his work clothes on. And I watched him walk away until I couldn't see him anymore. I didn't know whether to follow him, but then I finally decided it wasn't any of my business."

"How did you find out about the fire?"

"Well, after Isaac left I went in the kitchen to get some snacks for watching my program. I hadn't any more than got the TV on when the phone rang. It was one of my cousins. Her daddy had a police scanner, and she said they just heard that Jimmy's was on fire and it was burning to the ground. Well, I just had to get over there and see if Noel was all right, so I made my cousin come get me."

"How long did that take?" I asked.

"Not long. She lived close by, probably not even half a mile away. When we got over there, it was crazy. I've never seen anything like it in my life. It was so hot. I didn't expect it to be so hot so far away from the fire. And there were people everywhere, crying and carrying on, trying to make sure everybody got out okay. The fire truck was there, and a few cop cars, and they couldn't get people to stay back far enough. People were just too scared. They didn't have any sense."

"Did you ever find Noel or Isaac?"

"I saw Isaac leaving. I ran over to see if he found Noel, but I never did get to speak with him. When I got there, another cop had just pulled in and got out of his car, and he yelled at Isaac, asking if he'd give a statement yet. Isaac just ignored him and kept walking, and obviously the cop had more important things to do than go running after Isaac."

"What about Noel?"

"Well, here I am, I still don't know if Noel's all right or not, and I wasn't about to chase the man either. But I did find Noel pretty quick. Miss Linton, she went to the same church, she had Noel. Isaac had asked if she would keep Noel for overnight, and he'd come by in the morning with her clothes and school books. Once I saw Noel was okay, I got my cousin and we left."

"When Isaac left, was he walking or did he get a ride?"

"Somebody might have picked him up later, but when he left he was walking. It's funny though, because his car must have been at Jimmy's the whole time. I came by a couple of days later, and their car was still there. I went to get the keys to pick it up in case he needed it when he got out of jail—lord, I forgot the two things happened so close together."

"Yes. Actually, Vanda was murdered that same night, the night of the fire."

"Are you sure?" She suddenly looked old and confused, like her brain had shut down without her permission.

"Yes, I'm sure. I know you talked to the police about Isaac and Vanda, right? Do you remember that?"

"The police? Yes, yes I remember. They asked me about their fights."

"Did they ever ask you about what happened on that night? The night of the fire and the night Vanda was killed?"

"They must have. I mean, I'm sure they did. They came out a few times."

Here her mind began to clear. "That detective, the white guy with the funny name, I remember he looked me up and down every time he came by, and that was at least twice. And I'm sure I spoke to somebody else too. But in my mind, the fire and Vanda's murder aren't connected. I don't understand it, but I really don't think they asked me about that night, not about seeing Isaac and the fire."

The wheels were turning, but I think her mind was trying to protect her from what she wasn't ready for. I certainly didn't want to push it. She didn't deserve the guilt.

"Don't worry about it, Miss Johnson. You can only answer the questions the cops ask you, and if you hadn't answered their questions they would have come back and asked again. Obviously they were satisfied, and so am I."

I rose to leave. "Thanks for all your help, Miss Johnson. I can't guarantee I won't be bugging you again, but I probably won't."

"Well, that's okay. I'm a busy woman, but I believe in doing my civic duty, unlike most people nowadays. I hope you don't mind me asking, but what happened to you? I know you didn't have that contraption on your arm and those bruises the last time you came out to see me. You didn't have a run-in with some of those street punks, did you?"

"No, ma'am, I didn't. I, uh, I actually fell off the back of a pick-up."

I should get credit for a partial truth on that one. Besides the last thing Miss Johnson needed was another bunch of boogey men to worry about. She made sympathetic clucking sounds.

"Unh-unh, well that is a shame, but let me tell you, you were lucky. It just scares me to death every time I see somebody with kids riding in the back of the pick-up, just waiting to fly off and eat the pavement. That's so irresponsible, it ought to be illegal."

"Oh, I hear you. It's the same thing with dogs. You see people all the time with their dogs running back and forth in the pick-up bed, from one side to the other, leaning over the side. I'm always afraid they're going to fly out and land on the hood of my car every time one of those pick-ups goes around a turn."

Obviously Miss Johnson was not a big dog fan. She'd lost her momentary sympathy for me and was now looking at me like I was a circus freak. That's what happens when I break my own Number 1 Rule of Investigation—just nod your head a lot and make listening sounds when appropriate. Any time you make a contribution of your own to the conversation, you risk getting the circus freak look, or worse yet, pissing off an important and/or armed witness. Perhaps it was the thought of armed witnesses that made me remember the bulge in my purse.

"Oh, Miss Johnson, I almost forgot," I said, handing her the bodice-ripping paperback I'd bought the night I was attacked. "I thought maybe you hadn't read this one."

Her eyes lit up, all talk of dogs forgiven. She thanked me and hurried me out the door. I stood on her stoop and listened to the clicks and metallic grinding slides. I didn't count them, but in her eagerness to crack the cover I think she may have missed a few locks.

CHAPTER THIRTY-TWO

I was feeling pretty worn out when I left Miss Johnson's, so I headed back downtown to my motel to indulge in a nap. My brain needed to be in top form when I briefed Mike and Richard in the afternoon. It's likely Richard would have some resistance to what I had to tell them, and I wanted to make sure I was able to logically counter every argument. I left a message at the PD's office that he and Mike could reach me at my room.

While no longer so painful, disrobing was awkward, so I settled for removing my shoes and lying on top of the sheets. I was wearing thin-soled, hemp pseudo-Mary Janes, the closest thing to slippers I could find that I could still wear in public. I felt like a hippie Ninja. There was very little cushioning between the soles of my feet and the ground, but there was also good air circulation and very little to irritate the itching, healing skin. I resisted the urge to scratch and instead rubbed aloe vera on my feet. The combination of burning and cooling sensations was intensely satisfying.

When the knocking at my door woke me later, I saw that my unconscious mind had been disobedient, rubbing my itchy feet against the bed in my sleep. It was pretty obvious; my feet were still moving and they had a slightly fiery feeling. I didn't rub them on the carpet as I walked to the door, but I did indulge in very heavy steps. The door swung wide when I opened it and I left it that way, not bothering to wait for Mike and Richard to enter.

"Did you even look to see who it was?" Richard asked.

261

In fact, I hadn't thought to check the peephole. My one good hand tried to rub the sleep from my eyes but only succeeded in making them more difficult to open.

"Didn't have to. I could feel your pissy vibes through the door." Grin from Mike, more pissy vibes from Richard.

Mike pulled a folder from his bag and placed it on the spare bed that was looking like a desk. "I come bearing gifts, not pissy vibes."

"What's that?" Richard asked.

"A report on vehicles operated by Isaac and Vanda Thomas at the time of her death. It turns out they only had—"

"One car," I interrupted. Mike gave me the sad puppy face and I flipped open the folder to glance through it. "I know, but I didn't have the make and model and license plate. Thank you."

I picked up my recently amended report binder, scanned a few pages from a scene report, and nodded. "Got it," I said, and set the binder back on my bed.

They both seemed to be waiting for me to say something, so I obliged. "Okay, guys, what's the plan?"

"Why don't we start with the two of you telling me what you've been up to?" Richard said.

Still pissy vibes, and possibly innuendo. Mike looked distressed at the animosity, but I was still too sleep-groggy to care.

"Hey, don't look at me. She just asked me to look up that one thing, and she wouldn't even tell me why. I don't know what she's up to either."

"Gee, thanks, Mike. Remind me to call you whenever I want to be thrown under a bus." I tried to run my fingers through my hair, but they caught in knots.

"Look, just give me a couple of minutes. I wasn't expecting company. Or wakefulness."

I started some caffeinated coffee in the little coffee maker, then washed my face and tried to do something with my hair. It was starting to look like a scarf day. Once the baby pot stopped popping and burbling and I had a heavily sweetened cup of nectar, I felt ready to deal with Mike and Richard. They were watching a news channel on TV but turned it off when I joined them.

"There's coffee in the pot." Of course they'd heard and smelled it, but like good little guests who'd barged in on their hostess unannounced, they waited until I'd offered to pounce on my meager effort at hospitality.

"Okay, this will probably make more sense later, but I'll start with the car. I called Mike last night after you guys left because I got a little bug in my brain about Isaac and Vanda's car, or cars. I didn't know for sure then how many they had. I was trying to figure out their movements on the night she was killed. It's that simple."

I took a deep breath. "The rest of it isn't so simple, so just hear me out."

"You don't think Isaac killed her," Mike said.

Okay, he owed me a couple, but my jaw still dropped. "How did you know?"

"Because I don't think he did either."

We both looked at Richard. "Let me guess. You think that because I helped screw up the case and get him sent to prison, I don't want to think he's innocent. And don't start—I did help screw it up, but this isn't about blame. It's about finding the truth. Sydney, the first time we met, I told you I had doubts about his guilt. That hasn't changed. So tell us what you've got."

Could it be that simple? Probably not, not deep down, but I was too tired to worry about deep down right now. With that in the open and the deep down stuff still deep down, the tension was gone. We felt like a team again. I grinned in giddy relief. I told them

Miss Johnson's story, that Vanda had picked up Noel from her house unexpectedly and Isaac showed up later looking for Noel.

"I think Vanda had the car, and she drove herself and Noel to Jimmy's."

"Wait," Mike said. He rummaged in his bag again, then whipped out a flat object with a flourish. It was a small whiteboard, about 12" x 18." "I know it's not your monster board, but I snagged it from the office anyway. Thought it might come in handy."

"Perfect," I said, and starting writing out the timeline as I spoke.

"Okay, Vanda picks up Noel in the car at about 8:30 or 9:00, and they go to Jimmy's. At some point, X, Vanda leaves Noel there at Jimmy's. It seems likely she went home, but she didn't drive. Someone had to give her a ride. The report from the fire at Jimmy's lists her car—their car—as one of the cars sitting in the parking lot at the scene. Plus Miss Johnson says she got the keys and went to pick up the car at Jimmy's a couple of days later."

"At 10 o'clock, a buddy drops Isaac off and he goes straight to Miss Johnson's to get Noel. When he finds out she's not there, that Vanda took her, he starts walking to Jimmy's to find them. I don't know how long it would take to walk it, but we can check. Right now let's assume 10 minutes. At 10:06, the call comes in on the fire, and the fire department is on the scene at 10:15. Let's say Isaac gets there around 10:10. The fire is blazing, he's running around looking for Noel and Vanda."

As I turned from the board to look at Richard and Mike, a smear of blue caught my eye. Somehow the side of my hand was already blue from the whiteboard marker. It's a gift. I ignored it and went on.

"Miss Johnson finds out about the fire and her cousin drives her to the scene. The first cops arrive at 10:25, and cops continue to arrive. When Miss Johnson sees Isaac, a cop that just arrived is trying to speak to him, so let's just say it's 10:28. At this point, Isaac knows Noel is okay and has already made arrangements for her to stay with someone else for the rest of the night. He's pissed at Vanda—not only did she take their little girl to Jimmy's, but she left her there alone, and Noel could have been killed in the fire. It's going to be ugly when he finds her, maybe he's going to kick her out for good this time, so he has Noel stay with a friend."

"Isaac isn't thinking, or he just assumes Vanda took the car. Miss Johnson sees him walking home. Maybe he walks fast because he's pissed, maybe slower so he can calm down. Let's just stick with the same 10 minutes for now. That puts him at home at 10:38 PM. He's leaving when Rudy and the Sarge show up at 10:45. That only gives Isaac seven minutes to argue with his wife, hit her a couple of times, and strangle her before the cops arrive to find a body that I suspect was not that freshly dead."

Mike chimed in. "Don't forget the soot spots on her neck. According to the State's theory, he had to have killed her before he went to the fire or the rest of her neck would have been dirty. He kills her, goes to the fire, she hasn't revived when he returns so he check her vitals and puts the spots there. Is it possible that he killed her before he went to Miss Johnson's?"

"It is possible," I admitted. "Not likely, but possible. She says she heard the car pull up and he knocked on her door shortly after. She could have heard a different car, making the timing a coincidence. When she goes out to speak with him at 10 o'clock, the lights in the Thomas house are out. Whether Isaac killed her or not, by that time Vanda is already lying dead in the house. I didn't think to ask Miss Johnson if she heard another car earlier. If Vanda took someone home with her, he had to park somewhere."

This time Richard spoke. "So if Isaac were going to trial today, with a decent lawyer and a good jury, we might have enough for a not guilty verdict. But now, over 20 years after he's pled guilty and almost two years after his death, we don't have enough to prove him innocent. There's only one thing to do."

Richard looked at each of us in turn to see if we were with him. "We have to find the real killer."

Richard let his words sink in before saying he had some information for us as well. He'd gotten a couple of phone calls at work. In the morning, ASA Jim Gilbert had called. The idea of Gilbert calling when they were in the same building struck me as funny and emblematic of our lazy 21st century. That is, until I heard what he'd had to say.

"This is one those conversations that, after you've had them, never happened. Jim didn't even call me on the office phone; he called my cell phone. He's been concerned about the missing notes from the Thomas file. He hasn't figured it out yet, but he has some disturbing leads. He wants to meet with me tomorrow, me and me alone. We have lunch together a few times a month, so no one will think it's unusual."

"Why is he so paranoid?" I asked.

"I don't know, and I don't know what he's found out. He sort of hinted around that there may be additional records related to Isaac Thomas that could not yet legally be disclosed. And before you ask why, he didn't say."

"An active investigation," Mike said. I looked at him blankly. My experience with Chapter 119, the public records disclosure law in Florida, was limited. I knew that agencies were supposed to provide public records to the person requesting them, including records relating to criminal investigations, unless the agency could claim that an exemption applied. Those exemptions were set out in the statute. Mike clarified his statement right about the time I reached the end of my own logical deductions.

"There are probably dozens of exemptions from disclosure. That's one of them. Records relating to an active, ongoing investigation cannot be turned over because of the danger of compromising the investigation."

"Remember," I said, "someone did get Isaac transferred to Latham for a medical visit he apparently didn't need, just a few weeks before his suicide. That transfer could have been related to the investigation. The question is, what's the investigation?"

We brainstormed for a while, but we kept coming back to Vanda's murder. Someone from the State could have figured out Isaac was innocent. It may sound cynical (I prefer well-informed) but the three of us had been around long enough to know that, like most states, Florida does not correct its own mistakes. The State would never have initiated an investigation to exonerate Isaac. There would have to be something more, perhaps another murder. It would have to be something sufficiently similar for someone to make the connection to Vanda's murder and start wondering if the man who killed her was still out there killing more people.

"Seems like a long shot," I said.

"Yes," Richard agreed, "but right now it's the only thing we've got."

"We're forgetting something," Mike had obviously had his caffeine ration for the day because he was thinking circles around me. "What about Sydney's stinky attacker?"

"Maybe he's Vanda's killer," I volunteered.

Mike was skeptical. "Him and all of his buddies? It seems unlikely that Sydney's investigation of the 24-year-old murder of— forgive me—a crack whore would motivate half a dozen men to dress in black, kidnap Sydney and beat the crap out of her."

"Unlikely and ill-advised," Richard added. "All they've done is make her, and us, more determined to figure out what it is they're trying to hide. But your point is well-taken, Mike. We're missing a connection here."

We were spinning our wheels with the speculation so we moved on to Richard's afternoon caller, Rudy Nagroski. "He kept copies of all his case notes, and he's been going back through them, trying to find something to help us. I think he's trying to figure out how they could have missed the fire connection. Of course, he doesn't even know what Claire Johnson told Sydney today, but he can still put two and two together. He knows there's a good chance he helped put an innocent man in prison."

Richard turned to me. "Have you spoken to Noel about this stuff?"

"No," I said. I hadn't told Mike and Richard about our fight Monday, so I filled them in. "Quickest reconciliation and subsequent break-up in the history of, well, my life anyway. Today at lunch I left a message for her at her house, but I haven't heard back from her. I tried to let her know how important it was, told her we needed to talk to her about what happened the night her mother died, but I don't know if she'll call me. Richard, maybe she'd talk to you."

He nodded his head. "I'll get the numbers from you. It can't hurt to try."

"I don't know if I ever told you this, but Noel originally hired me, as she said, to find out why her father waited so long to commit suicide. I wanted to reconstruct the last months of his life to see if I could find some insight there, but we've sort of gotten distracted by Vanda's murder. I may follow up on that end some tomorrow, head over to WFC to make sure they didn't find any more records for me. There's also a woman guard that I'm trying to get to talk to me. She's pretty rabbitty, but it could be something totally unrelated to Isaac. Personal problems. Who knows?"

Richard liked that plan. "I think it's a good idea if you don't follow up on Vanda's murder until I've had a chance to talk to Jim tomorrow about this phantom investigation. We don't need you—" He stopped, looked briefly at me, then at Mike.

"Was that too patronizing?" he asked one of us, I wasn't sure which one.

"How patronizing is too patronizing?" I asked. I got a flicker of a smile, but Richard wasn't about to be side-tracked.

"You're not going to do something stupid just because you think I told you not to, are you?" That one was definitely directed at me.

"No," I said. "No Nancy Drew for me tomorrow. I intend to stay out of trouble. Better annoyed than dead, and all that stuff."

I really meant it. I did, but what's that aphorism about best intentions gone awry? I never was very good at those things.

CHAPTER THIRTY-THREE

We went our separate ways that evening. Well, I didn't actually go anywhere except around the corner for some magazines and candy bars. I had pizza delivered to my room and spent the evening hours vegging, falling asleep early to the sounds of a cooking show. There's nothing like a cooking show to lull a confirmed non-cooker to sleep, unless of course it's one of those cooking shows where the chef makes up for the impossibility of achieving his recipe by overwhelming you with his loud and eccentric charm.

I didn't set an alarm, just let myself wake up when I woke up, which turned out to be when the phone rang at 9:30 AM. It was Mike.

"Richard wanted me to give you call. He tried Noel's home number last night and this morning and couldn't reach her either. He said the beep on her answering machine was really long, so I looked up her work number—don't ask, it was a good use of taxpayer money. Her boss said she hasn't been at work all week. She came in Monday and said she was taking some personal time and they haven't heard from her since. They're a little worried. Apparently she's never taken this much time off before."

"Sounds like Noel. I'll drive over to her grandmother's and see if she's there."

The thought of seeing Grandma Harrison was enough to send me back to bed, but I persevered. As a reward for my diligence and professionalism in the face of adversity, I had some of my pizza for breakfast before heading out the door. (It was veggie; only a college freshman can eat pepperoni for breakfast.)

Shockingly, Mrs. Harrison was even less happy to see me than I her. In her words, "I thought I made it clear to you the last time you were here that you are not welcome in my home or on my property. You will never be welcome here. Now get out!"

The same daughter, Ginny, had greeted me and let me in. Bet she was in for a tongue-lashing, or maybe not. Maybe chewing me out made the old broad's day. Ginny had immediately made herself scarce (this time not even bothering with the bogus offer of drinks), but Mrs. Harrison's yells brought another younger woman from the back of the house to see the commotion. She looked a lot like Noel, but slightly older. I could imagine Noel facing her grandmother down. This woman looked like she wanted to do the same, but was afraid of looking at Mrs. Harrison directly.

"Mrs. Harrison, I just came by to see if Noel was here or if you've heard from her recently," I said in my very best 'don't bite me, crazy dog, I swear I'm not a burglar' voice.

"Don't you even presume to speak my granddaughter's name in this house. This is all your fault, you and your scam. You don't fool me. You're not really an investigator. You're just some sort of pervert who gets paid to nose into other people's lives and stir up trouble."

She rose, and I looked quickly around the room to make sure she didn't have a shotgun within reach. I saw the younger woman do the same assessment before stepping forward.

"It's okay, nana, I'll take care of it. Don't exert yourself."

She took me by the arm and led me from the house. Mrs. Harrison's loud insults followed me as far as my car, where the woman finally introduced herself.

"I'm Noel's cousin, Sarah. She's not here, and she hasn't been here since Monday. I'm worried about her. Can you meet me at the Pancake House out on the main road, say in about 15 minutes? I have something for you."

I agreed, and 15 minutes later we were seated in a booth with cups of coffee that Sarah had recommended. "The water here tastes pretty bad, and the tea's not strong enough to hide the flavor, but the coffee's okay with lots of milk and sugar."

"So you're Noel's cousin?" I asked, after heavily doctoring my coffee.

"Yes. Nana Harrison—she hates when I call her that, but I don't have the strength to really stand up against her, so I have to go the passive-aggressive route. Nana Harrison had three daughters: Viola, Virginia (Ginny), and Vanda. I don't know what she ate during pregnancy that made her psychotic with the V's. My mother was Viola. She died of cancer several years ago. She was diagnosed with cervical cancer within a few months after Aunt Vanda was killed. Noel had been staying with us, but Nana used that as an excuse to take her away from us."

"Why?"

"You have met my grandmother, haven't you?"

I grinned. "I gotcha. So Mrs. Harrison takes Noel because she's on her usual power trip."

"That, and Vanda was always her favorite. It wasn't just that she wanted Vanda's child, she wanted to mold Vanda's child, or at least her memories of her mother. She wanted Noel to see Vanda as she did—perfect."

"And she wasn't?"

"Far from it. I'm three years older than Noel, so I remember some of the stories they used to tell about Vanda. Let me put it this way, the stories they told after she died weren't anything like the stories they told about her while she was still alive. Of course, even

273

when she was alive, they had to tell them behind Nana's back."

"But you never really knew her, or her husband?"

"I think I met Isaac a couple of times, and Vanda a few more. All I personally remember is that she was a gorgeous woman, with a diva attitude to match. There was one time, not long before Vanda was killed, that she came to visit with Nana for a couple of weeks, but they kept all the kids away from her. Nana said she was staying there because her husband beat her, but mom said that was bullshit, that he sent her there to dry out."

"So your mom gets diagnosed with cancer, and Mrs. Harrison decides that with your mother's condition, it's best for the family if Noel leaves your home and moves in with her. Then what happens?"

Sarah smiled. "You've got her pegged all right. Well, mom and Nana fought all the time after Vanda was killed. Mom thought Noel should see her father, even if he had killed her mother, and of course Nana would have none of that. Mom also didn't appreciate the revisionist history of Vanda. She said she loved her sister, but Vanda was no saint, and Noel shouldn't be brought up to think she was. Mom was a fighter, and she battled the cancer off and on for a couple of years until she went into a real remission. It took a lot out of her though, and she was never the same. She just didn't have the energy to fight with Nana any more."

"How long was she in remission?"

"Eighteen months. Then it came back, and she was dead within a year."

"I'm sorry."

Sarah nodded her head. "It was hard for her. Toward the end, she felt a lot of regret over Noel, that she hadn't done enough or told her enough. When she knew she was dying, mom tried to see Noel, but Nana did a good job of keeping them apart. Mom died in the summer, and I think Nana had sent Noel away to some kind of Baptist bible camp."

The echoes with my own life hit me in the gut like one of stinky guy's punches. My throat started to burn and I thought I'd throw up my coffee.

"Are you all right?"

I took a deep breath and tried to shake off 18 years of anger. "Yeah. Sorry, something just didn't sit right with me for a minute. Do you know what your mother wanted to tell Noel?"

"No. I wish I did. But she had a box of letters from Vanda, and she asked me to give them to Noel. I don't think Nana knew they kept in touch over the years. She was furious when she found out. Somehow she got her hands on them and burned the whole box."

Sarah reached in her purse and pulled out a slightly discolored envelope. "Except this one. I found it in my mother's belongings, and I've been holding on to it ever since. I was pretty messed up after my mother died. I put this away and never got around to giving it to Noel. I forgot all about it until Noel told us about you, about what she was doing. I guess I've been waiting for the right time."

Sarah handed the envelope to me. "Noel came by Monday afternoon, absolutely furious. I don't know what they were arguing about, but she and Nana were screaming at each other. It's the first time I'd ever heard Noel raise her voice. They must have gone at it for about 15 minutes, and then Noel took off. She didn't say where she was going, and we haven't heard from her since. Nana sent Ginny to Noel's work and her home, but nobody seems to know anything."

"I haven't been able to track her down either," I said. "I'm afraid this is my fault. I told her some things about her mother and father that I'd found out, probably the kinds of things your mother

275

would have told her if she's had the chance. But I'm not family, and I didn't do it as tactfully as I should have. To make things worse, I wasn't straight with her about some other things."

I looked up quickly. I didn't see the familiar distrust or even disapproval in Sarah's eyes, but I heard myself babbling anyway. "It's nothing about your family. And it's not like I was trying to lie to Noel in particular. It was just personal stuff that apparently I lie to everybody about. It's involuntary, like breathing. I tried to explain. I don't think she trusts me anymore, and now she probably doesn't know who to trust."

Sarah smiled and squeezed my hand impulsively. "Oh, I think she does, or she will. Don't worry. She'll come around."

We left a couple of dollars in the booth and walked out to our cars together. I thanked her and said I'd let her know if I heard from Noel, and she promised to do the same.

"Sydney, you need to read the letter. In all those years, I only read it once. Maybe I was afraid I'd wear it out, folding and refolding it, or maybe it just stuck with me. Well, I know it stuck with me." She started to get in her car, then reiterated her thought. "I think it's really important that you read the letter."

I had one last question for Sarah as well, one that I'd tried to repress because it had nothing to do with the investigation, but I had to ask.

"Sarah, why do you stay?" She didn't seem offended, and she didn't need me to elaborate.

"I almost didn't, right after my mom died, especially when she burned those letters. I was so angry, and I did leave for a while. Like I said, I went a little crazy. And then I got that out of my system and came back. It's like egg-laying turtles or spawning salmon. I can't explain it any better than that. I had to come back here. I didn't have a choice. She's family."

I tried deep breathing when I left the Pancake House, sort of driving meditation. I was so sick of family secrets, of high-handed, self-righteous people who justified lying to their children and grandchildren because it was in the children's best interest. In actuality, it was nothing more than a power trip, a means to control the future by re-writing the past, a way to avoid answering difficult questions about decisions their egos would never admit had been wrong. My deep breathing kept going shallow and quick, so instead I drove too fast and listened to some of Mike's obnoxious music way too loud. I'm sure that didn't help in a healthy way, but it did help. In a scratch your poison ivy, pick at your scab, wallow in your resentment sort of way. I'd take it.

I'd calmed down and turned the music down by the time I saw the signs for WFC. I parked Mike's Jeep and sat in silence in the heat, looking at the envelope on the seat next to me. Well, shit, I thought, rolled down the window and pulled out the letter. For some reason I'd expected the handwriting to be perfectly vertical and plump, maybe with faces or things written in the margin. Instead, it was nicely proportioned with the proper right slant, the kind of handwriting they show you on flash cards in the second grade. One illusion shattered; what was next? I scooted the seat back a bit for comfort and began reading.

June 11, 1979

Hey Sis!

How's it going in good old Hainey? Exciting as usual, I'm sure. Has the old bitch driven you crazy yet, telling you all the many ways you're not perfect like me? That's okay, you and I know better, and I think somewhere deep down she does too. Right now her perfect daughter is going through all the motions, pretending to listen to her loving husband and beautiful daughter, cooking meals and cleaning house, when all she can think about is getting high. Don't worry, I'm still hanging in there, but it's so hard, Vi. It's so very hard. I wish I had your strength, or at least had you here to knock some sense into me. You're the one person I can never lie to. There's no point – you always see through me in a second.

How's your Sarah? Not so small anymore I guess. Hard to believe she must be bigger than Noel. Noel is my little grown-up, my little genius. She's so smart and so pretty, sometimes I can't believe she came from me. I wish she and Sarah could grow up together. I worry that she doesn't have that same sense of family you and I grew up with. Yes, the old bitch drove us crazy, and Ginny was always tattling to her, but we had each other. Us against the world. I think Isaac would agree to come back if I asked him to, if I told him how much I need to, but I can't face Momma, and I don't want her getting her claws into Noel.

Sometimes I think they'd be better off without me, Isaac and Noel. They could go live with his family. His mother's a stuck-up old biddy, but I know she'd welcome them with open arms, and his sister's okay. (She was at my wedding, the one you were too pissed off to come to. Sorry – my Harrison guilting must be kicking in.) Vi, I'm just afraid I won't be able to hold it together much longer, and I don't know what I'll do. Maybe that's why little Joshua didn't make it, because I'm going to screw up bad and he's better off not being here when I do. I know, this is where you smack me. I miss you so much, honey. I hope I get to see you again.

In the meantime, don't let the bitch get you down. Remember, deep down she really does love us. She's just too hateful to show it.

Love you always,
Vanda

She had written on 3-hole lined notebook paper, the kind you get in packs of 200. In some places she'd paused too long on a letter, and the ink from her pen had made little round spots. Holding the slightly yellowed paper in my hand, seeing the words of a dead woman on the page made my breath catch. I got that familiar feeling that comes over me once in a while, that it's all just so sad. The world is full of so much suffering, so many people who just keep shuffling on through it. I leaned forward to rest my head against the steering wheel, overwhelmed.

I was used to my own car, my own steering wheel with an air bag, not Mike's steering wheel, which apparently didn't have one. (Let's tuck that away for future reference.) Maybe I rested my head a little too hard. As soon as it touched the steering wheel, the car's horn went off. I jerked so hard I felt a twinge in my back, and a man walking by in a suit gave me a dirty look. I stuck my tongue out at him, and his look of outraged shock made me feel better. At least it had slapped me out of my malaise, mostly. I still had a slightly foggy feeling, an emotional hangover.

I like to think that hangover, not just simple stupidity, was to blame for what I did next. Whichever, the result was the same. As my grandmother would say, I sure did set a helluva shitstorm in motion.

CHAPTER THIRTY-FOUR

I checked at the front desk for records because I said I would. I didn't expect them to have anything, and I wasn't disappointed. The real reason I'd come was to see Sue Ellen. I had downplayed what she had to offer to get Richard off my back, but I had high hopes. My timing was perfect—lunch time once again, so I headed over to the cafeteria.

Stepping inside the administration building at WFC, a hallway stretched before me. It was lined by bulletin boards and a few closed doors on the right, the glass wall and doors of the cafeteria to the left. Two of the cafeteria's three interior walls were made of glass, framed but otherwise completely translucent. As you reached the end of the hallway and turned left, the cafeteria's other glass wall remained to your left, and there was a small seating area with boxy vinyl furniture and dusty plastic plants to the right. All traffic to the ladies room from the building entrance or the cafeteria had to pass that seating area. I picked up a newspaper and settled in to wait.

I was counting on Sue Ellen to be one of those people who doesn't take a bathroom break near the end of her shift, but instead waits and does it on her own time right before lunch. Either that, or she could be fastidious enough to wash up before eating, all but a lost art in our culture. She'd been so freaked out before, I didn't want to approach her in the cafeteria if I could help it. From here I could see into the cafeteria as well, but wasn't all that visible to the people concentrating on their Salisbury steak, so I didn't think I had to worry about losing her.

I'd read all about the upcoming livestock show and the latest plans to populate the Panhandle beaches to within an inch of their lives when I saw Sue Ellen approaching. Good girl—she headed to the restroom and I followed. I waited in the outer lounge area for her to conclude her business. The sound of running water heralded her imminent appearance, and in a moment the door swung open.

"Hello, Sue Ellen." The poor thing was so startled I almost felt bad for lying in wait. Almost.

"Oh, hi. Listen, I don't have time to talk right now. I have to get back out to the—"

"How did you know Isaac's daughter is named Noel?"

"I don't know what you're talking about." She began a frightened stutter, and I felt as though I could hear her heart pounding from where I sat.

"I d-, I d-don't know anything about Isaac, and I have to go."

Her fear fed my own adrenaline and cleared the fog from my brain, facilitating a logical leap I should have made earlier. "I think you do know about Isaac. In fact, I think you sent a newspaper clipping to Noel, a clipping about her father."

That's when Sue Ellen bolted. I jumped up, a little too quickly, to block her exit. I still had head rushes and lost my vision when standing up and sitting down.

"Did you hear about my little adventure, Sue Ellen?" I lifted my left sleeve and the back of my shirt, and the hem of my long skirt up to one thigh to show her some of more persistent evidence.

"Someone doesn't want me asking questions about Isaac. I'm being hunted, and the next time these people catch up with me, I might not be so lucky. I need to know what's going on, and Noel needs to know the truth about her father."

My little pep talk had the opposite of my intended consequence. Sue Ellen panicked. With the element of surprise and my nagging injuries, she was able to knock me out of the way with her petite frame. She ran out of the room and down the hall, past the cafeteria and toward the exit. My feet still weren't up for running, but I hobbled quickly in my hippie Ninja shoes. Sue Ellen slipped through a group of people who'd just finished eating outside the cafeteria and I lost her.

I scooted to the entrance, scanning outside and inside, trying to see if she'd re-entered some secure area I couldn't talk my way into without an appointment. Maybe Charley could help me. Stretching on tip-toes, I finally saw him outside, caught up in the crowd of people entering and exiting the building for lunch. I called to him and waved, and he motioned that he'd be right over.

I stood off to the side of the door, out of the way of traffic, while I waited. Still scanning the crowd and nearby areas for Sue Ellen, I didn't pay attention to anyone in particular until I heard a nasty raucous belch. All heads turned toward the culprit. It was Charley's nemesis from the Handi-Way and the cafeteria. The man next to him made a disgusted face.

"Goddamn, Deacon. That's just gross. It's not like you don't stink enough already. You ain't never heard of deodorant?"

And it was that simple. By that time, Charley had made his way to me and was saying something, but I couldn't hear him. I walked over to the man they'd called Deacon, gauged his size, and sniffed him.

"What are you, in rut or something?" He turned to the man who'd just insulted him and said with a nervous laugh, "This bitch is crazy."

I'd smelled enough. "Deacon—is that what they call you? I'll bet you hunt a lot, but do you ever watch the Discovery Channel?

National Geographic? That kind of thing?"

"What the hell are you talking about?" His buddy was starting to wonder too.

"Nah, you probably don't. In fact, I'll bet you couldn't tell a leopard from a zebra if your life depended on it."

He looked confused at first, then his tiny little pea brain finally made the leap. His face flushed red, and I thought he was going to have a coronary episode. I should be so lucky. The flush highlighted what I'd originally taken for a bit of acne at the side of his nose. I pointed to the corresponding area on my own nose.

"Glad to see the scratches healed. I'd hate for an infection to make your nasty face even uglier."

"Fuck you, bitch."

Deacon's right hand moved, and I thought I heard a snapping, shuffling sound. I'll be the first to admit that I'm not one of those movie investigators who identify guns with ease, by sight of the gun or cartridge, by the sound or the hole it's made in flesh. Nope, not me. Rifle or pistol. That's about where my expertise ends. Let me just say that I found myself with what technically looked to me like a big-ass gun, pointing right at my chest.

CHAPTER THIRTY-FIVE

My life didn't flash before my eyes. All I could see was the gun. No past, no future. It was hard to look away from the dull metal, even for a moment. I had this irrational fear (if any gun fear can be irrational) that it would strike of its own accord, like a snake, if I took my eyes from it. Still, my gaze was drawn to Deacon from time to time. I have on occasion inspired true loathing in a person or two or a few, so I've learned to recognize it. I got a good enough look at Deacon's face to see how much he loathed me, that he really wanted to kill me, and he was going to. Even surrounded by all those nice, credible law enforcement-type witnesses, Deacon was going to kill me. Consequences be damned. And he was going to enjoy every moment.

My peripheral vision was gone. The world shrank down to me, Deacon and The Gun. No one else existed, and somehow I knew that was true for Deacon as well. The look in his eyes reminded me of the clearing, when he'd forgotten the presence of everyone else, intent on doing things to me I didn't want to thank about. He was envisioning dark things again, and this time he was about to realize them.

The one thing Deacon and I hadn't counted on was Charley. Good old Charley. I love that kid. While Deacon was busy staring me down and wondering what my guts would look like splattered all over the sidewalk, and I was busy being the object of his stare and wondering what my guts would look like spattered all over the sidewalk, Charley had pulled his own weapon.

"Deacon, drop the gun," Charley said.

Fortunately his shouted order didn't startle Deacon as much as it did me or I'd be dead now, victim of a spastic trigger finger. I was so proud of Charley. His voice didn't crack, and he was in a very professional-looking stance, at least to someone who doesn't know how to use a gun. I wondered if it was the first time he'd ever drawn his weapon, and Deacon probably wondered the same thing as he stood, gun still pointed at my chest, assessing the situation. I doubted many of the guards were carrying, and no one else had pulled a weapon yet, or at least no one else was pointing one that I could see. Still, drawn weapons or not, it didn't seem like very good odds for a guy intent on inflicting mayhem, or so I thought at the time.

Deacon must have reached the same conclusion. A buffer of empty space had appeared around him when he pulled his gun, and it moved with him as he slowly backed away from me toward the parking lot.

"Remember what I said before. I'm not done with you yet, not by a long shot. There won't be enough left of you to bury."

Then he was gone, around the corner of the building and out of sight. There was a lot of adrenaline coursing through my veins, but my brain hadn't had time to interpret it as fear, and now the gun was gone. Instead I felt like Superman. I gave Deacon a three-count and ran after him.

The adrenaline must have affected my sense of time or ability to count, because I really would have needed super powers to catch him. The parking lot was full of pick-ups, any one of which could be his, or could be blocking my view of him. By the time I spotted Deacon, he was climbing aboard a truck parked on the end near the exit. He must have spotted me at the same time. A shot rang out, followed by the sound of a shattering car window to my right. I'd believed him when he said he wasn't done with me, so I didn't think he was really trying to hit me, but he could be a lousy shot and accidentally blow my brains out just as fatally as if he'd done it intentionally. Besides, we were in the parking lot of a maximum security prison. Someone could start shooting back.

I crouched down and began moving back up the row of cars toward the administration building. Grassy verges separated the sections of cars. Once the sound of Deacon's engine faded beyond what I theorized was bullet range, I sat down on the grass. Charley was the first person to find me, but I knew the whole area would be swarming with law enforcement officers from various agencies soon.

Charley's face paled when he saw me, the inverse of his usual blush. "Are you all right? Have you been shot?"

"No, no I'm fine. I just felt like it was time to sit down. Join me."

He sat down tentatively. "Are you sure you're okay? You've got a little blood here," he gestured at his right temple, "and sometimes people go into shock and don't know they've been shot."

I got to my knees and scooched over to the nearest car to peek in the side mirror. When I tried to adjust the mirror left-handed, it came off in my hand. "Whoops." I carried it back to the grass with me.

"We'll say Deacon did it," I whispered, while examining my temple. Charley grinned. "It's just a little cut, probably from the flying glass."

There was barely enough room on the verge for me to lie back, upper body on the grass while my legs extended over the pavement. I could hear voices, but as long as we stayed down we wouldn't have to deal with them. If I couldn't see them, they couldn't see me, I reasoned. Charley lay down beside me with a ragged sigh. His head tilted up and down, surveying my healing injuries.

"So what happened to you?"

"I'm pretty sure Deacon did." I told him about the attack in 25 words or less.

"Deacon did that? Daggone. I heard about it, but I didn't make the connection to you."

"Charley, what were you doing wearing a gun? Not that I'm complaining."

"I wasn't working inside today. We had some inmate transfers, and I was an armed escort. Deacon too."

One more mystery solved. Guards inside the prison don't wear sidearms, and I'd wondered how Deacon had his so handy. "If you don't mind me asking, had you ever drawn your gun before?"

"No, ma'am, I hadn't. Not in a real situation, I mean."

"Charley, please, call me Sydney. And thank you for allowing me to be your first." He blushed. "Seriously, thank you. I think he would have pulled the trigger if you hadn't drawn on him. And God knows none of the other guys were lifting a finger to stop him."

"Ma'—I mean, Sydney, I may just be pointing out the obvious here, so feel free to stop me. Didn't you say he had a bunch of guys with him?"

"Probably five, give or take."

"Well, didn't you ever wonder who those other guys were?"

Now I felt the fear I hadn't felt staring at Deacon's gun. How could I have been so stupid? I'd thought the odds were against Deacon a few moments ago, but now I had to wonder. My eyes involuntarily went to Charley's bare arms—no scratch marks. Still, I was lucky I hadn't been "accidentally" shot in the back while Deacon was fleeing. When I could speak again, I asked Charley the question I knew he couldn't answer, but I had to ask it anyway.

"Charley, do you know why they did it?"

"No, Sydney. I'm sorry to say I don't."

My malignant thoughts were interrupted by the voices of self-important uniformed men. They'd found us. Charley got to his feet, then gently helped me to stand as well. He leaned over to speak softly in my ear so the approaching guards couldn't hear.

"By the way, you're the one who did a good thing, not me." He was taller than I'd realized, as most people are when I stand next to them. He looked down at me, pink-faced and grinning. "Thanks to you, that asshole will never work here again."

I spent the next two hours being interviewed by a succession of LEOs. After a while I stopped trying to remember their names or who they worked for and encouraged them to skip the introductions. No vigilante, game-playing P.I. persona for me. I told them everything I knew, which was precious little. I didn't know the man, but he and some buddies had attacked me, and when I figured it out and confronted him (not the wisest move on my part, they all confirmed) he pulled his gun and took off. Why does such a short story take so long to tell?

Charley came over to say goodbye before resuming his duties. I gave him a couple of my business cards, adding Mike's and Richard's cell phones to the backs as well, and asked him to give one to Sue Ellen if he saw her. He said he'd get her to speak with me if he could find her. I knew that he would.

I'd left my own cell phone in the Jeep, and when I checked it I saw that I'd missed 11 calls in the last couple of hours. Every number was associated with Mike or Richard. I picked one at random and hit redial. It was Mike's, and when he answered I heard him call out to someone, presumably Richard, that it was me on the phone.

"Syd, where the hell have you been? We've been looking all over for you."

"I'm still at WFC. There was a little… incident over here."

"Yeah, we heard, but they wouldn't tell us if anyone had been injured or arrested, and we thought they would have released you by now."

"I haven't been injured or arrested, and they just said I could go, so I'd like to get out of here before they change their minds. I haven't had lunch yet, and I'm absolutely starving. Where do you want to meet?"

He named the place, a little burger joint with a shaded area outside for eating. I'd made a healthy dent in my cheeseburger and fries before anyone else arrived. Richard was next. When I saw him approaching, I waved him down and asked him to watch my stuff, leaving before he could reply. Surviving such a shitty morning was cause for a chocolate milkshake.

When I returned with a luscious shake so thick I could barely suck it through the straw, I saw that Mike and Jim Gilbert had arrived. I looked around furtively before sitting, then leaned forward and asked Jim Gilbert, "Are you sure you weren't followed?"

I was in an impish mood.

"Doesn't matter now. You took the cat out of the bag and swung it around the room."

I stared at Jim blankly.

"Sorry," he said. "Bad metaphor. How about this—you fucked up a two-year long corruption investigation."

I shoved down the rest of my burger and dabbed daintily at my mouth with a napkin. "I feel like that's something I would have remembered doing."

"You didn't shoot anybody, did you?" Richard asked.

I was beginning to resent the tone of this interrogation, if not the fact of it. "I don't even own a gun!"

"That's a relief," Richard said.

"You know what? I've had a long day already, and I don't need this shit. Call me a wuss, but being shot at tends to take it out of me. I'm going to go find a quiet place to finish my milkshake," I said, heading toward another table. "And then maybe I'll have another one."

"Wait, Sydney," Richard said. "We're just trying to give you a little taste of what's coming your way."

I sat back down. I hadn't actually been that angry. I think events in my life had been so dramatic lately it was hard not to act the part. "So what's this about me screwing up an investigation? What investigation?"

"No, you first. What'd you do to piss off this guy so much that he shot at you?"

I explained how I'd recognized the malodorous Deacon as one of my kidnappers, opened my big mouth for confirmation, and quickly gotten it.

"What are you, Deputy Dawg, sniffing out crime?" Mike asked.

"I don't recall that he used his nose," I replied. "That would be Buford the bloodhound. Deputy Dawg was known for injuring his tailbone. Now I think it's your turn. What investigation?"

Richard answered. "We always assumed your kidnapping had something to do with Isaac's old case, the murder of his wife Vanda. It appears we were on the wrong track."

Now Jim spoke up. "I did some digging when you asked me about the missing documents from our State Attorney file. I never did find the documents, but I did find out that about two years ago, Isaac Thomas was approached regarding another investigation. At first, I couldn't find out anything except that it wasn't local. Then I made some calls to the state Attorney General's office, and from there I went to the Department of Justice."

"It turns out it wasn't a local investigation for good reason. Some of this my contacts weren't willing to share until after your shoot-out at WFC, but here's how it lays out. A couple of years ago Isaac sent a letter to the State Attorney's Office. He found out that some of the guards were shaking down prisoner's families on their weekend visitation. I don't know how much you know about visitation—"

Probably more than Jim did, but I nodded so he would continue. "Inmates have to submit paperwork ahead of time to get anyone, even a family member, on their visitation list. Once approved, a visitor still has to get prior approval and make an appointment for each visit. Most inmates are allowed contact visits with family members, meaning they can sit together in an outdoor area and have physical contact, a hug, holding hands, whatever within reason. But if an inmate has disciplinary problems, he may lose his visitation rights entirely or be restricted to non-contact visits. Non-contact means he has to visit with his family through a pane of glass, no physical contact whatsoever."

Mike cut in. "This is all set out in the Department of Corrections rules and regulations, with procedures for inmate grievances and appeals, but when it comes down to specific cases, the rules don't mean a lot. I mean, it's obvious who has the power in this situation."

I could tell Jim didn't want to agree with Mike on principle, but also didn't want to get sidetracked. "It's a system that generates a lot of paperwork and vests a lot of discretion in the people implementing it. Some of the guards figured this out. We think it started out small, selling perks. Slip me a few bucks and I'll make sure your son can get special food from the canteen during your visit, or you'll get an extra half hour together. At some point the character of the exchanges changed, became more coercive. Things like, you're not dressed properly for your visit—regardless of what you were wearing—but for the right price I'll overlook it this time. Then it escalated to, if you don't pay me, I'll make sure the visitation yard is full and you'll have to have a non-contact visit. Or I'll lose your paperwork and you won't get a visit at all."

Mike piped in again. "Yeah, after you've borrowed money for gas and driven 300 miles to get here."

"So Isaac found out about these slimy bastards and sent a letter to the State Attorney. Then what?" I asked.

"I haven't seen the letter," Jim said, "but apparently Isaac gave enough credible details that eventually someone in the State Attorney's Office saw that DOJ got the information, and they started their own federal investigation. We're guessing they're the ones who had Isaac transferred to Latham for the interview."

"But they would have needed somebody local to tell them about the medical transfer scam," I pointed out. "And somebody at DOC had to be in on it, to make sure everything went through coming and going even though the paperwork didn't add up."

"Maybe," Jim admitted. "I don't know the details. It does seem likely the guards knew somebody was onto them. The investigation continued for a while after Isaac's death, but it didn't go far because the shakedowns stopped. There weren't any new complaints to investigate. The old victims were hard to track down, and nobody wanted to talk. But we think the guards started up again about six months ago. The feds were close to getting warrants, and they had some stings set up for the end of the month. That is, until you made one of their suspects go postal."

"Glad I could help."

"They'll bitch and moan a lot, but I don't think you've really hurt their investigation. If anything, you've just moved up the timetable. Deacon James is on the run, but we'll pick him up, and they're trying to get warrants on the other major players as we speak."

"Deacon James, huh? For some reason I always thought Deacon was his last name. Any names on the others?"

"No. I practically had to sell my soul to get what I got."

"Well then, you got the better half of the deal. Remember, you're a prosecutor. You don't even have a soul."

Jim gave me a look like he wasn't sure whether to laugh or be pissed. I was glad he finally settled for laughing, and smiled back at him. "Thanks for all your help, Jim. I do appreciate it."

And I was grateful, but I'm also greedy, at least when it comes to information. "What can you tell me about my stinky perv Deacon?"

"Not much. I think the only reason I got his name was because he tried to kill you, which made his involvement in all this pretty conspicuous. I did get the impression that he was the one they really wanted, the one at the top of the list. I don't know if he was the ringleader, or a bigger offender somehow."

"I need his personnel file."

"What?" Jim's goodwill had been replaced by red-faced disbelief.

"Not the original, just a copy."

Jim turned to Richard. "You tried to warn me about her, so I suppose I've only myself to blame. All right, I'll see what I can do."

I had a sudden paranoid thought. "Jim, you may not want to mention my name, or your association with me, when you're talking to the AG's office."

"Why?"

"Well, I said some uncomplimentary things about them a few months ago, and somehow those things sort of made it into print.

They may not have noticed, or maybe they've forgotten by now—"

"That was you?" He opened his mouth. Closed it. Opened it again. Closed it. Then he turned from me to Richard. "You..." he said, pointing.

Richard shrugged. "What can I say? From now on, I'll be more careful in my vetting process."

CHAPTER THIRTY-SIX

I felt sufficiently comforted after only one milkshake, comforted and ready for a nap. I had a lot to think about, but I felt certain I'd do a better job of thinking after sleeping off a little of my food coma. Mike and Richard insisted on following me back to my room, and I suspected they would try to watch me nap. If they did, I'd just have to tell them that watching me sleep was where I drew the line.

I leaned heavily against the elevator on the way up to the third floor, letting its wall support most of my weight. At my door I kept fumbling with the key card, so Richard took it from me and opened the door. I never got a chance to follow him in.

Richard practically threw me back against the opposite wall of the hallway. Mike glanced in my room without entering, then looked at Richard. "Elevator," he said.

The two men each grabbed an arm, none too gently considering my injuries, and dragged me to the elevator. It never even occurred to me ask them why. Mike pushed the down button. When the ding heralded the car's arrival a few seconds later, Richard pressed me back against the wall and stood in front of me, flat against me. The elevator was empty, and they pushed me in.

"Hold the elevator," Mike said.

Richard pushed a button and moved to stand with his back against one of the doors to keep it from opening. In the meantime, Mike moved back down the hall to my room and disappeared inside. He wasn't gone nearly as long as it felt like he was, soon waving the okay to us from the door. Richard and I left the elevator and returned to my room.

Maybe I watch too many movies. I was trying to prepare myself for the worst, and images of stewed bunnies, of entrails and blood smeared on walls flashed through my head as I stood outside the door, preparing myself. Maybe something that flamboyantly disgusting would have been less disturbing than what I found.

My room had been trashed, I thought. On second glance, I found that assessment to be inaccurate. My stuff had been trashed. Aside from the staple holes in the wall, nothing about the room or its furniture had been damaged. Both beds were still perfectly made, so the intruder must have been here after housekeeping. (I don't make my bed at home, much less on the road.) My clothing was strewn across the pristine beds and spilled onto the floor, along with the pages of a paperback novel I'd been reading, and pages from Isaac's files. Fortunately only my copies of Isaac's DOC records and trial attorney file had been in the room. I'd been so mobile lately I'd kept all of my notes from the current investigation and interviews with me, either on my person or in the car.

Not all of my clothes were scattered across the beds. In the bathroom, a white button-down shirt was hanging from the shower curtain rod, speckled with brilliant splashes of red. It was a perfect imitation of blood spatter, the red vivid against the bright white shirt. A perfect movie imitation, I should say. The red was too vivid, too crimson. I saw its source on the bathroom floor, an open container of nail polish. A couple of years ago I'd had a beach weekend planned for right after I returned from an investigative road trip. I had the idea that I might get bored in my motel, at loose ends with witnesses, and want to paint my toenails, so I picked up the red in a drug store. I never did use it, but the polish had been sitting in the bottom of my travel bag ever since.

There wasn't much he could do with my make-up, all pressed powder what little there was of it, but he had emptied tubes of lotions and cleansers, soap and shampoo all over the countertop and smeared my deodorant on the mirror. I always keep spare tampons in my bag, and those were sitting together on the counter. One had been removed from its plastic wrapper. A stapler was sitting on the counter next to it. Apparently he'd been interrupted before he'd finished.

Which brings me back out to the bedroom. I had only glanced at the wall coming in, choosing to see the rest of the damage before trying to assimilate this. There was a pair of scissors on the desk. He had used the scissors to cut my underwear in half, right across the forward seam of the crotch so that the entire section was intact. Then he'd stapled my underwear to the wall by that section, inside out, so the portion that was normally next to my skin was facing the room.

Once again, it was a random, trivial (slightly demented) thought that helped me to maintain my sanity. I'm not sure if it's endemic to my gender or was instilled by my mother, but I always take my best underwear when I travel. That bastard, I thought—he just ruined half a dozen pairs of my best underwear! Plus the pair I'd been wearing during the attack on my last trip that I lost to the hospital or the cops. Then again, if a bunch of cops had to see my underwear, at least it would be my best, not some kind of raggedy soiled grandma panties. The mothers' clean underwear in case of accident axiom suddenly made sense, although I don't think this is the kind of accident they had in mind.

If I'd had any doubts about the identity of my vandal, the whiteboard would have dispelled them. He hadn't signed it, but he had written on it in block letters, "I told you I'm not done with you yet."

Mike and Richard had patiently waited by the door while I inspected the damage, never speaking and I suspect even staying out of my line of sight. As I began a second circuit, peering over and under and around everything, Richard finally spoke.

"Don't touch anything."

"I know." Of course, what he really meant was, what are you doing? If he wanted to know, he could come right out and ask. Which he did, on my third circuit.

"I'm looking for tissues or paper towels."

One look at Richard and Mike's faces, like they'd eaten a bad grapefruit and looked forward to more of the same, and I could tell their minds were heading in the wrong direction. A revolting direction.

"I had my notes with me. I don't think there was anything in the room to indicate what new investigation had been done, who had been interviewed or what we suspected, with the possible exception of the whiteboard. I believe I cleaned it myself before I left the room this morning, but I want to make sure he didn't have to wipe it before leaving his own message. If he did, there should be some sign of it."

"If you find something, how do you know you didn't leave it this morning?" Richard asked.

"He was here after housecleaning," I explained.

This time Richard took my word for it. The three of us searched the room as best we could without disturbing anything, and didn't find what we were looking for. Richard had already used his cell phone to notify the police, and we went downstairs to wait in the lobby for them to arrive. Drake and Sutton hadn't been among the many LEOs crawling over WFC, at least not while I was there, but they had apparently heard about the incident.

"So," Drake said, "you've had a busy day today."

"Not really," I replied. "Deacon James is the one who ate his Wheaties this morning."

I detailed my movements throughout the day, including at WFC. I had debated about Sue Ellen, trying to decide whether to disclose our contact and my suspicions. I didn't want the cops to freak her out, and if she was going to talk to someone I wanted it to be me. Still, she could be in danger, so I played it safe and told Sutton everything while Drake grilled the guys about their movements and our arrival at the scene. I also gave Sutton, from memory, a list of people we'd contacted in connection with our investigation so they could be warned as well.

"I hate to state the obvious because people tend to get pissed off when you tell them how to do their jobs, but I'm going to anyway. Keep a tight lid on this list, and especially on Sue Ellen. Obviously Deacon had a bunch of buddies with him when he came after me, and now it looks like they were all prison guards. I'm not saying this is anything that goes beyond WFC, but you know how word travels in law enforcement circles."

Obviously I'd picked the right cop. Sutton simply nodded and said, "Got it," before heading over to join Drake again. Fortunately he was finishing up with Mike and Richard. We had closed the door behind us and all the hotel staff had been warned, so the scene was relatively secure. I hated to be squeamish, but I really wanted to be gone by the time the crime scene techs arrived and everyone went upstairs to look at my underwear.

Of course, Richard wanted us to have a planned destination before we left the hotel. "We're not going to stand out in the open and argue about this. Sydney, you might as well paint a bulls-eye on your forehead and be done with it."

As always, I appreciated Richard's optimism, but I knew he was right.

"All right, but before you start calling the airlines, let me just say that I'm not going home to Tallahassee, and I'm not taking any impromptu vacations. If getting at me is Deacon's primary objective, I'll be safer and he's more likely to be caught if I stay in Stetler County, where everyone knows him and is on the look-out for him. And if getting me isn't top on his list, then it doesn't matter where I am anyway."

It seemed like a sound argument to me, and Mike and Richard agreed. They probably wouldn't have if I'd given my real reason for staying, that I still had things to take care of in Stetler County.

CHAPTER THIRTY-SEVEN

We came up with a tentative plan. I wasn't looking forward to another motel room, and it was too dangerous for me to stay with Richard's family. I'd crash with Mike that night unless we came up with something else before then. Mike and I traded cars again, and he headed home in his jeep for some quick cleaning while I followed Richard to the PD's office in Cecil. We left Cecil in the parking lot and Richard drove me to Mike's.

I talked Richard into stopping off at one of those big box drug stores that tend to face off on opposite corners now. Not the most auspicious place for retail therapy, but I still managed to give my debit card a jolt. I stocked up on the necessities first—toiletries, a package of pastel granny-esque underwear (selection was limited) and matching bra, a pair of flip flops with flowers on top, and a few Florida T-shirts, including a big manatee sporting sunglasses that was long enough to wear as a nightshirt.

Having taken care of apparel, I went for comfort—a couple of magazines with more advertisements than copy, and lots of chocolate. I'd nearly made it to the check-out when I got distracted by the DVD display, as I always do. I was pleasantly surprised to see they had "The Philadelphia Story," which also went in my cart, and meant I had to go back for popcorn and ice cream. Those are the rules—Cary Grant movie = popcorn **or** ice cream. Cary Grant + Katherine Hepburn = popcorn **and** ice cream. Okay, so they're my own rules, but I'm sure I have them written down somewhere, so they are official.

When we got to Mike's apartment, Richard made no move to leave the car. I waited for his cue. He eventually gave one, but it wasn't quite what I'd expected. We'd taken off our seat belts and he turned to face me, left elbow up on the steering wheel as if trying to look natural.

"Sydney, I know lately I've been kind of—what's the word?"

"A hard-ass? I think that's considered one word if it's hyphenated."

He grinned. It's the first time I'd seen him really smile in days, and I'd forgotten how it took my breath away. "I was thinking taciturn, but I guess hard-ass works. It's just that I'm really worried. Sydney, I don't want anything to happen to you. I—"

His words stopped. He reached over to stroke my cheek, traced his fingers down my face and tilted my chin forward. Then he kissed me. His lips were warm and dry and felt impossibly hot as they pressed against my own, all four occupying the same space, defying the laws of physics for just a moment. When we slowly parted, I felt a quick moist flick from his tongue, followed by a corresponding electric jolt running from the roof of my mouth to between my legs.

It had been too easy. I sighed as I turned away, face toward the window. When I shut my eyes and squeezed the lids together, I could feel a tear run down one cheek. It was so goddamned easy. I thought of his words the first time we had dinner together, "My wife knows I've always been faithful." I wanted to throw them back in his face, but that would be too easy too. I turned back to face him, but I couldn't yet. My gaze dropped to the drug store bags I had by my feet, in preparation for leaving. Finally I turned back to him.

"Richard, I'm not going to lie to you. That's the best kiss I've had in a long time. A very long time. And your smile makes my knees melt. But so does Cary Grant's."

"Cary Grant's dead."

"It doesn't matter. It's the same thing. It's not real." I didn't want to say any more, and he didn't make me. He twisted back around in his seat, put both hands on the steering wheel, and stared at them.

"Okay then." He smiled. "Let's go. If your knees can make it. I'm not sure about my own."

If Mike noticed anything amiss when he let us in, he didn't say anything. "It's not much, but it's home," he said, standing aside to let us in.

"Jesus, Mike, are you sure this is your apartment? I've never seen it so clean."

Mike shook his fist at Richard in mock consternation, then smiled. "I figured Sydney's been through enough this week. The sight of my filth just might push her over the edge."

Mike was about to give us the tour (I say us since Richard was obviously unfamiliar with this incarnation of Mike's living space) when I interrupted him. "Wait—do you have a washer and dryer?"

He led me to his laundry nook. I kissed his cheek and patted it. "Then nothing else matters." After removing the tags, my recent purchases were dumped in the washing machine. When Mike saw what I was doing, he told me he'd found something I could wear if I wanted to wash the clothes I was wearing. He led me to his bedroom, where a garment was folded on his bed, then closed the door for privacy and retreated with Richard.

Mike's bedroom was small and contained only the bare necessities—bed and nightstand, both in faux distressed pine with dark metal hardware. There was no dresser, but his nightstand had drawers and the folding louvered doors on one wall concealed a

305

closet. A photograph collage was now the only wall decoration, but a few lonely nails stood testament to previous company. I resisted the temptation to look at the collage, to open drawers, and instead I stared at the light comforter covering his full size bed, abstract earth tones with a southwestern feel. What was I expecting—the Superfriends? Teenage Mutant Ninja Turtles?

My compulsion to snoop averted, I returned to my original purpose. Mike had folded the garment on his bed so its identity was hidden, probably so he could make a quick getaway before I started yelling. It was a Yankees jersey, something no self-respecting Red Sox fan would wear, but I was too tired to take offense. Beneath it was a pair of novelty boxers, Yosemite Sam on a galloping mule, if mules can gallop. The mule was apparently moving quickly enough to kick up clouds of dust. The boxers looked as if they'd never been worn, and they smelled of fabric softener. If I'd wanted to be daring, I could have gone without them—what is the female equivalent term for "going commando"? The jersey stretched nearly to my knees, but I did choose to modestly wear the boxers in place of underwear.

When I emerged, Mike and Richard were leaning against the kitchen counter nursing bottles of beer. I took the opportunity to drop the rest of my clothes in the machine and get it going before joining them. Mike's apartment was a two-bedroom, one-bath. The two bedrooms were in the back, with the bathroom and laundry nook next to one of the bedrooms. You entered the apartment through the main living/kitchen area, which had an open floor plan. The furniture was sparse and looked like a mix of Pier 1 and college dorm leftovers. Most of these walls were bare as well, eggshell white broken only by the silhouette of the entertainment center, except for one corner. There a black halogen lamp illuminated several maps of ancient geography and civilizations, trade routes, migration routes, etc., that looked like they'd been taken from magazines.

My wandering had finally caught their attention, and the three of us moved to the seating area, Mike and Richard on the couch and me on the recliner. They both tried once again to convince me to leave, either for home or for parts unknown, but I refused.

"We still don't know what's going on. What's the connection between Isaac, or at least my investigation of him, and the corrupt prison guards? We can speculate that Isaac was an informant, but it's still just speculation. We don't have confirmation on the letter, and we're not likely to get it soon. I don't see the feds sharing that kind of information before it comes out in court."

"So what do you want to do?"

"I told you that Sue Ellen is the key to this thing. I know it."

It was then that I recalled the clipping sent to Noel. I'd promptly tucked it away and forgotten about it in the drama of our second argument. At least that meant I'd had it on me when Deacon was going through my stuff. I retrieved it, then showed it to Mike and Richard and told them my suspicions.

"Once I talk to Sue Ellen, I'll be able to get my head around this, and I'll have something to tell Noel. Then I'll be happy to get the hell out of here. Believe me, I have no interest in being a martyr to the cause. The case. Whatever."

We seemed to have run out of things to say. Richard announced that it was past time for him to head home. Mike and I walked him to the door, then settled down in front of the TV. This time Mike had the recliner. It seemed to be his usual spot and had a vaguely Mike-shaped depression in its seat. Although we were both exhausted, neither of us was ready to sleep. One of the sports channels was running a "best of" video, and they flashed to an amazing catch in Fenway Park.

"Did you ever go see games there?" Mike asked.

"Once or twice." Something about his tone of voice or syntax had perked my ears up. "How did you know I lived in Boston?"

He didn't answer immediately. Maybe he was trying to figure out his answer, or how to answer, defensive or nonchalant. Maybe he was just watching TV.

"It was on your Autofind—apartment, utilities. But you didn't register your car while you were there, naughty girl. Most states allow 90 days or less grace period, and you were there for at least a year."

"You ran an Autofind without telling me?"

Mike clicked off the TV and set the remote on the floor before twisting in his recliner to face me. "Yes, I did. You acted funny when I brought it up, and my investigator's instincts kicked in. I'd known you all of five minutes, and I couldn't help myself. I'm sorry."

I should have been pissed at him. No, that's not quite true. It was in my nature to be pissed at him, at anyone, for such an intrusion into my hard-won privacy. But I wasn't. "So you know?"

"That you changed your name, or that you're almost as old as I am? Which is the bigger secret?"

I barely suppressed a smile. "Does Richard know?"

"About the name change? No, or at least I assume he doesn't. I didn't tell him. I didn't tell anyone. I skimmed through the report once, and a couple of days later I put it through the shredder. If you want to have a secret identity, it's no one's business but your own."

"Secret identity sounds much more exotic and exciting. All I did was change my name. But thanks anyway, for your...discretion."

"I'm a discrete kind of guy." We sat in silence for a while, and I thought that was the end of it. Until he went on. "Still, it takes

308

something pretty intense for a 19-year-old to go to the trouble of changing her name. You want to talk about it?"

This is when I should have told him to mind his own business, insulted him with impressive conjugations of profanity and walked out the door. That is, if I'd been myself I should have. If he'd been someone else, I should have. Would have. But I didn't. I surprised myself. Or maybe I became someone else.

"It's a long, boring story of familial dysfunction."

"I'm looking forward to a long, boring night."

I sighed and snuggled back into the corner crease of the cushions. "Well, our family wasn't exactly the Cleavers, but our dysfunction wasn't obvious either. My parents stayed married, and they never raised their voices. No one in our house ever yelled. My sister and I hated each other, and my parents were indifferent at best, with me and with each other. If it hadn't been for Allan, I would've felt like a freak."

I smiled at the thought of him. He always made me smile, or cry. "Allan was five years older than me—my sister was in the middle—and all the girls were hot for him. I remember the summer he turned 16, he used to pick me up every afternoon at the public pool. He'd beep and wave from the parking lot, and every bikini-clad female—not just the teenagers, grown women—would pick that precise moment to stretch and turn over, to walk to the diving board on tip-toes and dive in gracefully."

Mike chuckled, and I nodded. "It used to crack me up. Then we'd go out for ice cream, and I'd tell him all my gossip, and he'd actually listen. Sometimes he'd tell me stories about his friends. Of course I was just a kid, but I just, I can't even begin to explain what that meant to me, that this amazing person, the coolest guy around, chose to spend time with me instead of his friends. When he went away to college, I didn't see him as much, but every once in a while he'd just show up at my school. 'Hey Mongoose, let's go play hooky!' I'd hop in his car and we'd take off, go hang out in the park on the grass and stare at the sky."

"Mongoose?"

I blushed. "Yeah, that was his nickname for me. Something about how I was always picking fights with cobras. He said I didn't know when to back down."

"Imagine that," Mike said.

I tried to smile at him, but I was suddenly tired, and I didn't want to talk anymore. Then the buzzer on the washing machine went off. Saved by the bell. When I rose, my bare leg brushed Mike's jeans. When had he moved to sit next to me? I hadn't a clue, but I was glad he was there. Focusing on the weave of faded denim around his knees, I took a deep breath and willed the past away for the rest of the evening. It never went far.

"Are you really older than me?"

Non sequitur much? Mike didn't seem to notice. He let his glasses slide down his nose a bit and slipped into a professorial character. "Don't let the kid face fool you. I've got at least a few weeks of life experience edge over you."

In that extra few weeks and the intervening years, he'd never gotten around to watching "The Philadelphia Story," so we did that night. We shared a pint of ice cream on the couch while admiring the droll wit of Mr. C.K. Dexter-Haven.

"It was good," Mike admitted. "Not what I expected. The humor was edgier, funnier. Not quite as wholesome as I assumed anything in black and white would be. But it was a little too close to reality for me."

"Why is that?"

"I didn't get the girl." I blinked in confusion at his wry smile. "Jimmy Stewart's character Mike didn't get the girl."

"Yes he did," I corrected. "He didn't get Katherine Hepburn, but he got the girl he was meant to be with."

CHAPTER THIRTY-EIGHT

When I woke on the couch the next morning, Mike was still asleep in the recliner. He had offered me the bed, but I'd declined, and apparently neither of us made it there. Mike had retreated to the recliner after the movie, and we got sucked into late night TV. Of course, to my trained, suspicious eye the apparently accidental, casual sleeping arrangement was anything but accidental. The TV had been turned off, and I was covered with a safari print blanket I hadn't been wearing last night. I didn't confront him about watching over me, in part because I didn't want to make him uncomfortable about something so sweet, and in part because after I'd dropped it he hadn't brought up my past again.

It was nearly 9 AM. I got the shower before Mike did and dressed in a hurry, pulling on my new "Life's a Beach" T-shirt. We feasted on peanut butter and honey toast before running out the door. The plan was that I'd drop Mike off at the PD's office, then go by WFC to see if there was any word on Sue Ellen's whereabouts. If I couldn't find her, there wasn't much point in staying in this neck of the Panhandle.

We made it to the PD's office by 9:45. I thought Richard looked at us askance when we came in together so late, but maybe I was being paranoid. Either way, he recovered his equanimity quickly. Both men offered to accompany me to WFC, but I declined. I did agree to keep my cell phone on me at all times, to check in every hour and to notify them every time I left a location. Hopefully I'd remembered to charge it.

Sue Ellen hadn't shown for work at WFC. No one in the administrative office would tell me more. I'm sure all of the guards knew what was going on, but I wasn't looking forward to talking to any of them. There'd been nothing on the radio this morning about the investigation or arrests, but that didn't mean anything, and I felt as if everyone were staring at me. Fortunately I ran into Charley on his break. He hadn't seen or heard from Sue Ellen, so he'd checked with one of the supervisors. Sue Ellen had called in with an unspecified family emergency. She'd said she'd be out until the situation was resolved and hoped it wouldn't cost her job, but if so it couldn't be helped.

"That's not like Sue Ellen at all, so I called her mother. I didn't want to worry Miss Mavis, so I made out like it was some kind of scheduling thing. She hadn't spoken to Sue Ellen, and there wasn't any family emergency. Miss Mavis would have told me."

Charley's eyes locked on mine, and any trace of the unsure young man was gone. "I don't like it. She's not been answering her phone, but I'm going over by her house after work to see if she's there."

"Look, Charley, I don't have to be anywhere. Why don't you give me her address and I'll go check on her right now? There's no point in waiting until the end of the day."

Relief made his features soften, but not relax. His left cheek and eye were twitchy, unable to decide on an appropriate expression, afraid to hope but more afraid to mock hope. "That sounds good. That sounds real good. But you be careful, Sydney. I'd hate to think of you getting in another fix with nobody around."

I smiled, more because he'd remembered to call me Sydney than because of the sentiment. "Don't worry, Charley. I'll be careful. And I'll let you know what I find out."

True to my word, I checked in with Mike and Richard before leaving WFC, but I needn't have bothered. I didn't find any trouble at Sue Ellen's house, or anything else. She lived in a duplex, but there were no vehicles parked in front and no one answered my repeated knocks on either side. I tried to peek around her curtains and walked around the property, but I didn't see anything suspicious. Certainly nothing more suspicious than me casing the joint, but there were no neighbors to report me. No curtains rustled. No dogs barked. No one answered my knocks.

I considered sitting for a while, "staking the place out" in old P.I. parlance, but it wasn't worth it. Instead I called Mike and Richard, advising them that I was on my way back to the PD's office and asking that they let Charley know I'd struck out. Charley was the only person who'd been pleased to see me at WFC. I was afraid if I called and left a message for him there, he'd rocket up to the number two spot on the office shit list, right behind me.

As I passed the Handi-Way, I decided at the last minute to pull in, jolting over a curb to make the turn. Well, I rationalized, that's what Jeeps are made for. I hadn't spoken to Annie since I'd been attacked. I'd meant to, but I just hadn't gotten around to it yet. Now that I'd caused all hell to break loose at the prison, I wished I'd done so earlier. Most of the town, thus most of Annie's customers, worked at WFC. I might not be one of her favorite people right now either.

She glanced up when the bell announced my arrival, then looked down quickly at her book, as if she hadn't seen me or didn't recognize me. I took my time getting a sports drink and a candy bar and headed to the counter. She rang me up without speaking.

"Hi Annie." No response as I counted out the cash.

"How's tricks?" Still no response.

"So I take it I'm on your shit list too?" That got her.

315

"Well, let's see. A bunch of guys were arrested at work this morning, and you got half the town wondering if they're next. Yeah, I guess you could say a lot of people aren't real happy with you right now."

Charley hadn't mentioned the arrests. Maybe they'd happened after I left. I should have felt relieved, but I didn't. Not yet. "Annie, do you know why they were arrested?"

"I don't know and I don't care. If you got what you came for, I'd like you to leave."

"Deacon and his buddies kidnapped me a couple of weeks ago. You probably heard about that. You might not have heard that they beat the crap out of me, and if I hadn't gotten away Deacon would have raped me, possibly even killed me."

Annie's eyes locked on her counter, her lips wrinkling as she squeezed them tightly together. "Those boys never would have allowed that."

"Maybe. I'd like to believe that. It'd help me sleep better at night. Of course, it was Charley who saved my life yesterday. No one else lifted a finger."

It was then that I remembered Annie's nephew. "Annie, 'those boys' weren't arrested for attacking me. I can't even identify them. You want to know what they were capable of, what they actually did do? They were shaking down prisoners' families for visitation. And I'm not talking about bribes for illegal perks—$100 gets you a conjugal visit with your girlfriend. I'm talking about extortion— $100 or we lose your paperwork and you don't get to see your son. How would you feel if someone made you pay to visit your nephew?"

Annie still wouldn't look at me and still didn't speak, but her mouth had relaxed. She rocked a bit on her feet, back and forth, while she looked up at the ceiling tiles. "Look, Annie, I'm sorry. I know you have to live here, and I'm not trying to get you in trouble. I just dropped by because I'm trying to find Sue Ellen."

That finally got through to her. She narrowed her eyes at me and asked, "Why do you want to talk to her?"

"I'm worried about her. Those other guys might be relatively harmless, but Deacon's still on the loose, and he could be after her."

"Why? Why would he go after Sue Ellen? She's just a child."

Sue Ellen was in her mid 20s and was qualified to carry a hand-gun, but I didn't want to argue the point. "I think Deacon is in deeper than the rest of the guys, probably did some dirtier stuff, and I think Sue Ellen knew about it. She was scared to death of him, and now she's disappeared."

"If you see her, please tell her to call me." I pulled out a card and wrote every phone number I could think of on it, then held it out to Annie. She hesitated.

"Annie, please. If Deacon was mean before, he's psycho now, and he's got nothing to lose."

"Okay," she said, taking the card. "I'll tell her."

CHAPTER THIRTY-NINE

Even with the extra stop and chat with Annie, it couldn't have taken more than 20 minutes total to get to the PD's office, but Mike was waiting in the parking lot when I got there.

"What took you so long?" he asked. He took my bag from me and practically dragged me into the building. There was an armed guard at the entrance I didn't recall being there on my last visit.

Even Melinda's composure seemed ruffled, or perhaps I should say her hair was ruffled and her clothes were slightly rumpled. Dr. Seuss rhymes danced through my head—a late-blooming symptom from the head trauma? More likely my usual batty self. Maybe she was ruffled rumpled stumpled because she was working on Saturday. No, wait, today was still Friday. The real reason for Melinda's dishevelment and Mike's impatience became evident when we entered Richard's office. He had a full house.

Richard, Jim Gilbert, and Rudy Nagroski rose when I entered the room, and I began to feel claustrophobic. They all made the proper greeting noises and Rudy tried to negotiate the bodies to get out the door, explaining that he was just leaving.

"Wait," Richard said. "Tell Sydney."

Rudy blinked as though the thought had never occurred to him. "Oh. Oh yeah, sure." He seemed unsure where to begin.

Mike spoke softly. "Rudy, tell her who it was."

Rudy's eyes focused, and he nodded. "Well, you were asking about the Thomas investigation, about who Chet Hawkins used for his legwork. I could see the guy clear as day, but I couldn't remember his name. That is, until I heard the news this morning. It was that guy on the news, the prison guard that went crazy. Deacon James was his name. He was Chet Hawkins' investigator."

While Richard thanked Rudy for coming by and walked him to Melinda's door, Mike led me to a chair and made sure I landed in it rather than on the floor. I should have seen it coming. I took a deep breath, trying to let the self-recriminations go and clear my mind for useful cogitation. It worked.

"Are you all right?" Mike asked.

I tried to smile. "Yes, thank you. Would you hand me my binder, the one with the police reports?"

He did, and I'd found what I was looking for by the time Richard returned to the room.

"No luck with Sue Ellen?" he asked. I shook my head.

"Rudy showed up about half an hour ago. He's been looking through his notes, trying to figure out what went wrong. What he did wrong."

Richard shook his head, likely clearing his own self-recriminations. "Then Jim got here a few minutes ago. All things considered, I thought he'd want to know as well."

Jim smiled. "Yes. Rudy was able to find out what I couldn't. Deacon James' personnel file is a valuable commodity, and I'm afraid I didn't have enough pull to even set eyes on it, much less get a copy. We now know Deacon worked at the police department, however briefly, before he went to work as a prison guard at WCF. Rudy made some calls, but no one seems to know the circumstances of Deacon's departure from the force. For what it's worth, the consensus is it was something shady."

I spread the binder on Richard's desk, opened to the report. "Remember when I said I assumed Deacon was his last name?" I pointed at the name at the bottom of the report. "Officer D. James was one of the officers at the fire at Jimmy's."

"Pretty common name, James," Jim said, but he sounded as if he didn't believe in coincidence any more than I did.

"It's him."

We were interrupted by Melinda's knock at the door. "Richard, I know you said you didn't want to be disturbed, but there's a woman on the line asking for Sydney. She won't give her name."

They all looked at me. "It has to be Sue Ellen," I said. I moved to Richard's desk and picked up the line.

"Is this Sydney Brennan?" a breathless woman's voice asked.

"Yes. Sue Ellen?"

"Yeah. I got this number from Annie when I stopped to get gas. I tried all the other numbers first, but nobody answered." Her voice got higher as she trailed off at the end.

"Sue Ellen, do you know what happened at the prison? Yesterday and today?"

"I don't know what to do," she whispered. "I'm scared." Little "eeee" noises like baby sobs came from her end.

"Sue Ellen, listen to me. Do you know where the Public Defender's Office is? It's in the same building as the State Attorney. Sue Ellen?"

"Yes."

"That's where I am right now. Meet me here, and we'll keep you safe. I promise. I'll wait for you in the parking lot. Okay? Can you do that?"

"Okay."

The men (my little posse of over-protective chauvinists was growing) vetoed me standing in the open parking lot. Instead I waited just inside the door with the armed guard. Richard had warned him to be particularly vigilant.

"If trouble starts, it's usually because she brought it with her," he said, pointing at me. "Little Miss Tempest in a Teapot."

I didn't argue.

Fifteen minutes later, a car arrived in the lot. I knew it was Sue Ellen and hurried out the door before someone could try to stop me, reaching her as she was locking her car door. She recognized me and tried to smile. When I put my hand on her elbow she didn't flinch or pull away, so I wrapped my splinted arm awkwardly around her shoulder and drew her inside. The guard came out as we approached and backed in after us. I thought he'd seen too many military movies.

I led Sue Ellen to Richard's office. We had agreed that I would speak to her alone first, not inviting the men in until I'd had a chance to explain their presence. On the way through I asked Melinda if she could find us some hot tea. Like most government buildings, the PD's office kept the air conditioning at least 10 degrees cooler than I would have preferred, and I hoped the hot beverage would soothe Sue Ellen's nerves.

For a few minutes, we said nothing of substance. I kept repeating the same reassuring phrases, waiting for her to get comfortable in her surroundings. She was wearing a pink T-shirt and jeans, her bony little elbows held close to her ribs, as if she were afraid to touch the chair. Her breathing had begun to even out, and her eyes weren't as wide, when we heard a knock at the door. She still jerked at the sound. It was Mike, carrying a tray with cast-off mugs of steaming liquid, the yellow Lipton tags still hanging over the side. He'd added sweetener packets of various colors and toxicities as well.

"Thanks, Mike," I said, waving him in. I motioned for him to stay.

"Mike is an investigator here at the PD's office. You know I've been looking into Isaac Thomas's case. A couple of weeks ago, I decided I was in over my head and asked some people to help me out. Mike is one of those people, and two more of them are waiting outside. Would you mind if they came in while we talk?"

Some of the color had returned to Sue Ellen's face. Maybe it was the three sugars she had dumped in her tea. "No, I don't mind. I know it sounds silly, but I think I might feel safer with them here."

Mike went to the door and let Richard and Jim in. I introduced each of them to her by name and position. Once again the space was tight, and there were only two chairs in addition to Richard's. Sue Ellen and I sat opposite Richard in the two guest chairs, and Jim perched on the windowsill behind Richard. Mike sat on the floor on our side of the desk, his back against a bookshelf.

I'd been afraid Sue Ellen would have difficulty, that we would have to coax her story out of her, but she'd only needed a safe place to tell it. She began with no prompting.

"Isaac was a very kind man. Sometimes it's hard being a female guard, but he didn't, well, you know, say things like a lot of the guys. He wasn't like that." She looked down at her hands.

"I think he just liked having a woman to talk to."

"Is that how you knew about Noel?" I asked.

"Well, yes. But not at first. I mean, he didn't tell me right away. He didn't talk much about his life on the outside or anything like that. I didn't even know what his crime was until Deacon told me."

"What did Deacon tell you?"

"He said—I feel awful, but it's what he said—that Isaac killed his wife because she was a whore. He said she got what was coming to her."

"Did you ever hear that from anyone else?"

"No. I don't remember talking much at all about Isaac to anyone, except maybe Charley. Definitely not about Isaac's case."

"Did it seem like Deacon had something against Isaac, or there was something between them?"

"Not at first. Not until Isaac started asking about visitation."

"What did he want to know?"

"Well, different days he'd ask who was on duty, who'd be handling the visitation and how it worked. Isaac was smart. He knew all the operating procedures and everything, but I don't remember him ever having a visitor while I was there. He knew what happened on paper, but he'd never had the experience, if you see what I mean. What's on paper and what goes on day-to-day can be two very different things at the prison."

"Did he tell you why he was asking?"

"No, but as time went by, he started asking more specific questions. Then one day, it must have been a Friday, he asked if I'd be helping with the visitation next day. I told him I was, and he asked me if I'd do him a favor. One of the guys on his wing had a little sister coming to visit, and Isaac wanted me to stick close to her. He wouldn't say why, but he said to be careful, not to be too obvious about it. He didn't want to get me in trouble."

"And you did it?"

"I couldn't see in any harm in it, and Isaac was real good to me, so I kept an eye on her. She was a young girl, maybe about sixteen. It seems to me like she had to bring a parental waiver. At some point, I don't remember if it was before or after the visit, I looked around the visitation area and I didn't see her. There was a place where you were out of sight if you went around the side of the building, so we always had someone posted right there, but I didn't see anybody. I thought that was kinda strange so I walked around the corner and there she was."

Sue Ellen's voice started to crack, so I moved her tea cup within easy reach. She took a tiny sip before going on. "The girl was up against the wall. She was wearing a skirt, a long one that came below her knees but he'd hiked it up, so he could get to her. She was crying, real soft, and I—I didn't even think. I just couldn't believe what I was seeing. I walked over and I said, Deacon, what the hell are you doing? He just stared at me, still leaning against the wall, belt hanging down. He hadn't, you know, really got to her yet, and while he was looking at me the girl took off."

Sue Ellen's head dropped. I reached over impulsively and grabbed her hand, giving it a gentle squeeze. She still didn't look up, but she squeezed back and continued.

"He asked if I was volunteering instead. I didn't know what to say, and before I knew it he was standing right next to me. He grabbed me real hard, between my legs, and he shoved me up against the wall. Then he just walked away. I thought that was it, that he'd scared me bad enough, but that evening he was waiting for me. I got in my car, and he knocked on my window for me to roll it down. He looked around, and I guess there wasn't anyone close enough to see, because he pulled out a gun."

Sue Ellen's voice didn't change, but tears began trickling down her cheeks. "I closed my eyes, but I could still feel his gun, like a cold smooth rock against my head. He said if I ever told anyone, he'd kill me, but before he did he'd…"

She took a deep breath and looked up at me.

"He'd do things to me someone like Charlie could never imagine."

"Did you tell Isaac?"

"No! No, I didn't tell anyone. I avoided Isaac for a while. I was afraid he'd be able to see it, just by looking at me. I thought everyone would, especially the way Deacon kept looking at me, saying little things here and there, so I wouldn't forget. Charlie suspected something, but then he got transferred. Nobody else saw it."

When she spoke again, her voice held an angry edge, the edge that I hoped would help her through the next few months. "That's what I thought anyway, that nobody else saw it, but Annie told me this morning what they were up to. They just didn't want to see it. Oh sure, there were little things that I ignored too. Like some of the guards would make the inmates give them honey buns they'd bought from the canteen, just to take a shower. Or when one of the inmates comes up positive on a drug test. I knew they had to get the drugs from somewhere. But making people pay to get visits, making girls have sex to see their brothers?"

She shook her head in disgust.

"Did Isaac ever figure it out?"

"He never said it in so many words, but he did. Not long before he died, maybe a couple of weeks, they were shuffling the wings and the shifts around and I got transferred too. A few days before my transfer, I went to talk to Isaac, I guess to say goodbye. Usually we wouldn't get to talk that much, but I think Deacon was out and the other guys were cutting me some slack, so we got to talk a lot the last couple of days. That's when he told me about his sister. He said she was having a rough time now, but he was hoping to get a visit from her soon. And he told me about Noel too, how he wanted to see her, but he didn't want to see her here, in prison. He wanted to wait until he got out."

"When I dropped by for the last time, my last shift on his cell block, that's when I knew for sure Isaac had figured it out. He apologized to me. He said he was sorry for getting me in the middle of the things that were going on, but he said not to worry, that he'd taken care of it. He said Deacon would never hurt anyone again."

That must have been after he'd written the letter, right before his medical transfer for an interview. Isaac knew he'd set the investigation in motion, and he'd trusted in the system to work, trusted that people would do their jobs. After his own experience, how could he have been so naively optimistic?

We'd gotten enough from Sue Ellen for our purposes, but I knew a lot of other people would want to speak to her. The question was what to do with her in the meantime. None of us felt comfortable turning her over to the police until we knew for sure Deacon's corruption hadn't spread beyond the prison to his old employers. Jim had worked on a multi-agency corruption case a few years earlier and had access to a safe house in Destin, with no questions or interference from other agencies when he used it. We finally settled on keeping her there until he could make some progress with the Feds, and someone could make some progress apprehending Deacon James. After confirming that this plan was okay with Sue Ellen, Jim and Richard began making calls and putting things in motion.

Before they left with Sue Ellen, I realized there was something important I'd forgotten to ask. "Did you send the newspaper clipping to Noel?"

"Yes. After Isaac died, I sent an anonymous letter to the State Attorney's Office."

She smiled at Jim. "Obviously it never made it to your desk. Nothing happened. This might sound crazy, but I couldn't shake the feeling that Deacon had something to do with Isaac's death. I don't know how, but the why is pretty obvious. I didn't know what else to do, so I just let it go. A few months ago, I began to suspect that Deacon was… taking advantage of people again. I didn't know about the other guards, but it makes sense that they were too. It probably wasn't the best idea, but the note to Noel was the only thing I could think of."

"Did Deacon ever mention Noel?"

"No, but I do remember something else he said. You asked me before about Isaac's wife. He knew her name. I remember because it was so unusual—Vanda. He said, just like Wanda, except with a V."

CHAPTER FORTY

While Richard and Jim were running around settling Sue Ellen's arrangements, I took the opportunity to review my notes and make a phone call. It was a brief call, but by the time Richard returned, the Reverend Robert Johnson had confirmed my suspicions.

"Let's go get something to eat," I said.

Richard objected. "We've got a lot to talk about, and we can order in."

"Believe it or not, there's no law yet that says we can't talk outside. I'd like to get the hell out of here, if you don't mind."

Richard obviously wasn't happy, but he knew he couldn't hand-cuff me to a radiator. The new building had central heating. We got barbeque sandwiches from a woman in a cart around the corner. I wanted to walk to one of the downtown parks and eat there, but Richard and Mike both objected, so we compromised. Instead we got in Mike's jeep and drove to a city park a few miles away. I rolled my window down and let the wind whip my hair until it stung my eyes. After a couple of blocks of airing out, Mike turned the air conditioning on, but I left my window down, eyes closed and face tilted to the sun.

Some sort of organized day camp had started for the summer at the park, and teenagers in matching yellow T-shirts led lines of children snaking around playground equipment. Their game was unrecognizable from our vantage point, but I could hear their squealing laughter. We'd chosen a relatively secluded area a hundred yards away. Our nearest neighbors, a couple of teenagers discreetly feeling each other up, left at our approach.

I set my lunch on a peeling red picnic bench. It was well-shaded with a small stream trickling nearby, which tricked my brain into thinking it wasn't quite so unbearably hot. I thought of the tourist T-shirt I'd passed up, *It's not the heat, it's the stupidity.* My feet led me to the stream and I peered down at the water. The ground beneath was comprised of reddish-brown goop, and I wondered what nasty surprises lurked in the water, waiting to be discovered in a few decades. I wasn't in the cheeriest state of mind.

Mike and Richard waited patiently for me, and when I sat down we unfolded our barbeque wrappers into placemats and ate in silence. When I'd finished, I balled up the aluminum foil and tossed it in the trash before moving to sit on the ground, my back against a tree trunk. Its large trunk was able to accommodate multiple people, and Mike sat at a right angle to me. Richard moved to face us from the bench and began speaking.

I didn't really listen to what he was saying—like I said, I wasn't in my happy place—but he droned on about Sue Ellen, about things we already knew, about how dangerous Deacon James was. He stopped to stare at me, his unspoken question hanging in the air. *What are we going to do with Sydney?* He probably knew if he asked it aloud I'd start walking back to Tallahassee in my flowered flip flops.

"Now with Sue Ellen, the Feds have everything they need to arrest him on the corruption charges, and the police have a warrant for him on the WFC assault. The Feds already arrested his buddies, and it's just a matter of time before one of them breaks on your kidnapping as well. It's just a matter of time before they pick Deacon up. There's nothing else we need to do."

"You're forgetting something," I said. "He killed Vanda

Thomas."

"What?"

I couldn't see Mike, but Richard's mouth had dropped as he spoke. Agitated, he rose from the bench and paced a small circle, causing puffs of dirt with his heavy steps.

"And he probably killed Isaac too, but I'll never be able to prove it."

"Oh, so you're saying you can prove he killed Vanda? This I've got to hear."

"No, I didn't say I could prove it, but he did it."

I could feel Mike slide around the tree and sit closer to me. Whether his movement was to reassure me or just hear me better, I didn't know. Richard's face was still a mask of condescending disbelief.

"Let's look at what we know. Deacon James was a cop when Vanda was killed. He was at the scene of the fire, practically next door, the night Vanda was killed, and after Vanda was killed. He was Chet Hawkins' investigator, his go-to guy, on Isaac's prosecution. Chet Hawkins, a meticulous prosecutor, is dead, and none of his personal notes, none of his correspondence or memos, nothing that could detail Deacon's efforts in the case, or even the fact of his involvement, remains in the State Attorney's file."

"There's a strong argument that the presence of Isaac's sooty prints on Vanda's body actually indicates that he did not kill her. Somehow the investigating officer wasn't aware of the fire at Jimmy's, or at least the significance of its timing, and you and Sammy never received any reports from the fire."

"Legal arguments to the contrary aside, practically speaking, Chet couldn't turn over what he didn't know about."

"And you don't think that should have come up in conversation with his investigator, who was at the scene of the fire? I'm not

JUDY K. WALKER

impugning Chet Hawkins. Don't you think it's odd that Deacon never would have said, to Chet or to you or to Rudy or someone else, 'No, I wasn't at the murder scene because I was still at the fire —remember? Boy, that was a big mother. Never seen anything like it. Funny thing, those happening the same night.'"

I thought I heard a snicker from Mike at my flip Deacon impersonation, but Richard looked even angrier. I continued. "He told Sue Ellen that Isaac killed his wife because she was a whore. You and Sammy never knew about her sexual escapades. He also called her by name—'Vanda, like Wanda, except with a V.' Robert Johnson had said those exact words when I spoke with him about the fight at Jimmy's, so I gave him a call after Sue Ellen left. He said that was part of Vanda's routine, sort of a tag line that she used with all the men."

"So what?"

"So Deacon knew her. He knew Vanda from Jimmy's, and I do mean in a biblical sense. We know he's been shaking down women, and even girls, at the prison for sex. Is it such a leap to think he was doing that with prostitutes when he was a cop? That's not exactly an unknown phenomena, and it could be what got him kicked off the force."

"Fast forward 20 years. Doesn't what he tried to do to me seem a little extreme for someone afraid I'll uncover his little prison corruption scheme? And the connection to Isaac is too tenuous. Isaac may or may not have kick-started an investigation at the prison, but he died a year and a half ago and nothing's happened. No one's been arrested, and no one was going to be."

"Not until he pissed you off," Mike said. Richard looked at both of us. His face was flushed, and his belt seemed too tight. He left abruptly, heading toward the place where the teenagers had been making out.

332

"That probably wasn't the best thing to say," Mike admitted. "At least it stopped the escalation."

He scooted around until his shoulders brushed my own.

"He's just scared, Sydney. He doesn't want anything to happen to you. He's right. Deacon is a dangerous guy, he's really gone around the bend, and I just reminded Richard that you're number one on the psycho's hit list."

When I didn't respond, Mike kept talking. "And this whole case has floored him. Intellectually, we've all been at this long enough to know that these things happen. A convergence of inadvertent fuck-ups results in what's euphemistically known as a miscarriage of justice. But it's something else to find out, 20 years after the fact, that you were one of the converging forces and didn't even know it. It'd be easier if Rudy or Chet had been dirty, but they weren't."

He sighed. "I'm sure Rudy's going through the same thing."

I knew Mike was right. It was one thing to reassure a colleague that everyone makes mistakes. Learning to live with your own, extending forgiveness to yourself, was much more difficult, sometimes impossible. I felt bad for Richard, I really did, but right now that sympathy took a backseat to doing what was right, finding the truth. In my position, Richard would feel the same way. I had to keep going, and I had to stay alive in the process. Those things didn't leave room for much else.

My thoughts were interrupted when I felt Mike's hand slide under my own. He didn't look at me when he spoke.

"What Sue Ellen said about Deacon... he was like that with you, wasn't he?"

"Yep," I answered. My voice was flat because I felt nothing.

Mike release his breath again in a deep sigh, and in my peripheral vision I could see his head tilt back so he looked at the sky. He sprang up suddenly, pausing halfway up to kiss the top of my head.

His lips felt soft through my hair. Then he extended a hand, grabbing my left arm above the elbow where the worst injuries had been bruises, and helped me to my feet. Ever the peacemaker, he walked toward Richard, now sitting on another bench. I followed.

Richard smiled rather than growled as we approached, but it was a sad shadow of a smile. "You're probably right, Sydney. I just don't see how we can ever prove it. We have nothing to test for DNA. We have no witnesses. I just don't know where we can go from here."

This time Mike and I both extended arms, helping Richard up, and we all walked back to the car arm in arm. Three jaded musketeers, tilting at windmills, to mix my literary metaphors. Richard rode in the back seat, and as he lifted a leg to leverage himself in to the Jeep, I patted his shoulder.

"Don't worry," I told him. "I'll figure something out."

In fact, I already had.

CHAPTER FORTY-ONE

I had figured something out, but I knew my posse wouldn't like it, so I wasn't telling them. When we got back to the PD's office, I pled exhaustion and Richard arranged for me to sack out in a vacant office with a sofa. It was what I would diplomatically call a vintage piece of furniture, obviously carried to the new building for sentimental reasons. I suspected the stains on the worn upholstery had been around longer than most of the attorneys, but that didn't matter. I wasn't planning on sleeping on it. Instead I headed for the phone.

First, I left slightly cryptic messages for Annie and Charlie to let them know that Sue Ellen was safe. I was sure they'd figure it out, and if not they had the number at the PD's office. Mike or Richard could set them straight. Next, I determined that Noel was still AWOL. Neither her employer nor her family had heard from her. (Thankfully Ginny had answered rather than Mrs. Harrison. I might really need to lie down on the nasty couch after a tongue-lashing from that woman.) I checked my home and work answering machines but learned nothing. It was time to take action.

Melinda informed me that Mike was in with Richard, discussing another case, and sent me on through. Good—two birds with one stone.

"Hey," I said, peeking around the office door. Richard motioned me in as he finished a phone call. I took the chair next to Mike.

"You were right," I began, the most effective sort of beginning with most men. "There's nothing else we can do right now. Hopefully the Feds will turn up something with the other arrests, or maybe when the case gets back in the spotlight a witness will come forward, someone who saw them leave Jimmy's together."

I slid my butt forward until my slouching form barely remained in the chair and sighed. "Right now, I'm worn out. I've been beaten up, shot at, and lost my best underwear. It's time for a little retail therapy, maybe a few days at the coast with a good book. I'm heading home, boys."

"Now?" Mike asked. He might be reading me too well.

"If I leave now, I'll be home in time to make all the arrangements tonight and head to St. George Island tomorrow."

I don't know how much either of them believed me, but what could they say? I'd told them I'd leave after I spoke to Sue Ellen, and now she was in protective custody. Both men had been practically begging me to leave for days, to do exactly what I had just announced I was doing. I agreed to check in as soon as I got home, and again tomorrow when I got where I was going.

I patted Cecil's dash in greeting and told him I'd missed him, but he was too pouty to respond. I looked forward to taking some of the back roads home with the top down. Mike and Richard had walked me to my car, and stood like fond parents waving their only child off to college. No, not really. More like wise guys waiting to see if their buddy's car will explode when he turns the key. I wondered about that for a moment myself. Unfortunately I have a very vivid imagination, and I held my breath as I turned the key.

Nothing. No boom. No click. Nothing. Cecil wouldn't start. The engine wouldn't even turn over.

Now Deacon James was really starting to piss me off.

Mike had a good friend who happened to be the rare mechanic

BACK TO LAZARUS

who makes house calls. He said there hadn't been any damage to Cecil. Deacon had just removed a few crucial parts, and once those were replaced his engine was purring again. Mike's friend only charged me for the parts, so $56 and three hours later I was finally on the interstate. Because of the delay, the sun was just short of setting, and my psyche wasn't ready for driving back roads alone in the dark in a convertible.

The way I figured it, at this point the only person who could prove Deacon killed Vanda (and possibly Isaac) was Deacon himself. I was hoping he was just stupid enough to do it too. I didn't know when he'd tampered with Cecil, but tomorrow morning he'd see that Cecil was gone and know that I'd left town. Probably. Just in case, I'd put a call in to Annie and Charlie to spread the word. I had no doubt someone would tell Deacon. And Deacon would come for me.

I'd be waiting. Not much of a plan, I know, but I had until tomorrow to fill in the details. Ralph might have some ideas, but I was afraid they'd all involve him sitting in my living room with a gun. No way was I letting Deacon near Ralph, so I guessed that left me on my own. What else could I do? Sue Ellen was in hiding, Noel had vanished, Richard was on the verge of a breakdown, and I wouldn't be far behind. I had to do something. It had to end, and I had to end it now.

It was nearing 11 PM. Tallahassee time when I exited the interstate. I hadn't seen any rain, but apparently we'd gotten a much-needed shower. The roads were wet and the temperature had dropped into the 70s. Traffic was light. Even on Monroe, the bane of my traffic existence, I was one of the only cars on the road. I rolled down the windows and let the air cool my cheeks. It might be a nice night to turn off the AC and sleep with the windows open.

337

Instead of pulling directly into the carport, I paused at the head of the driveway long enough to check my mailbox. It was empty. Ben was fulfilling his job as good little neighbor. In fact, it looked like he was still on the job, this time as "unannounced house guest," or whatever title required him to raid my fridge and watch my TV. I saw the TV flickering when I coasted up the driveway, and I could hear it when I got out of my car. Sounded like wrestling. Good. I'd pop some popcorn and we could play "Who's the Ho?," making up biographies for the skanky women characters that always show up at the end of the match and help throw things.

It was good to be home. I took a moment to stretch out the kinks and see if the banana spiders had taken up their summer residence at the corner of the carport yet. The porch light wasn't on, so I had to squint in the dark, and my eyes were drawn to the moonlit backyard. I started daydreaming about a barbeque in the back with the posse when this was all over. Maybe I'd invite Ralph over and they could tell war stories. I'd like to see Ralph and Jim go head-to-head. He's never met a State Attorney he could tolerate, much less like, but he might make an exception for Jim. Or maybe he'd just convert Jim to the defense.

My lovely daydream was interrupted by the tickling of hungry mosquitoes and intruding thoughts of the latest West Nile virus statistics. Grabbing my keys and the soda I'd nursed on the drive, I left my bag in the car. I was too tired to carry it in right now, and Ben would be happy to play the part of the long-suffering lackey. I said as much when I walked in the kitchen and put my soda in the fridge. He didn't answer.

He had camped out in the comfy chair, watching TV in the dark, and fallen asleep. I couldn't decide whether to wake him and give him grief, or just watch him sleep. The little imp sitting on my shoulder voted for waking him, and just now her vote was carrying the day. I set my keys on the counter and crossed the living room to give him a shake.

I was almost close enough to touch him before I could see the ropes holding Ben upright in the chair.

Chapter Forty-Two

Supposedly there's a part of the brain dedicated to instinct, to self-preservation, to survival. Until that moment, I'd never been sure that part of my brain was functional.

I twisted and lifted my arms to shield myself while shifting away from the dark spot in the room. Deacon must have been waiting in the hallway, just at the edge of the living room. His first blow landed on the fleshy part of my arm where it meets the shoulder rather than on my head, but the power of it still knocked me to the floor. Whatever he hit me with, it felt like my arm was broken. My body curled around the pain.

He must have swung again and missed as I fell, or maybe it was his follow-through. Glass shattered, and the flickering light from the TV died. Now the only light in the room was from the small bulb in the exhaust hood over the kitchen stove. After the sound of glass faded, I could hear the grating nastiness of Deacon's voice, but I couldn't make out the words. Then his boot kicked the back of my thigh so hard my leg spasmed involuntarily. I rolled onto my knees and tried to crawl away, but his foot caught my ribs next, not as hard as the last kick but still with enough force to lift me from the ground.

Darkness. I couldn't see. I was on my back and someone was slapping my face hard. I finally realized I wasn't blind; my eyes were closed. When I opened them, maybe it was the shock of Deacon looming over me, my brain finally figured out that I was supposed to be breathing. I sucked air into my lungs so hard it rasped in my throat and burned it raw. My chest continued to heave, too hard, and tears ran from my eyes. I felt like I had died, but I was still dying and I couldn't stop. I couldn't get enough air, I couldn't stop gasping, and I knew I was going to black out again. Deacon pulled my legs out straight and put his hand in the middle of my chest, above my breasts.

"Shit, girl," he said. "You got to calm down and breath right, or you're not gonna be no good to me. And you definitely won't be no good to your little friend."

That eventually penetrated the layers of panic. All I could see from the floor was Ben's knees, but I concentrated on them until my vision cleared and breathing grew as even as it was likely to with a psychopath in my face. Deacon stood, and I backed away from him on my butt until I hit the wall. I looked at Ben. In the dim light, I could see a rope or extension cord or something around his chest, and another around his neck. It was tight enough to keep his head upright, but beyond that I couldn't say. His face was bloody and his eyes were closed, maybe swollen shut.

"Don't worry, he's alive," Deacon said. "I haven't decided for how long. After all, the boy's seen me."

I forced my voice out through numb lips. "It doesn't matter if he's seen you or not. They'll know you did this. When you're done with me, some of your old buddies might think I got what was coming to me, and maybe they won't put in too many extra hours trying to track you down. But kill an innocent 15-year-old, and your own brother'd be after your ass. Kill the boy, and your own brother —not to mention every cop in Tallahassee—might not care if you're brought in dead or alive."

Probably bullshit, but it was the best I could do under the circumstances. Deacon leaned back against my counter and shook his head, smiling. He probably thought he looked like a bad ass. I thought he looked like a crazed fat freak. His shaggy dark mustache mirrored his caterpillar eyebrows, and together they emphasized his bulging eyes. His hair was wet with sweat or rain, and he pushed it away from his forehead with the back of his hand. He was wearing a thin blue windbreaker and dark jeans. I wasn't surprised to see the pigeon-toed boots beneath them; the pointy fuckers looked just like they felt.

"You are cold, you know that? I been thinking about that bitch a lot lately, thanks to you, and you remind me of her. Thought I was gonna call her a nigger, didn't you? Yeah, you did—don't deny it. I could see it in your face. Well maybe I'm not such a dumb-fuck cracker after all." He laughed.

"Hell, when it comes to screwing, I'm downright liberal."

He reached beneath his windbreaker, exposing a belly that strained shirt buttons and fell over his belt, and pulled out a gun. I didn't know what kind of gun, but it was plenty big enough to have bullets and that's all I needed to know.

"Yeah, you got that same attitude. Neither one of you could ever tell when to keep your goddamned mouth shut."

He set his gun behind him on the counter.

"As you can see, I came prepared, but to be honest I'd rather not use my firearm. I have other plans for you. Besides, shooting somebody just lacks that personal touch."

I thought of his marksmanship at WFC.

"Really? I thought you just couldn't hit the broad side of your own fat ass."

For a big man he moved quickly, and my living room is small. In two long steps he'd back-handed me, and my head fell back against the wall. When it bounced back, he smacked the other side of my face. Maybe he switched hands, to keep from over-working his right. The second one caught my nose, bringing tears to my eyes. The stinging pain was almost rejuvenating.

"Now see, that's what I'm talking about. Just can't keep your goddamned mouth shut."

I tried not to stare at the counter, at his gun, but I couldn't help it. Deacon may have "other plans" for my demise, but I was sure none of them included me walking out of here alive, and I had no illusions about Ben's fate once I was gone. I had to get the gun. Deacon looked that way and nodded.

"Anytime you think you can get that gun, you go right ahead and try." He took a shuddering breath. "Kinda spices things up a little, huh?"

He came down on both knees, pushing my own legs down flat so they were pinned beneath him. Then he grabbed both my arms around the wrists and held them down at my side. I had a feeling of déjà vu as his rancid body odor swept over me. His voice was soft when he spoke, an attempt at intimacy.

"You're one of those people, you just won't be satisfied until you know what happened, will you? Yeah, I can tell. You just gotta know *the truth*. And it ain't just her truth either, but you knew that, didn't you? Somewhere deep down. Just like you know there's only one way to find out what happened to her, to *them*, only one way you can ever really understand it."

He leaned against me and whispered in my ear. "*You gotta live it.*"

My splint made for an awkward grip, and I think Deacon's hands loosened the slightest bit in anticipation of slipping them around my neck. I smashed my head against his face, but pinned down I had no leverage. It was just enough to get my splinted right hand free. He was so close I couldn't reach his face, but I raked my nails across his neck and tried to dig in. He snarled, or maybe it was me.

344

I'd hoped to get free, but instead my scratching just made him more pissed. With his free hand, he gripped my throat, pushed my head back against the wall and began a slow, measured squeezing. I went for his eyes, but I was moving through thick water. He still held my good arm, and I smacked my splinted one against him ineffectually.

Through the building pressure in my ears, I heard a distant sound. Deacon stopped squeezing and looked up. It was the kitchen screen door slamming. Deacon released my throat and started to his feet, but it was too late.

Noel stood on the other side of the counter, holding Deacon's gun in her hand.

CHAPTER FORTY-THREE

If, as Deacon said, Vanda was in me that night, she was in each of us, most of all in Noel. The woman pointing his gun at Deacon was her mother's daughter, a figure of impervious calm. Deacon was still crouching, like a man facing an attack dog, trying not to make any sudden moves. He spoke in the same soothing voice.

"Easy there, honey. That thing's loaded, and you might hurt somebody."

"Don't worry. I know how to use it."

"We were just messing around, and maybe I got a little carried away, but it's nothing to get excited about?"

"Really? You must be Deacon."

I wondered how long his legs could support him in his crouch, but he didn't move, except his head. He looked Noel over, top to bottom. His eyes narrowed. "Do I know you?"

"It's been a long time, but I hoped you'd recognize me." Noel gave him an icy smile. "I'm the whore's daughter."

The recognition wasn't instantaneous, but it happened. I'd expected him to leer, make some crude remark, but as he'd said, maybe Deacon wasn't such a dumb-fuck cracker after all. He lunged quickly to his left, and when he returned to his crouch he was holding a crow bar. My shoulder throbbed in recognition. He edged back slowly, closer to me. Closer to Ben.

"Put down the gun, I head out the front door and we all walk away from this in one piece."

347

"I don't think so."

He held the crow bar with both hands and settled it across his right shoulder. "Okay, let me put it another way. Put down the gun, or you'll spend the next couple of weeks trying to scrub all the boy's brains off the wall."

I looked at Noel, at Deacon, at Ben, and made some quick calculations. They all added up to, no way in hell could I get to Deacon in time to stop him if he wanted to take a swing at Ben. I began edging toward Deacon and Ben. I hoped Noel wasn't lying when she said she knew what she was doing. I'd never been shot before, and it wasn't an experience I looked forward to. I kept my eyes on Deacon as Noel spoke.

"How about *I* put it another way? You're not leaving here alive."

I wasn't sure any of us was getting out alive. There was too much adrenaline, and too many unknowns. It wasn't just the crow bar I was worried about. If Deacon was carrying another gun, where would it be? Not his ankle, not if he wanted to get to it quick. He was too heavy. Small of the back? Could he draw with the crow bar in his hand, or would he have to switch off? I had to distract Deacon, get his focus and his body away from Ben if Noel was to have a chance at stopping him.

"No matter what happens here tonight, Deacon, this is my last chance," I said.

He didn't shift his body or his gaze away from Ben and Noel, but I could tell he was listening to me.

"It's my last chance to ask you what the hell you were thinking when you killed Isaac Thomas."

Both he and Noel swung their gazes toward me. I was afraid that would happen, with what I had to say. *Come on Noel, don't fail me now. Keep watching Deacon. Keep your eyes on Deacon.*

"You thought he knew, didn't you? You thought he knew that you killed Vanda."

He didn't speak, but I had his full attention now.

"Of course you did. Why else would he be transferred to Latham?" Deacon's head started to nod involuntarily, and I saw something in his eyes. Something…

"You were afraid of him, weren't you? Afraid of what he would do to you for killing his wife."

"I'm not afraid of anybody, least of all a fucking inmate."

"No C/O with a bit of sense isn't afraid of the inmates. It's too easy to hide a shiv, or get somebody to do it for you. Besides, Isaac might not have been an inmate forever. Sure, now life means life, but when he was sentenced it was 25 to life. He might have gotten out one day, and you couldn't take that chance."

I gave Deacon a smile so acidic it nearly burned my lips. "You never were very bright, were you? Isaac didn't have a clue about Vanda! He was turning you in because you couldn't keep your pathetic little pecker in your pants. You had to go around black-mailing teenagers for sex. Once you'd made it through all the hookers, what else could you do? Plus, blackmail a teenager and she doesn't talk back. Blackmail a virgin and she doesn't know any better, doesn't know how inadequate you are. Is that what happened with Vanda? It is, isn't it? She told you what a lousy lover you were, and you couldn't take it. You killed her for telling the truth."

Deacon's bulk shifted. Gun or crowbar? Me or Ben? I looked toward Noel, and my gaze was somewhere between her and Deacon when I heard the gunshots. One, two, three. The first one was so loud, I didn't really hear the next two, but I could feel them in my organs. I never thought a gunshot would be so loud. My eyes saw bright ghosts, like headlights in the rearview mirror at night, and the smell made me think of a lightning strike in an industrial area. I stood dumbly until the worst of the ringing in my ears faded away, but I still couldn't hear very well. Then I realized I had my hands over my ears. Removing them helped.

Noel hadn't moved. She stood still, one hand bracing the other, holding the gun. "Noel, put the gun down."

My voice echoed in my ears, coming from inside me, but I wasn't sure if Noel had heard. I finally looked around at the rest of the room. Deacon was lying on his back on the floor, and Ben was still sitting in the chair. Beyond that, I couldn't tell. My eyes were still spotty.

"Noel, I need light."

I spoke as if to a hearing-impaired old man. I didn't watch to see if she complied, but in a few moments the kitchen lights came on. I flipped the rest of the switches in the hallway and went first to Ben. I couldn't decide if he looked better or worse for the illumination, but he was breathing. When I touched his bloody face, he moaned softly.

"Hang in there, kid. Everything's okay now. Syd's here."

I didn't want to, but I went to Deacon next. Blood had seeped from his chest through his shirt and onto the floor, and there were drops spattered randomly across his face. His eyes bulged open, as they had in life. I knew he was dead, but I went through the motions anyway. It wasn't because I thought he might leap to his feet or haunt my dreams if I didn't see for myself that he was dead. My paranoid, pragmatic mind was already assessing the possibilities, trying to determine the legal consequences of Noel thrice fatally shooting a law enforcement officer (albeit a psychotic one) with his own gun. I considered looking for his second gun, maybe even putting it in his hand, then rejected the idea as too risky. We had to do everything by the book.

I couldn't bring myself to touch his neck, so I grabbed his

wrist. My hands were slippery with blood—his, Ben's, or mine, I couldn't tell. It all looked the same. No pulse—big surprise. Now what? I took a deep breath, but it didn't have the calming effect I'd hoped. The smell of blood made my stomach queasy. Blood and pain. My adrenaline was starting to wear thin, leaving me strung out and exhausted. I had to get us out of here while I could still think.

Noel was still standing behind the counter, leaning a bit, but she had set the gun down. I stood up. My voice stood sounded hollow in my ears.

"He's not going anywhere, and we need to get Ben to the hospital. Don't touch anything else, and don't move anything. We're going to lock up, leave everything as it is, and call the cops on the way. Let them deal with the mess."

We were able to slip the chest rope up and over Ben, but I had to cut off the rope around his neck. There was no slack, so it bit into his neck while I hacked at it mostly left-handed with my scissors. My right hand was pretty useless again, and I didn't trust Noel's hands or my own with a knife. Ben's breathing was shallow, and as the rope tightened he started coughing. I stopped to let him catch his breath and wiped the tears from my eyes, probably smearing my face with blood in the bargain. Looking at Deacon, my hand tightened around the scissors. Dead or not, I wanted to carve him up into little pieces for what he did to Ben, what he would have done to him.

One of Ben's arms was swollen and discolored, probably from the crow bar, so we tried to avoid it as we half-carried, half-dragged him to Noel's car. She'd parked on the street, but I'd sent her to pull up the yard to the front door while I worked on Ben's ropes. It was a straighter shot out the front door than the kitchen to the carport, and I didn't want to drag him through the worst of the crime scene if I could help it. We used Noel's car because it was a

351

4-door, and there was no way we could wrestle Ben into my Cabrio. I wasn't sure I could get into it myself.

We settled Ben across the back seat, then I went back around to the carport and locked the kitchen door from the outside. I slipped a key in my car frame above the right front tire so the cops didn't feel compelled to break my locks. When I stood up, I suddenly noticed how much it hurt to breathe. Thank God Noel was driving. She'd left the passenger's door open for me, and I relied too much on gravity to shut it. The dome light had gone out, but when I turned for my seatbelt, I could still see space between the door and frame. Screw it, and I wasn't wearing the seatbelt either.

"Shit. I forgot my cell phone."

Noel backed out of the driveway with such speed I almost reconsidered the seatbelt. "Mine's in the glove box," she said.

I leaned forward, wincing, and after a couple of tries got the button to catch so it would open. When the tiny bulb came on, the first thing I saw wasn't her cell phone. It was a gun.

"This isn't Deacon's gun, is it?" I was pretty sure it had been on the counter when we left.

"No," she said. "It's Grandma Harrison's."

I was so full of adrenaline my mind wouldn't stop racing, even when I wanted it to. How long had Noel been carrying her grandmother's gun in her car? Had she taken it in with her? Would she have used it if Deacon's gun hadn't been on the counter? I didn't want to know. I really didn't want to know. I managed to retrieve Noel's cell phone without touching the gun and slammed the glove box shut. Instead of dialing 911, I tried my old buddies in Stetler County. No one I knew was in the office, but a secretary managed to track down Sutton at home and work some kind of technological magic so I could speak to him.

"Deacon James is dead in my house."

"Where are you?"

"On the way to the hospital."

"I thought you said he was dead."

"He is, but the rest of us aren't."

I gave him a brief explanation of what had happened and told him the crime scene was secure and he was welcome to it.

"I haven't called the Tallahassee cops yet, so you'll probably want to do that."

"Well, considering the man was killed in their jurisdiction, yeah, I think I just might."

Sutton wasn't pleased with the situation, but he didn't tell me to go back, and he didn't waste my time telling me what I should have done. Probably because he couldn't come up with any better ideas. Noel pulled up in front of the emergency room entrance.

"I gotta go. I'll be at the hospital if you need me."

I hung up and handed Noel her phone instead of putting it back in the glove box. She tucked it in her purse. Call me superstitious, but I didn't want to be shoving a gun out of the way in front of the emergency room. Noel helped me get Ben inside, then ran back out to park her car. A guy in uniform was eyeing it hungrily.

Things went downhill after Noel left. A young man helped me get Ben into a wheelchair, took one look at me and left to get another. Initially I protested, but then they started asking questions. Ben was obviously a minor, so was I his mother? If not, where was she? They needed a waiver to treat him. Where was his insurance information? I tried to lie, to say he was 18, but they weren't buying it. Of course, then I couldn't turn around and say I was his mother. I realized belatedly I didn't even know his mother's name, and that we should have stopped by his house on the way. By the time the young man returned with the wheelchair for me, I was ready to sit in it. Just for a little while.

JUDY K. WALKER

Someone began wheeling Ben away, and that was when I lost my tenuous hold on reality. He was Ben, but he was my brother Allan, and they were taking him away, and they wouldn't let me see him. He would die, and I'd never see him again. The blue and white coats explained that they couldn't treat Ben without parental permission, which they hoped to get soon, but they were going to evaluate the extent of his injuries. Of course, I was beyond being rational and made an exemplary scene for the small audience in the waiting room. Noel's appearance finally cut my drama short. She squeezed my shoulders hard trying to focus my attention. The resulting crow bar pain did much more to snap me out of it than her stern gaze ever could.

"Sydney, he's not dying. I promise. When they're done checking you out, they'll let you see him."

Whether it was due to my histrionics or the subsequent arrival of several cops very interested in what I had to say, I didn't have to wait long to be seen. My arm and ribs were x-rayed, but I had emerged relatively unscathed. No broken bones, not even my bloody nose. I'd be sporting lumps and bruises for a while—nothing new there—but the only real casualty was my strap-on wrist splint. It was soaked with blood and had its own internal injuries. It didn't quite flop like a soggy french fry, but it definitely no longer served its splinting function. I was issued another splint and told that my antics had bought me an extra two weeks in the new one. If I was lucky. Why are doctors always so damned optimistic? Maybe it's just the ones who meet me.

CHAPTER FORTY-FOUR

The cops were interviewing Noel when I was released, so I slipped over to see Ben. I couldn't believe they were really letting me see him. Of course, I did sort of slink into his room, so maybe no one noticed. Ben had been cleaned up a bit, but until his mom arrived they couldn't treat him. Apparently it had taken a while to track her down, but she was on her way. I sat with him for a few minutes before he opened his eyes. His cracking voice squeezed my heart.

"Syd, I'm sorry."

"For what, you goober?"

"He said he was a cop. He had a badge and everything."

I reached out to stroke his hair gently, mindful of bruises. "It's okay, hon. Everything's okay now."

"Where is he?"

"Don't worry. He can't hurt you anymore."

"Syd, he beat the shit out of me. Where is the mother fucker?"

"He's dead."

He sighed and let his eyes drift shut. "Good. You okay?"

"Yeah, I'm fine."

"You don't look fine. Is that what happened the last time? Him?"

"Yeah."

"He said he was gonna kill you, Syd." His voice started to crack at the end. I reached for his cup of water, as if I thought a parched throat and not emotion was responsible. He shook his head, a few slow fractions of an inch.

"Well, he didn't." I snorted, trying to abort a laugh. I knew laughing would hurt, and laughing might lead to uncontrollable crying, which would hurt even worse. "But the asshole killed the TV."

"Man, that's cold. That's okay. Your TV was too small anyway. I'll help you pick out a new one." He groaned and shifted. "So when do I get some drugs?"

Soon, apparently. A commotion drew Ben's eyes toward the hallway and I turned to watch through the glass. A woman, maybe a few years older than me, was screaming and gesticulating wildly. I couldn't make out the words, but her mouth stretched wide and her face flushed with anger. Noel seemed to be her target, facing her in the hallway. Noel responded calmly and the screaming stopped, but the woman still didn't look happy.

"That's my mom."

"Yeah, I kinda figured. Time for me to go, kid." I leaned over and kissed the top of his head. He tried to make a face at me, but winced at the effort. "Easy there. Your disgust has been noted— don't hurt yourself. I'll check on you again soon."

When I left Ben's room, his mother slipped past me without speaking, carefully avoiding any physical contact. Her mascara was smeared, whether from concern for her son or having just crawled from someone else's bed I didn't know. She had taken the time to brush her hair and pull it into a ponytail at the base of her neck.

"What was that about?" I asked Noel.

"She didn't want you seeing her son anymore. Something about you getting him killed, her getting a restraining order. Blah, blah, blah."

"Can't say I blame her."

"I can." The corner of Noel's mouth slowly curled. "I made a few observations about the kind of nighttime activities one engages in that take you away from your home and keep your child from getting emergency treatment until 2 AM. She reconsidered her position."

"Thanks."

"Any time. You know what the funny thing is?"

"There's something funny? Please tell me."

"She didn't know you were a woman."

"Noel, I know I look like crap right now, but I'm really finding it hard to see why that's funny."

"No, that's not what I mean. She apparently knew Ben was spending time with 'Sid,' but she didn't know Sid was a woman."

"Really? That sneaky little twit. I'm lucky I didn't end up on America's Most Wanted as some kind of perv with a teenager in tow."

"Uh-huh."

We almost made it out the door unmolested ourselves, but a local cop caught me by the arm, none too gently, as the automatic door began to whoosh.

"I'll be waiting outside," Noel said, with a sour look at the assembled uniforms. Her first interrogation apparently hadn't been a pleasant experience. I wasn't looking forward to it myself, but I was glad to see that Sutton had made it to Tallahassee. I guess when you're a cop you can drive as fast as you want to. Sutton didn't speak, just nodded at me once and listened while I told the Tallahassee cops my story.

I said Deacon had started to swing at Ben when Noel shot him. It felt true enough to me, and no one contradicted me. In fact, they took it easy on me. When they said I could leave, Sutton walked me to the door.

"Thanks for coming all this way to see little old me."

"It's the least I could do when you closed a couple of my cases in one night. Of course, you prompted those cases by being attacked, so it's your fault I had them in the first place, but hey, why split hairs?"

We'd made it to the front and lingered, leaning against the wall.

"I hate to break it to you, but I may have opened a few more. I'm coming out your way next week. We can have a sit-down then and I'll explain everything, but for now you may want to start looking through missing person reports, especially prostitutes. Also any unsolved homicides of women, and closed cases where Deacon was an investigating officer. It's something he said right before he tried to choke me to death."

I hadn't seen a mirror yet, but I hoped Deacon had left bruises on my neck. They'd add automatic credibility and gravity to everything I said while they lasted.

"How far back?"

I had the grace to squirm. "Early 1980s."

"No wonder Drake can't stand you."

My mouth dropped at the honesty. At least he'd said it with a smile.

"I'll make sure he's in the office when you drop by next week. Don't forget to call ahead."

Noel sat on the curb waiting for me, and I settled gingerly next to her, another exercise in controlled falling. It seemed neither of was quite ready to go anywhere else. The city was quiet, as it almost always is away from campus. With no sunlight to dry it, the curb still felt damp beneath my butt. No wonder. You could see the fine mist of the humid air in the streetlight halos. I breathed the cool damp into my lungs, leaning back to ease the pressure on my ribs.

I hadn't told the cops about the gun that didn't kill Deacon, the one still in Noel's car, not even Sutton. In fact, I would never tell anyone else about it, about the length of those moments between Deacon's threats and the bullets that ended them, and I wouldn't lose a moment's sleep over the omission. But there were other things gone unspoken for too long. I gave up trying to take a deep breath and plunged ahead.

"You remember that message you took, from Lisa? She is my sister, but we haven't spoken since my mom died about 10 years ago."

"Sydney, you don't have to explain."

"I know I don't, but I want to. I had a brother too. Allan. He died. I guess you could say he's the reason I have issues with hospitals."

"Syd—"

"There's more. Let me just get it out, and then you can—whatever. A few years after he died I wanted to make the break from my family official. I changed my name."

I look at Noel's face carefully. I didn't see anger or revulsion. I wasn't even sure I saw comprehension. "Sydney Brennan isn't the name I was born with."

Noel leaned over until her shoulder bumped against mine. Even now, after everything that had happened that night, her posture was still too stiff for the gesture to look casual, but she had tried. She smiled, taking my hand, or more accurately the fingers protruding from my splint.

"Thank you, but it doesn't matter. I know who you are now."

I looked up to see Mike standing over us. I didn't know how long he'd been standing there, but it never occurred to me to question his presence. I just patted the curb on the other side of me. Noel apparently had a tighter grip on reality, the barriers of the space-time continuum that usually separated us from Mike.

"So what brings you to Tallahassee at this late hour?" she asked.

"I got a call from Sutton. He said you might need bail money."

We laughed. It was too close to the truth to be funny, and laughing intensified the physical pain, but it relieved the tension.

"Richard sends his regards. He wanted to come, but his wife's away and he had to stay with their kids. So how about an early breakfast?"

Since it was after 9 PM, all-night breakfast/trucker food was all we'd be able to find in Tallahassee. "We look like rejects from a war movie."

Mike reached up and, after a few tugs, managed an asymmetrical rip in his plain gray T-shirt. Then he walked over to the landscaped grasses and shrubs and dug through the mulch until he reached damp dirt, which he smeared on his face and forearms. He came back to us grinning.

"Moral support."

Mike drove. I found that I was ravenous, devouring an omelet and hash browns. I'd missed dinner, and almost getting killed takes it out of you. We lingered over our meal, chatting as if it were a normal night and every eye in the place weren't on us. When we got up to pay, a brave soul finally broke societal taboos and asked us what had happened. Noel and I were at a loss for a reply. It's easy to say something like, "car accident," but that wasn't true and would probably elicit more inquiry. "Run-in with a psychopath" had the advantage of being true, but I really didn't want to have that kind of effect on a stranger this time of day. Mike saved us.

"Movie extras," he said. "In a student film over at FSU. Swear to God, the kid's the next Scorsese."

When we went back to the hospital for Noel's car, we found out that Ben had been released. Nice to have some good news. Noel headed home. She said she'd be all right, and she'd call me this evening after we got some sleep. Mike drove me to my house, a.k.a. the crime scene. He didn't turn the engine off immediately, apparently so I wouldn't get out before he was ready.

"You knew, didn't you?" He glanced at me once, quickly, then gripped the steering wheel with both hands and tried to bore a hole through it with his eyes. When he spoke his voice was rough with emotion—anger, frustration, and other things I couldn't identify. "You fucking knew this would happen, didn't you?"

Had it been anyone else, I would have gotten defensive and vented my own emotions. Instead, seeing Mike that far from center helped me maintain control.

"No, I didn't. I knew we'd never catch him otherwise, never prove what he'd done. And I knew he would follow me. I didn't know he would be waiting for me. And I didn't know he'd grab Ben."

Mike still didn't look at me, but he nodded and turned off the engine. "I'll wait for you."

The officer in charge was nice enough to let me in to pack an overnight. He gave me little booties and a female officer for an escort, I'm sure not because I'd get lost in my own house, but to guarantee I didn't take anything of interest.

They had nearly finished processing the scene, but Deacon's body was still there. In life it had been easy to see the sneering menace, but hard to think of him as truly dangerous. In death, it was even more difficult to see the threat in the big middle-aged body, but obviously it had been there. He had killed Vanda. I believed he had killed Isaac and other women yet to be discovered, and I knew he would have killed Ben and me, and Noel once she had arrived.

The officer in charge was obviously wondering the same thing, trying to see the "victim" as a boogeyman, without the benefit of my experience. He was youngish, maybe a year or two younger than me, clean-cut. I wondered if he'd ever been afraid for his life. Not in the sense that many cops are daily, dealing with unknown potentially deadly threats, but in the imminent gun-at-your-head, "barring divine intervention I'm about to die" kind of way.

"Three shots to take him down, huh? Well, he was a pretty big guy." He looked me over, no doubt assessing that I was in no way a pretty big guy.

"Yeah. Three shots instead of three dead bodies seemed like a pretty good trade to me. Of course, I'm biased, being one of the potentially dead bodies."

"Yeah, I guess you would be."

At that moment, someone in a white jumpsuit called out from the floor where a couple of guys had just rolled Deacon's body over onto its belly. He was massive enough that the body lay at an angle, compensating for the protuberant belly. "Mitch, we got another gun here. Small of the back."

Not that there was anything small about Deacon, in his back or anywhere else. I tried not to smile.

CHAPTER FORTY-FIVE

I knew Ralph and Diane were early risers, so I gave them a call when I got to Mike's car. They were glad to have me for a couple of days until my house was released and back to normal, and I got Mike to drop me off there. I was slow getting out of the car. All right, I'd started to doze. I woke up when Mike opened the passenger door to let me out. He leaned across me to unhook the seatbelt and helped me step down to the ground from my Jeep perch. I was a little unsteady on my feet, and Mike held my shoulders gently, gazing into my eyes until he could see them start to clear. One hand moved up to rest against the side of my head, and I tilted against it, mashing my fuzzy hair.

"You okay?" he asked.

I nodded. His hand slid to the back of my head, and he pulled me toward him, his own body meeting me halfway. I could feel the steady thud of his heart as he held me against his chest. I hadn't realized he was so tall.

"Ben's gonna be okay, too," he whispered to the top of my head.

I didn't respond. I just wanted to stand there against him. He didn't stroke my hair. His body asked nothing of me, just offered support. It was something I'd never felt before, an embrace from a man with no demands, no expectations. At least I hadn't felt it since Allan died.

It was the thought of Ralph watching from the window that

finally made me move, step back from Mike. "Thank you."

"Sure. What are friends for?" He walked back and got in his Jeep before I could answer. He didn't leave though, just sat in the car waiting until Diane opened the door for me. Then he gave a small wave and drove away. I could see the speculation in Diane's eyes, but she didn't ask.

"Come on in, honey."

Ralph was at the kitchen table having his coffee, and I'm sure he was dying for details (of my adventures, not any possible love life) but Diane wouldn't hear of it. I wasn't a stranger to their spare bedroom, so I suspect she led me there simply to act as a Ralph buffer.

I smelled the fresh sheets and looked longingly at the thin quilt folded at the bottom, an item I might need in their generous air conditioning. When Diane handed me a pile of fresh towels and a spare robe, I realized another reason she had escorted me to the bedroom. Covered in blood and sweat and who knows what else, I was in no fit condition to touch her furniture. I took a shower to get the muck off as quickly as possible, but I was looking forward to a bath later in their claw-foot tub.

I slept all day, and when I woke mid-afternoon Diane made me a turkey sandwich, sliced diagonally with chips and a pickle on the side. She set my plate on a place mat and joined me at the kitchen table with a glass of iced tea. When she brought out a box of Little Debbie's snack cakes, I felt like I was 8 years old again visiting my grandmother. I unconsciously began to swing my legs and was surprised to find my feet touched the floor. But still just barely.

Now that I had enough sugar to sustain me through any maternal tirade, I called Ben's house. He answered the phone, sounding slightly groggy. The big news was that he had a broken arm, courtesy of Deacon's crow bar was my guess, so I'd better think of

364

something creative for his cast and I'd better do it soon. Kelly (girl Kelly) was coming over tomorrow, and she was welcome to do anything she liked with it. I'll just bet she was.

I called Noel next, and she was groggy as well. She said she'd been awake for a while—really, she had—but I'd told that lie myself too many times to believe it. Ralph and Diane had plans for the evening, so Noel said she'd drop by with supplies and her baking expertise. We were going to try to make a batch of my no-bake oatmeal cookies more diabetic-friendly for Ralph. It turns out Grandma Harrison is diabetic, so Noel had some experience. Maybe that's why the old bag was so mean. She just couldn't tolerate sweet.

When Noel arrived, I was waiting on the front stoop. She handed me a six-pack of Mexican beer she'd no doubt seen in my own house, and I took it from her awkwardly.

"The most important supplies," she said, then went back to retrieve a bag from the health food store. It contained things I'd never heard of and things I'd sworn I'd never try, but having eaten Noel's cooking, I was willing to give her and her ingredients the benefit of the doubt.

We went in the kitchen and mixed everything up, or rather she tasted and measured and mixed and I watched, and sometimes tasted. The cookies had to set up in the fridge, so we took a little cooler of beer and went out back. Diane's patio was lovely, but we opted for bare skin on the grass. Once we'd gotten settled, I handed Noel the only thing I'd brought outside with me—her mother's letter that her cousin Sarah had given to me, presumably to give to her. It was time.

Noel read in silence. I'd stretched out flat on my back, looking up at the sky to give her privacy. It really was beautiful, so green and lush and steaming with life. It's easy to forget how beautiful the world is when you're busy living in it every day. The sky directly above me was pale blue, and dense banks of clouds moved quickly through my field of vision. I sat up with a pained grunt to get a better view and brush an adventurous ant off my calf. We were about to lose the sun to masses of clouds, and the sky to the west was a deep dark blue-gray that smelled of metal and promised lightning. I love that color. It reminds me of the ocean at dusk.

When Noel had finished, she folded the letter and placed it back in its envelope. "Sarah gave it to you?" she asked.

"Yes." I told her about the box of letters Viola had wanted her to have, and how her grandmother had destroyed them. Noel shook her head, but she didn't seem angry.

"Typical grandmother." She leaned over on one elbow and began fidgeting with the grass. "When I got that clipping in the mail, I started thinking a lot about my mother and father. I hadn't thought about either of them for years, not about my memories of them. Maybe that's why it was so hard. I just couldn't remember what my life with them was like, what they were like. When I did remember things, I wasn't sure if it was real or another one of my grandmother's stories. I had nightmares about things I couldn't recall, and I'd wake up terrified without knowing why. The first time I had one, I threw up next to my bed before I could make it to the bathroom."

"Then you started telling me things about my family, things I didn't want to hear but I needed to. That's when I began to remember. It's as if suddenly I had permission to remember the bad things. I wasn't making them up, and I wasn't being disloyal, because they were true. After I left your house, the day I took the message from your sister, I went to see my grandmother. I told her I wanted to know the truth about my mother, and we had a huge argument. I don't think she even knows the truth anymore. That's when I knew it had to come from me."

She took another sip of beer. "I went to the coast for a few days, didn't tell anyone where I was." She smiled. "As you noticed. Sorry. But that's where I found my memories, and I keep finding more every day. My mother was an amazing person. She was every-thing my grandmother said, everything you told me, and more. And my father loved her passionately, so much that he stayed with her even when she couldn't stand to be with herself."

Noel held up the letter. "I didn't remember the miscarriage, but I did remember the nursery. For a long time, it smelled like talcum powder, even though the baby never made it there. Mom some-times slept there after the miscarriage. I'd find her when I got up in the morning for school, and I'd lie with her for a while and let her spoon me. Then when she started having... substance problems, she slept there again, but I knew it was different. The room didn't smell like talcum anymore. It smelled like Jimmy's—cigarettes and sweat and vomit. She wouldn't wake up when I looked in her. She'd just lie there, sleeping, holding a little stuffed lamb."

I reached out to touch her hand. "I'm sorry, Noel."

"I'm not. She's a person again."

"How did you know last night? About Deacon?"

"Well, I knew what you and the guys were up to, what you'd found, and I started putting some of the pieces together, but I didn't know until after you did. When was it? I've lost my days. I guess it was the night before last, the day all hell broke loose at the prison. It's funny because I hadn't turned on the TV all week, and I happened to turn on the late news that night. Maybe to check the weather, see if there was a storm in the gulf, I don't know. They had a story about it. They didn't give your name, but I knew it had to be you. Who else could it be? They did give the suspect's name —Deacon James. That's what did it. That's when I remembered that night."

"The night your mother was killed?"

Noel nodded. "She picked me up at Miss Johnson's. I don't know what possessed her to take me to Jimmy's, but she did crazy things sometimes. Jimmy's always scared me, but it was exciting too, to be out so late with my mother. Everyone knew her, and she had to introduce me to each one of them, all these men. I tried not to be shy. I knew I was too old not to speak. Then a man came up and whispered in her ear. He was a white man, pretty unusual in Jimmy's, but I think he was also wearing a uniform, which might have made it less unusual. I don't know. That was when my mother had to leave."

"There weren't many women in Jimmy's either, but she took me over to one—I can't remember her name, skinny woman—and asked her to watch me until she got back. Whoever she was, she disappeared about five minutes after my mother did, took off somewhere with a man. It was so loud in there, you had to yell to be heard, and I remember my mother saying, 'Deacon, my ass! If that prick ever set foot in a church he'd burst into flames.' They both laughed, and mother said she'd be back soon, not to worry, that it wouldn't take long. They both laughed at that too."

Noel began picking at the label on her bottle, waiting until she had every bit of paper and glue before pulling it from the bottle, a couple of millimeters at a time.

"I never saw her again. When the fire broke out in Jimmy's, one of the men grabbed me and carried me outside, but then he left and I didn't know what to do. People were screaming, and I didn't know anyone. Finally my father came. I knew he would, but instead of staying with me, he went looking for my mother. He didn't know she was already dead. She must have been."

"When I heard Deacon's name and saw his face, the picture of him, even after 20 years… and he shot at you. I knew it had to be him."

I nodded. "Noel, when did you—"

When did you get your grandmother's gun, before you went to the coast or after you came back? That was the rest of the question, the part that went unspoken. It went hand in hand with, did you bring the gun in with you and decide not to use it once you saw Deacon's on the counter? And the doozey, had Deacon really started to swing? Really started to go for a second gun?

"When did I what?"

"Never mind. It doesn't matter."

The air had grown cool and the sky darkened to twilight. A nearby rumbling vibrated through my body to the ground. Pine tops swayed and palmetto fronds curled and tickled the air like windblown hair, the sound of their rustling both reassuring and spine-tingling. Noel and I rose together and headed inside to avoid the approaching storm. As I slipped through the sliding glass doors, a solid mass of rain began to pelt the patio unrelentingly. The force of the impact caused a fine spray, but I stood there, smiling, getting damp, marveling at the wonder of it all. I'd never imagined there could be answers I didn't want to know.

EPILOGUE

Over the next few months, we filled in some of the gaps. I say we, but it was mostly Sutton and Jim Gilbert. In 1983, soon after Isaac pled guilty to Vanda's murder, Deacon had been investigated for "inappropriate behavior" with prostitutes. There were never any charges or official findings of wrongdoing, but the investigation led to his voluntary resignation. He did private security work for a year or so before getting on at WFC. While not officially designated as missing, some of the women mentioned in the investigation could not be accounted for, although Sutton continued to try. With some help, I suspected, from Rudy Nagroski.

Deacon had manipulated the investigation into Vanda's murder from the inside. How much couldn't be determined 20 years later, especially after what Deacon had done to the investigative and State Attorney files. It seemed likely that he'd been responsible for crucial follow-up interviews, had failed to pass on information and sown misinformation. Claire Johnson had confirmed that Deacon interviewed her, although she could no longer be sure of the substance of their conversation.

Mike discovered that Deacon had also been influential in the shuffling of personnel prior to Isaac's alleged suicide. Most of the people working in his area at the time of Isaac's death were now under indictment for their involvement in Deacon's visitation extortion scheme. They universally denied any knowledge of wrongdoing in Isaac's death, as well as any knowledge of Deacon's sexual extortion tactics. People who still cared (i.e. Jim Gilbert) maintained high hopes of turning one young man who seemed particularly disgusted with their actions. Was he the masked man who'd let me escape, that night that seemed so long ago? And perhaps the spelling-impaired author of the warning that reached me too late?

When Deacon was killed, the enthusiasm for discovering the depth and breadth of the corruption surrounding him died with him, at the state and federal level. I wasn't surprised. My thoughts often lingered on connections, connections made and unmade. Vanda's death, the 1983 prostitute investigation, Isaac's contact with and probable initiation of the corruption investigation 20 years later—all connected, and yet the connection had gone unrecognized. Or had it? I didn't think so. While investigating Deacon, while investigating Isaac's allegations and credibility, I felt sure that someone somewhere had figured out Deacon's connection to Vanda. Figured out that it was likely Deacon killed her, and even more likely that an innocent man pled guilty and would spend his life in prison. That is, until Deacon killed Isaac too. Or maybe I'm just cynical and paranoid.

After all, why would an innocent man plead guilty to murdering his wife? I found out from Sutton that when Deacon's body was searched, there were condoms in his pocket, so I asked Sutton to do a little more checking. He confirmed that Deacon had a practice of using condoms with the prostitutes and women he coerced to have sex. Yet there was no evidence of a condom at the scene. I now knew that, as he'd been so proud to point out, Deacon was not a stupid man. Perhaps he'd taken the evidence—the condom— with him. Of course, this was years before DNA testing. Maybe he wouldn't have taken it because he thought it didn't matter. So long as they couldn't tie him personally to the scene, evidence of sex with another man gave Isaac motive to kill his wife.

There is an alternative explanation. Imagine that a man discovers his wife dead, apparently killed by one of her many lovers. Imagine further that in a moment of profound but misguided love for his dead wife and for his daughter, this man decides to alter the scene, to remove the evidence most damaging to his wife's character and memory. In minutes he can have the items in his own or his neighbor's garbage cans, which go unsearched when he is arrested at the scene. He doesn't intend to take responsibility for her death, but the police arrive—recall the anonymous tip by our savvy killer —before he can leave the scene. He can't bring himself to explain his actions, and even if he did, who would believe him now?

Or maybe not. That's the version that feels right to me, but we'll never know. So many questions unanswered. I knew I'd left things in good hands with Jim Gilbert, and I think he shared many of my suspicions, though we didn't speak of it. Had I really found the unthinkable—an honest, justice-minded prosecutor? Perhaps he was the exception that proved the rule. Occasionally I'd hear stories from Mike, who was as shocked by Jim's character as I, about Jim's dogged pursuit of the corruption investigation, and the corruption investigators. He was determined to fix the system, to prove it could still work.

As for me, I was healing, physically and in other ways. Loud noises, quick movements still made me flinch sometimes. It had been hard to stay out of my head at first, hard not to wonder what would have happened if Noel hadn't shown up when she did. Would I have lived? Would Ben? I don't think about it much anymore. That son of a bitch gave me enough nightmares already— I'm not volunteering for any more.

Still, I found it difficult to muster interest in the big picture, particularly on this day. Noel and her newly rediscovered aunt Ida had spoken on the phone a few times, and yesterday I finally drove Noel to meet her. Noel said she needed the moral support, and I needed to reassure myself that something good had come of the chaos I'd created. Their speech and their touches had been tentative at first, but they'd gotten along well, as I knew they would. Ida had made up the guest room and asked us to stay overnight so we could do something special this morning. I knew what she had in mind.

I'm sitting in the car, a discreet distance away, while Ida and Noel visit Isaac's grave. Noel asked me to accompany them, but this is something she needs to do without me. Not to worry. Now that I know he's here, I'll be back. Alone. There are things I have to say to him, this man I never met, that no one else, least of all Noel, needs to hear. It's a good time to be here though, already muggy but early enough that the heat hasn't yet baked the dew from the grass. I found a shady spot to park and put the top down. There's the scent of something sweet blooming nearby, as there almost always is in north Florida, and birds are the only creatures audacious enough to break the silence. It'd be a downright idyllic scene if it weren't for the man digging a fresh grave two rows over. The mask that protects his lungs from the toxic earth of Lazarus lends a touch of the surreal.

Before Noel left the car, she handed me a slip of paper and left her cell phone on the seat, "just in case." It's my sister Lisa's phone number. Little does Noel know I've been carrying it, on my own cell phone, in my purse for weeks. Waiting for the right moment. The imp on my shoulder says that would be my most masochistic moment. Maybe, but I think I'll take Noel's hint. What else do I have to do, sitting in a hot car in a cemetery on a Sunday morning?

THE END

ACKNOWLEDGMENTS

Thank you to my husband Paul for the patience, love, support, and pancakes (pasta or otherwise) that keep me going. My resilient mom Sandy has always believed in me, no matter what, and probably still has my first marker-rendered books in a drawer somewhere. Thank you to mom-in-law Gloria as well, and her not-so-subtle nudges of support (*Judy, there's someone I want you to meet*).

I spent a chunk of time working on death row appeals, so this book draws on my exposure to that world. If I had stayed, I'd be very unhealthy and quite likely insane. Some amazing people have dedicated their own lives and sanity to it, several of whom I've been lucky enough to get to know. Thank you to them for keeping up the good fight, and for allowing me to be a part of it for a while. Thanks also to my guys, who are always with me, whether they know it or not.

On the literary front, I've kept Michael Koryta's kind words of encouragement in my pocket (well, in my inbox) for several years, pulling them out from time to time as needed.

And thanks to the indie publishing community, for being so generous with everything they've learned. We're listening.

About the Author

A recovering criminal attorney with a Master's Degree in Tropical Conservation Biology, Judy writes from her home in Hawaii, where she is surrounded by husband, dog, cat, and assorted geckos. If she's not tapping away at her computer, she hopes she's in her snorkel fins.

Back to Lazarus is Judy's first novel, but expect more Sydney Brennan adventures in the future. You can explore Sydney's world and connect with Judy online at her website:

http://www.judykwalker.com

Sign up for Judy's Newsletter there and be the first to learn about her upcoming New Releases and Special Deals. Thanks for reading!

Made in the USA
Lexington, KY
17 December 2015